About the Author

I trained as a nurse in the eighties, having to give up due to a family member being terminally ill. I returned to nursing as a health care assistant for six years. I then left to work for the family business and retrained in book keeping. I had to stop work because I became seriously ill. I still have ill health and found writing a means of escapism. I love reading and the fulfilment it brings me. I hope this book brings much joy to whoever reads it. I now work for the NHS as admin assistant for Discharge Planning. I have a very supportive husband of thirty-one years, and one son. We live in Bedfordshire.

Happy Birthday Sue,
Thank you, for coming on my journey.
It means a lot and I really do appreciate
it. I hope you get much joy from reading
the book?
Happy Reading
Best Wishes
Joanne Gregorer

Forbidden Love

Joanne Gregorec

Forbidden Love

Olympia Publishers
London

www.olympiapublishers.com
OLYMPIA PAPERBACK EDITION

A CIP catalogue record for this title is
available from the British Library.

ISBN: 978-1-80074-380-9

This is a work of fiction.
Names, characters, places and incidents originate from the writer's imagination.
Any resemblance to actual persons, living or dead, is purely coincidental.

First Published in 2023

Olympia Publishers
Tallis House
2 Tallis Street
London
EC4Y 0AB

Printed in Great Britain

Dedication

I dedicate this book to my husband, Roman, and son, Daniel, who kept
believing in me.

Acknowledgements

Thank you, Margaret, for always being there on this journey and for proofreading the final draft.

Thank you to my friends and family who have contributed to the many hours of proof reading, it means a lot that you are coming on this journey with me.

Chapter One

Daisy Peters was on her way home from school, the one she had attended most of her young life, at nearly seventeen she had passed her school certificate with flying colours, words couldn't describe how she felt, she was ecstatic, the nerves that had been there earlier had finally settled in her stomach, she was getting hungry now to the extent she was starting to feel sick, her stomach suddenly reminded her of how hungry she was by making a rumbling noise, she hadn't been able to tolerate breakfast when her mum had prepared porridge earlier that morning. She felt for the paper certificate and tightly gripped it with pride and hurried on home.

School had closed now for the start of the summer holidays and sadly this was the end for Daisy, she wouldn't be going back. She had been extremely happy at school. her parents had encouraged and sacrificed a lot for her to stay on and get her qualifications, not like most of her friends and sister Mary who had left school at fourteen either to get work or help look after younger siblings.

Daisy was quite tall for her age; she had striking blonde hair and lovely blue eyes that shone like the ocean and an attractive figure to match. Her clothes were nice and well made, mostly by her mother. Daisy knew she looked attractive, and all the boys would stop and watch her when she walked by them.

The weather had so far for July been very warm but it had changed today; there were low lying clouds in the sky which had turned an ugly darker grey colour during the morning, it was also trying to rain slightly, but it still felt humid and warm. Nothing, though, could dampen the mood she was in. Daisy pulled her light raincoat closer to her.

She had always loved school from a very early age, the teachers and her parents had encouraged and praised her, they could see how intelligent she was and that she had a promising future ahead of her. Not like her brothers and sister, who didn't like school and only went under protest, and usually only did the bare minimum amount of work.

Daisy always wanted to do well, her dream was to be a qualified nurse; it was a very good profession for a young lady to have although she thought it was going to be very hard work and would take a lot of dedication. Following being in hospital, having her tonsils out when she was seven years old, Daisy had admired the nurses in their crisp light blue uniforms and starched hats, bustling around the children's ward, caring for the sick; she knew then nursing was for her, and she had worked tremendously hard to gain these qualifications. Daisy remembered the care they had shown her, this had planted the idea of the career she wanted to do once she got older, it had never waned.

She hastened her pace as she wanted to get home; the rain was coming down quite heavy now. How she wished she had brought an umbrella and, looking down at her hands she didn't want to get her certificate wet. She turned the corner of her street and quickened her steps, the excitement growing with every step she took. She couldn't wait to tell her mum the good news, pausing at the green door to her home. Daisy thought how proud her parents would be.

Hannah and Jack, her parents, were loving and caring, both born and bred in Luton and had lived close to each other as children, and their schools were also near each other. As they grew up friendship had turned into love, and at eighteen they had got married with permission of both sets of parents who hadn't been surprised. Daisy and Mary had been born a year later. They were twins, Daisy was the eldest, being born fourteen minutes earlier than Mary. Their family life had so far been a happy and fun filled one, both parents having enough love for all their children.

Jack worked as a supervisor of a hat factory in the centre of Luton. There was a chance the country would soon be going to war, well that was what he thought quietly to himself, reading the newspaper; Hitler was not going to be stopped. The factory, he thought, would soon be making military hats and uniforms. He hadn't expressed his thoughts to his wife as he didn't want to worry her unnecessarily so had kept them to himself for now.

Daisy took a deep breath put the key in the lock and turned it, opening the front door. She entered and called out, "I'm home." Standing in the hallway she carefully took off her wet coat, trying not to splash her certificate, and hung it on the coat hooks by the side of the door so it could dry. Pushing back her wet hair out of her eyes, she waited for the rush of her brothers, sister and mother. Mark, her youngest brother, ran from the kitchen, straight into her outstretched arms, wanting to be picked up. He loved Daisy as she was his big sister and had taken care of him as a baby, helping her mum when she had clients for her dressmaking business that she ran from her front room.

"How did you do, Daisy?" asked Mark. Beaming up at his sister. Being five, Mark was Daisy's favourite, he didn't really understand what was happening but had gotten caught up in all the excitement. He was getting too heavy to be picked up, but he was a happy, loving little boy. He too had piercing blue eyes and blond hair. Daisy passed her dry certificate to her mum who glanced at it and picked Mark up; who gave her a big hug, burying his head in her neck.

Her mother and other brother and sister were now waiting for the answer... Hannah looked down at the certificate in her hand and saw that her eldest daughter had passed.

"Well," said Mark again with enthusiasm.

"Yes, I have passed," yelled Daisy above the noise, her other brother, George, and sister, Mary, were making as they started arguing with each other.

"Will you two pack it in," their mum said. "Are we going to have this all summer?" she said in mock annoyance, but couldn't stop the tears of joy running down her face as she looked at her older daughter with pride.

Wiping her eyes on the edge of her apron she said, "Wait till you tell your father when he comes home from work. I'll put the certificate safe in the front room and you can show him later." Hannah walks and opens the door to the front room. "This calls for a celebration tea today," she says walking back towards the kitchen.

Their home was modest but homely, it being a three-bedroom terrace, with a small indoor bathroom and separate toilet that had been built on the back of the property, which most homes didn't have. The family knew they were very privileged. Daisy carried Mark and the other two followed behind, entering the warm kitchen which was heated by a small range.

The kitchen smelt lovely thought Daisy, the cakes that her mother had just pulled out were cooling on a rack on the side. The kitchen wasn't particularly big, but it was comfortable, and it was the heart of the family's home. It always smelt lovely and Daisy loved it when all the family congregated there. There was a little table with chairs around it which they could all sit around at a tight squeeze. Everyone gathered around and the two girls helped their mother prepare lunch for them all.

The younger of the twins, Mary, was reluctant to help, and she wasn't too pleased that her sister had done well. She didn't want to admit it, but she was jealous of her sister, she always thought that Daisy was the favourite of the two of them. Hannah got the thick loaf of bread out, butter from the cold storage and block of cheese that she had purchased that day, Daisy got the plates and glasses. Mum made a pot of tea for her, Daisy and Mary, the boys would have milk or water.

The boys were playing on the floor with Mark's tin soldiers, trying not to get in the way. They really wanted to be outside in the street playing football with their friends, but it was raining heavily.

The cakes would be finished later with them all putting icing on top, once they had cooled down. Hannah had also made a trifle for teatime.

Once lunch was over Daisy and Mary helped to wash up. Mary reluctantly finally helped to dry up, but was whining the whole time. Daisy carried on washing up the plates, rolling her eyes at her sister who carried on regardless.

"You did really well." Hannah praised her daughter as she spoke, still beaming with pride, Mary was trying to hide the hurt she felt growing inside, she looked over at her sister. Daisy couldn't help smiling back at her mother with love and gratitude.

Hannah glanced at the old wooden clock on the wall, she noticed the time, she had to prepare as she had a customer scheduled for a fitting for a new outfit at two.

Daisy would be helping her mother with her dressmaking business and helping to look after her siblings until she turned eighteen. Then she would hopefully start her training as a nurse at The London Hospital in Whitechapel in the East End of London — well that was her first choice.

"It's a shame it's raining because you could have taken Mark to the park for an hour or so," her mother said glancing out of the window into the small garden.

Daisy said, "Don't worry, I can keep him amused while you're occupied."

Her mother observed her daughter, she was proud of the young lady Daisy was turning into. She didn't say it enough, but she would miss her dearly when the time came for her to leave but would never stop her eldest daughter following her dreams. She thought Daisy would make a good nurse as she was caring and warm-hearted. Two o'clock soon came around and their mother welcomed her client and the two vanished into the front room.

In the corner was a tailor's dummy with a beautiful handmade dress placed on it. On the other side of the room was a large sideboard where Hannah kept her best plates, cutlery, cups and saucers and few valuable ornaments that she owned. There was a large worn looking settee as well, but it was comfy, also a small table where her mother produced her wonderful garments and kept her materials and her pride and joy; her Singer sewing machine.

There wasn't much room left, it was a tight fit. Hannah peered over at the dress she had worked long into the night to get finished and was waiting for the reaction from Mrs White.

"Oh, it's beautiful Hannah," Mrs White exclaimed as they walked into the room. Mrs White, or Flora to her friends, was a neighbour to the Peters family and thought the world of Hannah and Jack. She had even babysat for them when the girls were small, having watched Jack and Hannah grow up and then settle down together and have a family of their own.

"I hear Daisy has passed her exams? News spread very quickly around the street. You must be very proud?"

"OH! We are, but Jack doesn't know yet as he is still at work, so please don't say anything if you see him?" Hannah looked at Flora who nodded back in agreement.

"Now, would you like to try on the dress?" Hannah asked, carefully taking it off the dummy. "And then we can have a cup of tea unless you are in a hurry to get back to your family?"

Mrs White, having tried the dress on, was very pleased with the result, dipped into her purse and payment was made. They both made their way into the kitchen where the rest of the family was playing.

"Well done, Daisy," said Flora, smiling over to the young girl."

"Thank you, Mrs White," replied Daisy shyly.

"Are you going to help your mother now, until you go away in a couple of years?" she asked, turning and sitting down at the table.

Everyone knew Daisy wanted to become a nurse, it was the worst kept secret as it was all she talked about.

"Yes," said Daisy, feeling a little apprehensive. She was happy that she was going, but enormously scared as well as she had never been away from home before. She let the feeling drop, as it made her nauseous to think about it. It was still a long way off, but she knew two years would fly past, and knew she would suffer from homesickness, but she still wanted to go.

Shortly after Mrs White left, Hannah went to make ready another garment for the morning, leaving Daisy to occupy her siblings. Sometimes her mother worked long into the night. Daisy thought she was very dedicated.

George being the next eldest at nearly fifteen, thought he was big enough to take care of himself, but Daisy knew trouble was always around the corner. George was starting work with their father in September, and he couldn't wait.

Daisy remembered when George had left the front door open, and a stray cat had got in with a mouse in its mouth. Her mum and dad had a terrible time trying to prise the dead mouse out of the cat's mouth and getting the cat out just in case it had fleas. Mary had screamed the house down, while the rest of the family had tried to catch the stray cat.

"What shall we play till we can help Mum ice the cakes?" Daisy looked at all three, waiting for an answer.

"Hide and seek," said Mark.

"We can't really play that in here, we really need a bigger space," said his big sister.

"I know, I will read to you. Go and fetch a book," Daisy said. "And by then, Mum should be ready to finish the cakes."

The afternoon went quickly, Mark had chosen his favourite book with torn pages, all the siblings enjoyed sitting around while Daisy occupied them with stories.

Mum entered the kitchen at four thirty and they all helped to ice the cakes. Mark, standing on a chair, liked to lick the wooden spoon. Daisy and Mary helped prepare tea.

Chapter Two

Dad arrived home at five thirty, rushing through the back door that led into the kitchen. As it was still raining, he took off his wet jacket and hung it on the back door to dry.

On seeing all his family together, he cheerily called, "Well, how's my favourite gang? All okay?" he asked cheerfully, looking at each one in turn.

"Yes, Dad!" came the reply in unison. His eyes caught Daisy's, her blue eyes shining bright back at him.

"Well, how did you do, my girl?" he enquired smiling at her warmly.

Daisy couldn't contain herself. "I passed, Dad," she said with a big smile on her face.

"Oh, that is wonderful news, I am so proud." Her dad pulled her to him and gave her a big kiss on the cheek. He peered down at her and thought 'she is going to break a lot of boy's hearts as she gets older'. Mary, on the other hand, he thought, was nice but she would use people to get what she wanted in life and was not as warm as her twin. They looked very similar, you could say they were almost identical. Jack noticed, when he caught Mary looking at her sister, it was always with a slight scowl. Jack knew Mary was jealous of her sibling.

Daisy loved the warmth that radiated from her dad, she hugged him tight, tears prickling her eyes. Wiping her eyes, Daisy reluctantly let go and walked to the front room to get her certificate to show him. Jack looked over at Mary while Daisy was out of the room and decided later to have a quiet word with her.

Hannah and Daisy came into the room, and Daisy handed the certificate to her father to look at. Hannah asked Daisy to set the table for tea. Daisy liked this time as they all sat round the little table and could all talk about their day; it was family time.

Jack went over to Hannah and gave her a quick kiss and cuddle. "How's my favourite girl?" he whispered into her ear.

"Flora came today and picked up her dress, she was very pleased with the result."

He kept hold of her. "Oh, that is good news, but I'm not surprised as your work is exceptional," he said with pride.

"I put the money in the tin on the sideboard," said Hannah, embarrassed.

The tin on the sideboard is where she kept the money she received. Hannah was uncomfortable taking money from clients, she would happily do the work just out of enjoyment, but Jack had said no, she needed to charge them, and it helped the family finances. She didn't have a bank account yet, Jack had been talking of opening one as the business grew. Jack reluctantly released his wife and put the certificate down.

"Let's eat," said Hannah. They all sat around the table, it was a tight squeeze, and everyone enjoyed their tea.

Later Daisy helped bath Mark, splashing the water and making Mark giggle. She loved this time with her younger brother, he smelt lovely from the soap she used. Once done she wrapped him in a fluffy towel and got him into his pyjamas, and she took him to his room, which he shared with George. She snuggled him under the covers and sat by him to read a story.

"Thanks, Daisy, I really love your stories." He cuddled into her more.

Soon his eyes were getting heavy and drooping, and Daisy called her mum and dad to come up to say goodnight. He wrapped his arms around both of them tightly.

"Love you," came a sleepy voice. "Please can you leave the little night light on until George comes up?"

"Yes, of course," replied his sister.

He had always been afraid of the dark, so the family always made sure the light was left on. Daisy made her way into the kitchen, the wireless was on quietly playing in the background, her brother and sister were listening to it.

She dropped down beside them and sat quietly waiting for her parents to enter the room. Once they entered, they sat talking until the BBC news came on, some of the news recently had been serious and the repercussions on Britain could be huge. Her parents listened intently and the news was not good; it was all about what was happening in Europe with Hitler and Neville Chamberlain, the current Prime Minister, was trying to install peace at all cost.

Her dad listened attentively, he looked worried and so was her mum, they were both in a sombre mood, both trying not to show it. They had both seen what had happened during the First World War and the memory was still fresh there. How it had torn a lot of families apart, and some families had never recovered to this day. The news ended and Jack went over to turn the wireless off, it was looking more likely that there would be a war. Both parents were left with their own thoughts and concerns.

Daisy observed but kept silent, her parents would say something when they were ready. Soon it was time for George to go to bed. Mary usually went up with Daisy, but tonight, she went up early. They had normally had their baths on a Saturday night like Daisy, but Mary had asked to have her bath tonight. It left just Daisy and her parents in the room.

"What an eventful day," Jack said picking up the certificate. He walked out into the hall, closing the door behind him to keep the light from shining out, walked into the front room and over to the sideboard. He found what he was looking for and placed the certificate down, he would have to get a frame for it and came back into the kitchen carrying a thin small box wrapped in coloured paper. Jack and Hannah had been saving for a few months for this gift.

"This is from both of us." Passing it over to his eldest daughter, she pulled the coloured paper off, being careful so it could be used again. Once she had opened it, she couldn't believe what was inside; she saw a long gold necklace and cross.

"Oh, it's beautiful!" whispered Daisy, it was like nothing she had seen before, let alone owned.

Her mother picked it up, unclasped it and put it around Daisy's neck, it sat perfectly.

"It's for all your hard work and the help you give me at home, congratulations again," Hannah said.

"We may not tell you enough, but we are grateful and appreciate all the help you give with your brothers and sister, and for passing your exams," said Dad proudly.

"Are you meeting up with Bobby tomorrow night to go to the cinema?" enquired Mum.

"Yes, he is taking me to see a film and then to have fish and chips for supper after." Daisy glanced down at her neckless as she talked, she couldn't take her eyes off it.

Robert, or Bobby to his friends, was a boy from school. They had grown up together and their parents were friends. Bobby wanted to be more than friends but Daisy was reluctant, it's not that she thought he wasn't boyfriend material but he was more like another brother to her. He was very nice, she even thought he was attractive; he was tall and had broad shoulders, but his hands were red and sore from being covered in motor oil all day. He was very kind and, most importantly, he adored Daisy.

Bobby lived in hope that she would change her mind and that she would learn to love him. Even so he would not give up. Robert had left school at fourteen and was working with his dad at his garage, fixing cars, he was lucky to have a job. Bobby had a younger sister Julie who was friends with Mary, they were roughly the same age. Just after ten o'clock Daisy yawned, and she said her goodnights. It had been a long but exciting day; she made her way up to bed.

Daisy shared a room with Mary, they had to share a large bed, she didn't mind, especially in winter when it was cold as they kept each other warm. Sometimes in the summer when it got too hot, it was unbearable but she didn't grumble. She knew they were better off than some of her friends who lived nearby, they just accepted it.

Mary wasn't asleep when her older sister came up, Daisy got undressed quickly and slipped her nightie on. Mary had noticed her necklace.

"Is that what Mum and Dad got you?" Mary's voice was harsh.

"Yes," Daisy replied guiltily.

"It's lovely," she said. She couldn't help feeling just a little bit jealous, and she hoped her voice didn't give it away.

"If you work hard and do well, I'm sure you will get one," said her sister sincerely, but Mary wasn't sure, she wasn't as clever as her older sister.

Mary's only interest was getting a boyfriend, then getting married, settling down and having a family. As she laid in bed, she had a secret that she hadn't told her family, that she had an interview at the local greengrocers in the morning. She wanted some independence and money of her own.

Her mind went back to boyfriends, well there was only one boy exactly, Bobby. She knew he only had eyes for her sister. Well, she would bide her time and wait, he would notice her soon, once he worked out that Daisy wasn't interested in him. Daisy climbed into bed having come from the bathroom.

"Budge over." Nudging her sister.

Mary moved over so Daisy could get in, the two girls lay there looking at the ceiling, lost in their own thoughts for a while. Daisy pushed back the blanket as it was warm, both yawned, and they said 'goodnight' to each other. Tomorrow was another day, thought Daisy. Soon sleep took them.

Chapter Three

At seven the sun was just coming through the curtains; it was going to be a beautiful day; the rain had gone. Daisy got up even though it was the holidays, she had jobs to do, and she still had to help her mum. She was quiet so as not to wake her sister as she wouldn't be too pleased. Daisy quietly put her dressing gown and slippers on, walking to the door, she made her way first to the toilet, which she knew was a luxury, and then to the bathroom for a quick wash in the sink.

She laid out on the bed a yellow summery dress her mum had made for her the year before and got dressed. Dad and Mum were up already, she could hear them downstairs. Closing the bedroom door, she made her way downstairs, leaving her sister sleeping.

She entered the kitchen, where her mother had got the range working, making the room warm. She said, good morning, to her parents and helped set the table ready for breakfast.

Mark had heard her and was carefully making his way down the stairs, she caught him on the last step and made him go back upstairs to get his clothes on. A few minutes later she heard him again and this time he came down fully dressed and was laughing. He entered the kitchen and gave his older sister a big hug and kiss and then he turned to his mum and hugged her.

"Love you," he said in his little voice.

Dad finished his breakfast and picked up his lunch box and made for the door, he picked up his light rain coat off the back door which was dry, he slipped it on and popped his peaked cap upon his head. He left for work at seven thirty as he had to walk into town to get to the factory. He enjoyed that time as he liked to think things through. He kissed his wife, son and daughter goodbye and was gone.

Hannah turned around and looked at her eldest daughter.

"What do you have planned today?" she asked.

"Well, to help you of course!" came Daisy's reply.

Hannah wasn't surprised by this response. By eight Daisy's sister and youngest brother had decided to join them down in the kitchen.

Leaving them Hannah got herself dressed ready for the day ahead, making outfits for her clients who were coming in today and the rest of the week. She left Daisy to keep an eye on the rest of her family for the morning.

Daisy automatically put the wireless on, listening to the news while playing with her youngest brother. It was difficult to keep him occupied as he wanted to go out with George and Mary. George went off to meet his friends and Mary had her interview at the local greengrocers, as a Saturday girl, with the hope of going full time when she could.

Mary had told her mum of the interview over breakfast; their mum had not been too pleased which is why she hadn't said anything earlier! But Hannah let her go for the interview as most of their friends were now at work or being used for babysitting, and her daughter was nearly Seventeen, she couldn't really stop her without Mary causing a scene.

Daisy was left minding her little brother, and when she could she helped her mum prepare the garments. She was a good sewer; her mum had taught her well.

The morning flew by and by twelve-thirty she had prepared lunch and had prepared tea ready for the evening; she was not eating with them tonight as she was going out with Bobby on a date.

Mary got home mid-afternoon saying she had been successful and had got the job, everyone congratulated her. Following the interview, she would be starting there next Saturday; Daisy was truly delighted for her sister. Maybe she would be a lovelier person now she had a job and her own money? Daisy hoped so.

Bobby was collecting her at six-thirty for them to make the seven showing at the Roxy cinema, and then afterward they would have fish and chips.

At five-thirty Daisy went and got herself ready. She put on a lovely grey dress, sandals and cardigan just in case it got chilly later. Mary had even helped style her hair, and she wore light make up, as she didn't like a lot. By six-thirty she was ready, it hadn't rained today, and it was still very warm for a summer's evening.

Bobby arrived dead on six-thirty looking smart in casual shirt and trousers, he knocked and walked into the kitchen. Mary shot up out of her seat, flashing a big smile at him. He didn't notice as he only had eyes for Daisy, who he thought looked like a princess. Daisy peered over to Bobby nervously.

"Off you both go and have a lovely evening, see you later," said her dad smiling. "But no later than ten-thirty," he said, as an afterthought, checking his watch.

Bobby and Daisy walked out into the warm evening. He wanted to hold her hand like a real date, but he knew Daisy was reluctant so kept it down by his side. They made their way into town to the cinema and joined the queue. They enjoyed the film; he turned to her and took her hand and held it like he had done all through the film. Unbeknown to him she had a small smile on her face. Was she actually beginning to enjoy the feeling of being with him?

The nerves were receding. Watching the news reel before the start of the film had been worrying, especially the latest news about what Hitler was getting up to in Europe.

"There will definitely be a war," said Bobby.

Daisy looked at him and said, "Do you really think so?" She couldn't stop the worry in her voice.

Daisy also couldn't stop a chill running down her back when she thought of it. It was getting dark when they left the cinema. They stopped off at the fish shop and Bobby treated them to fish and chips, and they found a place to eat them out of the newspaper. They tasted nice as they were piping hot, and Bobby had put plenty of vinegar on them. Once finished they made their way along a path by the River Lee walking towards home.

Talking to one another about what they had seen on the film screen, they were quite at ease with each other. Daisy's nerves were returning but Bobby didn't notice. As she spoke, he watched her lips moving slowly, mesmerised, he wanted to kiss her; she had lovely lips, he thought, he bet they felt soft.

Daisy knew Bobby liked her, but she didn't want to get his hopes up, but she did like him. She stopped, turned around and he held her tight and slowly his lips met hers in a slow kiss. After a few moments they pulled apart. He was right, her lips were soft and very welcoming.

Bobby spoke first. "Will you be my girl Daisy? Whatever happens I will always protect you and love you."

Daisy knew things had changed between them in the last few seconds. After what seemed a few moments, she said, "Yes." A big smile spread on Bobby's face.

Unbeknown to him though, Daisy wasn't sure if she had just been caught up in the moment, and she still had a little doubt. They walked home slowly enjoying each other's company, Daisy trying to keep the doubt from forming in her head.

Luckily, they made it to Daisy's house by ten-thirty, Bobby had kept checking his watch as he didn't want to upset Daisy's father. They kissed again on parting, and she made her way into the kitchen.

Her parents were still both up.

"Had a good time?" enquired her father.

"Yes," she replied.

He noticed the small smile spreading on his eldest daughter's face, she had gone out a young girl and came back a young woman.

Daisy ran upstairs to use the toilet, and she then came back down to say "goodnight" to her parents, kissing them both on the cheek, and went up to bed.

Her sister was still awake and asked, "Did you have a nice time?" Daisy noticed the envious tone she had used, trying to keep the jealousy out of her voice but failing.

Daisy sat down on the bed and started to get undressed. She looked up at her sister. "Yes, it was lovely." But didn't go into too much detail.

Mary noticed the smile on her sister's face, and she thought more had gone on than her sister was saying. Mary had to find out what had happened, she wanted Bobby for herself.

Daisy climbed into bed pulled the covers up and rolled over to sleep. She really did sleep badly that night. Looking over at her sister who was sleeping soundly, she reflected on what was she going to do about Bobby and her feelings.

Chapter Four

Over the next few days, the same routine continued. They all got up, her father went to work, and her mother did her dressmaking. Daisy took care of her brothers and sister. In the evening she would meet up with friends from school or Bobby would come around and they would sit in her mother's front room talking, holding hands and stealing a few kisses.

She didn't see the jealousy that was oozing from Mary. Why does he like her better than me? I'm better looking, wear better clothes and would be a better girlfriend than her, she deemed angrily. Any how she would bide her time and when Daisy went away, she would show them. It was time to hatch a plan. With that she turned and walked away.

At the beginning of September, on a Monday morning, George was up early, dressed and ready to leave with his father for his first official day at work.

Everyone else was up to see them off and Hannah thought how grown up he was. She couldn't stop the tears as she was very proud.

They all settled into a routine, George loved his job and was learning a lot doing his apprenticeship, and the look when he had brought his first pay packet home had been a delight.

Before long it was coming up to Christmas, the summer had long gone and the nights had drawn in.

Mary was enjoying her job and earning money for herself, what she did earn mainly went on make-up. She also helped her sister and their mother during the week.

Little Mark couldn't wait for Father Christmas to come. The weather had changed, it was much colder, and the snow was trying to fall, not heavy but it still left a slight whiteness on the streets.

Her parents had bought a lovely real Christmas tree that sat in the corner of the front room, and it had been decorated, each child helping — even Mary had joined in! The lights shone and twinkled brightly making the room look homely. The old fairy sat proud on the top, pride of place where she belonged.

Hannah stopped having customers just for two days so they could all have a real family Christmas together. Daisy had been to the market with her mum and they bought a large chicken for Christmas Day dinner and picked up fresh vegetables and potatoes.

At the end of October Mum had made the Christmas pudding and that would be ready for Christmas Day. They all looked forward to finding the two threepences that she had put in them.

Daisy had bought Mark a little toy lorry, Mary some make up and George a cap to wear for the wintery days to keep the rain or snow off his head. For her parents she had bought gloves for her mum and cigarettes for her dad; Bobby had gotten them for her. For Bobby she had bought a cigarette case with his name engraved on it, she didn't enjoy the smell on his breath when he did smoke but she let it slip as a lot of men smoked, she supposed she would just have to get used to it. Her dad wasn't a heavy smoker, but he did enjoy them on special occasions.

Christmas Day soon came around. Their mother was up early preparing the chicken and vegetables for lunch time, and to get the chicken into the range to cook. Both girls came down to help, they got to work on the potatoes and fresh vegetables. The family settled in for a nice day together. Bobby came around in the evening, after he spent the day with his family. As the day had been very cold and it was still trying to snow, they had decided to sit in the front room while the rest of the family was in the kitchen listening to Carols on the wireless.

Jack had been in earlier to light the fire so the room was warm. They sat close together on the settee and were holding hands. Bobby turned and leaned in to kiss her, it left her with a nice feeling.

They shared a few more kisses, and it was getting more heated. Daisy noticed a smell of ale on his breath, mixed with cigarettes. He was feeling brave as he had been allowed to have a couple of glasses of beer at lunchtime. Bobby slowly worked his hand up her jumper, and he felt her breast.

"What are you doing?" she asked firmly, she was shocked.

"Bobby we can't. I'm not letting you touch me like that. I want to do my training and become a nurse, I thought you would wait until we at least got married? I'm not that type of girl," she said, blushing,

Little did they know but Mary was standing by the closed door listening again. Mary knew her sister wouldn't sleep with Bobby, and that alone, would probably spilt them up. Off she went back into the warm kitchen, smiling as she went.

Daisy sat quietly, the atmosphere had changed, and she sat looking into the flames. She knew what happened, and how babies were made but she couldn't help the warm feeling down below. Her hormones were all over the place, making her cheeks blush red while Bobby had kissed and touched her. She knew the risk was too much, but her body had felt so alive; it took all her reserve not to. They both sat there silently, and then Bobby got up.

"I had better be going home," he said looking guilty.

She looked at him, glad in a way as she was tired emotionally. She walked him to the front door, normally he used the back one. She didn't want him seeing her parents or she might blush again and then they would know something had happened.

New Year came and they settled into January 1939. After that night things settled down again and Bobby and Daisy met up regularly, went out or stayed in either at her house or Bobby's. His parents were quite taken with Daisy and they enjoyed it when she went around.

He was good and behaved himself. She put it down to the drink he'd had. By the spring their friendship was stronger, he was falling helplessly in love with her and she was with him, or so she thought.

Underneath it all, Daisy was being pulled in two, she wanted to be with Bobby, and she wanted to go away and do her training in London if they accepted her. She hadn't worked hard to throw it all away.

Mark was growing up too, he had lost his baby charm and was a young boy, and was liking school. Mary was Mary, they may be twins in looks but they were so different in so many ways.

Daisy would take and collect Mark from school and help her mum during the day. Life was good, in the background Hitler and Germany was still causing problems in Europe and the mention of war was becoming more realistic. Mum was worried, she tried to hide it but that was difficult.

Daisy only had to go to the end of August, and she would be off to start her training at The London if her application was successful. She had written lots of letters to various hospitals around the country, and had heard from a few, some had said a firm 'no', others 'yes'. It had taken a while for an answer to come from The London, but she had gotten her wish at last and had been called up to London for her interview with Matron.

So, on a cold blustery day in March she made her way up to the city, she had never been so nervous, and had never been on a train before, let alone the underground on her own. The hospital was made up of very old buildings, each one having many hidden secrets or tales to be told within their walls, it was daunting and intimidating to someone like Daisy who came from a small town.

Daisy was terrified but having asked at Reception where to go, she made her way to Matron's office. She tried to calm her nerves by taking deep breaths, sitting outside the office on a hard chair, she tried to think of nice things.

Dead on eleven, she heard, 'enter', in a stern voice. Daisy stood up and knocked on the door took one more deep breath and entered. Matron's office was cosy with a fireplace in the corner, a large desk sat in the middle of the room with a couple of chairs positioned in front of it.

Matron was a tall thin lady with very high cheek bones, and looked very stern, she wore a black uniform and had a very small pillbox like, white starched hat on her head. Daisy waited to be told to sit down, not daring to move as she spoke to Matron, accurately answering the questions that were being asked.

She asked why Daisy wanted to nurse and why at The London? The interview lasted an hour. Daisy came home unsure how she had gotten on.

She must had answered them correctly as she had received a letter in the post a few weeks later, congratulating her on getting in. They wanted Daisy's measurements for her uniform and told her where she was going to live and all the additional things she needed to buy and bring on Sunday, third September 1939.

Daisy was nervous but excited all at the same time, her family was ecstatic for her, apart from Bobby who wasn't keen for her to go.

He tried to make her change her mind, saying, "Let's get engaged and then married later this year, like your parents and mine had done."

Daisy was annoyed, that was not what she wanted or had worked hard to achieve but trying to explain it to him had been getting more difficult.

He said, "I have a good job. I can take care of you." Gripping her hands in his. "You can work with your mum, and learn dressmaking."

But Daisy wanted more, she wanted to go away, maybe even see the world if she could. London was just a start; little did she know it would change her life completely. Mary was becoming more jealous, telling her how lucky she was to have someone like Bobby, and if he were hers, she definitely wouldn't treat him like Daisy did. Daisy just took it as if Mary had a crush on him.

In July Hannah helped Daisy prepare for going away at the beginning of September, made her some new clothes, night dresses, bought some pyjamas for the winter nights, got her a new dressing gown and she had knitted a regulation blue cardigan which was really nice. Also, two new pairs of black flat heeled shoes and text books from a list that Daisy would need for her training, had been bought. Most importantly her parents had bought her a fob watch for her uniform, it was beautiful, and she had cried when they had presented it to her.

Her father brought a brown suitcase down from the loft, that was her mum's before she got married, which she put in the corner of the room ready to be packed.

Mary was really pleased she was getting her own room and bed at last, but her biggest wish was getting Bobby as well. Soon it was the end of August, and the summer had been hot. Daisy had packed her case. Hannah had helped her daughter, trying to keep the tears at bay, but she was still emotional. Once packed it was ready to leave with her in the morning, she had said goodbye to Bobby the previous night, which hadn't gone too well.

She sat on her bed and her mind drifted back to the events of the evening. It had started well. Bobby had picked her up at Seven-thirty and they had gone to the Lord Nelson public house where they had celebrated her eighteenth birthday a few months back. Bobby gave her a lovely gold bracelet, it was beautiful, and had placed in on her wrist. Daisy thought back to when Mary had first seen the bracelet the jealousy had oozed from her. Daisy quickly put the thought to one side.

They had entered the pub, through the double doors, the room was full of lingering smoke. Men were standing at the bar talking with the landlord, mainly the topic was about the upcoming war. Daisy found a table in the corner away from people so they could talk by the fire, the glow making her relax slightly.

Bobby went to the bar and got Daisy a port and lemon and he had a pint of bitter. He came over and sat down. Lighting a cigarette, he sat back.

They had started with small talk and then he said, "You're really going then?" Rather harshly. He regretted it as he hadn't mean it to come out like that.

"Yes," she replied curtly. "You know I am, this is what I always wanted." She was pretty angry with Bobby's attitude.

He had drunk the beer quickly, stabbed out his cigarette in the ash tray, aggressively pushed the chair back, got up and went to the bar, and got another.

When he sat down again Daisy said, "I will write, and you can come up to London and visit. I will still be becoming home for the holidays."

He replied, "You will soon forget me with them fancy doctors."

"Are you jealous? I haven't even gone yet," she nearly shouted at him. The conversation between the two of them was rather stilted after that. Both decided to call an uneasy truce and they kept off the topic of Daisy leaving.

After a few more drinks they left the pub and headed home and ended up in a quiet place down by the river. Bobby pulled Daisy to him. He kissed her roughly and his hands began to wander, one even ended up on her breast. The other was moving downwards.

Daisy pulled away sharply. "What the hell are you doing?" she shouted.

"I love you Daisy. Just this once, please show me," he slurred his speech.

"No," she hissed. "Get off me."

She pushed his hand away and just then a man walked by, and asked if everything was okay? This stopped Bobby in his tracks and had brought him to his senses, they made their way home both lost in their own thoughts.

Daisy said, "I think you should leave." When they reached the front door.

Bobby turned around, head down and headed down the road angrily, embarrassed and upset with himself. Daisy entered the house ran upstairs to her room and burst into tears.

"What's the matter, has something happened?" asked Mary concerned at seeing her sister upset. She was sitting on her side of the bed.

"Nothing," came the reply.

Daisy didn't mean to raise her voice but she was upset, and she didn't see her sister smirk; she would find out what had taken place, Mary thought.

The next morning after sleeping badly, Daisy had tossed and turned all night going over what had occurred the evening before, and blaming herself in the end, she got up, not feeling herself.

She went downstairs once she had dressed, having laid her clothes out the night before, and had breakfast. Daisy couldn't eat much as she was so nervous, by eight everyone was up to see her off. They all set off together to get to the station by Nine-fifteen a.m. They entered Luton Station, and noticed the concourse was heaving with men in uniform, they were regular soldiers on the move, there were families saying goodbye to loved ones, her father looked around with a worried expression on his face…

Hannah was crying, but trying to be strong for her daughter. The train was in, and Jack opened the carriage door. He passed her the suitcase through the door, placing it to one side, and she stepped down. He pulled his daughter to him tightly, at that moment he felt so much love for his girl.

"Just be careful!" he warned with a wobbly voice.

Now she started to cry, she let go reluctantly and climbed aboard again. Daisy put the suitcase up above her seat on the rack and went back to the door, pulling the window down. Gently the tears slowly trickled down her face, it was a wrench to leave.

Both her parents were crying they had been disinclined to let her go as the threat of war was real now, but life had to carry on. Mark wanted her to hold him, but his mum held him tight, otherwise he would have wanted to get on the train as well.

George wished her well and she kissed his cheek. Mary said a curt "goodbye," and Daisy just smiled at her.

Take care they called as the train began to pull out of the station, steam bellowing out of the engine. She had hoped Bobby would come but there was no sign of him, she had looked around and looked down at the bracelet he had given her. Her feelings were one of relief that he hadn't shown up as she didn't want to have an argument with him in front of her family.

Mary too had noticed Bobby hadn't come, and she smiled to herself.

"Well, he's mine as Daisy isn't here now," she thought as she turned towards her parents.

Daisy sat back in her seat as the train departed the station. Well, here's to my new life she thought, wiping the tears with the clean pressed hanky her mother had given her. She wondered what the future held for her, only time would tell.

Brewing in the background was the threat of war, a very large threat. Another passenger in the carriage, an elderly gentleman, had asked her, if she was all right?

Daisy had replied, "I am fine, thank you."

Daisy pulled herself together and stared out of the window at the fields and the train rocked on its way to the big city and a new life for the eighteen-year-old. Little did she know that later that day the country would be at war!

Chapter Five

Lady Elizabeth Fenton, daughter of Lord Clifford and Lady Margo Fenton of Newton Hall Warwickshire, was Sixteen nearly turning Seventeen over the summer and had just left the prestigious boarding school her mother had insisted she attend — much to Lizzie's distaste.

Elizabeth had been collected from Warwick Station by the family Chauffeur, Geoffrey, dressed in his liveried uniform. Her Mother, whose birth name was Margaret but liked to be called Margo, thought she had given her daughter an adequate education and now it was time for her to find a husband; and Margo had found just the perfect man.

As she sat in the back of the family Rolls Royce against the cream leather upholstery, staring out of the window as the car drove down the sweeping grand entrance to the family home, a feeling of trepidation came over her, and she really could have done with a cigarette. Her Mother hated her smoking; she had picked up the habit from School.

The car swiftly pulled up to the front entrance and Elizabeth took a deep breath and opened the door before Geoffrey could get too do it. The heat of the summer's day hitting her as she got out. All of a sudden, she came over feeling nauseous, but she quickly pushed the feeling away.

Once out she was greeted by her mother, father and Dinky the black Labrador. Elizabeth greeted her parents with a kiss on their cheeks and a pat on the head for the dog.

"Welcome home Elizabeth," said her mother in a jovial voice.

Her mother had married into money and wanted the same for her daughter, Elizabeth looked at her mother closely and thought the years were telling on her face, she was stern, had no maternal bone in her body, both herself and her brother had been brought up by the family nanny.

Her father on the other hand was warm and loving, he gave her a warm welcoming hug and took her by the elbow. His family had made their money in shipping and he wanted a good and happy life for his only daughter. They entered a magnificent grand hall with a sweeping staircase straight ahead, there was a coat of arms in the corner. On the walls were paintings of old family members, too many to count, and along the wall were suits of armour gleaming in the sunshine. To the left were the library and drawing-room.

Geoffrey in the meantime had unloaded her belongings and these were being taken up to her room by the butler. They entered the drawing-room, and she was told to sit by her mother. Taken back by the tone of her voice she did as she was told.

"My darling girl, we have wonderful news, but first tea."

A maid in a black dress came in, carrying a tray of teapot cups and saucers. She placed it down gently on a lovely oak table and her mother said, 'she would pour' and she waited while the maid left the room.

"Well, Mother, what is this wonderful news you have to tell me?" Elizabeth asked in a sarcastic voice.

Her mother straightened her back and told her that she had met Lord Charles Holmes and his family, her mother knew his mother, they were old friends. They had come to an agreement that when the time was right, both children were to get engaged and married.

Elizabeth's face fell. She felt sick as she had heard of this man, he was a friend of her brother and apparently not very nice. Yes, he had the looks by all accounts but was snobbish, arrogant and more importantly he was cruel. He only wanted a trophy wife, and it was not going to be her, Lizzie had decided she wanted to marry for love. He had only become friends with Edward at School because he too had a title and money.

Elizabeth glared at her father for support, he just smiled, and she could see he was at a loss of how to help his daughter get out of this situation. She felt trapped and wanted to get away, she felt claustrophobic, so made her apologies by saying, 'she felt unwell' and headed up to her room.

Her mother called after her, "I will speak to you later young lady!" As she closed the door.

Elizabeth flew up the grand stairs and headed for her room along the landing, she opened the door, flopped on the bed and immediately burst into tears, that she had been holding back. Her room was medium size, a large bed was to one side and chest of drawers to another, with a large full-length mirror to the right. A Persian rug laid down on the floor by her bed and the rest of the floor was covered in carpet.

This was not happening, she thought, she didn't want to meet anyone, nor did she want to get married yet. She wanted to be a nurse and live in London, that was her dream — away from her mother. After some time and when she had cried enough tears, she saw her suitcases and trunk in the corner.

She unpacked her clothes and put everything away neat and tidy, boarding school had taught her to be tidy. Lizzie had enjoyed her time at school, she had made some good friends, but some were not desirable, if her mother had only known some of the girls she had mixed with, what a bunch of unscrupulous girls she had met. Some were nice but the others were, how to put it, unsavoury.

The air in the room was stuffy, so she opened the large door which opened onto a balcony, she looked out onto the sweeping green lawns and nicely kept gardens at the back of the house. Looking down she watched as the gardeners were hard at work keeping the hedges neat and tidy. When she was younger, she used to enjoy assisting them, much to her mother's annoyance, Lizzie did it on purpose to make her mad. It was cooler here as the sun was at present at the front of the house.

Edward her brother, aged eighteen, arrived home a few hours later and knocked on her door, it was end of term for him as well.

"Enter," she called, demoralised, thinking it was her mother come to gloat. Her brother came into the room and gave her a big hug.

"Hi sis, how is everything?" But he stopped once he saw his sister looking so downcast.

"Oh, Eddie. Mother wants me to meet Lord Charles Holmes with the hope that I end up marrying him."

Eddie took a step back and said, "She is meddling again with no thought to how you feel." Taking pity on his sister as he didn't like Charles one bit. He felt sorry for his sister.

"I don't want to meet or marry him! Please help," she implored. Eddie, knowing Charles, knew this was a bad union for his sister.

"Okay, let me get settled and then we will talk."

He gave his little sister a hug and she held him tight, her sad look she upset him. Edward turned and left the room and made his way to his room next door. He opened the door and turned, closing it, he leaned against it and sighed. He knew how she felt, their mother was also doing it to him, she wanted him to meet Lady Francesca Owens with the plan to also get married.

Oh god, he thought, how were they going to deal with this?

He really wanted to join the Air Force as a pilot, he knew war was coming; he had spoken quietly with his father and the boys at School. That man Hitler had to be stopped at all costs. Eddie opened his case and started to unpack his clothes.

Lizzie finished unpacking and had a thought that if she could get her father on her side, he may be able to persuade her mother to change her mind and let her decide what she wanted to do. Deep down, she knew it wasn't going to happen, her mother was very strong-willed, and no one ever got the better of her.

Lizzie decided to have a bath and went into the bathroom just off her bedroom. She turned the taps on, filling the lovely white enamel tub with hot water, adding cold to get it just right. Undressed, she climbed in and sat down, letting her worries go to the back of her mind. She laid down and enjoyed the feeling of hot water and bubbles against her skin and washed herself with exotic smelling soap. Too soon the water started getting cold and she got herself out and dried off using a lovely white fluffy towel embroidered with the family coat of arms.

Wrapped in it, she made her way into her bedroom and got dressed for the evening. She chose a lovely light olive green dress and sandals, she looked at herself in the long mirror and thought, 'not bad', she tied her hair up.

Lady Elizabeth was a strikingly pretty young lady; she wore little makeup; had blonde hair, blue eyes and a very nice figure, her only vice was that she smoked. On hearing the dinner gong, Lizzie set off down the stairs for the dining hall and another battle with her mother.

"Glad you could join us," her mother said to them both.

She had met her brother coming out of his room on the landing. They both entered the dining room at the same time, which was a splendid room with a large Edwardian table covered with candles and had chairs positioned all around. On the walls were portraits of various landscapes by different artists.

"Please take a seat both of you. We have lots to discuss," she continued.

Both siblings looked at each other and sat down. Once the soup was served their mother began in earnest. Firstly, she aimed at Edward about Francesca and then it was Elizabeth's turn. She held her breath as her mother started saying how Charles came from a good family, and the marriage would be good for the family. Lady Fenton kept on relentlessly until she had had enough.

To stop her mother, she said, "I will meet him soon." But really, she wasn't interested.

On hearing this her mother's face lit up. The rest of the evening flew by and at eleven Lizzie had had enough, she excused herself, mentally exhausted and made her way up to bed.

As it was a warm night, she left the door to the balcony open, and she got undressed and listened to the animals as they said goodnight to each other in the pitch black. Whether it was the heat or what her mother had said, Lizzie slept badly that night, tossing and turning. She woke to the sound of birds singing and pulled the sheets towards the bottom of the bed and got up.

Quickly getting dressed, she pulled her hair into a ponytail and made her way down to breakfast. Both her parents were up and already seated at the table. Elizabeth hoped her mother would be quiet about the subject of marriage today, but she knew it very unlikely. Just as her breakfast was brought to her, Eddie arrived for his.

"Isn't this nice, all of us together?" said her mother cheerfully.

Their father looked up and smiled as if agreeing in his own way. Once breakfast had finished, Elizabeth wanted to get her letters for Nursing off to the hospitals. Over the last few weeks, she had completed the letters and was ready to place them in the envelopes and send them off. Something made her hold off as she wanted to hear what her mother had to say today, if she didn't agree then the letters would be posted tonight.

"I will speak with you both at eleven in the drawing-room. Don't be late," their mother had shouted as they left the room.

At eleven both siblings arrived promptly and were met by their mother.

"Sit down both of you." She waved her hand at the vacant chairs. "As you know it's about time you both found yourself a husband and wife."

"But, Mother," both said together. She glared at them for interrupting her.

"Let me continue. These are two good matches and I want you now to agree to meet them. I have liaised with their families, and they are happy for this to go ahead. Edward, you will meet Francesca on Friday as she will stay the weekend, and the same for you Elizabeth, Charles will be doing the same."

Both looked at each other and felt dread and a cold, icy feeling ran down their backs.

Chapter Six

Friday was the day they both feared with dread. It turned out to be overcast, and rain was looming, but it was still warm. Up to then it had been hot but now the weather for the weekend didn't look so good.

They were both told to meet by the door at eleven-thirty, that was when both parties were arriving. First to arrive was Francesca, driven by Geoffrey. He had picked her up from the station. Shortly after, Charles turned up driven by his family chauffeur in the Bentley. Lizzie knew Francesca from School. They weren't close friends but she knew of her, her brother could do a lot worse, she was a pretty girl but a bit dreary.

They were shown to the guest suites and left to unpack. They were to meet up for lunch at twelve-thirty for drinks prior to sitting down at one. Lizzie sat up in her room looking at the pile of written letters waiting to be posted and she made up her mind to post them today. She sat back, and relief flooded over her. Her mother was not going to be stopped in finding her a husband, but she was going to a least train as a Nurse first.

Drinks were served in the drawing-room; Charles entered the room looking charismatic in dark blue trousers and white shirt, and he made his way straight over to Lizzie.

"It's nice to finally speak with you."

Lizzie did her best to keep out of the way of Charles, but he stayed by her side, and at one stage he grabbed her arm when she tried to walk away while he was talking. She looked up at him and glared.

"You are hurting me, let go," she said, looking down where he gripped her wrist.

"Sorry," he hissed once he saw everyone in the room looking at them.

The gong went for lunch, and everyone made their way into the dining room, Lizzie hoped her mother had seen what Charles had done, but knew it wouldn't change her situation. When Lizzie got her lunch, it tasted unappealing. Once lunch was over, Lizzie couldn't wait to get to the safety of her room. Lady Fenton spoke.

"Elizabeth, will you show Charles the grounds and gardens later?"

Lizzie rolled her eyes, that was the last thing she in fact wanted to do.

"Yes, Mother," she replied dutifully.

Edward butted in, "We will come too!" Glancing at Francesca, who agreed readily.

Lizzie mouthed a 'thank you', to both and Fran smiled, she knew what Eddie was up to.

So later that afternoon they met at the bottom of the stairs, and they all set off for a walk. It was warmer than earlier, the rain had not come but the sun had come out, the party headed off in the direction of the summer house and lake. The grounds were spectacular, there was a herb garden, rose garden and a large greenhouse.

Fran and Edward were happily talking, and Charles was walking in front with Lizzie, Dinky had joined them as she knew she had to keep an eye on Charles. They headed to the summer house, passed the large lake with white swans swimming on it, they must have got lost as Fran and Eddie were nowhere around.

Lizzie froze as Charles pushed her into the summer house door, his face leering at her. He pulled her near and pressed his body against her; she felt his hardness.

"I want you!" he hissed."

Luckily Lizzie kneed him in the groin and he fell backwards clutching it with his hands, just then Edward and Fran walked in.

"What's going on here?" Edward shouted, glaring at his sister and friend lying on the floor, rolling around in agony.

Once Charles' pain had gone. "I was just getting to know your sister better." He stood tentatively and winked at Edward. Edward wanted to hit his friend, but Fran placed her hand on his arm stopping him.

"Let's get your sister back to the house," Fran said in a concerned voice. Lizzie walked with Fran while Edward walked back with the winded Charles who was sulking, thinking it was a big game and Elizabeth was his prize at the end.

Edward wanted to tell his mother but Lizzie had asked him not to as she would not believe it.

"I don't think he will try that again," she said laughing, but Edward wasn't so sure, he knew what Charles was like and he didn't give up very easily.

Later that evening Elizabeth got the maid to post her letters on her way home. After what happened today, it had made her more determined to follow her dreams.

The rest of the weekend passed by without any further major incidents and Fran and Charles left on the Sunday evening. Lizzie was pleased as she couldn't take many more attempts by Charles to grab her at every opportunity. Both would miss Fran as she was in fact a very pleasant person, and if Eddie did have to marry someone then Fran was nice enough and would make a good sister-in-law.

Both children were summoned to the drawing-room by their mother. Well, the weekend had been a success she thought. They sat there looking at each other, hoping they could leave and get up to their rooms. Their brains were tired tonight, and they hadn't the fight to argue with their mother, she was in a good mood and so took pity on her children, seeing they appeared tired, she dismissed them.

Once upstairs, Lizzie knocked on her brother's door, and waited for the "come in." She entered and made her way over to his bed. Sitting down on his thick eiderdown.

"I hate him Eddie," she said with as much venom in her voice as she could muster, Eddie sat by her and held her in his arms.

"Don't you worry, I will protect you," he said, rubbing her arm. "It's late, let's sleep on it and take stock in the morning."

"Oh…, how did you get on with Fran?" she enquired.

"Yes, she is nice, but I don't want her as a girlfriend or to marry her," he said, looking sadly at his sister. "I think she has a secret, but she didn't say," he said.

"I'm sure it will come out," replied his sister, wondering what the secret was.

"Now time for bed. Good night, sis." Eddie looked at Lizzie as she let herself out of the room and into hers.

She slept badly that night tossing and turning as her mind worked, hopefully she would get a reply and get an interview for nursing, surely some hospital would take her?

Just after Christmas Elizabeth received a letter inviting her up to The London Hospital in Whitechapel, London for an interview with Matron in March. She had received many other replies, but this was the one she truly wanted.

Now all she had to do was convince her parents that it was a good idea, well especially her mother. First, she told her brother, who was delighted. She then found her mother sitting in the drawing-room.

"Elizabeth, my darling girl, have you heard from Charles," she said.

"No, not yet!" Came the sombre reply. "But I have some news for you and Father," said Lizzie who was nervous as hell. Her father entered the room.

"Our daughter has some news for us Clifford," said her mother. Her father took a seat,

"Please tell." Lizzie took a deep breath. Here goes, she thought.

"Well, I have applied to train as a nurse at The London," she said. "I have an interview on seventeenth March, if I get in, I start the beginning of September."

Margo turned a bright shade of red and exploded with, "You are not going young lady."

"Mother, Father, please, it's what I want to do," she pleaded.

"It's not a job for a Lady, Elizabeth, you have Charles to consider."

"Why?" Lizzie shouted. "How is he involved?" Lizzie said.

"Because, young lady, he is going to be your husband." Her mother looked solemnly at her daughter.

Once she had calmed down, she asked, "Why Nursing?"

"Because I want to do something worthwhile with my life and have a professional career at the same time," replied Lizzie. She felt sick as if everything was falling apart around her.

"Please, I beg of you, just let me go to the interview, I might not even get accepted." Lizzie knew she would be accepted, just by having her name the hospital would want her, and the prestige that went with it.

Edward entered the room; he had heard the commotion from outside the door.

"Mother, Father, let her go," he said patiently.

Her father turned to his wife, and for the first time he said, "Margo, let her go. If we don't, she will only try and find a way to do it without our knowledge."

His daughter waited with anticipation and held her breath; finally, her mother said, "No, and that is my final word."

Lizzie turned and stormed out of the room, and headed up the stairs to her room. Slamming the door hard, God, she was fuming. How could her mother be like this!

About half an hour later Eddy knocked gently and entered her room.

"All right old girl?" he asked soothingly, sitting down by her side on her bed.

She fell into his arms and cried, "How can a mother be so cruel?"

"I don't honestly know! Well, we had better get her to change her mind," he said smiling.

Lizzie smiled back feeling slightly better. The next day, both siblings, before entering the breakfast room, took a deep breath, looked at each other smiling, nervously, and opened the heavy wooden door. Taking their seats, they waited for their mother to speak first.

"Good morning," she said in a curt voice.

"Good morning, Mother," both replied.

Lizzie gave her father a weak smile hoping for reassurance, but he just looked down at his breakfast and carried on eating.

Mother scowled at her daughter and began by saying, "I have spoken with your father and I have changed my mind." Lizzie glanced over at her mother not quite believing what she had just heard. "We have agreed you can attend the interview only if you agree to marry Charles once your training is finished!"

"But Mother!" Lizzie replied.

"I will hear no more and I want your answer now!"

Lizzie thought quickly, she had two choices, to say no and have a major argument, which would not go well for her, or say yes and hope things would transpire in the future to alter things. At this moment, she prayed this to be the case.

Lizzie glanced at her mother and said very quietly, "Yes, I agree to your terms." Why did she feel her fate had just been sealed?

Her mother's face lit up and she turned and looked at her daughter. "You have made the right decision."

Breakfast was very awkward; Lizzie couldn't wait to escape up to her room. She felt her life was over before it had even begun.

The seventeenth of March soon came, and Elizabeth made her way by train up to London, and took the tube to Whitechapel. The London Hospital was big and formidable looking, the old buildings standing majestically. It held a lot of history thought Lizzie, I want to make some memories here too.

She found her way to Matron's Office after asking the head porter in his hut where to go. She sat waiting for the allotted time and was called in by Matron, who was a tall stern-looking lady in her black uniform and white cap. The next hour was the most harrowing Elizabeth had ever experienced; her career was in the balance.

Walking along the corridor Lizzie noticed the sign to the canteen, and she made her way there. She had a cup of tea and reflected on what had just taken place. She thought she had done well, answered all the right questions and had asked the right ones too. 'Well, I can't do any more now it is over', she thought, and Lizzie knew that Matron wanted her at The London, or more exactly, her family's wealth and title.

She finished her tea and made her way out, then she walked along the road to the tube and home. Lizzie arrived home early evening and found her family in the drawing room having drinks, she poured herself a gin and tonic.

Her brother asked, "How did it go?"

"Well, I think I have done well," was her simple reply.

Her mother huffed but made no comment, inside she hoped it had gone badly for her daughter just to prove she was right.

Her father said, "Well done." And leaned in to kiss her cheek.

Lizzie finished her drink and was heading for the door when her mother said, "Charles called and wants to come for the weekend again? He really likes you Elizabeth," she said, smiling sweetly at her daughter.

Lizzie felt sick and looked at her mother and said, "I'm tired from travelling and I'm off to bed. "Good night to you all."

Lizzie nearly tripped over her own feet as she ran out of the room. She couldn't wait to get away to her bedroom and as she ran up the stairs nearly knocked the butler over as he came down the other way.

"Sorry!" she called over her shoulder.

Lizzie could hear her mother shout, "Don't run, Elizabeth."

Eddie came up later and knocked on his sister's door, he entered before she said come in, saying, "Don't worry, I will be around when he comes".

Lizzie said, "There is something not right about him, but I can't put my finger on it."

"There was a rumour at school about a girl and Charles, but it was hushed under the carpet by his family," her brother said cautiously.

"Can you find out what happened and let me know?" she pleaded.

The next morning it was arranged that Charles was to arrive in a month's time. Eddie had asked Fran to join them too as it would be to their advantage.

A few weeks following her interview, Elizabeth received her letter. She had been successful and was to start her training at the beginning of September, 1939. Lizzie was over the moon with happiness and so was her brother, not so her mother! Lizzie braced herself for the abuse she was going to get from her.

Elizabeth entered the drawing room and went up to her parents, and looked at her mother.

"I am begging you please to let me do this?"

"Why should I?" she replied curtly.

"I am eighteen and I want a career and profession, mostly I want you to be proud of me, Mother!" Lizzie implored.

"Remember you have agreed to marry Charles once you have finished your training?" Lady Margo reminded.

"Yes, I haven't forgotten!" Lizzie said. She was mentally drained and could not wait to get away from her mother, for her sanity.

Her mother had won again and was controlling her life, and there was nothing she could do about it at present. Charles and Francesca arrived a few weeks later and heard the wonderful news.

Charles wasn't happy about the nurse training but the marriage part he was smug and arrogant about, he could wait three years. It was easy to take some willing lovers on the side. He thought to himself that he had Lizzie where he wanted her; in his grasp. If she ever put a foot out of place, he would make sure that he would put her back in her place. It didn't stop him from having his fun behind her back.

The weekend went quickly, Lizzie kept her distance and tried to not be alone with Charles as best she could. Her brother, with the help of Fran was brilliant. Her brother had found a good partner, if he indeed married her, but Lizzie sensed Fran still had a secret between them, they would work it out.

Her mother was over the moon and wanted to start making engagement plans straight away, but Lizzie was reluctant. She kept making excuses that she wanted to begin her training and kept putting it off, much to the frustration of Charles and his family.

The last few weeks soared by, and Lizzie went shopping in London for items on the list, she got her flat black shoes, blue cardigan and found a book shop for an anatomy, physiology and hygiene and nurses' dictionary, it also had all the other books she would need.

Her Father bought her a fob watch; secretly, he was extremely proud of her. In his own way, he didn't want his daughter to marry that obnoxious Charles and hopefully he would find a way to help his daughter when the time came.

The night before Lizzie was due to leave, her case and trunk all ready, he knocked and entered her room. He sat down on her bed and asked Lizzie to join him. Lizzie apprehensively walked over to the bed and sat by her father, he pulled out the black box.

"Open it," he said gently.

She snapped it open and inside was the fob watch made from solid silver. Turning it over her name was engraved on the back.

"This is for you, and remember I am very proud of what you have achieved."

Tears trickled down her face, and her father held her like he had when she was a small child.

"Thank you for being so understanding," she said sincerely.

Lizzie went to bed that night with a terrible feeling and slept very badly. She woke early, got washed and dressed, and had breakfast, which she couldn't eat. Her mother hardly said two words to her, but that was fine.

Finally, it was time for her family to take her to the Station and send her on her way. She was as excited as she had packed the night before, she couldn't help but think of the life and the adventures she was about to have. Even with the threat of war, a real worry following the news on the wireless last evening, this couldn't shake her from her excitement.

The family all gathered and took the Rolls to Warwick Station. Geoffrey unpacked her case — her trunk would be sent on. On the platform, Lizzie stood talking to her brother.

"Keep in contact old thing, and let me know how you're getting on?"

Lizzie was trying to be strong and not cry. "You do the same Eddie." She had a feeling her brother would be in the Air Force as soon as war was declared, as he had a love of aeroplanes.

The concourse was busy with uniformed men. They all stopped what they were doing to look at Lord and Lady Fenton, and especially Elizabeth. Luckily, dead on time the train slowly pulled into the Station and came to a stop. Lizzie opened the door, and Geoffrey placed her suitcase in with her, she found a seat in first class and Geoffrey placed her case up on the overhead rack.

She said her 'goodbyes' and looked out the window at her parents, she smiled and waved. Finally, she heard the station master blow his whistle and the train slowly pulled out of the station. Elizabeth sat back, rested her head against the seat, and considered what her future held. She looked out of the window as the train passed lush green fields on its journey towards the city and her new life.

Chapter Seven

The train slowly pulled into the spectacular St Pancras Station. Daisy stood up, collected her suitcase from the rack above her and placed her handbag on her shoulder. Once the train had stopped, she made her way to the open door and stepped out onto the platform. She looked around and then followed all the other passengers and made her way to the exit, it was very noisy.

There were a lot of men in uniform here too, rushing to and from trains along the concourse. Many couples were saying tearful goodbyes. She gave her ticket to the station master at the barrier and looked for the sign to the underground. Daisy noticed there were a lot more people about and she had an uneasy feeling that something bad was going to happen.

She found her way to the underground and the ticket office and asked for one way to Whitechapel. She handed over her money and took the ticket. Looking at the map on the wall, she found Whitechapel and made her way to the Hammersmith and City line. Down the wooden noisy escalator, the warmth hit her and she made her way along the platform to stand and await the train.

A few minutes later she heard the train approach and felt the rush of warm air. Daisy picked up her case and waited as the doors slid open, and people pushed to get off. She then got aboard and found an empty seat. The doors closed and away the train went, picking up speed, Daisy couldn't get over how astonishing the underground was. After a few stops, the train arrived at Whitechapel, and she made her way up to the street. The glare of the sun hit her as she came out of the station, and Daisy made her way down the road, walking towards The London Hospital.

Her eyes were wide with all the different activities going on around her. Looking up into the light blue sky with white clouds scattered around, she suddenly stopped, looking at an unusual sight. She noticed large balloons floating high up in the sky, they were held by a large solid cable to the ground. People, she noticed, were putting up black out curtains in their property windows, and also there was more traffic than in Luton, especially the buses and trams, which she hadn't noticed when she came for her interview.

All the shops that lined the road to the hospital were colourful, with the wares they sold sitting on stands proudly. She took in the sights and smells, she had never experienced anything like it before.

When she arrived, she found the head porter in his hut, listening to a wireless.

"What's going on?" Enquired Daisy worriedly, observing his sombre face.

He looked up, his expression solemn.

"War has just been declared," he answered sadly.

She was in shock, thinking of her family she had just left, but then she remembered why she was there. Shaking herself off, she asked for 'Home Sister'.

Before she heads off in the direction of the nurses' home, she asks, "Can you tell me what those large balloons are doing?"

He looks up to the sky. "They are barrage balloons and they are supposed to protect us from German planes as they fly over the city. It won't stop them bombing us!" he said in a solemn tone.

He smiled warily. "By the way, my name is Tom, and if you require any assistance just pop and see me anytime."

"Thank you," Daisy said.

He directed her to the nurse's home, where Home Sister was waiting outside with a clipboard. She was dressed in a dark blue dress with a white cap, very similar to Matron, her hair in a tight bun, and sleeves pulled down.

"Name?" Home Sister barks.

Daisy stutters, "Daisy Peters," she replied timidly.

"Follow me."

Daisy picks up her case and follows the tall imposing lady with her dress swishing against her legs, into an entrance of the nurses' home. Workmen were busy putting up black out curtains and anti-blast tape to all the windows in all the rooms around the home. To the left were the stairs that take you to the first floor and other floors above. Home Sister took her up to the second-floor; room Seven.

Using the key she opened the door to a large room with two cast iron beds, one dated looking large wardrobe and two sets of drawers and a sink in the corner. On the wall is a large full mirror.

"That's for checking your uniform is correct," she said, looking at Daisy when she noticed her staring at it.

All Daisy could do was nod her head and take it all in.

"Meal times are, Supper from six and breakfast is at six, lunch is served from twelve midday in the dining hall," Home Sister said.

"You will make up your bed, making sure you do envelope corners, unpack, and report to the sewing room to collect your uniform as soon as possible. They will make any adjustments while you are there. Lights out at ten and you will be in your room promptly. Meet me downstairs in the common room for a welcome meeting at seven sharp, where you will meet all your other new colleagues. Smoking is not allowed in your room, only in the common room or outside." With that she turned and left.

Daisy could hear her rushing down the stairs. She sat down on the unmade bed and put her head in her hands and wondered, had she made the right decision, especially with the country now being at war?

'Pull yourself together she thought', for the second time that day. As soon as she could she would write to her parents and let them know that she had arrived okay and was safe. Daisy collected her sheets and blankets off the bottom of the bed and got to work making it. She didn't know how to do an envelope corner but she did the best she could, little did she know that soon she would be able to do it with her eyes closed!

Once done she looked at her handy work, smiled to herself and threw her case onto the newly made bed and got unpacking. She chose half the wardrobe and drawers nearest her bed and hoped her new roommate, when she turned up, didn't mind. Half an hour later she was done, as she didn't own many clothes. On the wall was a bookshelf and she positioned all the brand-new books she was asked to get, all lined up neatly. Once she was satisfied, she got herself ready to make her way to the sewing room. She hoped it was easy to find as her navigation skills were very poor. Daisy was about to leave the room when the door flew open, and the most stunning looking girl entered behind Home Sister. Walking into the room Elizabeth looked around, taking in her surroundings. Standing in front of her was a young girl her age, first impression she thought, friendly looking enough.

"So this is your new roommate, Daisy Peters. She arrived today as well. This is Lady Elizabeth Fenton," said Home Sister. "I will let both of you introduce yourselves and get to know each other, then you can settle in."

Home Sister turned on her heel and flew out the door, walking quickly to the stairs. Both girls were left standing in the middle of the room, looking at each other and they broke into nervous laughter, the ice was broken.

Elizabeth stepped forward. "Hello you can call me Lizzie."

"And I am Daisy, nice to meet you."

Daisy had never met a Lady before. Should she curtsy? No, she thought. Both girls shook hands attentively, and Elizabeth looked around the room, getting her bearings.

"Let me help you make your bed up." Daisy said. Lizzie nodded. "If you don't mind, I took the bed by the window?" Daisy said, as she helped Lizzie. Picking up the sheets and blankets she headed towards the empty bed, and both got on with the job of making it up.

Luckily, Lizzie knew how to do envelope corners from her days at school and helped Daisy with her bed as well. The girls were chatting with each other as if they had been friends for a long time once the initial awkwardness was overcome.

"Please, don't call me your ladyship, I'm happy with Lizzie, and it makes me feel old." So Daisy never did.

Once the beds were done, Lizzie packed her clothes away from her suitcase. Daisy was sitting on her bed admiring the quality of the clothes, which Lizzie was putting into her side of the wardrobe, she was slowly running out of space. Lizzie knew she had bought too many with her and next time she went home, would take some back or give some away, and her trunk had not even come yet! She saw Daisy admiring them, so she offered Daisy to look through and take anything she fancied.

Daisy couldn't believe her luck. "Really?" she asked.

Then Lizzie put her other items into the chest of drawers. Finally, all her books were placed on the shelf next to Daisy's. Once everything was packed away, they left their room and made their way down the stairs to the door and off into the main part of the hospital to find the sewing room.

They stopped at reception and a nice lady slid the panel open and asked, "How can I help you young ladies?"

"We are looking for the sewing room?" They both said together.

"Down the long corridor to the right, small room to the left. You can't miss it," she said smiling.

Both girls followed the instructions to a tee, finding it after a few minutes. The girls knocked and entered and found a lovely small lady of Italian extract who took one look and welcomed the girls.

"Come in, come in," Mrs Alonso said.

The girls gave their names and Mrs Alonso got their uniforms out.

"Try these on behind the screen and I will check them, hopefully the measurements that you gave are correct."

Each girl went behind the screen, coming out fully changed. First nurse Peters. "Perfect fit." Mrs Alonso's expert eyes noted. "You can go and take it off," she said waving her hands. Daisy looked in the long mirror and couldn't believe her eyes, standing in front of her was a totally different person. She blinked and felt like she was on top of the world. Then her mind wandered to the fact that the country was at war. Mrs Alonso spoke, and Daisy returned to where she was.

"Now nurse Fenton." It took a moment for Lizzie to realise that she was being spoken to. She stood in front of Mrs Alonso. "Just needs the hem taking up a bit, two minutes and then you are done. Take it off and I will run it through the Singer."

A few minutes later it was all finished, both girls left happy with their brand-new uniforms, capes and cap. They took them back to the room where the uniforms were hung up on hangers, pride of place on the front of the wardrobe. Capes were put away in the wardrobe and the caps were put to one side for the morning. They would be shown how to assemble them in the morning at the school.

"What shall we do now?" asked Lizzie.

"What time, is it?" said Daisy, both looked at their watches. It was one o'clock.

"Shall we get some lunch, I haven't eaten since breakfast, and I am famished. Then we can gather our thoughts and plan the rest of the day," said a hungry Lizzie. Both girls linked arms and made their way to the dining hall.

They followed the smell along the long corridor, pulling the door open, it was a large room with white walls, and it smelt of stale food. Full of long tables and chairs filled with nurses and doctors having lunch, and there was a hatch at the end where the food was dished out. They noticed sisters sat at one table, staff nurses another table and doctors had their own table, although sometimes they did mix. The noise level was particularly high.

Everyone was discussing the news that Britain was at war. Their lunch consisted of mince, potatoes and cabbage, apple pie and custard for pudding, it was plain, hot and edible. As the girls were very hungry, they didn't care! Once the girls had eaten the lot, they took their trays and cleared away and made their way towards the door.

"I need a cigarette," said Lizzie in a desperate tone, so they headed back to the nurse's home and to their room. Lizzie found them in her drawer by her bed where she left them.

"You don't mind, do you? It's a bad habit I picked up at boarding school, one of many," she laughed.

Daisy looked up. "No, I don't mind, my father smokes occasionally; I quite like the smell, it reminds me of him."

But she didn't like the smell on Bobby's mouth. The young girl sat down on her bed and a pang of homesickness drifted over her. Doubt flooded her mind. Had she done the right thing? She could be safe at home with her family, helping her mother run the dress-making business. Instead, here she was in the big city starting a new adventure, was she mad!

Hearing Lizzie say, "Can I smoke in here?"

"No," said Daisy a bit too sharply. "You are only allowed to in the common room or outside."

Lizzie stubbed out the end of the cigarette she had lit, trying to disguise the smell.

"Let's go outside and you can finish it. It's a nice day," Daisy said cheerfully.

Both girls headed for the door. Firstly, they explored their new surroundings, where they found the bathrooms and toilets and a small kitchen area where they could make tea along the corridor. Next they made for the stairs and exploration of the rest of the hospital that was to be their new home for the next three years. Once outside Lizzie lit her cigarette and took a deep breath inhaling it. Once finished she felt better, calmer and more relaxed.

"Where does one begin?" Lizzie asked. "Well, we know where dinner is served, let's find the School of Nursing ready for the morning."

Both girls followed the signs on the wall, and both had high admiration when they saw a smartly dressed very young-looking nurse rushing past them down the corridor, which had a slight smell of disinfectant. After getting lost once and having to ask a junior doctor they found it.

They turned around. "Now what shall we do?" Lizzie asked looking around.

"Let's head back and see if anyone else in our group has turned up," said Daisy.

Going back the way they had just come; both were feeling unsure as to how the rest of the day would go. They wandered back towards the nurse's home passing young men wearing white coats deep in conversation with each other. Once back outside the nurses' home, Lizzie found a quiet corner out of the way, where she lit up another cigarette and puffed on it.

"It's nerves," she said to Daisy who had a raised eyebrow, but Lizzie saw her eyes laughing! "Right, Daisy, tell me a little bit about yourself?" asked Lizzie. She was inquisitive to know about her new roommate.

So Daisy told her about her family, Mary, the boys and mentioned Bobby. How she came to wanting to nurse and end up at The London. Half an hour flew by, it was Lizzie's turn. Lizzie talked about her parents, brother and Charles, leaving out about Charles was her fiancé and a Lord. She felt uncomfortable lying but thought she would declare the truth once she knew Daisy better. She also told Daisy how she had come to want to train at The London and why nursing.

Chapter Eight

As the afternoon carried on the two girls entered the nurse's home and made their way up the stairs to their room. As soon as they made it to the top, they heard laughter coming from the room next to theirs and went to investigate. Both girls stood outside the open door, Lizzie knocked and both girls entered before hearing a come in.

"Hello," both girls said together, as they entered the room. They both looked to see the layout was exactly the same as theirs. Staring back at them were two nervous young girls.

"Shall we introduce ourselves," said Jenny. "Well, my name is Jennifer Baxter, and this is my new roommate, Claire Hudson."

All the girls shook hands and acquaintances were made; Jenny had come from Brighton and Claire was a local girl from Woolwich who wanted to live in the nurse's home. Jenny was small built and had a lovely bubbly infectious laugh. Claire being a bit taller was the quieter of the two, all four girls felt they could be friends.

Once their beds were made, with the help of Daisy and Lizzie, the girls all flopped down on a vacant bed and went through what they had found out and done today. The biggest news being that the country was at war, people had long heard the rumours now it was very real.

"We had better take you two to the sewing room and get your uniforms." Checking the time on their watches.

All four made their way along the hospital corridors, each girl trying to remember the way. Once there, they found a queue had formed and they had to wait to be seen. An hour later the girls decided to head straight to the dining room for tea, once uniforms were hanging back in their room on the front of their identical wardrobes.

Again, leaving the nurses' home and crossing over to the main building, heading down the long corridors of the hospital they reached the dining hall. The two new girls were looking around trying to take it all in and get used to their new surroundings. All four girls got their tea and made for the long bench, which they could use, being new. Tea consisted of sandwiches cake and tea or coffee. No one spoke as they ate, all being nervous. Once finished the girls slowly headed back through the hospital and to the common room ready for the talk by Home Sister, which was to start dead on seven o'clock.

As they entered the room, they saw it was already filling up with other girls in their set. In the corner was a small group of girls and in the middle was a tall blonde pretty-looking girl they found out later was called Hilary Swinton. She turned and looked over as the girls made their way to four empty seats in the middle of the room.

Daisy sat down looking around. She could see the room was quite big and not furnished much but it was comfortable. There was a couple of arm chairs, a settee, and a book case filled with reading books. A big bay window looking out into a small courtyard which now had its black out curtain attached…? She heard her name being spoken by Lizzie.

"Are you okay?" She turned and looked at her new friend.

"Yes, just nervous. You?"

"The same," came the reply.

Just then Home Sister entered and made for the front of the room, all the girls stood up.

"Please sit," she said in a loud voice.

All the young nurses did as they were told, awaiting the next part of the presentation. Home Sister stood straight and began.

"Welcome," she said. "This is a new chapter in your young lives. For some of you it will be the first time away from home. This can feel very daunting and scary. For others it will not be anything new but tomorrow and onwards it will be. You will be learning and seeing things new every day. Learn and experience all the new challenges that you will face with pride and courage, especially in this uncertain world we live in at present. I know this is a worrying time for you and your families who you have left behind, but together we will defeat Hitler."

She carried on for another half an hour about the rules and of pride of being chosen to train at The London. By Eight the group of new friends had been dismissed until the morning, they left the room and headed up to their room. Jenny and Claire came in as well.

"Well, that was interesting," said Jenny.

Jenny sat on Lizzie's bed and Claire did the same, but on Daisy's bed. Lizzie knelt down, pulled up a loose floor board and liberated a bottle of whiskey that she had hidden earlier. Alcoholic drink was banned but that didn't stop Lizzie. She poured four glasses of golden liquid and passed them around. Each girl took a hesitant sip and the warm liquid hit the back of their throats, it burned.

Daisy coughed but she didn't dislike the taste; she could get used to it. The others agreed it was nice and so began a daily meeting in the evenings when shifts permitted.

"What did you make of Home Sister's talk?" Jenny asked, looking around at the others.

All the girls replied, "interesting. …So many rules and regulations to remember!"

"We will help each other out, that's a promise!" said Daisy.

The four girls sat talking until nine forty-five, when they noticed the time. It would be lights out soon and they had a long day ahead tomorrow.

Claire and Jenny got up, picking up their dirty glasses and headed to their room, both saying, "Goodnight, see you tomorrow for breakfast."

Daisy and Lizzie got washed and ready for bed, both talking quietly to each other, both recounting what had happened today and what tomorrow would bring.

Both the uniforms looked impressive hanging up ready for the morning. They both lay in bed once the lights had gone out and Daisy thought back to what had occurred today. She thought of Bobby, how he was, and finally she was thinking of her family and were they missing her like she was missing them. A small tear trickled down her face which she brushed away. Lizzie was doing the same but thinking of Charles and how to get out of the engagement, her parents wishing they were both all right, and finally her brother that he would get his wish to join the Royal Air Force and to stay safe.

She looked over to where her new roommate and friend lay and said, "It does get better, the home sickness."

"Thank you," came a muffled sound. Lizzie didn't know if to get up and go over to give her new friend a hug? She decided against it. Daisy would soon manage it and it did get easier. Soon the room fell silent.

The bell rang at five-thirty, each new nurse opened her eyes and fell out of bed; an older nurse popped her head round their door.

"Breakfast is at six in the dining hall, hurry," she called, as she closed the door behind her.

Both girls quickly gathered their wash bags, went to the washroom and were back in record time. They both helped each other into their new uniforms, taking a look in the mirror, the finishing touches were the hair and caps.

Lizzie pinned Daisy's hair up using a mix of Kirby clips and a band. Daisy repeated the procedure, both girls looked impeccably dressed.

Now pleased with the end result they left their room, both girls knocked on the other girls' door and entered. All four looked each other up and down, admiring the view in front of their mirror. All the girls looked good and professional; they all felt extremely nervous.

By six they were seated in the dining hall tucking into stodgy porridge as Home Sister had warned them to eat a good wholesome breakfast. She did not want any girl fainting through lack of food.

Daisy looked around the hall. The noise was deafening with girls chatting away, many waiting to go on an early shift. Lizzie wasn't overwhelmed as she thought it was just like being at boarding school. Soon it was time to leave the room with full bellies and get ready for a day in the classroom.

Lizzie and Daisy were trying to calm their nerves as they made their way back to the nurses' home to brush their teeth and collect their books. The four finished off getting themselves ready by eight-thirty and they all wandered over to the school.

All four girls had made it to the classroom and found seats together. Over in the corner was a skeleton, the girls looked over at it thinking it was staring back at them, all four turned away from it.

Dead on nine o'clock the Sister Tutor entered, walking with her back ramrod straight in her neat, starched uniform.

"Welcome," she said in a steady voice. "This will be your home for the next two weeks followed by an exam. "You will be learning all aspects of nursing before you are allowed on the wards."

All the girls sat up straight, paying full attention as Sister Tutor spoke, there was an eerie silence in the room. Daisy sat in her chair, she could feel her heart beating very fast, you couldn't hear a pin drop as the lecture began.

The morning flew by, the trainee nurses were taught how to do envelope corners, make hospital beds and started to learn anatomy. By lunch their heads were pounding with everything they had learnt that morning.

Following lunch, the girls went through what they had learnt and exchanged notes and got ready for the afternoon lectures which were given by the consultants.

By five it was time to leave the classroom and head to their rooms to get ready for teatime. The girls were exhausted, on entering their room, all four flopped down on the made beds.

"I could sleep for a week, my brain is exhausted with all that information," said Jenny. "Let's have tea then we can relax."

All four made their way to the dining room. Tea was sandwiches and cake washed down by lukewarm tea. By seven o'clock Lizzie and Daisy were back in their room getting out of their uniforms and putting them away ready for the morning. The girls changed into pyjamas and sat around talking, they were joined by Jenny and Claire a few minutes later.

"Well girls, we made it through our first day of training," said Lizzie, handing each girl a glass filled with whiskey.

"We are officially trainee nurses," they all said in unison. "Here's to us and the next three years."

They raised their glasses all together. Talk turned to the war and what was about to or could happen. Daisy talked about her father making military uniforms and hats, maybe he would even be called up?

Lizzie mentioned her brother joining the Air Force and Charles joining the army; both as officers. Even mentioning Charles made her feel uncomfortable, but she tried not to show it to the others; but Daisy noticed.

Jenny mentioned her brother, Freddy, who also wanted to join the army and Claire had a sister who wanted to be a Wren.

All four girls sat back and felt this war was going to affect them all in some way, good or bad.

Lizzie got them to go through the notes from today's lectures and decided that the girls needed cheering up.

"I heard there is a dance next Friday at the Roxy Dance Hall. Anyone interested?" she queried.

It was four yeses, so plans were made for the following Friday. It was getting late, and Daisy and Lizzie decided to head for a bath while the others headed to their room, agreeing to meet in the morning to walk over for school.

Daisy decided to write to her family and Bobby. Soon Home Sister was going around saying 'lights out', and Daisy put her half-finished letters away, promising herself she would finish them tomorrow.

Lizzie wanted to write to Charles; wanting to end the relationship, but she knew it would upset her mother and, more importantly, make Charles angry, so she thought that she would leave it for now. In the end she wrote a short note to her parents. Just before lights out Lizzie stood by the opened window having a final cigarette of the day, making sure the smoke drifted out, mulling over her dilemma.

Daisy had turned the lights off in their room, so you could only see the tip of the lit cigarette. Once Lizzie had finished, she stubbed it out, threw it out of the window and climbed into bed.

The rest of the week was lectures given by consultants and learning to take a temperature, pulse and respiration on a patient and learning to take blood pressures. The evenings were used for revision for the four girls, who were quickly becoming firm friends.

Time flew by and Friday soon came around. The girls were up in their rooms getting ready for the dance that evening. They found earlier that week that it was Claire's birthday, she was the oldest of the four and the decision was made to celebrate at the Roxy. The Roxy was not far from the hospital, and they had decided to leave by seven-thirty, the dance was starting at eight. Jenny and Claire knocked on the girl's door dead on time.

"Ready?" They called as they stood waiting.

Shortly Lizzie and Daisy came out. All four looked lovely in summer dresses and sandals as it was still warm in the September weather. All four girls carried cardigans for later in the evening for when the temperature dipped.

"Right, let's go and enjoy ourselves, let our hair down," said Daisy.

Lizzie led the way down the stairs and out into the cooler evening air. By eight the girls entered the hall, it was just filling up nicely with local people. The band was playing band music and some couples were already moving around the great room to a waltz. Some men were in uniform but mostly they were dressed up in suits.

"Shall we get a drink and find a place to sit?" asked Daisy.

All four headed for the bar first.

"Four gin and tonics please," said Lizzie, she had to raise her voice over the music.

The bartender brought them their drinks. Picking up their glasses, they found a table in the corner of the room and sat as they watched couples dancing.

"Happy Birthday to Claire!" said Lizzie.

All four raised their glasses and clinked them together. A bit later Daisy noticed Hilary had arrived with her gang of followers, these were the girls that worshipped every word that Hilary said and did.

Daisy turned to her three friends and said, "Hilary has arrived."

The group turned and acknowledged the other group of girls. Hilary spotted the girls wandering over she couldn't help herself and bragged about how home Sister had also given them late passes. Getting no response from the other women she swiftly turned and walked back to her group of friends.

Jenny turned and said, "Forget her, let's have a lovely evening of dancing and freedom from studying." Everyone agreed.

Before long all the girls had found willing dance partners and were being swirled around the dance floor. Daisy had been partnered with a young lad of eighteen called Thomas, known as Tommy to his friends. He was a local lad from Poplar and his friends had all teamed up with Lizzie, Claire and Jenny.

After a few dances Daisy asked, "Can we sit down for a bit, my feet hurt?"

The hall was getting very warm, Tommy took her hand and they headed to the table and chairs that they have vacated a few dances ago. Tommy went off and got some more drinks. The conversation was loud and they had to speak up over the sound of the band.

Soon the others arrived with their partners and the group had a pleasant evening, talking and dancing some more. During the evening the hall was getting hot due to the amount of people, so the girls sat back down to get their breath back.

Before long it was ten o'clock and the girls said they had better make a move as it was getting late. They all had late passes, that were reluctantly given to them by Home Sister, only because they told her it was Claire's Birthday and they wanted to celebrate. Also, they were new probationers and having been up early all week, they were all extremely tired.

Tommy and his friends asked if the girls would be coming again, but due to starting on the wards soon they all said, "we will see". Tommy and his friends didn't know if they would be back, they could soon be called up, so they left the invitation open.

The four friends said goodnight to four young men and wished them well. All four girls walked back to the nurse's home, they could not believe that the country was at war after an evening like this. The stars were up in the clear sky, but it was now chilly, all four looked up, lost in their own thoughts.

The girls had a lie-in on the Saturday and, after breakfast, they all chose to have a bath and just relax, later all of them met up in Daisy and Lizzie's room.

"What shall we do today?" asked Lizzie.

"Well, we have to revise for the test next week. If we don't pass then we have to leave!"

Daisy was quietly confident, as was Lizzie, but Jenny and Claire needed some help. So, they spent the morning revising, and after lunch, they all went out for a walk around the streets of Whitechapel as it was a nice day for September.

Over the week, the girls had gradually gotten to know each other, and it turned out to be a pleasant afternoon. By evening they found a local fish and chip shop, Lizzie had treated them all to a bag of Fish and chips. Back in their room and a glass of whiskey later, the girls were talking about their home life. Jenny talked about her life in Brighton, Claire about her home in Woolwich, across the Thames. Daisy talked about her life in Luton and Lizzie about her life at Newton Hall and boarding school. Each girl had a story to tell and that evening the bond grew stronger.

Jenny had grown up in Brighton not knowing her father but was brought up by her mother and her uncle who lived nearby. She had an older brother, Freddy, who was going into the army as soon as he could enlist. Her mother worked in a hardware shop but her uncle helped his sister when he could. Jenny never knew what happened to her father.

Claire had a mother and father, a sister called Emily who, when she was older, wanted to be a Wren, and a smaller brother, Arthur, who wanted to join the navy, but at present they were both still at school. Her mum worked in a factory now making parts for spitfires. Her father was an engineer.

Lizzie talked about her parents, her unwanted engagement to Charles, her brother Edward and how he was going to be a pilot in the Air Force. She felt comfortable to tell them she was a Lady, which Daisy already knew. All three girls took it in their stride and Lizzie felt relief wash over her that she was accepted for who she was.

It was Daisy's turn, she talked about her mum and dad, her twin sister and brothers. Then she mentioned Bobby and how he wanted to get married but she had doubts!

It was late by the time the girls had finished their stories and they made their way to bed. Sunday was quiet, they could go to church if they wished. Claire went as she got enjoyment from going and her family was catholic, once she was back then they spent the afternoon studying as the girls all wanted to do well and pass the exam, no one wanted to leave.

Monday, came again, and the girls had classes, lectures by consultants and study. The week flew by and the exam was soon here. All four couldn't believe that the time had flown by and soon hopefully, they would be on the wards, they felt satisfied with the amount of revision they all had done.

Hilary and her group kept on about how they were going to fly through the exam. The others just kept their heads down and hoped that the questions would be on what they had learnt and, more importantly, knew. Friday was the exam day, and the results were due out on the Sunday Morning.

The ward rotation would be out Sunday afternoon and the girls then would know what ward they were placed on, assuming they passed their exams. The girls walked into the classroom, took their places, took deep breaths, and looked at each other, silently wishing each one well and waited for the instruction from Sister Tutor to start. These exams went towards the prelim exam that they would sit later. Papers were turned over, and the exam began. Two hours later it was all over and now they just had to wait.

Chapter Nine

Sunday morning Lizzie woke up and yawned, and looked over at Daisy who was still asleep. She got up, used the toilet and entered back into the room.

Daisy heard the door open, rolled over to look and said, "Good morning," to her roommate. "What time is it?"

"Eight-thirty," replied Lizzie. Both girls rushed to get ready, knocking on the room next door.

They were met by Jenny and Claire saying, "Are you both ready for breakfast?"

By the time they made their way back to the nurse's home, having eaten hardly anything through nerves, they saw Home Sister walking away from the notice board. The list went up at Ten. The three others looked at Lizzie who shot them a look.

"What?" queried Lizzie.

"Please go and look?" They all said in unison.

Lizzie walked to the board, scanned it slowly and turned around beaming, all had passed except two girls who they didn't know well. They had all beaten Hilary's marks; it was a relief now the girls were probationers.

Hilary pushed past them, not saying anything and glaring at the four girls as she went. All four were trying not to laugh, but failing miserably. They all wandered back to Daisy and Lizzie's room, and once inside they couldn't help but laugh.

"Did you see the look on Hilary's face as she read the results?"

"That certainly brought her down a peg or two" Daisy said. "She will be even harder to live with now."

The rest of the day was spent pleasantly relaxing as all four had done well. Finishing letters home, they made their way to the common room to listen to the radio, it was all about the phoney war as nothing was happening at present. The only thing that had happened recently was the air raid siren, which meant all the girls in the set had to go down into the basement of the hospital, but it turned out to be a false alarm. All four were talking about it on the way back to their rooms.

The ward list went up later that day; again, on the notice board. Daisy had female surgical. Lizzie had male medical. Jenny, Gynaecology and Claire had male surgical. It finally dawned on them; they were going to be let loose on patients tomorrow!

Sleep didn't come easily to any of them that night, as nerves about tomorrow got the better of them. Daisy could hear Lizzie moving around the bed.

"Are you asleep?" she whispered.

"No," came the reply. "Do you want to talk?" Lizzie whispered back.

Both girls lay in the darkness talking about their fears well into the early hours. Talking seamed to soothe them and sleep soon came.

It was now the end of September and the mornings were getting darker, but the days were still warmish.

Daisy and Lizzie woke early, long before the official time of five-thirty, ready for the first day on the wards. Both made sure their uniforms were immaculate, hat on straight and held on by plenty of Kirby grips. Breakfast was a rushed affair with the girls meeting up with Jenny and Claire who had also slept badly. All four looked immaculate on the outside but inside were feeling nervous, but the adrenaline was pumping. They made their way to their assigned wards along different corridors, ready for the full day ahead. Saying, goodbye and good luck, the girls went their separate ways.

Daisy walked along the corridor towards her fate, she could smell the faint whiff of bleach and it kind of calmed her. She took a deep breath, entered the ward, pushing the heavy doors with her right hand. On entering, a tall stern blonde-haired girl greeted her.

"Are you the new probationer?"

"Yes," Daisy replied. "Student Nurse Peters."

"Get your cape off, find a locker and then back here quickly. Sister Williams will be along any minute to check us all, get to the end of the line. I'm Staff Nurse Phillips."

Daisy did as she was told, she found the locker room, hung her cape up and made sure she headed to the end of the line. There were two staff nurses, one third year student nurse, one second year student and another first year, a few months above Daisy; but looked the same age. The ward maid was coming out of the kitchen, carrying a tray to put in Sister's office, for her tea with the consultant.

You could hear a pin drop, all the patients were quiet as if they had been told to behave. Daisy looked around, then all of a sudden Sister Williams appeared out of her office at the end of the ward. She glided down the ward like an angel, towards her staff, stopping to check each one's hair was regulation up, nails short and clean and finally uniforms were spotless. Sister stopped at Daisy, looking her up and down.

"Are you the new probationer?" she asked.

"Yes," replied Daisy quietly.

"Speak up girl!"

"Yes," louder this time.

"Get your hair cut or put it up better!" said Sister Williams carrying on. "Once we are done find a mirror and correct it, I don't want to see a hair out of place."

Daisy just stood open mouthed and gazed as Sister Williams headed back to her office to await the ward round of Matron and Mr Moses.

"And stop looking like a goldfish," she boomed.

Staff Nurse Phillips gave the jobs to be done for the morning. Daisy quickly found a mirror with the help of the other first year, called Dora, and corrected her hair. It was so tight it hurt but Daisy didn't care, she was not getting on the wrong side of Sister again.

Finally, she was presentable and had rolled up her sleeves and put her cuffs on, she then put on her apron, and she made her way onto the ward to start work.

She finally could take in her surroundings, the ward was long with twenty beds on both sides, and a large table in the centre. The nurse's desk was down the end with a lamp sitting on it.

"Make yourself useful," said Staff Nurse Phillips. She took Daisy into the sluice room. "Clean the bed pans and make sure they are spotless."

Dora followed her in and showed her what to do.

"Empty the solids in the toilet here then wash them out in the sink. I will be back in thirty minutes." Dora turned before she left to tidy the lockers by the beds. "Oh, by the way, Mr Moses and Matron arrive around ten, just keep out of the way. Sister will greet Matron at the door, once Staff Nurse Phillips warns her, they are on the way. Good luck."

With that she vanished and Daisy was left to her own devices with a pile of dirty bed pans. She pulled a face and got to work. Welcome to nursing she thought. She wondered if the others were having a similar morning? Daisy got hold of a full bed pan but as she was tipping it out the contents splashed her leg, luckily, she righted it, no harm done she thought.

Later Dora returned. "Now we clean the toilets, and after that it's break time. Remember to take your apron off and pull your sleeves down when you leave the ward."

Daisy was allowed her break at ten thirty where she met the others in the dining hall. They all had similar experiences to tell of their first morning on the ward.

Once back on the ward Daisy helped with lunch and she was finally allowed to talk to her patients. She was told who could eat and those on fluids only and the ones nil by mouth as they were going to theatre later that day. Once lunch was over Staff Nurse Phillips released the rest of the staff for lunch one by one.

Daisy, being the newest, had lunch last. It was almost two when she got to the dining hall, and she was starving. Today was liver and onion mash and cabbage followed by spotted dick and custard. Daisy didn't care she was so hungry; she galloped the food down. Jenny, Claire and Lizzie were all late to lunch, they were eating their dinner as well and talking about their experiences from the morning. They made plans to meet up later in their room at eight to catch up.

Daisy said her 'goodbyes' and rushed back to the ward. When she arrived back, she remembered to put her apron on, and rolled up her sleeves, meeting Sister as she left the locker room.

"Mrs Jones, bed three. Prepare her for theatre, second year Student Nurse Henley will show you what to do. The porters arrive at three sharp."

Mrs Jones was just about ready to be taken down to theatre. Student Nurse Henley explained Mrs Jones was having her gall bladder removed having gotten gall stones.

"See, look at her jaundiced skin." It was tinged with yellow. Daisy looked at the poor woman's face, feeling empathy for her. "She will be nursed one to one through the night on the ward. Tomorrow she will have a bed bath and stay in bed for a week, then she can get up once Mr Moses is happy. She will be on fluids only and a light diet later, at the end of the week."

The rest of the afternoon was spent in the sluice again on bed pan duty till she was told to go home. Daisy was spent, her feet ached, and she was tired, all she wanted to do was go back to her room and collapse on her bed. Daisy collected her lukewarm food and found a seat, being so hungry she devoured it washing it down with tea. Sitting back, she nearly forgot the others were coming over later.

Lizzie met up with Daisy in the dining hall. "I could fall asleep in my tea," she cried.

Both girls got up and headed to their room to get changed and wait for their friends to turn up. Just before eight, Jenny and Claire knocked on the door.

"Enter," came the reply. "Make yourselves at home."

Both girls flopped on the nearest bed. "We will not stay long as we need our sleep, it's been a long day, not used to standing on our legs all day, it's very tiring!" said both girls in unison.

"Here is a whiskey night cap," Lizzie handed the girls a glass each. "Now, tell us about your day."

"Well, Sister is terrifying, some of the Staff Nurses are all right, and the senior student nurses think they know it all, otherwise I spent the day in the sluice on bed pan duty," answered Daisy. "This is real Nursing!" she said sarcastically.

"The junior doctors are a nuisance, they keep thinking they are god's gift to women. Don't get me wrong, they seem nice but boy, I wish they left us alone," said Jenny.

"I had the same problem, every time I turned around a junior doctor was hovering and getting in the way," said Claire.

"Well, you are both lucky, I didn't get to see anybody as I was stuck in the sluice as well," said Lizzie. "Hopefully it will get better tomorrow?"

"Have you posted your letters home?" asked Claire.

"Yes, managed to catch the last post last night," both girls answered together.

Daisy was looking forward to hearing from her mum and dad and especially Bobby as they had left on bad terms. Lizzie on the other hand was not looking forward to hearing from her mother about her pending engagement to Charles.

"Well, I think it is bed for me," said Jenny yawning. "Are you coming, Claire?"

"Yes," said Claire, yawning away as well. "See you girls in the morning." And with that both girls left.

Lizzie sat on her bed and looked at Daisy, lifted her glass and said, "Here's to day two tomorrow."

Both girls got ready for bed and by ten lights were out and both were snoring gently.

Next day Daisy entered the ward at six-fifty, just as the night staff were getting ready to leave, she had spent extra time doing her hair, making sure it was as neat as it could be. She had got Lizzie to pull it tight adding extra Kirby grips where they were needed, nothing was going to move this hair or cap to come off. She placed her black cape on the coat stand near the lockers and made her way to stand in line ready for Sister Williams to do her daily inspection.

Once Sister was happy, Staff Nurse Johnston passed out the daily jobs to be done and Daisy made her way to the sluice for bedpan duty, it was becoming a regular job. Dr Reynolds popped his head round the door.

"Hello," he said in a bright and cheerful way.

Daisy looked up from the sink. "Hello," she replied shyly.

"You're new?" he asked.

"Yes," replied Daisy, still in a quiet, nervous voice.

Daisy just wanted to get on, but Dr Reynolds had other ideas. Just as he was going to ask another question Staff Nurse Johnston came looking for him to examine Mrs Jenkins, as she had abdominal pain and was feeling sick.

Left alone, Daisy got on with the job in hand, she thought he was very nice, but she knew he wouldn't fancy her, she was just a silly nervous probationer. Daisy put the thought to the back of her mind and got stuck in.

Break time came and again she was lucky to meet up with the other girls. Before long it was time to get back to the ward. Dr Reynolds bumped into Daisy as she was entering through the swing doors.

"Well, hello again," he said smiling. "Where have you been?" He already knew but just wanted to speak with the pretty new nurse, she was very beautiful he thought.

"Having my break, sir," replied Daisy.

Dr Reynolds stood in Daisy's way and, as she tried to push past, he stood his ground, she could see his eyes sparkling with merriment. Daisy, being quite nimble managed to get past and got to where Staff Nurse Johnston was dealing with a patient.

"Go put your apron on and roll up your sleeves," she barked at Daisy.

Daisy moved sharply and did as she was told. Meanwhile Dr Reynolds was watching her intently by the door, grinning. Why did he make her feel nervous? She put the thought quickly out of her mind again.

Lunchtime meant helping give out dinners and feed patients who couldn't manage it themselves, and for Daisy it meant she kept out of the way of Dr Reynolds, the orderlies helped too.

It had been another busy day with patients coming and going to theatre and taking care of post-operative patients. Daisy was taught how to do observations; now this was progress.

She made her way to the dining hall. Once finished, the four friends headed back to the nurse's home for a quiet evening. Lizzie, once out of her uniform, turned off the room's light, opened the room's window, letting in the cold night air and lit her cigarette. After a few puffs, aiming the smoke out of the window so Home Sister couldn't smell it, the room was getting colder, so Daisy put her cardigan on and dragged a blanket over her legs. Lizzie didn't fancy walking to the common room or outside.

"How was your day, Daisy?"

"Okay," replied Daisy. "But I had to keep dodging Dr Reynolds." She sighed, good job it was dark as she was blushing.

"I heard he is going out with Student Nurse Henley from your ward?"

Daisy sat up and shot Lizzie a look and she knew that she would have to be careful of Dr Reynolds. She couldn't put her finger on it, but it gave her a nice feeling down below, she couldn't stop thinking about him.

"Right, we had better do some studying for our next round of exams," said Daisy.

Both girls pulled out their textbooks and so began an evening of studying, Lizzie had closed the window once she had finished the cigarette and already turned the light back on. Both girls were still waiting for post so Daisy decided next day she would check with Home Sister on her return from the wards. Hopefully some would turn up soon.

Over the next week the girls fell into a routine of getting up, working on the wards and returning early afternoon, when they had a lecture given by a consultant in school and then back on the ward till late evening. In the evening all four women would study together, unless they had a late shift that then finished at nine.

Daisy did get some mail and so did Lizzie. Daisy's arrived on the Wednesday, and Lizzie's on the Thursday. Daisy had two letters, one from her parents and the other from Bobby. Daisy opened her parents' letter first. Both were well, her siblings were all fine, Mary was enjoying having the room to herself. Mark and George were both missing her and asking when she was coming home for a visit. Daisy didn't think her sister was missing her as much. Little did she know that her sister was planning to get Bobby to notice her! George had settled into working at the hat factory and he was growing up before her mum's eyes. They asked how she was doing on the ward and asked that she wrote soon with all her news about her new friends.

Then she picked up her letter from Bobby, and with some trepidation she looked at his handwriting on the front which she knew by heart. She carefully opened it, pulled the sheet out and began to read. He first apologised for his behaviour and hoped she could forgive him for the way he had acted. Of course, she would, they were friends, well more than that. He told her about the garage and that petrol was soon to be rationed, meaning fewer cars would be on the road. Only essential people and the military could use their cars. He went on about the war and wanting to join the army if they would have him, but his father wanted him to stay at the garage. He hoped she would be home soon for a visit and to let him know her news and when she would be coming. He signed off, 'affectionately Bobby'.

Daisy sat on her bed looking down at the letter. She thought about what Bobby had said. Yes, they were back in school in a month or so, and then would have one week annual leave. Yes, she would be going home then. So, she got out her writing set and responded to her parents and to Bobby's letters.

Meanwhile Lizzie had opened her letter from her mother, she began by saying that Charles and his family had been in contact and were pressing for a date for the engagement. A chill ran down Lizzie's back, she really didn't want to marry this man. How was she going to get out of this mess? She would write to her brother Eddie asking him to help, then she would reply to her mother.

Once they had annual leave, she would go home for a few days then come back if things got too bad. Relieved she had a plan she began her letter to her brother. Firstly, she asked how he was? Then she asked if he was going into the RAF? How did the medical go? It would be good for him to get away from their mother. Finally, she asked about Francesca and had he seen her? Then she mentioned Charles and that her mother had received a letter from him asking her to set a date for the engagement. She then asked him to help her get out of this predicament and said that during her holiday she hoped to see him.

Once done she folded the letter and sealed it ready for posting. They both got into their pyjamas as the evenings were getting colder and they laid in bed talking about their day. Both girls were beginning to enjoy this part of the evening, it was making them become much closer.

Lizzie and Daisy, over the weeks had gotten used to being woken at five-thirty, they still didn't like it, but it was part of being a student nurse. Lizzie entered her ward; Male Medical a few minutes to seven, having posted her letter to her brother in the post box outside the hospital. She felt calm and knew her brother would help her. He knew what Charles was actually like and felt that between them they could deal with the current situation. Eddie had gotten her out of difficult scraps when she was younger. She checked herself in the staff room mirror, hung up her cape, put on her apron and checked her cuffs, and she joined the end of the line awaiting Sister Warnock's attention.

Once Sister Warnock was happy, Staff Nurse Evans and Staff Nurse Moons then handed out the jobs for the day. Over the weeks Lizzie had learnt a lot and was progressing nicely under the supervision of Staff Nurse Evans. The Staff Nurse couldn't understand why a titled lady would want to be a nurse, but who was she to stand in the way of this very strong-willed young lady.

Lizzie had arrived on the ward raw but over the weeks had learnt to handle the men from the East End. They, in return, had a great respect for the posh probationer from Warwickshire. She could handle herself, no doubt.

It soon got to the end of November, both girls had settled on their wards and soon they would be back in the classroom for a few days, another exam, then annual leave.

The war was progressing slowly, there had been a sinking, HMS Royal Oak which was part of the home fleet. An enemy U-boat got through, had fired off a torpedo and the battleship had gone down in just a couple of minutes, killing everyone on board. The battle in the Atlantic had begun and the weather was getting colder and the dark nights were coming in fast. Everyone had been issued with gas masks which they had to carry everywhere, Lizzie had heard back from her brother and the news was good, he was joining the Royal Air Force as a spitfire pilot. He had also heard from and seen Francesca before going for basic training. She was doing all right and would like to meet up with them both as soon as possible. He hadn't heard from Charles but that was not surprising really as Charles was going into the army as an Officer. She felt sorry for the men who would be under Charles as she felt he would treat them unfairly. Lizzie had no time to dwell as she was busy with her training.

All four girls made it to the classroom and more lectures. It was sad to leave the wards they were on, but they were looking forward to new challenges that lay ahead. Daisy was sad about leaving her ward but not about getting away from Dr Reynolds, over the weeks he kept turning up. She had not ever encouraged him but still he tried to get her to go out with him. Staff Nurse Phillips had made a few comments but Daisy had told her she was not interested in him. Daisy thought if he acted like this when he had a girlfriend, he wasn't worth bothering about. Finally, one day just before Daisy was leaving the ward, Dr Reynolds came into the kitchen on the ward and announced to everyone that he was joining the Royal Army Medical Corps. On hearing this news Daisy felt upset as she wouldn't be seeing him around, it made her feel quite sad, a tear was prickling her eye which she quickly wiped away. She wondered if their paths would ever cross again during this war.

The week of lectures in the classroom had flown by and the girls had spent the evenings studying and drinking, they all wanted to do well and beat Hilary, who wanted to do better this time. The bottle of Whiskey had emptied, and it was Daisy's turn to buy it, so after lectures one cold day she wrapped up warm, headed out into Whitechapel to a local pub near the hospital, and with the help of Lizzie had purchased her first bottle of alcohol. Trying to smuggle it back into the nurse's home under the watchful eye of Home Sister was difficult but they achieved it. They hid it under the loose floorboard in their room.

Finally, the exam was upon them. All four made it into the exam room, and this time the nerves were still there but they were prepared as best they could. Like last time the results were out on the Sunday morning and the girls were heading home on the Monday for their holidays. The wait, like last time, was nerve wracking, all the girls were agitated with each other, but they all knew it wasn't meant. Sunday morning, they were all up early and breakfast completed, the girls stood by the notice board waiting for Sister Tutor to arrive with the list.

Again, the girls got Lizzie to look, and she turned around beaming. Daisy was of course top, Lizzie second, Jenny and Claire joint third and Hilary was below them again. She took one look at the smirk on the girls' faces and left to find her friends. Hilary knew when she was beaten.

They all entered Daisy and Lizzie's room and made a circle, arms joined, "Well done!" they screamed. "We have passed." And the atmosphere in the room was electric.

The rest of Sunday was spent packing and Daisy was due off Monday morning, as was Lizzie and Claire by train. Daisy from St Pancras, Lizzie from Marylebone, Jenny from Waterloo and Claire, well she only had to cross the Thames.

Monday morning was a grey and cold morning, and their cases were by the front door ready for them to leave after breakfast. They all said their 'goodbyes and see you in one weeks' time'.

Once back, it soon would be Christmas and the girls would be working on new wards. Daisy had Men's medical, Lizzie had Gynaecology, Jenny had Female surgical and Claire Female Geriatric. Daisy had warned Jenny about Dr Reynolds but hopefully he had left or was leaving to do his training very soon.

Chapter Ten

Right, got everything? They all said, looking at the four cases by the door all packed. All four girls nodded with excitement. The girls picked up their cases and handbags and they made sure they had their gas masks and walked through the grounds of The London, making their way to the entrance. They all had noticed that sandbags had been put in place by all the entrances. Daisy and Lizzie went to the underground and so did Jenny who was walking behind with Claire who was going to catch the Woolwich Ferry to take her across the Thames and home.

Once reaching the underground, there too were sandbags by the entrance. Tickets were purchased, they all hugged each other. "See you in a week's time." With that they went their separate ways. Daisy went one way Lizzie went another and Jenny another.

Daisy waited for the train to approach; the station was full of people in military uniforms a lot more than when they had arrived back in September. Looking around the platform it was still a novelty to ride on the underground. Within a few minutes she could feel the warmth of the approaching train and she waited for it to slow down. She was still nervous about travelling on the 'tube' as the locals called it. Once on board she got a seat and waited for the train to leave the station and for it to pick up speed. She caught the eye of two sailors who smiled at her, she smiled back politely but her immediate thought was about her impending trip home. All had promised to be back on Sunday afternoon to exchange stories of their visits.

Soon Daisy arrived at her destination, she pulled her coat tighter to her, and made sure her gas mask was on her shoulder with her handbag. Daisy entered St Pancras; it was heaving with service personnel of all services as were all stations around London. They all looked impeccably smart in their new uniforms. You couldn't move for bodies. Daisy made her way along the concourse to the ticket office, purchased her ticket and made her way to the platform, having had no time to visit the Buffet. The train was in for Luton, so Daisy made her way to the carriage and got on, finding a seat between two men; she placed her case on the rack above the seat. Ten Minutes later the guard blew his whistle and the steam train slowly picked up speed.

Before long the grey skyline of the city turned to green countryside. Daisy looked out of the window and thought you would not believe that this country was at war. Soon they arrived at Luton station, Daisy got her luggage down from the overhead rack and exited off the train. Looking around she stood and thought how different she was from the shy young girl that had left a few months ago. She made her way out of the station, pulling her coat round her body and tightening the scarf her mother had knitted around her neck. Daisy took the quickest route to her family home; it was hard going with her case and a bitter wind was blowing but Daisy was stronger since starting her training.

She made light work of it and arrived at the end of the familiar street she called home. Daisy walked to the front door and knocked firmly; she didn't want to use the back entrance. She waited patiently for the door to be opened. Next thing she knew her mother was standing in front of her telling her to come in and why had she not come around the back, her mother stood back and examined her daughter carefully, and then gave her a big hug and kiss on the cheek.

Her mother pulled the blackout curtain over the front door, one, it kept the light out, but also two, kept the heat in. They made their way to the kitchen which was nice and warm as usual. Daisy took her coat, gas mask, hand bag and scarf off and went to hang it up by the front door. Only her mother and Mary, who had joined them in the kitchen, were at home as Mark was still at school and George was working with their father now but was looking forward to joining up when he was old enough. Mary was working full time at Woolworths now but had today off as her sister was coming home, well she had been told to take the day off.

"Here, sit down, Daisy." It was nice to be home. "How have you been?" asked her mother? What have you been up to?"

She answered the questions.

"I'll put the kettle on," said Mum as Daisy took her case up to her old bedroom, the one she once shared with her sister.

Her sister sat at the table looking miserable that Daisy was home. Daisy could hear the jealousy in her voice as Mary spoke, but she could not for the life of her work out what she had done to deserve it. Her mother noticed the atmosphere between the two sisters and she decided to find out why there was animosity, when the time was right, as for now, she would just watch and wait.

Daisy in her letter to Bobby had arranged to meet him later that evening. He was to come over after the family had tea and her father and brothers had time to catch up with their sister. For the rest of the afternoon Daisy helped her mother with her dressmaking while Mary took herself off to see friends as she was off work.

It was nice to spend time with her mother; she had missed her greatly. They chatted away like old times and before long it was time to collect Mark from school. Daisy went with her mother to collect her brother, who as soon as he saw his older sister ran out of the classroom as soon as the bell went.

"Daisy," he shouted, running straight into her arms.

His sister scooped him up and gave him the biggest cuddle she could manage with his big winter coat on. They held hands and walked back to the warm house that was waiting for them that winter's night.

Hannah closed the blackout curtains all around the house putting the electric lights on. They closed the winter's night out and the house felt like home to Daisy, sitting in the kitchen waiting for her brother George and their father to come home.

The lovely smell of the dinner her mother had prepared wafted around the kitchen, ready to be dished up once everyone was home. Mary had arrived home just after Daisy and her mother; she came into the kitchen and took her seat at the table.

"Had a good afternoon?" asked her mum.

"Yes," she replied. "It was nice to catch up with my friends." But Daisy could sense there was an uneasy mood as Mary spoke.

Daisy sat taking it all in, it felt lovely just being back home, but she still could feel the uneasy tension that she felt coming from her sister. Just as she was going to mention it, her dad and brother walked through the kitchen door.

"Well, hello my girl," her dad said cheerily.

Daisy got up from her seat and threw herself into her dad's arms. He wrapped his strong arms around her and gave her a kiss on the cheek.

"It's lovely to be home, Dad," said Daisy honestly.

George came up behind his dad, Daisy noticed that since she had been away her brother had grown and was as tall as his dad now. He was turning into a young man, working with his dad, it was doing him so much good she thought.

"Hello, George." She gave her brother a hug which he returned with a shy grin.

"You have changed, Daisy," he observed. "You have grown up," he said.

She said the same back to him. They all took their seats at the table and Hannah dished up the dinner. Beef stew and dumplings on this cold night, Daisy was in heaven, she didn't mind the hospital food but you couldn't beat her mums cooking. They sat talking, catching up with each other's news. Hannah glanced at her husband and caught his eye and gave the look that said all her family were back together.

Once all the dinner plates had been stacked up to be washed, pudding finished, Daisy and her sister helped her mum wash up. Daisy excused herself to get ready for her meeting up with Bobby, she was so anxious and nervous; she hadn't seen him since the last time, and she didn't know how he would be with her.

She thought it was odd that at seven Bobby knocked on the back door, her dad let him in.

"Hello, Bobby," everyone said, but they all noticed how Mary was unusually quiet.

"Daisy will be down in a moment, have a seat lad."

Bobby happily accepted, and he caught Mary looking at him lovingly. He looked away as if ashamed. Daisy on the other side of the door took a deep breath and entered.

"Hello, Bobby," she said with confidence she didn't really feel.

He stood and gave her a nervous peck on the cheek.

"How have you been?" he asked nervously.

"Fine, thank you," she replied back. "Come on let's go for a drink and catch up."

Both gathered their coats and headed for the back door, and closing the back gate, headed down the entry and out into the street. Bobby awkwardly took Daisy's gloved hand and they walked down the road to the Lord Nelson. Bobby pushed the door open and was told quickly to close it, pulling the blackout curtain back in place.

Bobby asked her "what she wanted?"

Daisy replied, "A whiskey."

Bobby looked, open-mouthed. "Really?" he asked, stunned.

"Yes!" she replied.

He headed towards the bar, stopping to talk to a few men he knew from fixing their cars. Once he got their drinks, he returned to the table that Daisy had found in the corner, away from the noise and the darts match going on in the other corner. She fancied learning to play and would mention it to Lizzie once they were back.

Bobby took a sip of his pint and glanced over at Daisy, she looked different he thought, more grown up even after this short period of time away, he wondered if he had changed as much?

Both started to talk together but Bobby said, "You go first."

He wanted to hear about all her news. She took a deep breath and told him about all the girls she had met, and some doctors too but she didn't mention Dr Reynolds for some reason, she thought better not too as she might show her emotions. She told him about Sister Williams, Staff Nurse Phillips and some of the patients she had met and taken care of. Bobby listened intently to every word that Daisy said, only stopping to have a drink. Once she had finished then she asked about what he had been up too.

He took a sip and told her all his news and that he wanted to go into the army if they would have him, hopefully the Royal Engineers. Daisy wasn't surprised at the news she was hearing; he would be good as a soldier and people would be using less cars once the petrol was rationed which was happening soon.

"When is your medical?" she enquired.

"Oh, I haven't applied yet, but I want to soon."

He wanted to ask the next question but was very nervous, even reluctant, but he continued fiddling with his pint glass. Bobby took a deep breath and came out with it.

"Have you thought any more about us getting engaged?"

Daisy looked into his eyes and said, "No, as I have been too busy."

"You still do want to?" he asked optimistically, his heart beating fast.

Daisy couldn't answer, the words got stuck in her throat. She wanted to say 'yes' but something was stopping her, and she couldn't make out why.

So, she said, "Please, give me more time?" She could see she was hurting his feelings.

Reluctantly, he said, "Yes, but I will not wait forever."

The atmosphere in the room had changed and he said, "Let me walk you home, and if it is okay, I will pop over tomorrow night to see you after work?"

"Yes," she replied to both questions.

Both finished their drinks and got ready to leave the warmth of the pub. They made their way back home through darkened streets using a torch that had a slit in it, but they both knew the way back. They said their goodbyes by the entry to the side to the house, he gave her a kiss on the cheek. He really wanted to kiss her lips, but at present he thought this was for the better, until he could gauge her better. She walked down the entry, opening the back gate and through the back door to the kitchen.

Everyone apart from Mark was still up, she looked at them all, said her 'goodnights' and explained that she was tired from the travelling. Daisy took herself upstairs to bed, she was emotionally drained even after this short length of time being with Bobby. Why could she not commit to him she kept asking herself?

She unpacked her case, had a wash in the bathroom and got into her pyjamas, preferring them to a nightdress as they were warmer. She lay in bed; their mother had put on a stone heater, so the sheets were warm. She was waiting for her sister to come up, she was thinking about the events of the evening, they kept going through her mind, tomorrow she would see Bobby again. Daisy didn't hear Mary come to bed as she must have fallen asleep, it was seven-thirty when she woke, hearing her dad and George heading out to work. As she lay in bed, she was wondering how Lizzie was fairing at home with her parents. Her sister was just waking and jumping out of bed to get ready for work. She thought she had better get up too.

On entering the kitchen, she saw her mum at the range and Mark had already had his breakfast and was getting ready for school.

"Will you take me and pick me up please Daisy?" he begged.

"Of course," she replied. "Let me have breakfast first — which was a bowl of porridge — and I will get ready."

Soon they were ready, Daisy helped Mark with his shoes, and both had big winter coats on, scarves wrapped round their necks from the biting wind and Mark had a tight grip of his sister's hand. They made good time walking to school, both were talking like she had never been away. They stopped at the school gate, Daisy knelt down and gave her brother a hug.

"Have a good day and I will see you at three-thirty." With that he got up, turned around and headed towards the classroom and his waiting teacher, turning once more to wave at her.

Daisy quickly walked home. She had promised to help her mum with some dresses today and she wanted to speak with her sister before she left for work on why she was behaving like she was.

Daisy made it back in record time, just as her sister was walking down the road the other way into town. 'I will catch up with her later', thought Daisy watching her sister turn the corner and disappear. On entering she heard her mother.

"Right, will you wash up and then help me in the front room?" her mother asked. "Your sister has left for work already," her mother continued.

"Yes, I saw her."

"Come on then, let's get these cleaned away." Her mother turned around and carried on.

Daisy wondered if she had been imagining how Mary had been towards her? But she put that thought to one side, she wasn't going to rock the boat today.

Mother and daughter worked well together and chatted between them; they had the wireless on as they worked. Daisy thought it was nice to be home. Daisy made her way into the front room where Hannah already had the fire lit. It felt really cosy and warm in there. Hannah gave her jobs to do and she happily got on with them, chatting away as she worked. The morning flew by and before long it was lunchtime. They had lunch together and tidied up and Hannah had a customer during the afternoon for a fitting.

Daisy kept out of the way. Hannah had managed to get chicken fillets to make a stew and she got to work getting tea ready. Before too long Daisy got her shoes and winter coat on, picking up her handbag and gas mask, she went to collect her brother as promised from school.

On her way Daisy met neighbours she had grown up with, they kept stopping to ask her how she was and how she was getting on. Daisy stopped and spoke with them and finally she arrived at the school. Daisy waited in the cold November day as Mark came rushing out when he spotted her and took her hand. They walked home chatting away about his day.

Chapter 11

When they arrived home, they took shoes and coats off and made their way into the warm kitchen.

"Are you hungry?" Daisy asked her brother.

"Yes," came the reply.

"Let's get you something to eat."

Daisy headed for the cupboard, got the biscuit tin and took two biscuits out and gave them to her brother, who looked at them with anticipation and she poured him a glass of milk. He sat there munching away while Daisy got the table set, ready for the family tea.

Soon Hannah entered the kitchen having finished with her customer, she finished preparing tea and they waited for Dad and George to come home. Daisy called her sister and Mary came down from the bedroom, having been reading a magazine. She had come home from work, and not wanting to speak to her sister had gone upstairs. The warmth of the kitchen hit her as she entered the room. Hannah welcomed her daughter.

"Come on, we need help setting the table for tea."

Both girls got on with it, both being lost in their own thoughts. Daisy thinking about seeing Bobby tonight which, if she was honest, filled her with dread and made her feel physically sick. Why was she so worried if she really loved him! Mary couldn't contain her jealously, so she thought it was best not to say anything, but her sister had noticed the way her sister was looking at her.

I will speak with her later when we are upstairs alone and get to the bottom to what is going on, Daisy thought. A few minutes' later Dad and George entered the kitchen, took off their winter coats, hats and scarves as it was bitter outside and warmed their hands by the range.

"It's nice to be home," both said.

"Had a good day?" Hannah asked.

"Yes," both replied, "getting big orders for uniforms and hats now."

"Will have to get more machines to cover the orders?" Hannah asked.

"Yes," replied Jack.

At least both were going to be busy for the future, Hannah thought.

"Come on, let's eat." And she dished up the chicken stew that Daisy had prepared earlier that afternoon.

The talk turned to war and the lack of things happening, Jack was to join the Air Raid Precaution (ARP) as a warden, his first meeting was to be tomorrow night at the local church hall. The country was preparing for when the bombs would fall. They talked a bit more and Hannah brought the pudding out, which was eaten in silence.

Daisy excused herself to get ready for Bobby to come around. As she sat on the bed she shared, putting her make up on, her mind drifted to what she was going to do about Bobby. She could not lead him on, so he would have to decide once and for all. The clothes she had decided on for tonight was jumper and trousers her mother had made, she thought trousers were safer than a skirt. Having got changed she ran down the stairs, Daisy took one more look in the mirror, she liked what she saw looking back. Just then she heard a familiar voice coming from the kitchen, Bobby had arrived! Time to face the music she thought.

Daisy entered the kitchen and she greeted Bobby with a big smile which didn't quite reach her eyes. Mum had put the fire on in the front room earlier so when they both entered it was lovely and warm. Both were nervous as they sat down on the battered worn settee; Bobby took her hand.

"Daisy, please let's not argue again."

"I don't want to argue either, but you don't make things easy, do you?" she said.

Bobby went to his pocket and pulled out a black case, got down on one knee and opened the case saying, "I love you Daisy, will you marry me?"

Daisy looked at Bobby and no words would come out of her mouth.

"Well?" he said with a worried look.

Daisy looked at Bobby and at that split moment she decided.

She said, "No, I don't want to get married at the moment, as I said last night. I have not changed my mind she said with more force than she wanted to. I want to finish my training and we don't know what the war is going to do to us all."

Bobby was furious, he got up and looked at Daisy. "You string me along, well there is plenty of more girls that would say yes and offer more."

He started swearing at her saying unkind things, but she knew he was hurt so she just let him carry on, but she was shocked by the things he was saying.

Jack, once he heard the swearing opened the door, and stood glaring at Bobby.

"I think you had better go and cool down at home lad."

Bobby turned and, head bowed, left. Mary stood watching with a keen interest and thought 'this is playing right into my hands'.

Hannah came into the room and sat by her eldest daughter, taking her hands.

"Are you okay?" she asked concerned, glancing at her daughter. "Do you want to talk about it?" she asked.

"Yes, but not at the moment," came the reply with a shaky voice. Daisy sat looking at the burning flames and wondered how her life had got so complicated.

Her mother saw the anguish in Daisy's face and said, "Let's get you up to bed, tomorrow is another day."

"I am all right to go up on my own." She headed up to the bedroom and got ready for bed, but sleep wouldn't come easy that night. Her thoughts kept going back to earlier and she felt shamefaced. Had she made the right decision? She heard Mary come up a little later.

"Do you want to talk?"

"No!" she said curtly and have her sister gloat! "I just want to sleep. Thank you," said Daisy a bit more politely.

Mary smirked in the darkness, she would leave it till her sister went back on Sunday and then she would go and see Bobby to comfort him and make him hers. Both woke early, Mary got up and sat at the edge of the bed looking at her sister's red eyes and dark circles now formed under her eyes, she had been crying.

"Are you sure you are okay?" Mary asked, alarmed.

"Yes," replied Daisy. "But I don't want to get married, I want to enjoy life, you understand that!"

Mary looked down at her sister. "Yes, I did." Which shook her a bit.

"I have never meant to string Bobby along, but he began to keep pushing to get married and wanting other things." Which she didn't elaborate on. "I want a career!" said Daisy, unwaveringly. "I have a new life nursing and what that can offer." She was so tired it showed in her voice, she felt deflated!

Her sister didn't answer but just looked at her older sister and thought she was silly to turn him down, she would have jumped at the chance of being his wife. Mary finished getting dressed and made her way downstairs to get ready for work. Only a few days left till she went around to see Bobby, see if he wanted to take her out on a date instead, she wouldn't turn him down that was for sure and she didn't feel guilty either.

Daisy soon followed her sister into the kitchen.

"Can you take Mark to school again today?" Hannah asked. She thought it might take her mind off her troubles.

The day was the same as yesterday with the exception she wouldn't be seeing Bobby. She hoped he was okay with her decision. She still cared for him.

Hannah was worried about her eldest daughter, but she knew in her heart she had done the right thing, she was still young, her life was just beginning, and she had a new career.

The rest of the week flew by, and Sunday soon come around. Daisy had packed the night before, ready to go back to London early on the Sunday morning. For the rest of the week, she hadn't seen or heard from Bobby. Mary had seen him in town when she had been out with her friends at the local dance.

She had gone over to him at the bar and asked, "How are you, Bobby?"

He stood and looked straight at Mary and the first thing he asked was, "How is Daisy?"

"Oh, she is getting ready to go back to London," Mary said.

"Did she tell you that she turned me down when I proposed the other day?"

"Yes, she did," replied a smiling Mary. "I'm really sorry, but I think she is being a big fool. If I was her, I would have said yes."

Bobby then looked at her and said, "Well, let's see what the future holds, anyway I am joining the army soon, thinking over the last few days I want to live a little, perhaps your sister has done me a favour."

With that he turned around to speak to his friends, he called back, "See you later Mary, I'm off to have fun."

Mary followed him as he walked away and thought this is going to be harder than she thought, she wasn't just going to fall into his arms.

Sunday arrived and Daisy stood in the warm kitchen putting her thick winter coat on ready for the walk to the station. Mum, Dad and her siblings all got ready as well.

"You don't have come with me," she said.

"But we want to," they all replied, even Mary agreed.

Dad carried her case out into the cold grey November morning, they chatted about everything to try and keep the journey short, you could see their breath against the cold as they talked. Daisy and Mary held Mark's hand and lifted him up into the air, he laughed with joy.

Even though she was going away again her heart felt lighter than it had felt for a long time, maybe saying no was the right thing to do. Forty minutes later they found themselves waiting on the station concourse, the train was just emptying of passengers. The concourse was full of military personnel and some families getting ready to travel.

Daisy stood with her family. "Please write, and I will too," she said. "I will be home as soon as I can, we may get busy due to the war," she warned.

The guard came along calling the London train was ready. She turned to her family and gave them one more family hug.

"Love you," she shouted, picked up her case, and made sure she had her handbag and gas mask.

She could hear her father say, "Be careful and stay safe." As she walked to the train, a tear started to trickle down her face. Would she ever find it easy to leave them?

Chapter 12

Once Elizabeth had left Daisy and Jenny at the underground, she took her train to Marylebone, where she too found military personnel swarming the concourse, it was a sea of khaki. Lizzie sat in the warm buffet drinking a hot mug of tea and eating a freshly made cake, her thoughts turning to home and what she expected to happen when she saw her mother, suddenly the cake was hard to swallow.

Once her train was called, she hurried to her carriage, climbed aboard, placing her suitcase on the overhead rack, and settled back in her seat, her thoughts turning to home and her mother and Charles.

She would have to put her best actress face on for her mother and play along until Eddie and she came up with a plan to stop them. She sat by the window looking out onto the countryside as the train sped towards Warwick. A couple sat to her right, and a vicar sat across from her. He chatted to her, so this passed the time. The journey was quick, soon they arrived at the station.

The family chauffeur, Geoffrey, was waiting by the Rolls Royce, he still had enough fuel to run the big old car, luckily, he was alone.

"Welcome home, Lady Elizabeth," he said and opened the rear door for her as he took her case and gas mask, she kept her handbag by her side.

The ride was one of mixed emotions, as she got closer to home, she wanted to see her parents, but on the other hand, it filled her with dread. Soon they were driving down the long driveway, and the house soon came into view, it looked stunning in the November sunshine!

The car pulled to stop and as normal Lizzie had let herself out before Geoffrey could do it. As she opened the door the cold air hit her and sent a shiver down her back, Dinky ran up and tried to get into the car behind her. Dinky was one person who Lizzie was happy to see. She could hear her mother long before she saw her; her father was following quietly behind.

"Welcome home, Elizabeth," her mother said in her high, irritating voice.

She greeted her mother with a kiss on the cheek and then a big hug for her father, who smiled back at his daughter with pride and whispered, "Welcome home."

Lizzie loved her father very much. The butler took her case, and gas mask and the family followed into the great house, the house looked old and cold, and the blackout blinds were all in place.

"Come into the drawing room and have drinks," ordered her mother.

All Lizzie wanted to do was head up to her room, have a long soak in the bath and see if Eddie was around. Still, as always, her mother had other ideas. The room was not cold but it wasn't hot as the windows lost a lot of heat and the wind whistled through them but it wasn't unpleasant. The fire was crackling in the background.

Once seated Lady Margo asked Lizzie, "How are you, and are you enjoying London?"

Then they talked about the war, or lack of it. Lizzie answered the questions but kept a few things to herself, what her mother didn't know was for the best. Then her mother got onto the subject of Charles, this is what Lizzie had been dreading the most.

"Darling, have you spoken with Charles, and can we announce the engagement in the Times? He wants to formally ask your father for your hand in marriage, but he will not until you agree."

Lizzie looked like a dear caught in headlights, so quickly she said, "No, I have not seen Charles, but I am happy to go ahead and set a date once my training is over as agreed."

In her head she hopefully thought that was still a long way off, this news seemed to satisfy her mother for the present. Her father sat and listened; she knew he would speak to him later.

About an hour later, she could excuse herself and headed up to her room. She had learned her brother would be home in the morning on a twenty-four-hour pass from his training. Lizzie entered her room and collapsed, exhausted on the bed; there was a warm feeling as the fire was lit, and she hugged her pillow to her, staring into the flames. What was she going to do about Charles? At least he wasn't here, he was doing his Captain training at Sandhurst, and then he would be sent to his battalion, by then Lizzie would be back in London and away from him, Eddie couldn't come home quickly enough!

There was a knock at the door. "Enter," said Lizzie. "Oh, Jean, I will run my own bath from now on."

"But your mother, Lady Elizabeth."

"Oh, don't worry, I won't tell her if you don't," she said, looking at Jean.

"I won't say anything, Miss."

The maid left, clicking the door shut quietly, shaking her head but smiling. Lizzie made for her bathroom and ran the bath putting bath salts in it, once full she climbed in and relaxed for the first time that day. Once clean, hair washed and clothes changed, she couldn't bear to go down to see her parents till lunchtime, there was another gentle knock of the door and her father entered, he came and sat by her on the bed.

He held her hand and said, "I can see you are happy being away and training to be a nurse, but I can see this episode with Charles is causing you a lot of anguish."

She thought carefully before she answered. "Yes," she replied not daring to look at her father as she would start to cry.

"Let's see how it goes, and maybe the country being at war will help with your dilemma," he replied. "Don't give up hope just yet?"

"Thank you, and I hope you are right, papa," she said with feeling.

She fell into his open arms; she could smell his aftershave. Oh, she felt safe and secure.

"Right, ready for lunch?" he asked.

He took her arm and led her downstairs into the dining room, the fire was not lit, and it was quite chilly.

"Why don't you and Mother eat in the kitchen when it is just the two of you?" she asked the both of them.

Lady Margo's face went red, and she was just about to rip into Lizzie about social standing, when her father rested his hand on her mother's arm and said, "She was only trying to help."

"What this country has come to and what would the servants say," replied her mother curtly.

"I'm sure they won't mind," replied her daughter. "They may be quite pleased," she carried on. Turning a shade of red, Lady Margo was inwardly fuming, how dare her daughter speak to her like that. No way would she let this of happened if Elizabeth had stayed at home.

Lunch was served and an uneasy truce was met. After lunch Lizzie wrapped up warm and took Dinky for a long walk around the grounds of the house; it was bitterly cold. The walk had woken her up, after being in the company of her mother, she thought she would be happy to go back to London and then her thoughts turned to Daisy and about how she was getting on at home, and how she missed her friend.

Soon the light was fading, and it was getting dark. Lizzie made her way back and entered the house through the kitchen, there was lovely smell coming from the oven and it was warm and inviting as she watched cook prepare tea.

"Fancy a cupper, Lady Elizabeth?" Edna the cook asked.

Lizzie knew her since she was a child, she would get a scone and jam with it. "Yes please," she replied, licking her lips. "You know me too well, just don't tell Mother." Lizzie winked at Edna.

"Your secret is safe with me, young lady," came the reply.

Lizzie took her seat at the large oak table in the centre of the room, cook spread everything on the table and Lizzie licked her lips with anticipation, it smelt and looked good.

"Help yourself, I need to feed you up before you go back to London." Lizzie took a big bite and was in heaven, Edna did the best baking.

She sat, telling cook all about the new friends she had made, the training and how tough but rewarding it was, Lizzie felt alive talking about it to someone who was interested, and she took a sip of tea and bit into the scone.

Much later she lay in bed listening to the howling wind that had gotten up, which was hitting the window and the rain lashing down, how it felt strange not having Daisy in the other bed to talk to. She knew the week would fly by and she would soon be back with her friends. Anyway, Eddie would be here in the morning, she couldn't wait to see him and catch up with all his news. Lizzie turned on her side, watching the few dying embers in the fireplace as she fell into a deep sleep.

The day started by opening the blackout curtain and it had stopped raining, and the wind had died down. Lizzie got out of bed and quickly got dressed, hurried to sort her hair out, putting it up into a ponytail as she would normally put it into a bun for work. She flew down the stairs and into the dining room for breakfast, her parents were already seated.

"Good morning," she said cheerily, kissing both their cheeks and taking her seat.

She waited for her mother to start but she stayed quiet, much to the relief of Lizzie. After breakfast she was at a loss with what to do while she was waiting for Eddie. Around eleven she could hear his car approaching and rushed out to the front of the house, watching as her brother advanced.

As soon as car stopped, he jumped out. "Hello sis," he said, she fell into his open arms. "What's the matter?" he said worriedly, pulling her tight. "We will talk later," he whispered, as their mother was fast approaching.

"Welcome home, Edward," Lady Margo said.

While he was talking to their mother, his sister had a chance to look at him in his new uniform, and she thought how grown up he was, no longer a boy but a young man that was ready to fight in the war.

The butler took his bag and greatcoat, that left Lizzie to take his arm and walk into the drawing room. Mother rang the bell for tea and then asked how "Edward was getting on?" Edward answered all her questions.

Lady Margo next asked about Francesca. "Have you seen her?"

Edward sat for a moment contemplating his answer.

"No," came the reply. "I have been too busy and in the wrong part of the country to see her."

Once tea was drunk, Eddie was free to go up to his room, Lizzie followed.

"Come and see me in fifteen minutes, once I am out of my uniform," he said.

Lizzie went to her room and sat looking at some magazines that Jean had given her to read. As she was flicking through, she was thinking how nice to be home with her brother, it felt like old times. Once outside his door she took a depth breath and knocked.

"Enter," he shouted. "Come sit with me." He had changed into a shirt, trousers and comfy jumper.

Lizzie then spilled all her news, telling him about her new friends, her life at The London and how happy she was.

They talked about the phoney war and how his training was going, and he said seriously, "Things will change, Hitler will either try to invade more countries or will bomb us soon."

This sent a shiver down Lizzie's spine. "Are you sure," she asked.

"Yes," he replied. "I'm sure, we must be ready," he said adamantly.

At that news, the worst was yet to come she thought, but she kept that to herself.

"Tell me about Charles," he asked.

"I haven't seen him," she said relieved. "But Mother wants me to get engaged and married once my training is complete. Oh, Eddie, I am happy, I don't love Charles." Sighing, she continued. "Why does she think he is good for me? Let's put our heads together and come up with a plan to stop this mad idea from happening,"

"Well, perhaps with us being at war, things might change without our intervention," said Eddie, praying he was right.

She gave her brother a hug and felt lighter and happy since talking to him.

The twenty-four hours flew by, and Eddie had to return to his squadron, it was sad to see him go but when he spoke about flying it was with enthusiasm, she had ever seen him so alive.

He gave her kiss and hug. "Be careful," she said sincerely, and she watched as the car drove down the driveway and away into the distance.

Her parents turned and entered the house, leaving Lizzie staring into space.

Chapter 13

Only a few more days and she would return to London and her new life, a life hopefully without Charles and marriage. She wanted to get married, but to someone that she loved with all her heart and had chosen herself, and in her own time. Once up in her bedroom she laid on her bed and thought how and what to do for the rest of the day, she made up her mind and headed downstairs to see cook.

"Can I help you?" she asked, hopefully.

"Of course you can, but don't let your mother catch you," came the reply, and they spent the rest of the morning making cakes and preparing lunch, having a pleasant time together.

The cook and Lizzie were chatting away when they heard footsteps coming.

"You had better go out the back door it may be your mother come looking for you?"

Lizzie cleaned her hands, and she made a quick escape and shot out the back door and ran around to the front of the house letting herself in.

Her father was walking through the hall when he spotted her. "What are you doing?" he laughed, covertly.

"You must promise not tell Mother but I have been helping cook and having a lovely time in the kitchen, then we heard someone coming and we thought it might be her."

"She is looking for you," he said apologetically. "Run up to your room and come down in a couple of minutes," he conspired with her.

Lizzie gave her papa a kiss on the cheek and hurried up the stairs as quick as she could. As soon as she was at the top, she turned around and then descended the stairs to find her mother at the bottom.

"I have been looking for you everywhere, young lady?" said a rather cross Mother.

Lady Elgar and her daughter are paying us a visit this afternoon, you were at school with Louise.

"Yes, I know of her, but we were not friends," answered Lizzie, bored already.

"Well, just be nice and pleasant for me?" Lady Margo glanced at her daughter.

"Yes, Mother." Lizzie rolled her eyes at her mother behind her back, causing her father to notice and laugh.

"Clifford!" she said in her stern voice. "Lunch is served, come along you two."

Clifford took his daughter's arm and led her into lunch still laughing to himself. The afternoon was actually pleasant. Louise was all right and very funny, and found talking to Lizzie rather enjoyable, and hearing about her life in London to be interesting.

"Oh, how I wish my life were like yours," Louise whispered. "Maybe I will join one of the services, like the Wrens or the Air Force!"

"Why not?" said Lizzie. "The war is opening up things to all different people, the war won't be finished by Christmas, you wait and see," Lizzie said stubbornly.

"I hear you are getting engaged to Lord Charles Holmes?" said Lady Elgar enthusiastically.

"Yes, once I have finished my training," replied Lizzie reluctantly.

"You must be extremely pleased, Margo?" said Lady Elgar looking across at the Lady Margo.

"Charles will make a very good husband for Elizabeth; she can't do better than him," Lady Margo agreed.

Louise picked up on Lizzie's unhappiness. "Tell me what's wrong?" she enquired as she rubbed Lizzie's arm soothingly.

"I don't love him or want to get married, but Mother has other ideas," Lizzie sighed.

"Well, don't, there is a war on remember!" said Lady Louise.

This made Lizzie laugh, much to her mother's displeasure.

"Oh, darling, of course you want to marry Charles and I want grandchildren very soon."

That surprised Lizzie as her mother had no time for them as children.

Lady Louise gave a sympathetic smile to Lizzie, which Lizzie returned. The rest of the afternoon flew by and both girls were sad to see it end, Lizzie watched as her friend departed with her mother with a promise to keep in touch.

The rest of the week passed without any incidents, Lizzie kept out of her mother's way as much as possible and soon it was Saturday.

Eddie had phoned a couple of times over the week and said he would be up in London, and if her shifts were okay, could they meet up and go to see a show in the west end, or go dancing?

Of course, she had jumped at the chance to see her brother, even if she had to change shifts with someone. Daisy and the girls could come too. Up in her room packing, she looked in her wardrobe and took out more clothes to take back with her as she thought some of them would look nice on the others and they were wasted being left here.

While in bed that night her thoughts turned to her mother again and she wondered why she disapproved of her daughter wanting a career. Everyone knew that this war would change how people like them lived forever, big stately homes were becoming a thing of the past and the cost of the upkeep was very expensive. With that she rolled over and fell into a deep, restful sleep.

The following morning, Lizzie had breakfast with her parents and said 'goodbye' to cook and the rest of the servants, she wasn't sure how much longer they would be working for her parents, but she kept that thought to herself.

The cook gave Lizzie a hug. "Take care of yourself and be safe," she said, Lizzie wiped the tear from her eye, and she left the kitchen, she always felt that cook was like the mother she really wanted, not the stone-cold Mother that she actually had.

Geoffrey was prompt and was waiting by the front door at ten-thirty.

Lizzie gave both parents a kiss on the cheek and said, "Please write, and I will be back soon."

"Telephone and let us know when you are coming up again," Father said. "And take care," he said in a warm manner.

Her mother just gave her a hard stony look. Lizzie sat back in the Rolls Royce, she couldn't look her mother in the eyes, so she settled in the seat looking straight ahead for the drive to the station. Once there Geoffrey got her case out, handed her gas mask over, and placed the suitcase on the ground.

She went over to him and gave him a hug. "Thank you," she said, "for all you do." She held his hand.

"Thank you, Miss," he smiled at the young woman.

"Keep an eye on my parents please," she said, as an afterthought.

At Eleven, the London train pulled in, it was packed with service personnel heading to the city and further afield. Lizzie had to stand, which she wasn't bothered about as she chatted to two sailors. She didn't ask where they were from as there were signs up saying loose lips, sink ships.

The signs on their hats only had HMS on it. She shared a sandwich with them that cook had given her, the look on their faces was worth it, soon the train made its way into London she said 'goodbye' to the two lads and wished them well, and Lizzie took the underground back to Whitechapel.

Once back, she headed straight to the Nurse's home, hoping that Daisy was back. Home Sister welcomed her back and said that Daisy was indeed already back and in their room. She hurried up the stairs and stood outside the room, took a deep breath, turned the knob and rushed in.

Chapter 14

On hearing the door open Daisy turned around sharply and saw her roommate heading into the room.

"Welcome back," they both said in unison. "We had better keep the noise down," they said, both laughing together.

Daisy carried on unpacking her case and hanging her clothes in the wardrobe, once done she stopped what she was doing, went over to Lizzie and they gave each other a huge hug.

"I have missed you," they both said together.

Lizzie took her winter coat off, hung her gas mask on the back of the door, then went over to her wardrobe and opened the door ready, laid her case on the bed and got unpacking her clothes as well. The wardrobe looked full already, they were chatting away telling each other about their week off.

"I have brought you back some more of my old clothes," said Lizzie. "Help yourself."

Daisy went over to Lizzie's bed to have a good rummage through, the clothes were beautiful she thought.

"When Jenny and Claire arrive; they too can have a look." Said Lizzie.

Once finished Lizzie asked about Bobby and then the floodgates opened. Lizzie rushed over to her friend and held her tight, she was shaking. Waiting for the tears to stop and once they had dried up, Lizzie pulled her friend to her bed, and they both sat down.

"Now, tell me what happened." Taking Daisy's shaking hands in hers.

Lizzie's hands felt cold from just being outside, but they felt soothing, so Daisy began. It was easy for her to explain what had happened, how in the end when she had turned him down, he had turned nasty towards her. Maybe, Lizzie said to her friend it is for the best and you are better off without him. Daisy having talked to her friend

100

weighing it up she had agreed and felt a lot better and not as guilty as she had. Maybe the feelings she had for him had been like having a brother and not romantic as she had been hoping for.

With the outbreak of war people's attitudes would be changing. A few months ago, she would have said 'yes' to Bobby's proposal, if she still lived in Luton. She thought that many people would be getting married at short notice with their loved ones going away and with an uncertain future ahead for everyone.

Once Daisy had finished her story, she asked Lizzie, "Have you seen or heard from Charles?"

"No," came the rather abrupt reply. "He is away doing his training and then joining his regiment straight after."

She really hoped she wouldn't see or hear from him for a long time. Her biggest fear was that he would turn up at the hospital and make a scene.

"Then we must keep our eyes and ears open, we are friends, that's what we do, we protect each other," said Daisy.

"My mother kept on at me the whole holiday and in the end, I just agreed to appease her," Lizzie told Daisy who was listening intently.

"How's Eddie?" Daisy asked, steering the conversation away from being about Charles.

"Oh, he is well, thank you! Really happy and enjoying his training. Maybe when he comes to London you could meet him with me, if our shifts allow it?"

"I would like that very much," answered Daisy with a smile on her face.

"That's better," said Lizzie. "No more tears today. Come on. Let's get back to unpacking and then we can go and see if Jenny and Claire have arrived back, we could go to the dining hall and see what delights they are cooking," laughed Lizzie. "I don't know about you, but I am absolutely famished from the journey back."

Both girls got to work and finished in record time. Half hour later they both stood outside the door of their neighbours' room, knocking on it.

"Come in," came the joint reply.

Jenny and Claire were both doing the same as they had been doing a few minutes before, unpacking from their journey. Both girls stopped what where they doing, moved the clothes and made space on the beds for all four to sit down. Each girl taking their turn to tell each other about their week away. Daisy didn't want to go into detail about her split from Bobby just yet, so she stayed off that subject and the others didn't mention it. Lizzie gave her a worried sideward glance but kept silent, which she was thankful for. In turn Lizzie didn't want to talk about Charles or her mother, so she too kept quiet on that subject. Jenny mentioned that the seafront at Brighton had been cordoned off with barbed wire and gun placements had been put in place, just in case of the invasion that the government was worried about, and her sister Dorothy had gone against her boyfriend's wishes to join the Wrens. The others could see she was worried about her mother being left on her own even if she didn't say anything. Claire mentioned that her brother Freddy had joined the army and was away training, otherwise her parents were both all right.

Finally, they all sat in the room with their own thoughts that war was becoming very real. Luckily talk turned to the next set of wards they were going to be on, starting the next morning. They all said that they were nervous, even slightly apprehensive, but not as bad as when going onto the first placement as they knew what to expect this time, but they had to get used to a new set of staff.

It was soon teatime, and the four friends made their way to the busy dining hall for tea, they caught up with other girls from their group and chatted about their holidays and being ready to go back on the wards. It was nice to catch up with everyone and Lizzie, following tea went and got her coat and cigarettes, Jenny joined her, having started smoking, and they took themselves out into the cold November evening and lit up one, both looking up at the full moon in the sky which was bright and clear. They finished the cigarettes quickly as the cold was biting through their coats and they both rushed back into the warm.

Once back in the room, Lizzie dug around the floorboard, she got the scotch out and the girls all had a drink.

"I think we should have an early night and get our uniforms ready for work in the morning," said Daisy sensibly.

All agreed yawning, and Jenny and Claire headed back to their room with a promise to meet up tomorrow evening.

Once they were both alone, Daisy went off to have a bath and that left Lizzie alone for half an hour, she prepared her uniform and made up her cap. She wondered how Eddie was getting on and she made a promise that she would write to him tomorrow evening after her shift. On reflection she thought she should write to Charles and her parents as well, but her heart wasn't really in it, so she would do that another time!

Daisy was back from having her bath, she quickly dried her hair which she had had cut a bit shorter while at home into an easier style to manage, and she too prepared her uniform for the morning. Once both were ready, they climbed into bed and lay there chatting in the dark. Soon their eyes grew tired, and they fell asleep lost in their own dreams.

They were soon woken at five-thirty, and sleepily they got up out of bed, the room was chilly as the heating hadn't kicked in yet. Both got ready for work quietly and quickly in the cold and made their way to the dining hall for breakfast, which was lovely and warm. Jenny and Claire soon joined them, the noise in the room was deafening with the chatter of girls getting ready for the day ahead. Lizzie on her way back to her room took a detour outside for a cigarette and wrapped her cardigan around herself when the cold morning hit her on the way out the door. She finished it in record time, followed by Jenny.

"God, that's cold out there," they both said together.

Once back inside, Lizzie made her way to her room and finished getting ready with Daisy, both girls checked each other over, making adjustments where needed in the mirror. Soon it was time to make their way to their new wards, both girls walked silently along the long corridors that smelt of disinfectant, both lost in thought to what the day would bring.

"See you later," they both said as they went their different ways.

Daisy headed to Male Medical and Sister Warnock and Lizzie down the corridor to Gynae and Sister Brown. Daisy took a deep breath, tried to calm the butterflies in her stomach, pushed the heavy ward door and entered the ward. Daisy looked down at the fob watch attached to her uniform, six forty-five, she was early, and she headed for the locker room, once inside she put her apron in a spare locker. Checking herself in the mirror, she thought she could do this with her eyes shut now, took another glance in the mirror at her appearance, liked what she saw looking back at her. Then quietly joined the end of the row of staff awaiting Sister's arrival.

Sister Warnock bustled up the ward from her office glancing around as she did so.

"Good morning, all," she said, her eyes came upon Daisy. "You must be the new probationer?"

"Yes, Sister," she replied in a near whisper.

"Well, I run a tight ship," she began. "Follow what the staff nurses tell you and you will learn a lot."

"Yes, Sister," replied Daisy.

Sister Warnock was a small, bubbly woman who Daisy thought was nice as she watched her bustle back to her office.

"We are very busy at the moment due to the time of year and the weather being so bad," Staff Nurse Evans said.

"Now go back to the locker room, put your apron on and roll up your sleeves."

Daisy heard a lot of coughing in the background and wanted to turn, and look around, but Staff Nurse was still talking, and she was trying to take in her new surroundings.

"The ward layout is the same as most wards at The London, kitchen to your left and the sluice down to your right. Linen cupboard by the main door, the pace is not as quick as surgical, but we are still very busy, understand?"

"Yes, Staff Nurse," Daisy replied.

Daisy noticed the ward maid was going down the ward putting water jugs on the patient's lockers, but as the same time, she was watching what Daisy was doing. I need to be careful she thought.

"Right, let's check the ward workbook and then make a start," Staff Nurse Evans said.

Daisy followed the staff nurse down the ward to bed six, with a very frail man in it.

"We need to change a bandage on his leg as he has got an ulcer on it that is infected. Go into the treatment room and lay a trolley for doing a dressing and come back," said the staff nurse.

Daisy rushed off trying to remember what equipment she needed.

Once in the store cupboard she found what she needed and then hurried back to the bed.

Once the task was completed, "Mr Jones in bed four needs a bed bath," said Staff Nurse. "Don't look so frightened, we will be doing it together." You could see the relief etched on her face.

She hadn't done much on her first ward. But she had heard from Lizzie, Sister Warnock liked her students to learn hands on. The morning flew by, and Daisy managed to meet up with the girls at break.

"How was your morning?" she asked.

Lizzie answered, "Gynae is all right. Sister Brown is strict but okay and we have been busy back and forward to theatre, I think I will enjoy it."

"I have been doing bed pans all morning!" Jenny said laughing. "And Sister Williams is more worried about my appearance! Which I can say was actually okay."

"That made the others laugh," said Lizzie, laughing too.

"Is Dr Reynolds still working or has he left?" Daisy asked, trying to sound as normal as possible.

"He has left to join the army," Jenny said, looking at her friend quizzically. Daisy was actually disappointed that he was gone, and she wondered if she would ever see him again? She had zoned out for a moment, lost in her own thoughts.

She was brought back when she heard Claire say, "Female geriatrics is really nice, Sister Douglas is lovely and really caring. We have quite a lot of very poorly ladies."

"Right, we had better be getting back," said Daisy, looking at her fob watch and stifling a yawn. "Sorry."

All four of them pushed back their chairs and went their separate ways.

"Meet up later?" Daisy called over her shoulder.

Quickly she rushed back to the ward, on entering Staff Nurse Evans found her putting on her apron and rolling up her sleeves ready to put her cuffs on.

"Oh, I am glad you're back, we've just had a new emergency admission in bed eight, he has pneumonia. See to him at once, make him comfortable as you can and await Doctor."

"Yes, Staff Nurse," she said obediently.

Daisy hurried down the ward to bed eight, where Mr Woods was laying on the bed looking very pale, and he was sweating. She wasn't sure what she was supposed to do, so she sat him up against the pillows.

"Is that better?" she queried, trying to sound confident but not feeling it at all.

Mr Woods nodded his head as he was so out of breath just from doing that. Daisy turned around and saw Catherine, a second-year student nurse, waving her over.

"He doesn't look too good," she said urgently to Daisy. "Better get Doctor Coleman."

"I will stay with him," said Catherine.

Daisy looked relieved and went to get Staff Nurse Evans to call the houseman. Luckily, he was only on the other ward and came rushing over very quickly.

"Where is he?" Came the commanding voice of Doctor Coleman as he came rushing through the ward doors, his white coat flapping behind him.

"Bed eight," Staff Nurse Evans replied, going with him to examine Mr Woods.

Daisy pulled the screens around the bed, her heart was pounding and waited outside for Staff Nurse's commands. Doctor Coleman examined his chest using his stethoscope, once Staff Nurse had pulled open his pyjama jacket.

"I don't like the sound of his chest, get a chest x-ray and oxygen tent ready."

"Yes, doctor."

He turned, walked off and over his shoulder said, "Well done."

Daisy felt her chest swell with pride, it felt good helping people, this is why she had wanted to come into nursing. Mr Woods went off for his x-ray when the porters arrived, while the nurses got the tent ready for when he returned. Sister had popped her head out of the office, wanting to see what all the commotion was about. Once happy everything was all right, she went back in calling the maid for her tea tray to be brought.

When Mr Woods arrived back, Daisy and Catherine settled him in the tent, and did his observations, Staff Nurse then sent them to lunch.

Daisy walked into the locker room, took off her apron and pulled her cuffs down. She heard her stomach rumble, luckily it was lunchtime, she thought.

Catherine looked over from her locker, a small smile on her face. "Hungry, are you?" she enquired.

Daisy answered, "Yes, come on." Both girls laughing, hurried out the door down the ward, into the long corridor down to the dining hall.

Lunch again was filling, dull but edible, both girls were so hungry that they didn't care. Daisy looked around trying to spot her friends, didn't see them so she sat talking to Catherine. They finished lunch and headed straight back to the ward.

The afternoon flew by and at five, the girls were released from the ward. Daisy was so pleased, but her legs and feet ached; they felt like lead, she didn't think she could walk back to the nurse's home. Once back in her room she found that Lizzie was not back yet, she took her shoes off, laid on her bed, feeling so tired she closed her eyes and drifted off. Next thing she heard was Lizzie opening the door and coming in.

Daisy sat up, rubbing the sleep from her eyes. "Sorry, did I wake you?" asked Lizzie.

"No! I must have dozed off for a few moments," said a sleepy Daisy.

She rolled off her bed and sat up. Lizzie sat on her bed, took her shoes off and rubbed her sore feet.

"All that standing all day is killing me," she laughed. "How was your day?" Lizzie asked. Interested in her friend's day.

"Really good, thank you but tiring, my feet were on fire when I got back," said Daisy

"Mine are the same, I will never get used to standing on them all day," said Lizzie. "I spent the morning preparing patients for theatre, helped put up an intravenous infusion, and was allowed to take one patient to theatre this afternoon," explained Lizzie. "We also had an emergency admission this morning, a lady was bleeding heavily and needed to go to theatre quickly, so that was exciting and an adrenaline rush. I feel we should be doing more though; it will get better, remember this is only our second ward, we are trying to run before we can walk," said a thoughtful Lizzie.

"How was your day?" Lizzie asked again.

"All right had an emergency too which was scary but in a good way," Daisy went on and explained what had taken place.

"Phew, that was exciting!" Lizzie managed to say between yawns.

Both girls put their shoes back on, made themselves respectable, and knocked on Jenny and Claire's door. Both girls were in, so they waited, while they got ready for tea.

Lizzie was too tired to bother to go outside for a cigarette and with it being dark and cold, so she thought she would open the window in their room when they got back. She had forgotten her coat as well. Once back in their room, Lizzie got Daisy to turn off the room light, she pushed open the window, and was taken aback when she was hit by the cool night air. Lighting her cigarette, she offered one to Jenny who had joined her, and both inhaled deeply making sure both blew the smoke outside.

While the two were smoking, Daisy and Claire went to the bathroom and had a long soak which was relaxing, the other two followed shortly and the plan was to meet up later for a chat once all the girls had finished their ablutions. By eight-thirty all the girls were clean and refreshed and sitting on Daisy's bed. Lizzie moved the floorboard and pulling the scotch out poured it into four glasses.

"Cheers," she said, and they all took a sip of their drinks.

"I needed that," said Jenny, feeling the warm liquid slip down her throat.

All the others agreed, they sat talking about their day, what they had learnt and what was coming up when they were back in the school. Talk turned to the war, pregnant women, women with small children and children in the cities had been evacuated to the countryside by the government. A lot of the stations had been busy but with nothing happening some of the children had come back to the cities.

"We should go to the cinema at the weekend," Lizzie suggested.

And we need to write some letters, the others mentioned. By ten, the girls were flagging.

"Bed, I think," they said.

They said their 'goodnights', and Jenny and Claire headed to their room. Daisy was lucky she was on a late the next day, which meant she started at lunchtime but finished at nine. Lizzie turned off the big light and turned on the small lamp by the bed. Both climbed into bed, Daisy pulled the sheets up and snuggled down, she could hear Lizzie doing the same. They talked for a few moments as they did most nights but sleep soon came.

Daisy could hear Lizzie getting up for the early shift. Getting dressed, she tiptoed out of the room so as not to disturb her friend. Daisy rolled over and went back to sleep. By nine Daisy was awake, she got dressed went down to the dining hall had breakfast. She thought, 'what can I do for the morning?'

It wasn't raining but was very cold, so she decided on a brisk walk. She pulled on her winter coat tied her scarf tightly round her neck, picked up her gas mask and headed out of the nurse's home into the cold grey air.

Walking past the head porter hut she stopped and said, good morning, to Tom, who looked up from his morning paper and grinned at Daisy.

In a booming cockney accent, he said, "Good morning, Daisy."

Surprised etched her face. "How do you know my name?" she asked.

"I make it my business to know all the new nurses," he said, laughing.

Daisy thought that was very nice that he knew everyone and carried on walking briskly, leaving the grounds of the hospital laughing to herself and soon she found herself in the high street. She quickly went into Woolworths to buy some make-up and stockings, which she was getting through very quickly as she kept snagging them on the side of the beds, being in the store made her think of her sister and home.

A wave of homesickness came over her and a tear slipped from a corner of her eye, she wiped it with her clean handkerchief. Pull yourself together she thought, but it didn't stop her from still missing her family, and especially her mum. She wondered what they were up to and hoped they were all right, she would write this morning once she got back to her room. Paying for her items, she headed along the street, stopping and looking at all the wonderful different foods you could get, but little did she realise that as the war went on food and other items would become scarce.

The raw chilly wind blowing off the Thames was making Daisy shiver, so she decided to head back to her room and write them letters.

She walked with a determination to get back and before she knew it the hospital was in sight; it was an imposing building she thought as it got nearer.

Daisy said 'hello' to Tom and entered the grounds, and she headed straight to the nurse's home and her room. Depositing her coat on the hook behind the door, she rubbed her hands together to get warm as she had forgotten to take her gloves with her.

Daisy got herself a cup of tea from the small kitchen down the corridor, settled herself at her desk and began to write. One letter to her parents and brothers, one to her sister and finally one to Bobby, this one was the hardest to write. She had decided to end the relationship definitely, following how it had ended while she was home on holiday, she was pretty sure he already knew it was over between them. It was a brief letter hoping that he met someone who would love him, and she wished him all the best for the future and she hoped they could still be friends. She sealed the envelope, attached a stamp, did the same with the others and decided to run to the post box, prior to going on the ward.

She had a feeling her sister would be pleased she had split from Bobby, because her mother used to say both girls knew what the other was thinking all the time, it was a twin thing! Daisy looked at the time on the watch on her wrist, stood up, stretched and got ready for work. Once in her uniform she retuned her dirty cup to the kitchen, washed it up in the sink and put it on the side to dry, and made her way back to her room and tidied her hair.

She took one final look in the mirror, and happy with what she saw, headed to the dining hall for lunch. Hurriedly she ate her food, which was hot and edible as always. Once finished pudding she checked her fob watch and rather smartly rushed to join the other nurses heading onto their late shifts. She walked speedily, making it to the ward with just a couple of minutes to spare, and swiftly took her cape off in the locker room.

Chapter 15

Daisy lined up ready for afternoon inspection, Staff Nurse Evans checked the girls over and work began. Daisy popped back to the locker room to roll up her sleeves and put her apron on, Sister had been called away to a meeting and would be back later during the afternoon.

A late shift was slightly different to a morning one, mornings were very busy but lates were quieter and not so hectic. There was less staff on, the first job was the back and bottom round, this meant turning patients and checking for pressure sores, rubbing cream into those areas. Daisy went around with Student Nurse Henley who had also switched to this ward.

"Have you heard from Dr Reynolds," Daisy enquired casually, not wanting to seem like she was actually interested

"Yes, he is enjoying training," was all the young nurse replied curtly.

Daisy left it at that, not wanting to push it. If it was visiting day, then the afternoon was taken up with the patients having their family to visit, only two people to a bed. Mainly relatives came on Sunday as they worked during the week, but if they could come then this was the highlight of the day. Sister was back from her meeting, she walked up and down the ward not missing anything. Satisfied with what she saw, she got ready to go off shift.

This left Staff Nurse Evans in charge. Daisy liked Staff Nurse Evans, she was fair and a good nurse. Observations done, tea served, patients were put to bed for the evening. Daisy was released by Staff Nurse for supper, and she made her way along the long corridor with its white-washed walls, smelling slightly of bleach. It kind of calmed her as she walked. As she made her way to the dining hall, she now understood why women went into nursing and that she knew she too had made the right decision, even though she had only been here just a few months. She walked the rest of the way to the dining hall with a bounce in her step.

The dining hall was quiet, Daisy entered and walked up to the hatch and for once she didn't have to queue. She chose cheese on toast, found a seat, and sat down to eat her supper, wondering how Lizzie was.

Back on the ward most of the patients were back in bed, some already asleep, and Daisy found time to speak with the patients still awake. She enjoyed this time, getting to know the men and listening about their home lives and families. She was quite taken with the cockney accent which she was getting used to and she talked about her family and why she chose London to train.

Having been chatting, she hadn't realised that the night staff had arrived. Staff Nurse handed over, and Daisy and the other nurses were then allowed to leave. Once she had said 'goodnight' to the patients, she got ready, said 'goodnight' to the other nurses and made her way down the ward and back to the nurse's home.

She couldn't get over how her feet ached as she walked up the stairs to her room on the second floor.

She entered the room and slumped down on the bed and Lizzie said. "Are you okay?" Concerned, she was looking over.

The day hadn't gone particularly bad but talking to Nurse Henley had brought up unexpected feelings again for Dr Reynolds. She pushed them to the back of her mind for now and concentrated on what her roommate had said.

"Yes," said Daisy. "I'm fine, just tired and still getting used to working these long hours."

"I'm afraid it's all part of the job," answered Lizzie.

Both girls laid back on their beds talking.

"I have sent letters home this morning," Daisy mentioned. "And I sent one to Bobby to end the relationship definitely, if we ever had one."

This information made Lizzie sit up, looked over to her friend, looking concerned again, she said, "How do you feel?"

"I feel surprisingly relieved actually, and contented nevertheless, I still have to see if I get a reply from him, we left on not very good terms. I feel it's like the end of a chapter and a new beginning is about to start. I feel much lighter and relieved," she said, looking over to her friend.

"Are you going to write to your family, and especially Charles, because you need to decide what you really want and to finally stand up against your mother. She doesn't own you; you know!" Looking over to

Lizzie, waiting for her to answer

"Yes, but she can cut off my inheritance!" Lizzie said, looking pale and drawn.

"Won't your father stand up for you?"

Sighing, she said, "I think he would at a push, but my mother is very forceful, and what she wants is what she gets." Said an angry Lizzie.

"Yes, but times are changing," Daisy replied. "Don't give up hope."

"All right, I will write to Charles and see what his response is and then we go from there, but don't hold your breath." Lizzie looked at her friend, she hoped that was all the bombardment she was getting tonight because she had had enough.

"I will also speak with Eddie as he may already have a plan and can help, but he has more pressing things to concentrate on, like the war." Lizzie needed to write to her brother, she should have done it days ago but being busy it had slipped her mind.

One girl felt like a very large cloud had been lifted, Lizzie on the other hand still wasn't sure, but time would tell.

"Right, that's enough contemplation for tonight, let's get to sleep!" said Lizzie.

Both slept but not particularly well, still troubled.

The rest of the week soared by for Lizzie. The next free time she had written to her parents explaining what she had done. She got Charles' address where he was training from Eddie and sent him a letter, basically asking if would consider not going through with the engagement, hoping they could be friends at least. Now she waited for the replies, she felt physically sick and very anxious. But she knew she was right; she even called her brother at the airfield he was training at and asked his advice and to get reassurance, he recommended giving it a go. And he said he would come to London to visit her as soon as he could.

A week later, the first reply turned up, it was for Daisy. Bobby was blunt and said yes it was over and he was joining the Royal Engineers, he did not wish her well and just signed off 'Robert'. She wasn't surprised at the response, but seeing it in black and white had hit a raw nerve. The other letter from her parents arrived a day later, they were all fine, missing her and hoping she was getting on okay. They mentioned that Bobby had left to join the army and that Mary was writing to him;

and there you had it. She wasn't surprised that her sister was writing to him as she always knew she had a soft spot for him, well she was welcome to him. She folded up the letter and put it away with the others for safe keeping.

A week later Lizzie found a letter in the pigeon hall, she noticed the handwriting was from her mother and she was not happy, in fact she was absolutely furious. Basically, the engagement, and the marriage would still go ahead. If it didn't then she would be cut off completely. Lizzie wasn't surprised but was still in shock when she read it. Daisy tried to support her but knew she was limited in what she could say and do.

Perhaps a letter from Charles would arrive and he would agree to not going through with this agreement. Luck was against her, the letter arrived two days later, Charles agreed with her mother and the engagement was still on, she belonged to him. 'Well not at the moment, I don't!' She thought. She showed the letter to Daisy, and she was angry.

The weeks raced by, and Christmas was upon them, most wards had been emptied, leaving only the really sick and infirm. To make up for this, the wards were all decorated really nicely and each one had a real tree sitting by the entrance, decorated with baubles and lights that sparkled. The nurses all loved this time of the year and they felt sorry for the poor patients stuck in hospital as it could be a lonely time.

As it grew nearer to Christmas, the hospital got really busy with emergency admissions, as the weather had taken a turn for the worse with heavy snow. On Christmas Eve, the choir would go around the hospital in the evening singing carols with the Salvation Army band, and at the end, had mince pies and a glass of sherry.

All four girls had been chosen to sing and had enjoyed it immensely, especially Claire who was booming out the carols at the top of her voice. Eddie had succeeded in coming up to see his sister just before New Year as flying had been suspended due to bad weather and heavy snow.

Lizzie and Daisy took the underground to Leicester Square one evening, it was trying to snow again. It was very dark as all the lights had to be turned off due to the blackout. Daisy took hold of Lizzie's arm, and both stood, trying to keep warm against the December evening and the bitter cold.

Eddie arrived out of breath. "Hello, sis," he called and hugged her close to him, she felt safe against his thick greatcoat and could smell his aftershave. Pushing him back she couldn't get over how dashing he looked in his uniform. Daisy stood looking, she thought so too.

He was formally introduced to Daisy and by the end of the evening they were firm friends. They walked together to the nearest Lyon's corner house, where they found a table, it was busy, filled with couples and groups. Eddie ordered cake and tea for all of them. They briefly talked about the war or lack of it. How Lizzie's training was going. Eddie then talked about his training as much as he could.

Both then mentioned their parents, especially their mother. "Why is she being like this?" asked Lizzie, her frustration boiling over.

Eddie explained, "At that moment go ahead and play along with the engagement and hopefully things should change."

It wasn't a solution to the problem, but Lizzie could live with this at present. The rest of the evening had been short but enjoyable. By nine-thirty the girls said their 'goodbyes' to Eddie and made the journey back to The London.

Chapter 16

The start of 1940 was cold and grey, the girls spent long days on the wards, learning all the time, attending lectures given by the consultants.

By the middle of February, the girls had finished their secondment on the wards for a while. Lizzie was sad to leave male medical; she had learnt a lot, but it was time to move on. The others all felt the same, and so Monday morning arrived and the girls were back in school for two weeks of lectures by doctors, and more exams at the end to go towards their first year.

Hilary was her usual self, saying she would do well in the exams and that she had excelled on the wards. They didn't take much notice of her and spent the rest of the week learning and practicing what they had been taught, in the evenings, studying was the norm.

The weather was still bad, made worse by the gusting wind blowing from the Thames, luckily the girls were happy to stay in. The girls, one evening to escape studying, went down to the common room to listen to the wireless, the only news was that some British troops had been sent to France and Belgium to shore up these two countries. Lizzie, looking around at the glum faces turned the wireless to some dance music to lighten the mood.

"Well, not much is happening, perhaps the war will be over sooner than we think?" said Jenny slightly hesitantly as they walked back up the stairs to their rooms.

The others doubted it. The exam they found out would be Friday of the next week and the results out Sunday on the board in the nurse's home as Sister Tutor liked to mark the papers really smartly. Following that, ward allocation would be out late afternoon and all the girls would know where they were working from Monday for another period of time, taking them to the middle of May and then annual leave again for a few days.

Friday morning the girls arrived in the classroom early, took their seats and prepared for the exam. Soon others started to wander in, some stood talking, but most took their seats. Dead on nine, Sister Tutor entered with the exam papers in her hand.

"Right!"

Quietly, all the girls sat ready. The papers were handed out.

"You have two hours, off you go," she said.

The two hours flew by and all four answered all the questions and departed the room once the exam was finished and papers collected.

Sister Tutor said, "Have a lovely weekend, you have all worked hard, remember results out on Sunday Morning."

Outside the door Hilary was her usual self, full of confidence and irritating. All the others just wanted to do was head back to their rooms, they quickly made their excuses and left.

Walking back to the nurses' home the girls couldn't help going over the questions.

"Are you sure it was that or was it this?"

"What about question seven?"

"Question eight was a stinker!"

In the end Lizzie said, "It's too late now, the exam is done, we can't change it. We will know when Sunday comes now come on, I need a drink." She hurried off towards their room.

Back in their room, Lizzie poured them all a small drink saying, "Only because this is a special occasion," the others laughed.

It felt good slipping down Daisy's throat, giving her a warm glow, putting the dirty glass on the side she said, "Right, who is ready for lunch?"

The other three agreed and finished their drinks and off they went to the dining hall, trying to avoid Hilary at all costs.

"What are we going to do this afternoon as we have no studying to do for once?" said Claire.

"I am going back to our room for a cigarette," said Lizzie.

"I am joining you too," said Jenny.

"Yes, okay, but what about later?"

"Let's play cards as the weather is still bad and it's too cold to go outside," uttered Daisy.

Since moving in, Lizzie had taught her to play and she was getting quite good, she wanted to learn to play darts too.

Both girls stood by the open window, puffing on their cigarettes, feeling the cold air entering the warm room. The afternoon soared by and all four had great time unwinding, having a laugh and letting off steam. The friendship was growing stronger all the time and they hoped it would last forever.

The weekend soon went, with some washing, cleaning of their rooms which had been neglected. Soon Saturday night drew to a close, the four sat together worried about the results coming out in the morning. The nerves were back and feeling sick, all four hardly touched their tea.

"Come on! it will be fine," said Lizzie, but not really feeling it would be.

They all slept badly that night, 'Why do we put ourselves through this all the time,' she thought, as Lizzie woke up from having very little sleep.

Looking over at Daisy who was still asleep, she slipped out the room to use the bathroom. Once back, she opened the door, and crept back into the room, not wanting to wake Daisy, but she noticed she was awake and sitting on the bed.

"Good morning," she said, cheerfully. "Slept well?"

"Not really," Daisy replied.

"Well, we will have the results soon, in approximately two hours. Come on, get washed and dressed, then we can grab the others for breakfast."

"I'm not really hungry this morning," said Daisy.

"Come on," came the reply. "Just try!"

The others felt the same. At least in a few hours they would be put out of their misery. Again, the girls were all congregated in Lizzie and Daisy's room, and they were counting the minutes till ten o'clock, and as soon as the clock struck ten, they sent Lizzie out to check the board.

Sister Tutor pinned up the list and the rush to check began. Lizzie managed to squeeze in and ran her fingers down the list. She turned and walked back to the others, standing by the door to the room, waiting with trepidation.

"Well?" They all asked in unison.

"Right, Daisy is first, I'm second, Jenny third and Claire fourth.

"Where did Hilary come?"

"Oh, way down."

"I bet she is fuming?" They all said together trying not to laugh at the news.

"Come on we are going to celebrate today, before we find out where we are going to next," said Lizzie, they all agreed.

The relief could be heard as they all got ready to brave the weather and go to the little café they had found near the hospital. Once ready, huddled together they left the warmth of the nurses' home and made their way along the High Street. It had stopped snowing a few weeks back and the wind had died down, it was slowly getting lighter but still extremely cold as they made their way to the small but inviting café.

Mr Rimi, the owner, greeted them as they entered.

"Welcome! Welcome! Girls. Let me take your coats?"

The coats were deposited on the coat stand in the corner of the room, the girls found an empty table and sat down.

Mr Rimi picked up four menus and gave them out. "Take your time, I will be back," he said in his lovely Italian accent, and he made his way to the counter.

After a few moments the girls had decided on what they were having, Daisy tried to look out of the window, but it was steamed up with condensation from all the warmth radiating from the room.

Mr Rimi came over, took the order. "Two coffees, two hot chocolates and four cooked breakfasts as we are celebrating our results." Mr Rimi scurried off with the order, leaving the girls to chat.

"Well, what an eventful morning," said Lizzie.

"Well done to all of us and for still being here, we deserve a pat on the back for all our hard work over the last two weeks."

They all agreed. The talk turned to where they would be placed this afternoon, before anyone could answer the food and drinks appeared.

"Tuck in girls, before it gets cold," the girls did as they were famished!

The smell was delicious. Once finished, Lizzie paid the bill on behalf of the others, they said their goodbyes to Mr Rimi and all four made their way out into the cold.

"Don't you just love egg and bacon," said Claire as they wandered back to the hospital with full bellies. "We won't need lunch today," she said.

Again, the afternoon was spent waiting for the list to come out so they could find out where their placement would be. Lizzie again was designated checker, so dead on four she made her way out of her room and headed for the board, but this time not with dread like she had this morning.

Lizzie heard giggling behind her as the others were peering out from behind the door, she turned and smiled.

"Right, let's have a look for the second time today," she mumbled to herself.

Just before she gazed up, the others were by her side, and then pushing her to the front of the now small crowd that had formed. Lizzie and the others scanned the names, with excitement she found Daisy's.

"You're on gynaecology."

"Oh, okay," she said.

"What about me?" Jenny asked.

"Female surgical."

"Claire, you got male medical and finally me, I'm off to female surgical."

Turning around and pushing through the throng of girls, all four walked back down the corridor to the empty room with the door left open. Sitting on the vacant beds, all four seemed happy with their choices even though they didn't have a choice! Daisy looked at the time.

"I don't know about you lot, but I am ready for tea, then I have to get my uniform ready for the morning."

The others followed down to the dining hall, where they sat with others from their group, talking amongst themselves about where they would be working over the coming weeks. Little did they realise that in a few months one of the first major incidents of the war was about to happen. By nine everything was ready for the morning, all girls were happy and were lying on the beds in Lizzie and Daisy's room, drinking whiskey from the hidden stash.

"It's your turn to buy it next," said Daisy to Lizzie, looking at the near empty bottle.

"Okay," came the reply. "But you need to come with me as I am not very comfortable when purchasing it, we may even have trouble getting it due to shortages."

They had noticed it was starting to get difficult to get certain things in the shops.

"If that happens, I will bring some back with me when I go home, we have plenty and father won't mind." Jenny yawned and stretched, and this made the others follow.

"Right, I'm off to bed, coming Claire?"

"See you both in the morning for breakfast."

With that they departed to their room, the others could hear their door being opened and closed. Once left alone the girls got into their night clothes and ready for bed. Daisy pulled on her pyjamas which she found to be warm in this weather, climbed into bed looking over at their neat uniforms hanging up in front of the wardrobe for the morning. A sense of pride came over her, she couldn't believe how far they had come in just a few months. Looking back over the day, the emotions that she had felt from being scared and nervous of failing first thing this morning to excitement this afternoon upon finding out where her placement was to be.

Tiredness took her and she said 'goodnight' to Lizzie, and both girls fell into a contented sleep.

It was the beginning of March, and the mornings were getting lighter, Lizzie woke first to the birds singing and the light trying to peep under the blackout curtain. She climbed out of bed and quietly made her way to the toilet, once back in the room, Daisy heard her and got up, she too needed to use the bathroom. Both girls now comfortable, got ready, both stood in front of the mirror, and touched up the bits they could see.

Once happy they knocked on the door of their friends and headed down for breakfast. It was becoming a routine that they fell into apart from when on a late shift. Following breakfast, they got back to their rooms brushed their teeth and gathered up their things. All four didn't want to be late so they hurried along the corridor. The surgical wards were all found on the same floor, near theatres, and medical wards were on the first floor, you could take the lift, but Claire said, "See you later." And flew up the stairs two at a time.

That left the others, male surgical was on the right and female to the left, gynaecology ward was down the corridor. The girls stood at the entrance and said, 'see you later', and then disappeared into their allocated wards. The routine was about the same for all the wards and was becoming a habit. The girls were settling in again, being back on the wards, they liked the routine and the structure it brought with it. Daisy's first morning flew by preparing patients for theatre, settling them once back on the ward, giving bed baths to the patients that needed it. Taking care of them if they were sick (some of the anaesthetics could do that), doing observations. By lunchtime things had settled down and Staff Nurse Beedon had released her for lunch, again she made her way to the dining hall. She was finding her way round the vast area with ease and would soon be able to do it with her eyes closed.

The dining hall was busy with nurses, doctors and porters all sitting around enjoying a well-earned break. Daisy spotted Lizzie seated with some members from female surgical so she waved and went over to join them. They all greeted each other politely and Daisy took her seat next to Lizzie.

"How is your day going?" she asked.

"Good, nice to be back on the ward," came the cheerful reply.

For the next ten minutes the two friends caught up with each other. They then talked about their shifts for the rest of the week.

"I have two lates coming up and then a late on Sunday," said Daisy.

"I'm the opposite," said Lizzie.

Daisy then tucked into lunch of mince and mash; it wasn't wow but it was edible.

The rest of the day flew along and soon the girls found themselves back in their room rubbing sore feet.

"Will we get used to having sore feet?" They said in unison.

The others had joined them for tea and by the time they had had their baths and done their hair it was bedtime.

"Where does the time go?" said Jenny as she said "goodnight" and made her way to her room.

The weeks went quickly, the girls were learning all the time, some of the experience was sad when a patient died. They had a feeling they would soon be seeing a lot more death very soon. They all pulled together when this happened, to comfort each other and give support.

Daisy liked the ward sister, Sister Brown. Again, she was strict but fair and was happy with how Daisy was progressing. She didn't want to leave the ward as she had settled really well, even the young medical students had been friendly. As the evenings were lighter and the days were getting warmer so the girls could get out and explore more — shifts allowing. There were sandbags everywhere you went, protecting the buildings from bomb damage that was yet to happen. Gun placements were going in at the local park, ready for the enemy planes. It was nice to hear the different languages that made up London and smells were different to the smells that they experience at home. Sometimes the smell off the Thames River was awful, but it was part of London.

More children were about, as many had returned from being evacuated at the beginning of the war.

Before long it was the middle of May and the girls were heading off on holiday again, and so the packing began in earnest. This time they were leaving on Saturday and coming back after three days, travel permitting. All the girls stood at the bottom of the stairs, and they said goodbye to Claire, who made her way to Woolwich.

Chapter 17

The others took the underground to their individual mainline stations, and were taken by surprise by the amount of troop movement all around them. The stations were heaving with service personnel and the platforms; you couldn't move for men, you had to weave through them all. Even women in uniform had increased since the last time they had been home.

The girls had made a deal to be back by Thursday, Daisy bought her third-class ticket and then stood on the platform at St Pancras waiting for her train. She listened to the noise all around her, watching people coming and going to their destinations, she was happy to be going home, specially to see her family as it could be a while until she saw them again. She was relieved that Bobby wasn't going to be there but didn't know how she would react to Mary seeing him romantically, but she really shouldn't care as they had split up. She pushed the thought to the back of her mind as she heard her train being called for departure.

Daisy, picked up her suitcase, hooked her handbag and gas mask on her shoulder, ran down the platform unsteadily, as her case was heavy, found a door open to a carriage and jumped in. She couldn't find a seat, so she ended up in the corridor with a group of young airmen. They laughed and joked, and she spent the journey to Luton chatting to them, where Daisy got off. The airmen carried on to Leicestershire, she wished them well as she got off the train.

Daisy hadn't told her family she would be home as she wanted to surprise them. Departing from the station, the warmer weather had brought smiling faces to people. She felt the warmth against her face which made her feel happy. Daisy was glad winter had finally gone, she looked around, seeing how dreary the place was looking and more sandbags were protecting the buildings in the town centre and outside the station. She dropped her heavy case and changed arms, carrying on, looking around as she went.

Soon she found herself at her front door, looking up and down the familiar street, it hadn't changed one bit, Mrs Robinson was out cleaning her windows, Daisy put her hand up to wave, and she waved back. Another neighbour was out cleaning her front step, she too stopped and waved to Daisy. Stopping at her front door, Daisy couldn't make her mind up whether to use the front or the back, so she chose the back as she knew her mother should be in the kitchen. Up the side entry to the back gate and pushed it open, into the familiar back door.

She knocked out of courtesy and found it was open and entered calling, "I'm home."

Hannah came through from the front room, covered in cotton, Mark was with her. He came bounding up to her and gave her a big hug, she knelt down and cuddled him.

She looked at her mum with a tear in her eye. "Hello, Mum?" she said smiling.

"Welcome home, love," came the reply from her mum, wiping her eye with the side of her apron. "And why did you not tell us you were coming?" Her mother asked Daisy, checking her daughter over as she talked.

"I didn't want to spoil the surprise," she said simply.

"Well, you certainly did that!" her mother said in a jovial voice.

"Where's Dad and George?" asked Daisy looking around the kitchen.

"Both still at work, lots of overtime at the moment," answered Hannah. "Which is good. Come sit down and tell us how you are getting on?"

Daisy dropped her case and hung up her handbag and gas mask. So, for the next two hours with plenty of tea, the two women caught up. Daisy enjoyed this time with her mother.

Finally, Daisy couldn't put it off any longer; she asked after Mary and Bobby.

"Both are fine," replied Mum, careful not to upset her daughter. "As you know Bobby is away, I think he is in France with his regiment, but we are not sure. Mary is at work full time now; she writes to him often. Between you and me I think she is sweet on him." Hannah looked at her daughter with a worried expression, but she didn't have to worry as the look on Daisy's face was a satisfied one.

"Let's take your case upstairs and get you unpacked; everyone else will be home soon." Hannah helped her daughter to take her suitcase up to her room.

It felt strange being back in it, she glanced around, her sister had put some posters up on the wall of current film stars.

Hannah eyed them. "That's all your sister's doing!" She raised an eyebrow and laughed at her daughter who looked back and just nodded.

Daisy turned and headed for the door and downstairs, working her way into the familiar kitchen. She helped her mum prepare tea, and soon her dad and brother arrived home, the look on their faces as they saw Daisy was a picture.

"Welcome home, love," said a beaming Dad, her brother she noted was looking taller and broader, he greeted her with a smile.

Dad pulled her into his arms, and she felt the warmth radiating from him, she could smell the sweat that he had produced from working all day; it didn't bother her one bit.

Mary was the last to arrive home; she greeted her twin with a wary greeting, unsure how Daisy would react to the news that she was writing to Bobby. Daisy didn't hang around; she put her sister out of her misery by saying she was okay with it; she wasn't going to wish them well, but that might come later as time went by. Mary was satisfied with that reaction from her sister.

Teatime was a happy affair, and they sat with the wireless on in the background, it appeared that Hitler had marched straight into Belgium and then into France without really any intervention at all. Everyone apart from Mark, who was playing with his toys on the floor, stopped what they were doing to hear the news.

"That doesn't sound too good," said Dad anxiously.

Hannah glanced over at Jack exchanging worried looks, and they sat down to eat, even Mark could sense something was wrong.

Daisy had laid the table earlier; Mary pushed her tea around the plate, trying not to think too hard.

'How was Bobby? Would he be okay?' She thought nervously.

The others left her with her thoughts, not wanting to finish tea, but you couldn't waste food at present, they managed to eat it.

Following tea, they sat around the table; Mary asked to go, and she went up to their room.

Daisy thought she would go up and see her, but Mum said, "Leave her, give her time! Go later," advised her mum.

Daisy said she would go up later to check on her, and this made Hannah content. Mark was all over Daisy, he couldn't get enough of her, she couldn't help but smile down at her brother, his smile being infectious. He had always been a lovely child, but today he was as bright as a button.

"How are you getting on at school?" she asked interested.

"I love it, Daisy!" Came the simple reply. "My teacher is nice, and I have made friends too."

"Oh! That is so lovely," replied Daisy. she pulled him to her and gave him a big hug.

She was proud of her family even though she didn't say it enough. Daisy situated herself on the floor by her brother, playing with him and making him laugh so much, that her mother had to intervene and tell her to quiet it down as she would make him nauseous.

"Will you help me have a bath and read to me, Daisy?" he asked with a toothless grin.

He just had to look at her with his big blue eyes, and she would do anything for him.

"Of course," came the reply. Daisy went upstairs to the bathroom, ran the bath and made sure it was the right temperature; she got his pyjamas and dressing gown ready as Mark climbed in. Daisy splashed the water at him, and Mark was enjoying it, she washed his hair and watched as he washed himself. Once done, she helped dry him off and got him into the pyjamas and dressing gown.

As she walked past her room, she heard a sniffing sound coming from inside; putting Mark down, Daisy would go and see her sister and comfort her if she wished her to.

Mark found his favourite book for her to read, she didn't have the heart to tell him she had read this a thousand times already, and she knew all the words off by heart. The pages were ripped, and the book was battered and old, but she would not disappoint her brother. They laid on the bed closely together and opened the first page, and she began. Daisy's voice was soft, and it was sending her brother to sleep, he was trying to fight it but, in the end, he gave in, and sleep came.

Daisy called her parents up, and they said, goodnight.

"Don't forget the light!" came a sleepy voice.

Her parents went back downstairs, leaving Daisy standing at the door to her bedroom. She knocked gently. "Come in," came a sorrowful voice.

Daisy entered and sat down by her sister, who was lying on her side. Mary feeling the weight of the bed dip, turned around.

"It will be okay, he will be back safe," Daisy began speaking softly.

"How do you know? You didn't want him? And what do you care anyhow?" Mary said in a poisonous manner.

Daisy was taken aback by the way her sister spoke to her; she never meant to hurt Bobby. She stood up, ready to leave her sister alone to wallow in self-pity. Her sister turned, back against the wall, and Daisy left her and came back downstairs.

Her parents looked up as she entered the room. "How is she?" asked Mum in a concerned voice.

"She won't listen to me!" said an annoyed Daisy.

"I will have a go later when she has cooled down," said her mother.

They talked into the evening, George had gone out with friends being a Saturday night, he had joined the local ARP.

Daisy stifled a yawn and said, "I'm ready for bed, I'll see you in the morning."

Daisy got ready to stand, but was stopped by her mother, asking, "What about Mary?"

"Don't worry, I'll talk to her myself." Daisy finally pulled herself up from the chair and said "goodnight" to her parents and wearily wandered upstairs to bed.

Daisy stood outside the bedroom door and took a deep breath, she opened the door and entered. Seeing her sister asleep, relief was on Daisy's face as she got undressed and into bed. Sleep would not come easy for Daisy, as she was concerned with her sister and Bobby. What was she going to say to her sister in the morning without upsetting her? Well, she decided not to dwell on it tonight, so she rolled over and tried to get to sleep.

By morning Daisy had managed a few hours of sleep and woke up lethargic, she noticed that her sister was awake when she woke to use the toilet, she hurried along the landing.

"Right." She sat on the edge of the bed. "I know you are awake," she said to Mary who rolled over and sat up.

"I am sorry for my behaviour yesterday, but I was upset," said Mary.

"It's okay," said her sister. "Are you all right, though?" Daisy asked in a caring voice.

"I will be when I see Bobby again here in the flesh," replied her sister.

"Keep believing," said Daisy sincerely. "Friends again?" Enquired Daisy, and she hugged her sister tight.

Both got dressed quietly and both made their way down for breakfast. It still being early for a Sunday, the girls set to work making the breakfast, a big pan of porridge and toast. Daisy thought it was nice working with her sister to provide breakfast and give their mother a rest. Hannah would do some eggs and bacon when she came down. Daisy got the porridge on the go and sat to await their parents.

Right on time, Hannah entered the kitchen followed by her father.

"Thank you for starting the breakfast," her mother said smiling, she noticed that both girls were friendlier towards each other. Hence, she thought they must have sorted out their differences, and she was pleased, she didn't like it when her daughters had disagreements, but she knew Mary was cantankerous and very stubborn.

Next to come down was Mark, who wanted a cuddle from Daisy as soon as he saw her, she picked him up and sat him on her lap and cuddled him, while Hannah took over the cooking. Breakfast was served as soon as George was up, it was lovely to have everyone at home thought Hannah looking around the table.

Following breakfast, the girls cleared up and helped their mother to prepare dinner for lunchtime. Once done, Daisy was free to do what she wanted to do, at a loss she decided, as it was a lovely day, she would take Mark to the park. She sat watching him running around and playing on the swings, she was happy to be home, but she couldn't wait to get back to The London and her friends. In the park she noticed that the gun placements had been installed to deal with any enemy planes, this gave goose bumps all up Daisy's arms, and it made her apprehensive about what was to come.

Looking at her watch, she made sure Mark was safe, and they walked back home. Lunch was lovely; she had built up an appetite and tucked into the delicious food her mother had cooked. By the evening, they all sat by the wireless, enjoying the music and everyone was preparing for work on Monday morning, except Daisy. Her mind drifted to how Lizzie was getting on at home?

Chapter 18

Lizzie had arrived at Warwick Station, with hardly any problems except for the trains being crowded with service personnel, which was to be expected. Geoffrey, the family chauffeur was on time, and she waved at him as she exited the station. Lizzie had time to telephone home to inform them she was coming from the station, and Geoffrey picked up her suitcase. Lizzie took her gas mask and handbag and he walked with her to the car.

"How are you, my lady?" Geoffrey enquired looking at her cheerily.

"Fine, thank you," replied Lizzie looking back at him. "And yourself?" she asked politely.

"I'm fine, my lady, thank you for asking," said Geoffrey, still smiling at the young lady standing in front of him. He thought she had changed.

Lizzie climbed into the back of the car, while Geoffrey put the case, and gas mask in the boot, she kept her handbag with her as it had her identity papers.

"Ready to go home, Lady Elizabeth?" Geoffrey asked, glancing in the rear-view mirror.

"Not really," came the honest reply, in an unhappy voice. "How is my mother?" she asked as she looked glum, glancing out of the window.

"She is quite well," replied Geoffrey as he started the car up.

This is going to be an unpleasant and tough experience! She thought as she sat back in the seat.

Geoffrey looked in the mirror and could see the strain on Lizzie's face, he felt for her, he wanted the Mistress to be kind to her daughter, but he knew how her Ladyship could be.

A half-hour later, she found herself being driven down the sweeping entrance to her family home that was very recognizable to her. Her mother and father, with Dinky by his side, were waiting at the door for her arrival; they must have seen the car.

God help me, she thought as the car pulled to a stop, she wasn't religious, but felt she could do with some divine intervention right now!

Geoffrey opened the heavy mahogany car door, and helped the young lady out and Lizzie said, "Geoffrey, remember when we are on our own, please call me Lizzie." Geoffrey tipped his cap in acknowledgement.

It was a warm spring morning; she felt the warm sun beating down against her face as she looked at her parents. She didn't know if the sweating was because of the weather or because she was facing her mother. Oh well, she thought, better get it over with, Lizzie made her way over to her parents, she first hugged her father, who warmly hugged her back.

"Hello, darling, welcome home," he said, genuinely smiling at her.

"Hello, papa," she warmly replied, hugging him tightly.

Elizabeth turned to her mother, kissing her on both cheeks. "Hello, Mother."

"Hello Elizabeth," her mother stiffly replied.

Looking at her daughter, giving her the once over. "Come, let's go into the house and get settled in the drawing room."

She sighed but followed her mother, her father took her arm as reassurance, which Lizzie was grateful for. The butler took her case and headed up the stairs to her room, her mother followed behind and walked into the drawing room; it was warm from the sun streaming in through the windows.

Elizabeth sat down on the Edwardian settee; it wasn't comfortable; she waited for her mother to speak.

"Elizabeth, I only ever wanted the best for you as you know, Charles would make an excellent husband."

"But, Mother!" Lizzie said, and so it had begun. "I don't want a husband yet," answered an irritated Lizzie. "I want a life, and I want to marry for love," she said determinedly and upset.

"What's love got to do with it?" her mother replied curtly. "When I married your father, glancing over at him not smiling at all. "I didn't love him," she said indignantly.

Lizzie looked over at her father; she felt sorry for him; he looked forlorn. She wanted to ask did she love her husband now? But stopped herself as it would only end in a big argument which she couldn't deal with right now.

Quickly carrying on. "Is it so bad that I want to marry for love?" She tried to ask again in a civilized manner. "Because I am going to marry for love." Lizzie was getting more infuriated as she spoke. "You may plot and scheme, Mother, but I won't agree," she said crossly, she could feel her face turning red.

Before her mother could say anything more, she got up and walked out of the drawing room, looking desperately at her father as she passed him, heading up to her room. If she had stayed, she would have said something she would probably have regretted later. How she wished Eddie was here, but he wasn't so she had to do this on her own, she wasn't going to let her mother bully her into this, she had decided.

Lizzie slammed the door out of frustration; the windows shook, and she went over to her suitcase, which was placed on her bed and got to work unpacking. She wiped the tears that stung her eyes. The room was warm so she opened her double doors letting in a light breeze and looked out onto the manicured gardens, how beautiful she thought this time of year was, you wouldn't think there was a war on here. Turning back into the room, it brought back happy memories of her childhood, and how carefree they were, but now things were more complicated.

Lizzie decided to go for a walk with Dinky as it was such a beautiful day, and she wanted to keep well out the way of her mother and to clear her head. She found her father, reading the daily paper and asked him to go with her. He agreed immediately, and they wandered into the garden and made for the lake.

Two beautiful swans were sat right in the middle of it, looking majestic, it was very tranquil. Both stopped and looked, having walked in comfortable silence.

"Your mother doesn't mean any harm you know?" her father said, gauging her feelings.

"What she said about you was horrible," he sighed.

"She says things in the heat of the moment, but doesn't mean it," he said, trying to sound convinced.

"Does she love you?" Lizzie asked awkwardly.

Her father looked back at his daughter kindly and said, "In her way, I think she does." He took his daughter's hand.

"But she doesn't show it," said Lizzie. If I were married to you, I'd show you some affection, for sure." He dropped her hand.

Lizzie could see he was uncomfortable talking about this as he kept rubbing his hands together, so she decided to change the subject but before she did her father said, "Don't give up."

Looking affectionately towards her father, she nodded her head as if to understand, she leaned over and kissed him on the cheek. She thought he was starting to look older; he had dark rings under his eyes. Father looked at the time on his watch, and she knew it was time to walk back, they walked back to the house in comfortable silence. They entered the house via the kitchen and when cook saw Lizzie, she wrapped her in her arms in a lovely hug, with her father watching on.

"Welcome home, young lady," said the bubbly lady dressed in her usual pinny. "We have some freshly baked biscuits that I made earlier."

Lizzie eyed them, licking her lips. Lizzie and her father sat at the large table and tucked into them with a cup of tea.

Cook enquired how she was getting on, and so Lizzie sat and told them of her life and friends she had made in the city. Her Father looked in awe at her, as she talked. It made him more determined that his only daughter would have a better and happy life.

"We had better not eat any more." Clifford glanced at his daughter with a guilty look. "If we don't eat our dinner, we will be in trouble with your mother, and we don't want that?" he said with mischief in his eyes, laughing.

Saying, thank you to cook, Lizzie joined him, and they went up the stairs to find her mother.

They found her in the sitting room. "There you two are!" she raised her voice. "Where have you been?" she nearly shouted.

"We have been out for a walk, is that a problem?" her father answered back. Lizzie felt guilty for taking him.

Lunch was a stilted affair, and Lizzie couldn't wait for it to finish, she made her apologies and headed up to her room, where she wanted to be on her own. I don't know how long I can keep this up; she thought as she lay on her bed reading a book. By mid-afternoon, she was bored; she found herself drawn to the warmth of the kitchen and the comfy environment of the cook. She stood at the door, hesitant, and cook told her to get herself inside. Lizzie sat at the table and spent a lovely afternoon, chatting with the cook who she found out was called Edna. She felt she couldn't keep calling her cook, the times were changing. Lizzie enquired about her family and learnt she had two boys, and both had just joined up, both in the navy, and they were away somewhere in the Atlantic. Her husband Albert had died a few years ago from cancer. Lizzie gave her condolences, and cook asked her more about her life.

The flood gates opened, and Lizzie explained about Charles and the marriage of convenience and her mother's interference. The tears just kept falling, after weeks of spent up frustration.

Edna held her, rubbing her back in a soothing way, Lizzie wished her mother would do this.

How on earth her Ladyship could treat her daughter in this way was questionable with it being the twentieth century. Edna sat down by Lizzie's side. "Look lovey," she began in her soothing manner. "You don't have to marry him."

"But I will lose my inheritance," she sniffled.

Edna passed her a hanky. "Does that matter, it's only money?" she said, which was the truth. "And somewhere out there is the man of your dreams, I promise."

Lizzie wasn't so sure, but Edna was sure there was. Lizzie had to laugh at this, she hadn't felt this happy in a long time, okay things hadn't been sorted out, but at least she had an inkling what to do. Talking to cook and spending time with her had been a revelation, and she left feeling relieved.

Supper was tolerable, Lizzie couldn't meet her mother's eyes. Once supper was over, she bid goodnight to her parents and went up to her room. Lying in her old bed with her quilt pulled up, listening to the animals out in the night, their noises were quite soothing, she went off to sleep.

Having slept in, Lizzie got herself up, had a soak in the hot bath and did her hair; it was nice not to rush around and not to be tired. The young girl who used to work for them had gone off to do war work, as it paid more and she wanted to get away from Lady Margo. Lizzie also thought it would be better than working for her mother, but she couldn't say that out loud.

Being late for breakfast was not good, it was bad etiquette in the eyes of her mother, so she braced herself for the onslaught, which came as soon as she entered the room.

"Where have you been?" she snarled.

"Morning to you too, Mother," replied her daughter. "Having a lie-in, if you don't mind," she said, glaring back at Lady Margo.

Her mother stared at her but said nothing, Lizzie went up to her father, giving him a loving kiss on the cheek.

"Leave it, Margo, let the girl enjoy her holiday, she has deserved it," he said glaring also at his wife.

Lizzie was in awe of her father. Lady Margo looked at her husband but bit her tongue; this was not over; they had breakfast in silence. Back in her room, Lizzie couldn't take this atmosphere any longer, so she decided she would give it till Tuesday and then make her way back to The London and the safety of the nurses' home, and wait for the others to come back the next day or so.

The rest of the days were spent in the kitchen with the cook, cooking wonderful things. Walking around the grounds of her home, enjoying her surroundings with her father and Dinky. She knew she was lucky, but it would be nothing without her brother and her father who made it all bearable. Oh! How she missed Eddie and promised herself she would write to him tonight.

She tried to spend as much time as she could with Clifford, keeping out the way of her mother, which was quite easy, considering the size of the house. She thought her father was doing the same; he seemed to come to the kitchen when he could.

Her mother didn't seem to come near the kitchen, making it pretty safe; it became their sanctuary. Lizzie explained to her father that she couldn't stay beyond Tuesday, he understood and was fine with it.

"Please try and visit your Aunt Lynn and her family when you get a chance?" he asked. "Maybe she can shed light on why your mother is like this."

That gave Lizzie an idea. Elizabeth felt bad; she hadn't seen her aunt for a while before starting her training, so promised she would visit her when she could.

"Why not before going back?" suggested her father.

"That's a good idea, if you don't mind?" said Lizzie. "I'll write to her tonight." She was going to be busy writing letters, that would keep her occupied, and more importantly out of the way of her mother.

Much later Lizzie had finished her last letter and was sticking stamps on them when she pulled a face, she would never get used to the taste; Lizzie would get them posted in the morning, then she would wait for the replies.

Lizzie received a reply from Aunt Lynn by return in the form of a telegram, a plan was made for Lizzie to catch the train up to Coventry and stay the night with her aunt.

Chapter 19

On Tuesday, she packed her bag, said "goodbye" to her parents, ran down to the kitchen and gave Edna a hug and off she went. Geoffrey took her to the station and waited with her until the train arrived. While waiting, they had an informal chat.

"Edna's nice," said Geoffrey shyly.

"Yes, she is, do you like her?" asked an interested Lizzie.

"I like her very much," answered Geoffrey honestly, blushing from head to foot. "Well, tell her soon, she likes you, Geoffrey, you could do a lot worse," said a serious Lizzie.

"It's not that easy," returned Geoffrey.

"When I come home again, I will help you," offered Lizzie. "That is a promise."

In the distance, they heard the train approaching. Geoffrey passed Elizabeth her case.

"Have a lovely time with your aunt," he said genuinely, smiling.

With that he was gone. Lizzie found an empty carriage which was unusual, found a seat, sat down and prepared to enjoy the ride. Her Aunt Lynn was so different from her mother; she was kind, funny and interesting; she had three children who were slightly older than their cousins Lizzie and Eddie. Charlotte, Henry and Alan, the boys had both enlisted in the army, both were in France, or so she thought, and Charlotte had joined the Wrens. She was based in Portsmouth.

It was only a short journey, Lizzie gave the street name to the conductor on the bus, and she told her where to enlighten. Lizzie found her aunt's house with ease and knocked on the door. Lynn came to the door and welcomed her niece.

It was a modest house, but it looked homely and clean. Once in, her aunt took her case, and gas mask and led her into the front room. Sitting on the battered settee, Lizzie looked around the place and it felt like home, not like her own home was at all.

Once settled. "Tell me, what's my darling sister done now?" Her aunt had seen how distressed her niece was.

Lizzie was overwhelmed, well that was it, the flood gates opened again, and she spit it all out. Not stopping for breath until she had finished. Lynn listened intently without interrupting; until she had finished, she sat back.

"Firstly, I am not going to tell you what to do." Which was refreshing. "Don't marry someone who sounds horrible and more importantly you don't love. Just because your mother married for money rather than for love, you don't have to, do you understand," Lynn said.

Lizzie looked at her aunt, glad she was on her side.

"Why did she marry my father?"

"She was pregnant with your brother, and his Lordship wanted to do the right thing, and Dad would have killed him if he had refused."

"How did they meet?" she asked her aunt with interest.

"My sister always wanted to be something that she was not, so when the chance to work at the big house came, she took it," she sighed. "Well, she caught the eye of his Lordship, he was young then, good looking, charming, engaged to another Lady but he met your mother and the rest is history."

"Dad, of course, was angry, so was your grandfather. When she found out the young lady broke off the engagement. Your grandfather wanted to pay your mother off which she refused and in the end the wedding went ahead, quietly, and your mother became her Ladyship when the older Lord passed away." She sighed again taking a deep breath. "I think in her way, she does love him now."

"But I wish she would show it," said Lizzie.

"It's a lot to digest in one go, you probably have lots of questions you want to ask. Tea?" Offered her aunt first.

"Yes please," replied Lizzie, she was thirsty and shocked by what she had just learned.

"Come into the kitchen." They made their way down the hallway, to the back of the house and the kitchen. While waiting for the water to boil, Lizzie found her voice.

"How are the boys?"

"Your cousins are okay, I think," replied her Aunt Lynn. "Haven't heard from them recently, so they must be all right. Charlotte is fine, she has met another sailor called Roger who is based in Portsmouth at present. They will be disappointed to have missed you."

"How is Uncle Edward?"

"Busy working as an engineer, making spitfires. You will see him later."

"Now, back to your mother." With tea in her hand, they stayed sitting at the kitchen table.

While Lynn prepared tea for them for later. "I have put you in Charlotte's room, hope that is okay?"

"Yes, thank you, you are too kind." Lizzie took a deep breath. "I couldn't stay there any longer as I would have gone crazy." Lizzie nearly cried but stopped herself.

"Well, you are always welcome here, so too is Eddie," said her aunt. "How is he? Still training?"

"Yes, nearly finished," replied Lizzie suddenly missing him dreadfully.

"Right, finish your tea, let me show you to your room, and then we will talk some more. I hope it has started to make sense."

The room was comfortable, with a single bed by the wall, wardrobe and mirror on a desk.

"Come down when you are ready," Lynn said.

Once on her own, Lizzie sat on the bed, reeling from the truth, her perfect mother was not so perfect as she made out to be. Oh! She had to blame her father, for some of it, of course. He had slept with her, but her mother had allowed it to happen, that is what disgusted Lizzie the most.

The delicious smell coming up the stairs must have woken Lizzie from her sleep, she wiped the sleep from her eyes and tidied herself up. Used the upstairs toilet and then headed downstairs to find her aunt. Finding her in the kitchen, finishing off tea, she heard her aunt talking to someone, as she approached the door, hearing a male voice that she recognised was Uncle Edward.

"Well, I had to tell her, she was in such a state," said her aunt in a whisper.

"Well, she knows now," said her uncle quietly. "How did she take it?" he asked.

"All right, but a bit shocked at how her perfect mother behaved."

Lizzie listened.

"Clifford was to blame, just as much," said Edward angrily. He couldn't keep it in his pants!"

"Edward," Lynn shouted.

"Well, it's the truth," he said giving a sidewards glance at his wife.

"Edward, really!" his wife said in a warning.

"I'm only telling the truth," he said, glancing at his wife who nodded.

Lizzie made out to cough, and she entered the warm room.

"Hello, angel," said her uncle standing up to give her a warm hug.

"Hello, Uncle Edward," she said warmly, hugging him back.

"I'm hearing you had quite the afternoon with your aunt." Pushing her back, and giving her the once over.

"Yes it was very informative," she replied, slightly irritated that she was thinking of her mother. She continued, "I have learnt a lot of things about my mother, it's all starting to make sense now." Lizzie kept peering at her uncle, while they chatted.

"I'm glad," replied her uncle.

While Aunt Lynn prepared tea, they sat talking, and they tucked into the delicious cottage pie. Lizzie tucked into the food, she had her appetite back and enjoyed the food immensely.

"What time are you off tomorrow?" Enquired her aunt.

Lizzie held her breath and asked: "Can I stay another day and leave Thursday instead?" she hoped her aunt would say yes.

"Of Course," replied her aunt enthusiastically. "We can go shopping, and it will be nice to have female company for a change as Charlotte is away."

So, Lizzie had a lovely evening with her uncle and aunt; after tea, they sat listening to the wireless. The news wasn't good coming from Europe with Hitler's troops invading France now. Her aunt couldn't keep the worry from her face, and her husband gently squeezed her hand to comfort her.

"Don't worry, they will be fine," he said reassuringly, but it didn't quite reach his eyes, he was worried about his sons, he silently hoped that they would be fine.

Lizzie and her aunt, after breakfast, walked into Coventry, both carrying a gas mask; it was getting easier to remember to bring them everywhere, some girls even used them as make up cases. They did some shopping, they had to queue in some shops. Items were getting expensive, but mainly it was all right. Some of the shops were getting low on stock, and the shelves were getting low. Lizzie enjoyed her aunt's company immensely. Why wasn't her mother liked this? She thought.

"You know, before your mother went to the great house, we were once really close, and she was a warm, caring person," she said sincerely. "We did everything together, and I do miss her," her aunt sighed and she took a deep breath.

"Do you think she will change?" asked a nervous Lizzie.

"Honestly, I hope so," said Lynn touching her niece's arm in reassurance. "Maybe the war will change her, or she will have to change," continued Lynn hopefully. "People don't have big homes now; she only has a handful of staff as it is."

"Many are leaving to do war work," said Lizzie.

"The Army may even take it over, you never know." Her aunt thought that might happen but kept that to herself. "They may not be able to keep it running, we will see, only time will tell," her aunt said anxiously.

"If it has to go, I for one won't be unhappy, it's cold and unwelcoming," Lizzie continued.

"But what about Edward, it's his on the death of Clifford," Lynn said.

"Eddie doesn't want it; he wants to fly. That's all he talks about."

"And what about Francesca?" her aunt asked.

"He hardly mentioned her or saw her, due to his current commitments," said Lizzie. "She is lovely, but I don't think it is serious" Lizzie carried on. "I will have to ask him next time I see him." Lizzie needed to speak with her brother.

Back at her aunt's, they had a lovely afternoon and evening, Lizzie packed her suitcase, as she was leaving first thing in the morning. Following an early night and saying goodbye to her uncle as he would be gone early in the morning for work.

Lizzie stood by the front door.

"Don't leave it too long to visit again," said her aunt, taking her niece into her open arms and holding her tight. "Promise me," she said, and she let her go.

Lizzie promised and with a heavy heart took off for the bus stop and the station. It was heaving with service people and families saying goodbye on the concourse. Her train was running late, so she sat in the buffet with a cup of weak tea, it gave her time to digest what her aunt had told her, over the last few days. There is no way I am getting pregnant and tied down with Charles or any man she thought. Finally, the London bound train was called, and she headed back to the city, that she was starting to call home.

Daisy's few days had flown by, and before long it was Thursday; she had spent the last few days, helping her mother, who was struggling to get material now to make new garments. It was make do and mend, so she had to start altering many customers' clothes, she had stockpiled some material luckily. She took her brother to school and collected him every day, met his teacher and his friends. Mark was proud of his sister.

Daisy packed her suitcase after tea, with both excitement and a sad feeling in her stomach about going back. She didn't want to leave her family, but on the other hand, she also wanted to go back to see her friends and the job she had started to love; she was being pulled into two. Homesickness always hit her when she least expected it, when back at work, but knew she had to go; it would be better when she was on the train and heading back to London. As it was Thursday, her family wanted to see her off, Dad carried her suitcase, he had taken time off work to see his daughter off. Mark held her hand tightly, and Hannah walked by her side. George and Mary stayed at home saying their goodbyes earlier before going to work.

The walk was pleasant in the warm sunshine, the sun was warm to their faces, and they were starting to sweat. Daisy was dressed in a summer dress made by her mum; she had taken her cardigan off; her sandals were well worn. She needed a new pair, but shoes were becoming scarce. At the station it was heaving, they couldn't move for the amount of people on the concourse, so Daisy said her goodbyes and found her platform for the London train.

Hannah hugged her daughter. "Now you take care, and we will see you soon." Hannah held her daughter tight.

"Yes, Mum," Daisy replied, wanting to cry but holding it together, just.

Her father pulled her close, slipped some money into her hand. "This is for emergencies", he said in her ear.

"Thank you," replied Daisy.

She knelt to Mark, who pulled her tight in a hug. "Take care, Daisy" he said. "And come home soon, I miss you." A tear pricked her eye. "I will miss you soon, but you are in my prayers every night, so look at the sky, see the stars and think of me." Mark looked lovingly at his sister, who promised.

The train was boarding, so Daisy picked up her case and walked to the gate. Walking alone by the carriages, she boarded and found a seat before the carriage filled up, sat back and took a deep breath, held it for a moment and let her breath out slowly.

"You can do this," she said to herself. She started to cry, and she let the tears fall down her cheeks. Ten minutes later the whistle blew, the train was picking up steam, and then it left the station.

A little later she found herself pulling into the city and St Pancras station, she must have dozed off! Daisy got herself ready and waited for the train to stop, and she got out. Finding the sign for the underground Daisy headed for the appropriate platform, weaving in and out of moving servicemen and women. The platform was packed, and the train was crowded but Daisy managed to get on, she held on for dear life as the train swayed to and throw.

By eleven-thirty she saw the entrance of the hospital coming into view. Tom was sitting in his hut. "Hello, Daisy, did you have a nice holiday?"

"Yes, thank you," she said cheerily back.

"Your friend is back, came back today as well."

"Who?" she queried.

"Lizzie, the posh one," he said.

Daisy laughed. She rushed off to the nurse's home.

Home Sister was guarding the door. "Welcome, Nurse Peters, Nurse Fenton is back already."

"Thank you," came the reply from Daisy, as she rushed past Home Sister and flew up the stairs.

"Don't run, only in Fire or haemorrhaging," she heard behind her, she didn't care.

Without knocking she turned the knob and pushed the door open, and there was her friend sitting on the bed, saying, "What took you so long?"

Daisy dropped her suitcase and walked over towards her friend. Lizzie stood up, and they hugged each other tightly.

"I am so glad you are back," said Lizzie. "I have so much to tell you," she said, looking at her friend.

"It can't have gone well because you're back already?" said a worried Daisy.

"It didn't, but I went to see my aunt, and she explained a few things to me."

Daisy couldn't wait for her friend to explain what had happened.

"I will explain later, but for now how about a cup of tea?"

Both girls were parched, and a cup of tea sounded perfect. "Yes please," said Daisy, starting to unpack, while Lizzie went off to make the tea in the kitchen down the corridor.

The girls sat side by side on the bed, Lizzie explained all that had happened, how her mother reacted and how her aunt explained how her precious mother got pregnant with her brother. While Daisy sat and took it all in, all the time holding Lizzie's hands. Daisy didn't say much, she just nodded, and she felt that Lizzie may now understand her mother better.

"It's made me more determined not to marry, and I will not marry Charles," she said defiantly.

"How was your time away?" Lizzie asked her friend. So Daisy told her about her time away and how Mary had behaved towards her.

By one o'clock the others were back, and they all went down to the dining hall for lunch. Lizzie and Jenny had remembered to bring their cigarettes, and as the weather was good, they went outside before heading back to the room.

They found a piece of grass, and as it was dry, they sat down and caught the warm sun to their faces. While the other two puffed away on cigarettes. They spent the afternoon out there, all talking about their holiday. Lizzie kept some news to herself. She would tell them later when it felt like the right time. After tea, the girls made their way up to their rooms and all headed for the bathrooms. Once washed and hair done, they met in Lizzie and Daisy's room for a nightcap. They were not late to bed, as they were all tired from travelling.

Daisy laid in bed, looking at the window; they had left the blackout curtain open, thinking of Mark and said a prayer for him as she looked up at the stars.

Friday was spent getting ready for going back into school for a few days, uniforms were hung, and caps sorted.

Daisy said, "The year is flying by; it will soon be our first year done."

Lizzie nodded in agreement.

Claire rushed into the room. "Can someone help me with my cap, it's gone limp!"

"Where is Jenny?" asked Lizzie.

"Gone to the sewing room."

"Come on," said Daisy. "Let's have a look."

The two women went off into the other room to sort out the offending article. Lizzie, left alone was looking forward to being back in school, but she was also looking forward to being back on the wards.

Monday morning was a struggle to get the girls out of bed, having some time off had made them lazy, and it took a few attempts to get them going. Breakfast finished, they walked across to the school, Sister Tutor welcomed them back and went on to explain what they would be covering this week, and what consultants would be coming to speak to them.

The exam would be the last Friday and results out the Sunday morning; then the wards allocation would be out on the board Sunday afternoon. The week went fast, and the girls spent the week studying intently, the lectures had also been intense. They all wanted to do well, and Hilary was at it again saying how wonderful she was.

"She doesn't let up, does she," they all chorused.

On days when weather was fine, they went outside and sat on the warm grass to study and to lay in the sun and catch up with sleep. Sitting on the grass was nice, to watch the world go by even with war raging around them. The exam was set for nine a.m. on Friday, all the girls were ready on time. It was a hot day, and the girls were glad the exam was in the morning and that in the afternoon they could get the thick stockings off and put summer dresses on.

Little did they know that things were about to change for the worse. Britain had appointed a new Prime Minister called Winston Churchill who was voted in by fellow MPs. Sunday the twenty-sixth of May Matron came rushing into the dining hall.

"We are moving all patients that are able to countryside hospitals as soon as possible and getting the empty beds ready for emergencies." And with that, she rushed out.

"What emergencies?" Everyone asked.

Senior nurses were seen rushing around as were the doctors. No one high up said a word. So, Sunday there were buses, ambulances and any other form of transport that could be used to move the patients that could be transported safely away from The London.

In between this, the results were out; all four had done well again, Daisy top, Lizzie second, and Claire and Jenny were ahead of Hilary. Ward allocation was put on hold until they knew how many injured would be coming and what ward they were being allocated to.

Monday morning, the injured servicemen came by train from Folkstone and Dover. The young men were battered and bruised, covered in sand and oil, most very wet, some with gunshot wounds, needing to go to the theatre immediately.

The injury you couldn't see was given the name shell shock from the first world war. It was a reaction to the intensity of the bombardment and fighting that produced an appearance as panic and being scared or an inability to reason, even sleepwalk, talk, these patients were taken to the psychiatric ward.

Daisy and Lizzie were put on one ward where they had to get blood-soaked, sand and sea uniforms, off battered bodies, before they could wash the young men and take care of the wounds. Some needed to go to the theatre straight away with life-threatening injuries; they would need to have one-to-one care all night.

No one slept, they all kept working long hours as the injured kept coming, no one complained, they caught sleep when they could. Some men, when crying out in pain, said, "The Germans are coming." The doctors gave them morphine to settle them. It broke Daisy's heart to hear them calling out in anguish, watching grown men getting upset wanting their mothers.

By the eighth day, there was a rumour that small boats of all shapes and sizes had gone to Dunkirk to rescue the British expeditionary force off the beaches, and so far, nearly all the men had got off safely. Some of the men told of how the German fighters were dropping bombs and shooting at them, while they waited on the beaches and in the sand dunes to be collected. They had to stand in line and walk into the sea in an orderly manner to the small ships; they were sitting ducks.

Daisy cried in anguish when she was safely back at the nurses' home so that no one could see her. How could people do this to other human beings? She thought. It made Lizzie worry about her cousins, and Daisy was worried about Bobby. She would, when she had some free time, try and get a letter to Mary to see how he was. Lizzie was going to do the same and get a message to her aunt to see if had she had heard from Henry and Alan.

On a rare night when they were both together, they had just finished their baths, which had felt marvellous, they had both managed to wash the grime of themselves from working nearly non-stop, their feet ached. They now lay in their warm, clean, comfortable beds, talking over what had happened the last few days. It had turned out the papers had called it Operation Dynamo and the full extent of the evacuation was starting to come out. It was amazing how many soldiers had been saved off the beaches and brought home so they could fight another day.

Lizzie had gone to the nearest call box and called her aunt, who had heard that her son, Alan had been killed on the beaches while waiting to be rescued, but Henry was safe. He only had been slightly hurt but not seriously and was on his way home for some hard-earned leave.

Lizzie was distraught, she wanted to console her aunt but knew her duty was to stay where she was needed at the moment. She said she would inform her parents, and she quietly hoped her mother would have some compassion in her, for her sister at this terrible time, and would go and spend some time with her. Before she put the phone down, she promised to get up to Coventry to see her aunt as soon as she could. Her aunt had said that Charlotte would get some leave as soon as was allowed and would come home with Roger if he was around then to accompany her home.

Daisy had written to Mary, and she had written back that Bobby was fine, a bit battered and bruised like the soldiers at the hospital, but safe and at home on leave, until he went back to his unit in a week to get new uniforms and kit, as most was left on the beaches.

Lizzie had a letter from her parents to say that the family home was being compulsorily taken over by the military, turning it into a convalescent home for injured service personnel. Her parents would have to move into two rooms in the west wing.

Lizzie had found the time to call them. "Hello darling," her mother had said. "It's frightfully bad news."

"Why?" said her daughter.

"Because it's ghastly that we have to move, but it's for the war effort."

Lizzie ignored the comments her mother was making; she was disgusted with her.

"Think of all the mess they are going to make to my lovely home."

"Oh, Mother!" Lizzie was lost for words with her mother's reaction. "Can't you think about more important things, like how Aunt Lynn is?"

Lady Margo went deadly quiet; "I will visit her when I can."

"Have you been to see her?"

"No, darling not yet." Lizzie was in despair. At least with this compulsory order, her mother had more important things to concern her, and she had forgotten about the engagement and Charles.

Her father was getting enthusiastic with the whole idea of injured soldiers coming and convalescing at the house. Clifford assisted the officers with preparing the house for its new arrivals that would arrive any day. Doctors and Army nurses had already arrived and were setting up in the great hall. The call had ended with Lizzie promising to come home when she could to help her mother move to the west wing.

Where was Charles? Lizzie thought, as she put the receiver down, had he joined his regiment? She hadn't received a letter from him. Well, no news at present made Lizzie happy. On the walk back to the nurse's home, she knew that she should call her brother but not tonight as her emotions were all over the place, she was all of a sudden too tired.

Daisy, on hearing her news, held her tight as she cried for her dead cousin. They talked for a while, but sleep soon took them, as the exhaustion of the last few days took over. Tomorrow they would be back on the wards caring for the soldiers, helping with their recovery, then when ready, to move them to the convalescence homes that were springing up all over the country.

Chapter 20

Both girls were indeed up early, one due to the mornings being lighter and also the thought of the day ahead, nursing the young men on the wards, it was harrowing but extremely worthwhile. Neither of them wanted to admit, but they were both thrilled and eager to get back to work as soon as possible, they were so exhausted that they couldn't eat much, looking at the greasy plate with the kippers sitting on it, made them want to gag, so they opted for bread and dripping. A cup of tea, sugar was now rationed, so both were trying to do without it.

After breakfast the girls hoped they might see Jenny and Claire as they hadn't seen them for a few days, only in passing. Once ready for work, the girls were happy with their appearance, they knocked on the door to see if their friends were prepared before heading to the ward. No answer, maybe later tonight, they would be back. The group of girls flew down the stairs dashing across to the main block where the wards were situated. They were still working together on the same department until the flow of military personnel had reduced, then they were to be split up again to continue their training as was the original plan. Lizzie looked her friend over; one more time, happy, Daisy did the same back. "Maybe you will meet a dashing officer?"

Straightening her bun and laughing at her friend as she made a face, they pushed the ward doors open and entered ready to start work. Sister Green was just coming out of her office at the far end of the ward, with a handsome man both girls had never clapped eyes on before. His was tall, blonde haired, blue sparkling eyes like the sea and a smile to die for and he was impeccably dressed in his Army uniform.

Lizzie grabbed and pinched her friend's arm so hard, that Daisy cried out, "Can you see what I see?" she said, staring over at the Officer.

The officer must have heard because he looked over at the two girls and stopped talking with Sister Green, who followed and looked over. Daisy could only watch as her friend was looking at the man with desire, and knew at once, Lizzie was in trouble.

He finished talking to Sister Green and he walked up the ward, as he went, he stopped and spoke to some soldiers and spent some time with each one. Soon he was standing in front of the girls. "Good morning, ladies," he spoke calmly. "I am Captain Jameson, of the Scotch Guards, here to see some of my men and enquire how they are doing."

All the time he was talking, he was only looking directly at Lizzie, and she was looking straight back at him. They, out of politeness introduced themselves but Lizzie left the Lady bit out when she introduced herself. Daisy looked over at her with a raised eyebrow but didn't say anything.

They saw Staff Nurse Anderson moving at a fast pace towards them, she didn't seem happy, both looking at her, Captain Jameson looked over too. Seeing he was running out of time, he turned back to Lizzie and said, "Will I see you again later?" With hope in his eyes.

"Yes, my shift finishes at six," replied Lizzie, a deep blush spreading across her face.

Seeing Staff Nurse Anderson getting nearer, Lizzie said, "I had better get on," she said, smiling up at the captain.

"I will be back later," said a smiling Captain Jameson back at the young nurse. With that he pushed the door open and was gone.

Staff Nurse Anderson arrived by their side at just at that moment.

"Get your capes off, then join us for Sister's inspection, otherwise I will mark you as late, then you will be reported to Matron."

Both girls scurried off and got sorted out in record time. Once Sister Green was satisfied, she dismissed them, Staff Nurse Anderson told them there was work to be done, ordering them that there were bed baths to do, with that she turned and headed back towards Sister Green, who had observed everything with some interest.

Lizzie and Daisy got sorted in the locker room rolling up their sleeves and putting a clean apron on. They found another nurse and orderly to assist them and got stuck into their work, they would talk later, hopefully at break. The morning sailed by; Lizzie was on cloud nine, watched very closely by her friend. As it happened, they were so busy that they had to go to separate breaks, but Sister sent them to lunch together for which they were grateful.

Once in the dining hall and queueing at the hatch, Daisy turned to her mate. "So, Captain Jameson seamed very nice?" Trying to catch Lizzie's eye.

"He is rather," answered Lizzie smiling and blushing, hoping her friend didn't notice.

They grabbed their food and found an empty seat side by side and tucked into their food, as were both hungry, having so little for breakfast.

"We had better get used to kippers," they thought.

"Come on, Lizzie, are you going to talk to him if he comes back tonight?" Enquired Daisy.

"Yes, I would really like to," came the reply.

Lizzie couldn't wait, she was so nervous, shy even, and her heart was racing, so that she kept making mistakes all morning, in the end Sister Green had to pull her into the office and warn her, if she didn't pull her socks up, she would have no choice but to send her to Matron for a ticking off.

That certainly did the trick, Lizzie knuckled down and was fine for the rest of the afternoon. She chatted to the soldiers as she tended their wounds and some of them mentioned Captain Jameson, saying how he was a good officer, cared about his men, and had made sure that he got every one of them off the beaches.

The more she heard, the more she was liking this man. One thing though was bugging her, Charles and her mother, what should she do? She thought for a second, I know, I will try and get hold of Eddie she thought, I will call his base tonight and with that she carried on with her work.

Much later the army Chaplain arrived to see if any men needed his guidance and prayers. Sister Green assisted him as he walked around the beds, offering comfort to some that were restless and lost, and those that were indeed dying from their injuries. As he left, he said he would be back each day and with that he pushed open the ward doors and was gone.

Daisy found that some of the men got relief speaking with the Chaplain who had also seen the effects of war first-hand. The ward orderly handed out tea to the men and the two nurses sat feeding the ones who couldn't feed themselves because of the bandages to their arms and body.

Just as Lizzie was giving up hope that Captain Jameson would come, the ward door opened, and he entered with a pretty female officer walking by his side. Lizzie's face was smiling but as soon as she saw the other officer, the smile dropped. She is beautiful, thought Lizzie, tall and elegant in her uniform.

Sister Green rushed up to greet them, they walked straight down the ward towards her office, Captain Jameson was scanning the ward for Lizzie, who had made a hasty escape to the sluice where Daisy was currently.

"What's wrong?" she said to her colleague when she noticed the concerned look.

Lizzie explained what had taken place.

Daisy, being the rational one said, "They may only be colleagues."

"But he had his arm on her back?" Lizzie could have cried, but she kept the tears at bay.

Daisy hugged her friend; "He may try and find you before he leaves." Daisy took a deep breath. "You have two choices, either go out there and see if he does indeed talk to you, or stay here with me and clean these bedpans."

Lizzie looked back at her friend and, as tempting the bedpans looked, said, "I would rather be back out on the ward." And with a swish of her uniform, she was off.

Her colleague was left cleaning but humming a merry tune as she worked, silently laughing to herself. It would soon be time to go off shift and she hoped to meet up with the others tonight for a well-earned catch up and a glass of scotch. The only slight cloud on the horizon where Daisy was concerned was for her friend, as she knew her heart was fragile, and she was falling heavily for the captain.

Lizzie came around the corner from the sluice room so fast that she nearly knocked over Staff Nurse Anderson.

"Will you watch where you are going, Nurse!"

"Sorry," replied an apologetic Lizzie, while all the time she kept an eye on Sister's office door.

"It's time you were off," said Staff Nurse Anderson.

Reluctantly, Lizzie went and found Daisy. "Come on, we have been dismissed."

They entered the locker room, got changed and made their way to the door. As they got to the last bed, Private Pickford called Lizzie over.

"Don't worry nurse, he will be back tomorrow, he's here every day until we are all discharged home."

With that her heart felt a little lighter. She was very grateful to Pickford for his kind words, she felt better for hearing them. Out in the corridor, she grabbed hold of Daisy's arm.

"Come on, let's have tea, then I need a smoke." Where she found Jenny talking to a porter called Leonard.

"Hello strangers," she called to them both.

As it was a nice evening, Daisy had come out with her. Two cigarettes later, and telling all to Jenny, they made it back to their room. Jenny went off next door to change and collect Claire, while the others got changed and sat talking on their beds until the other two arrived.

"I will never get over my feet aching so much," said Daisy, rubbing them.

"Well, I think we deserve a little tipple," said Lizzie, pulling up the loose floorboard and finding the unused bottle that she had brought from home, thanks to her father's continuous supply.

Claire popped back next door to collect the two clean glasses and brought them in, placing them on the side so Lizzie could pour the whiskey into them.

Lizzie, being generous poured in more than normal measures, which the girls drank slowly not wanting to be ill or worse, hung over. Lizzie, once the alcohol was working through her bloodstream, went on to tell the others, and mainly Claire, about her encounter with Captain Jameson today. How she wished she would see him tomorrow, and more importantly he would be on his own, she was on a late tomorrow, so would have a lie-in in the morning.

Daisy was on another early, she hoped that the captain did get to chat to her friend tomorrow, as she knew her mate was very keen on him, more than she was letting on. A little while later, with the whiskey drank, Lizzie went off to call her brother, hoping he was actually there and not gone to the pub with his colleagues. She got through, once the operator had put the call through. A fellow officer had answered and had gone off to find Flying Officer Fenton in the mess, it still felt strange saying it, but it suited her brother, after waiting a few moments, she heard his familiar voice.

"Hello, sis," he said cheerily.

Lizzie explained about their parents and how their mother had reacted badly, Eddie wasn't surprised, and then she had the sad task of telling him about Alan.

He had been shocked and said, "That's why they were fighting the Nazi's, because of Dunkirk."

Time was running out so she left out the part of meeting Captain Jameson, perhaps nothing would come of it. He seemed pretty cosy with that female officer. Lizzie couldn't put the thought from her mind, was in fact feeling jealous. Walking out of the call box Lizzie noticed how everyone around her was looking wary, and the atmosphere since Dunkirk had changed, she thought people were looking desolate, with no hope.

She walked across the road from the hospital into the summer evening, the alcohol was giving her a warm feeling. She made it back to the nurses' home and up to her room. The others were still sitting where she had left them, some thirty minutes ago, they sat around talking and got ready for bed. Once the others had left for the evening and she got into bed, Lizzie couldn't stop thinking about a lovely tall blonde-haired officer with no first name. She made it her mission to find out tomorrow what it was. With that she said goodnight to Daisy and had a very pleasant dream.

Daisy went off to work in the morning leaving Lizzie in bed to get up later. They had found out it was Jenny's birthday and the plan was to go to the local dance on the next available night to let their hair down, if they were indeed all off at the same time. Due to how busy they all had been, it had been put on hold but with the wards quieting down, they decided on Saturday night. It was something to look forward to, as the past week had been very hard on the young nurses.

Lizzie got up and had a bath, did her hair, and caught up with reading a book, until it was time to head for her lunch and then work. She got her uniform on, made sure it was perfect, did her hair and applied a light shade of make-up to her face. It wasn't really allowed but she didn't care, she wanted to look beautiful for the mysterious captain. Headed to the dining hall for lunch and by twelve forty-five and was heading up the familiar corridor to the ward. Soon as she was through the door, and was met by Daisy, who nearly knocked her over saying excitingly that he had been there that morning.

Lizzie said, "Asking for me!"

"He will be back later with Lieutenant Hopkins from family liaison," answered Daisy. "And I have found out that no, he doesn't like her, and she is married to a doctor in the navy."

The relief on her friend's face was worth it to see. "But how did you find this all out?" Lizzie enquired.

"I got young Pickford to ask him." Lizzie could have kissed her friend. "I couldn't stand seeing you being so unhappy today on the ward, to be honest."

She looked at her friend, who she had only known nine months, and hugged her tight. "I don't know how to thank you?"

"I don't want thanks; I want you to be happy and call your first-born Daisy if it's a girl," she laughed. "I think you first should thank Private Pickford over there," said Daisy, glancing over towards the young private.

Lizzie looked over at Pickford lying in bed trussed up in a traction splint and raised her hand to say thanks, today was getting better.

Staff Nurse Collins was on today and she saw Lizzie and Daisy talking by the door. Lizzie saw her coming and made straight for the locker room, Daisy headed in the different direction, to the sluice. Lizzie took her cardigan off, she hadn't brought her cape as it was getting hot, well it was June. She rolled up her sleeves and put on her cuffs and then found her white, clean apron, put it over her head and tied it around her. Lizzie couldn't help smiling, first thing this morning her heart had felt heavy, she had been forlorn, but now she felt ecstatic all thanks to young Private Pickford and her best friend. 'I really need to find out his first name as well'.

Staff Nurse Collins popped her head round the door. "When you are quite ready, Nurse Fenton, we have work to do."

"Staff Nurse, do you happen to know what private Pickford's first name is?"

"Albert, I think, why?"

"No reason, but thank you," said Lizzie.

The afternoon went really quickly. Lizzie helped Daisy with the back round, and then it was time to do dressings. Lizzie helped Staff Nurse Collins to wash down and make up an empty bed, putting fresh linen on the bed as the soldier in it had been discharged home that morning. Daisy went off early with other members of staff, including Staff Nurse Anderson, as Sister Green was at a meeting of all senior staff.

On her way out, Daisy went up to Lizzie. "I want to hear all about what happens, later tonight when you get back." She winked at her friend as she went.

After tea Lizzie managed to see Albert. "I owe you a thank you," she said smiling.

"The captain will be here soon," he said, smiling back at the young nurse that had caught the eye of his captain.

Lizzie was sent to supper by Staff Nurse Collins and still the captain hadn't come, she hoped she wouldn't miss him while on her break. Luck was on her side, as she was walking back from the dining hall, she glanced at the entrance of the hospital, which she had to pass to get back to the ward. She heard someone call, "Nurse." She didn't turn around at first thinking it was for someone else.

"Carry on walking," she said to herself, she felt someone touch her shoulder.

"Hello, nurse," they said again.

When she turned this time, she saw him, blue eyes met blue eyes, that melted into each other, and they stood in the corridor just staring at each other.

"Can I walk with you to the ward?" he asked politely.

Lizzie was lost for words, she nodded, and her heart was beating at such a pace, she thought it was going to come out of her mouth.

"Can I formally introduce myself? Captain Christopher Jameson at your service." He saluted smartly.

Elizabeth at last found her voice. "Elizabeth Fenton, nice to meet you," in her clipped accent, offering out her hand to him. "My friend's call me Lizzie."

"And mine call me Chris."

With introductions complete and Lizzy's heart stabilizing back to a slow beat, they walked to the ward in a comfortable silence.

Captain Jameson, asked, "When are you free this week, I know you are busy?"

"We are all going dancing on Saturday night at the Roxy." On impulse she asked, "Would you like to come?"

Chris stopped her by her arm gently as she was about to enter the ward.

"Yes, I would like that very much, it would be nice as I haven't had a lot of time to relax since arriving back, where do I meet you?"

"I am going with friends to celebrate Jenny's birthday, she's a fellow nurse, so can we meet you there?"

"Yes," he said smiling. "Say, seven-thirty?" And with that they entered the ward together.

Captain Jameson had to see Sister Green, who was now back from her meeting, she led him into her office. Lizzie relieved a second-year nurse so she could go for supper, she kept peering nervously at the door of Sister's office, hoping he would come out, but he was in there for some time.

Half hour later, he left Sister's office, he looked over towards her and he smiled but didn't say anything, went over to his men and spent time with each one. Once the bell had been rung for visiting to finish, more soldier's relatives were arriving every day, once they had been notified that their loved one was at The London being treated for their injuries, Captain Jameson got up from his chair by the bed, picked up his hat and got ready to leave. He said goodnight to his men, and left.

He got to the end of the ward by the door, before turning, he had one last look over at Lizzie, who couldn't help but smile back at him.

Could you fall in love with someone you just met? She wondered because she was falling fast, what would he think of her secret? Lizzie was troubled, what would Chris think of her title and would it scare him away? She certainly hoped not, she was buoyed with the hope that Daisy and the others had been fine with it so hopefully Chris would be too! What was his family like? What did he do before the war? All these questions were making her head ache. The one question she dreaded most was her mother and Charles' reaction and how would Chris deal with them both. Only time would tell, that's if they had time.

He left the ward, and the rest of the evening Lizzie and the other nurses made all the patients comfortable and ready for the night shift to arrive, she made her escape once Staff Nurse Collins had let them go, nearly running to the nurses' home, being told to slow down by Night Sister in the corridor.

"Sorry!" shouted Lizzie. Home Sister was waiting for the girls to come in and she said "goodnight" as she ran up the stairs to their floor. She made a detour into the bathroom before heading to their room.

Daisy was sitting on her bed reading, she had found a good book that she liked at the library, that was down the high street. She had found it when out on her last day off. She had better check the date, when she had to return the book as she didn't want a fine, luckily it wasn't for another week, she would finish it in plenty of time.

Her roommate couldn't contain her excitement. "He came! I spoke with him, he is coming to the dance on Saturday." Lizzie couldn't contain her happiness and excitement.

"Does he have a name?" asked Daisy.

"Yes," she replied.

"Well, what is it?" Questioned Daisy again.

"Christopher, or Chris to his friends."

Her friend couldn't hide her happiness, she was beaming. Daisy was truly pleased for her, but she was apprehensive as to how Lady Fenton would take to her daughter falling for a commoner. Only time would tell, but she promised she would be there for her friend at all costs.

"How was your day?" her friend asked, as they got ready for bed.

"All right," came the reply. "Come on, I'm tired. Let's get some sleep." Lizzie turned the light off.

Lizzie in fact didn't get much sleep as she was thinking of one blue-eyed captain and dancing on Saturday.

Chapter 21

Unusually, all four were actually off on Saturday, two had baths in the morning and two would have baths that evening. The girls went shopping but in the shops the shelves were low on stock. They decided to pool resources and borrow between the four of them, they were all different sizes, but they could manage with a little bit of luck, and Daisy's magic hands that she had inherited from her mother.

It had been a lovely day, nice and warm, and by the evening, Jenny was in a happy mood because of her birthday tomorrow. The girls had clubbed together and bought her some perfume, they had been lucky as it was in short supply. By seven they were all ready. You wouldn't recognise them as nurses all dressed in their lovely summer dresses and heading out the door to the dance. They all joined arms and were walking to the dance hall. As they turned the corner, standing by the entrance was Christopher, out of uniform in cotton shirt and trousers. Lizzie wanted to melt when she saw him, and he saw her, he went up to the group and introduced himself.

Once introductions had been made and he had wished the birthday girl a happy birthday, giving her a kiss on the cheek which made her blush, they all paid and entered the dance.

It was the same band, and they were just warming up, the hall wasn't very full, but there was a queue forming to get in. The group headed for the bar and Chris got the group their first drinks and they found a table and sat down. Daisy sat talking to Jenny and Claire leaving her friend to talk to the handsome captain. Over the course of the evening, they talked about everything and danced as much as they could, they got to know each other by the end of the evening and were falling more in love with each other.

Apparently, Christopher was from Edinburgh, Scotland and he was a schoolteacher, he enjoyed his job, and he loved the boys he taught. Both his parents were also schoolteachers up in Scotland but were looking to retire one day when the war was over. Before the end of the dance Chris took Lizzie by the hand and led her outside, they found a quiet space away from prying eyes, he wanted some time to themselves.

He held her tight around her waist and he pulled her in for their first kiss. Lizzie held her breath as their lips connected, it was magical and passionate. Lizzie felt stars before her eyes, yes, she knew she was in trouble, big time.

Chris stood back and he smiled down at Lizzie, meeting her eyes with his, that were full of love. "You are amazing and I've loved you from the first time we met on the ward," he whispered. They kissed some more.

Looking down at her watch, reluctantly, she said, "We had better be getting back to the others."

They went back into the packed hall full of people dancing and having a good time, picked up their stuff, found the others and headed home, Lizzie smiled when Chris took hold of her hand and did not let go. He walked back with them to the nurse's home, where he said "goodnight" and that he would see them again soon.

Daisy followed the others into the nurses' home and left Lizzie and Chris to say their goodbyes in private.

He looked at Lizzie lovingly. "I will see you tomorrow on the ward." And he took her in his arms again and kissed her passionately.

Once Lizzie entered their room, she quietly got ready for bed, Daisy was already in bed and waited for her friend.

"Chris is really nice," she mentioned glancing over at Lizzie who was blushing.

"Please tell him soon about your title, before he hears from someone else."

Lizzie looked over towards her friend and promised she would when the time was right, with that both soon fell asleep.

Over the next few weeks more soldiers left the ward, and more civilians were coming back to the hospital, that meant Captain Jameson was needed less, so he gave his details to Lizzie for her to write to him, and he promised to write to her, but she didn't tell him about her title.

He didn't know where the regiment was going next, but he promised Lizzie he would be back soon to see her. The day she dreaded came and he came to say goodbye, as all but Pickford had been discharged and Private Pickford would be going to a convalescent home prior to being discharged.

"Promise me you will write?" Lizzie's heart was breaking and she tried not to cry, but a few stray tears rolled down her cheeks.

She couldn't let the Staff Nurse see her, so she pulled him into the staff locker room and he took her in his arms, had one last sweet kiss, before he turned and walked up the ward and was gone.

Lizzie wiped her eyes with her clean handkerchief and went back to work with a heavy heart. The rest of the shift went in a blur, and she couldn't wait to get off that evening.

The girls would be back on rota to their proper wards to continue their training on Monday. The news from Europe was not good with Hitler posing for photographs in front of the Eiffel Tower in Paris. Next, he had his eye on Britain. The British people were bracing themselves for the invasion with Hitler and the German army only across the Channel, which was twenty-three miles away, it was only a matter of time.

In July 1940, The German air force, known as the Luftwaffe, were bombing British coastal shipping convoys, ports and shipping centres. At the beginning of August, the Luftwaffe was ordered to achieve air superiority over the RAF, and the aim was to incapacitate RAF fighter command, that was the news coming from the wireless.

Later in the month it shifted the attacks to RAF airfields and buildings. The Battle of Britain had begun in earnest, Lizzie was worried for her brother, he would be at the heart of the action, as he was flying spitfires. His squadron was on standby, so at present Lizzie couldn't see him.

The girls had been a week on their new wards, Claire and Daisy had been put together on Gynaecology, some of the sick patients had been returned or hadn't been deemed fit to move. Jenny was on male surgical as it still had a few soldiers recovering on it. Elizabeth went to female geriatrics, which was a come-down from nursing young soldiers, but it was part of the training and a break from dealing with life-changing injuries.

Now the possibility was they would soon be nursing wounded

airmen. War really was here and the residents of London were going to feel the full force of the German air force in a few months. Goring, wanted to destroy the RAF. Every day the news was about how the some of the British airfields along the south coast were being hammered on a daily basis, and badly damaged. Others escaped with minor damage. Many Air Force personnel got injured or killed and the worst injured were brought to the big hospitals in London.

Lizzie had gotten hold of Eddie, and the next time he was off, they promised to meet in London. By beginning of September, the Luftwaffe turned from bombing the airfields and dropped the first bombs on London, this was the start of the Blitz.

Many Civilians, including children were injured or died; the air raid siren would go off every night. In the background could be heard the ack-ack of the guns in the park firing up into the night sky, trying to hit the bombers. The search lights scanned the night sky for the enemy aircraft as they approached their targets.

The girls, if not on shift had to go to the hospital basement and take refuge there, it was damp and cold, and they would help their colleagues to bring patients down to shelter. The nurses on shift were given hard hats. Above them the bombs rained on down.

The first year of the war was over and now London was being bombarded, and the girls were starting the second year of training. It consisted of casualty department, theatres and maternity. Both Daisy and Lizzie had celebrated their nineteenth birthdays close together, but because of what was happening with the bombings, they both wanted little fuss, it didn't feel appropriate.

The girls had clubbed together and found some stockings and lipstick on a shopping trip up the high street a few weeks ago. What shook them the most was the devastation around them, the potholes and ruins where buildings had once been. The air was full of dust and fires were still raging by the docks which had taken a pounding.

The presents were given to them on a rare night off, sitting in the basement, waiting for the all-clear to sound. Lizzie had met up with Eddie at the Lyon corner house in Leicester Square, she had gone on her own this time.

Once sat down she looked at her brother, he looked grey and had a haunted look about him, he told of the long hours with little sleep. The loss of many friends who had gone off on a shout and never returned, seeing them fall into the channel, parachutes not opening. He was determined that the RAF would not be defeated.

His sister told him about Christopher and how much she was in love and she wanted him to meet him as soon as possible. A letter had arrived the other day from him, he was in barracks getting ready to be sent abroad again, once they were trained and replenished. She told him of the men who had died at Dunkirk.

Christopher wanted to meet up before he went but he had to go home to see his parents in Scotland for a few days. Her brother sat listening and could hear in her voice how happy she was. He didn't want to spoil her happiness but there was the little problem of their mother and Charles.

"Have you spoken with Mother yet?" asked Eddie.

"No," replied Lizzie curtly.

"If you are serious about Chris then you are going to have to tell her, sooner rather than later."

"I know, but I don't want to hear what she has to say on the matter."

"Have you seen Charles?"

"He wrote a letter a few weeks ago and wants to meet up next time he is on leave."

"Are you going to meet him?" asked a concerned Eddie.

"I don't know what to do," she answered truthfully, feeling sick with worry.

They would have to meet soon, and she would have to tell him she had met someone else that she loved. It was going to be difficult, but she knew in her heart it had to be done.

The only thing her brother advised was to be careful. "Charles has a temper and can be unstable." He didn't elaborate on the last comment. "Don't go on your own and stay in a public place he recommended."

Lizzie changed the subject and asked if he had seen Francesca?

"No, because she has joined the army as a driver and is stationed in Norfolk, somewhere by the coast, which apparently, she is enjoying, and she had grown close to another female soldier." He always thought she was different.

165

He didn't elaborate but his sister understood, she had met some girls like that at school. He did mention a girl he liked called Glenda and she was stationed at the same base in Kent, she was nineteen and a plotter. They had gone out a few times when not working and he really wanted his sister to meet her soon. He hadn't disclosed he was a Lord, as he was frightened she would not be interested, or worse even scared off.

Lizzie mentioned that she hadn't told Chris she was a Lady; they made a right pair. Soon it was time to part, Eddie had a train to catch, and the bombers would be coming soon, but looking up at the night sky, it was black but very clear, maybe they would be let off tonight.

"Keep safe," they both said together. They hugged and went their separate ways.

"Tell me how you get on with Charles," was the last thing her brother said as he went out into the street, hailing a taxi to take him to Charing Cross and back to the unknown.

Lizzie headed to the underground. While waiting for the train, she witnessed families bedding down for the night. Once on the train, she kept thinking back to what her brother had said, 'be careful of Charles'. She sat back in the seat and contemplated to herself, having changed at another station, she made her way along the road to the hospital.

Looking around she held her gas mask tighter, all the time praying no bombs would fall as she walked along the bomb-damaged pavement, ruins and damage were everywhere around her. Entering the hospital grounds, she noticed that the hospital had slight damage to the roof, a few slates had come away, workmen had been working on it that morning. Running across the grass, she pushed open the door of the nurse's home, a sigh of relief coming from her, and inhaled deeply, slowly she let out a breath.

Hurrying up the stairs she rushed into her room. Daisy was back from her shift and sitting up in bed reading a letter from her parents and she also had one from her sister, Mary waiting for her when she returned from work.

She laid back waiting for her roommate to arrive, her mind wandered, thinking about where Dr Reynolds was and more importantly, was he safe? No one she had spoken to had any news where he was but she would make it her mission to find out. She would start with Student

Nurse Henley tomorrow.

Hearing the room door open, she said, "Thank god you are back safe." Lizzie could hear the relief in her friend's voice.

"How is Eddie?" Daisy went on to ask.

Lizzie sat down on her freshly-made bed, we had clean sheets put on today, she could smell the freshness and it made her feel cosy and like being at home, a pang of homesickness came over her, she was missing cook.

"He is all right but looking very tired," she said. "He has met a girl called Glenda and she is stationed with him. I am pleased, he seems happy and with everything he is dealing with at the moment, constant stress and high alert, then let him have some fun."

Daisy gazed over at her friend. "I hope he is being careful!" she said in a cheery tone.

Lizzie glanced across at her fellow nurse and rolled her eyes. "I'm sure he will be." She quietly hoped and prayed he was not like their father! "I'd better get ready for bed." And with that, Lizzie got into her nightdress, pyjamas were too warm in this heat, and both girls hoped no bombs would be dropped tonight as they wanted to get some sleep.

They had just got off to sleep when Daisy heard the siren wailing. She had to shake Lizzie, who woke with a start, and rubbed sleep out of her eyes. They quickly put on their dressing gowns and slippers, grabbed a nearby torch they kept by the bed and grabbing the gas masks and tin helmets they had been given, they hurried to see if their neighbours had heard it.

The others had indeed heard it and were exiting their room at the same time as them. Following the others and Home Sister, who was barking orders like a sergeant major, the girls all headed for the basement, urgently and as quietly as possible. Once down in the damp dark room they found a space, chairs and camp beds had been placed down there. The four girls sat talking and they all knew they would get hardly any or no sleep tonight.

Daisy, settled on a chair, turned the torch on, the basement had lights but were not very bright, pulled her letters from her pocket and sat reading the first one from her parents.

They were all well, Mark was getting over a cold but was getting better. George was enjoying his job and wanted as soon as he could to join up but was still too young, he kept begging his father to let him join up earlier, his father told him the war was not going to be over any time soon. Luton had been bombed but luckily their street had been missed but a few houses in the next street had been hit. Dad had put an Anderson shelter in the garden, which they went into and Mum had made it comfortable and homely. Dad, did fire watching on certain nights at his factory and other nights he was an APR warden. Mum had joined the Women's Voluntary Service and had started to go to meetings, she had made a lot of friends and her skills were in big demand.

Daisy turned to her sister's letter. She was okay, Bobby had recovered from his ordeal at Dunkirk and had re-joined his regiment. She was missing him terribly. She was pleased for her sister, Daisy didn't have any feelings for Bobby now, she just wanted to be friends.

Mary told her sister how she hated the bombing, and it scared her. Daisy thought, well, she should live in London! With eyes hurting from strain, she folded the letters, turning the torch off to save battery life and to rest her tired eyes, pushing the letters back into her pocket. Settling down to listen to Lizzie telling the others about her evening with her brother.

Just then there was an almighty bang, the walls shook, all four held each other and said a silent prayer as dust fell around them. Hilary piped up, they must have hit the hospital. Still, they sat and listened as the bombs rained down around them, it's the docks they are after, everyone agreed. Daisy's thoughts turned to Dr Reynolds and again said a silent prayer to keep him safe, she couldn't understand why she felt like this towards a man she hardly knew.

The all-clear sounded around five a.m. and the girls made a weary walk back upstairs to their rooms. Luckily everything was untouched but they couldn't see outside.

Lizzie and Jenny said, "They needed a cigarette desperately."

But the other two said, "Hold off just in case a gas main has been hit nearby." Although they couldn't smell gas. For once, all four were on earlies and they quickly got ready, had a quick wash and breakfast before heading to the wards. They had started their second year of training. This was their last week on the wards before being back in school for a week, then either in theatre, casualty or maternity after their annual leave at Christmas.

All four couldn't wait but didn't get too excited as it was still a long way off. Walking out of the nurse's home, they saw that part of the hospital had been hit, slightly. It looked from the front that most of the wards were untouched. Matron had a while ago sent non-service personnel to local hospitals in the country, which meant that their relatives having longer journeys to make.

The hospital was now mainly filled with service personnel and some civilians unlucky to be caught up in the bombing raids. Daisy had talked with a porter one lunch time and found that the mortuary was getting full, so they were having to build mass graves for the dead. She had felt sad hearing that news but wasn't surprised, especially at the rate the raids were taking place all over the country.

On the wireless the government was calling this the Blitz, and the Royal Air Force were undertaking night-time raids in Germany. Lizzie had some more bad news; Coventry had been bombed and even the cathedral had been totally destroyed. Hearing this news, she had quickly called her parents at the hall, and found out that her aunt and uncle had been staying with them and were both safe.

Her mother was still adjusting to having various different people in her home, her father was in his element and loving it. Cook apparently was very busy and Geoffrey and her were finally engaged to be married. Lizzie wasn't surprised at this news and promised she would try and get home for the wedding. Her mother wanted to ask about Charles, but the operator had cut them off just had Lizzie was going to explain.

Charles was coming through London on his way to see his parents before being sent away again with his unit, so he had written to finally meet up. He hadn't told her of the girls he had been frequenting at a house near his barracks in Aldershot. They were very willing companions and he spent nearly all his free time there or drinking with his colleagues. He thought that he would keep this information away from Lizzie and especially her righteous mother.

Remembering the warning her brother had given her, she wanted a busy area full of people, so she decided on Marylebone station, as Charles could then carry on his forwarding journey home. The girls had been back in school a couple of weeks and were now learning about the operating theatre, casualty and delivering babies.

"God help me," said Jenny, "if I have to do that, I will probably be sick."

"What about the poor women?" said Claire.

While everyone caught up with letters, studying or washing their underwear, which was now imposable to buy in the shops because of rationing, Lizzie made her way to meet with Charles. On seeing him her apprehension intensified and she felt physically sick. Oh! how she had wished now that she had taken Daisy's offer to come as well, or to have Chris with her.

He was abroad, all she knew, from his last letter she had received a few days ago, was he needed to wear summer clothing and it was extremely hot, which the sensors hadn't blacked out like they had the rest of it. In the future they would need to make a code, so they would both know where he was in the world.

Charles looked over at her as she walked towards him, he kept looking up and down, examining her curves as he did so.

"What a leach!" she thought.

"Hello, Charles," she said trying to be pleasant, "shall we head to the buffet for a cup of tea or coffee…?"

"I don't want coffee if it's not real," he moaned.

She finished, "…if you have time?"

"My train is due soon, if not delayed due to all this bomb damage," he replied. He was speaking in a tone like it was an inconvenience.

They found a table and Lizzie got the tea and coffee; 'he couldn't even help do that,' she thought to herself. While she was waiting, her heart was hammering inside her, Charles sat patiently till she came and sat down.

"I am being sent away soon," he began.

"Where?" she asked, before she could stop herself.

"You know I can't tell you."

"Sorry," she said.

"I still want to get married once you have finished your training," he continued."

"What if I have changed my mind and don't want to get married to you," she answered sarcastically.

"You never really wanted to marry me!" he said with a sneer. "You are only going through with it only to please your mother." He laughed.

"Maybe," she replied, she was getting more uncomfortable and nervous as the time went on. Happy she had chosen to meet at that particular site.

"Let's cut to the chase," he carried on. "Your family are very rich and my family want some of that wealth, so we get married to please your mother and then we live as a married couple, but we see other people, we both win."

"I don't want to get married," she said. "Not to you."

"Well, we will see about that, there is still plenty of time and I am not going anywhere," he sneered again, facing Lizzie.

Following this he said, "Next time I am up in London, I will get a hotel room, then you can show me a good time!" Laughing.

Under the table she had crossed her fingers and hoped that would never happen anytime soon. As Lizzie was going to reply Charles's train was called, which was thankfully on time, and she made her way back to the underground feeling sick with worry. Her only hope was that something terrible would happen to him while he was away, she felt terrible thinking this and she thought she would end up going to hell. At this time though she didn't care. Before walking away, he had grabbed Lizzie's arm and yanked her towards him, he gave her a rough kiss and with that was gone, laughing.

Arriving back at the nurse's home, the others asked, "how the meeting had gone?" By the look on her face, they knew it hadn't gone well at all so they didn't press, she could feel the taste of his lips on her mouth, and she felt nauseous.

All four had tea in the dining hall, Lizzie just played around with hers, Charles' words still ringing around her head.

Lizzie and Jenny got their coats and gas masks and headed outside in the cold and had a cigarette, or two in Lizzie's case. Jenny kept quiet and let Lizzie talk when she felt like it, perhaps she would open up to Daisy later, they weren't out too long as the evening was very cold.

Much later, and with a glass of whiskey in her hand, she felt much better and opened up a bit about what had happened. When she told them about the hotel room, they were first all shocked and then angry.

"Are you going to tell Christopher?" Jenny asked.

"Not at the moment, he doesn't even know that Charles exists and I am not going to worry him while he is away fighting. Next time I see Eddie, I will talk to him and get his reaction."

Luckily, that night no bombers came as the night was very foggy and so they all had a restful night's sleep, apart from Lizzie who kept tossing and turning going over in her mind what had happened today.

The rest of the week, they were kept busy with lectures and studying for exams which would take place on Friday as usual. Daisy had found out that Michael, or Dr Reynolds to his colleagues, had been sent abroad, and was at this precise moment probably sitting in the sun somewhere. She was pleased to know that he had definitely split up from Student Nurse Henley, who on her part, didn't seem too upset, as she now had another boyfriend — another doctor.

Daisy, on hearing this news was silently pleased and hoped in the near future their paths would cross again and she kissed the cross on her neck that her parents had given her all that time ago.

"Please, stay safe," she thought to herself.

Sunday the list was out and as usual the girls sent Lizzie to look at the board, they were all watching intently from the door.

"Right," Lizzie said, laughing. "In first place, as usual is, can you guess … Daisy. Second me and you two not far behind." Looking at Jenny and Claire.

Lizzie went on to say that Hilary was at the bottom and would be seeing Matron in the morning. The girls were happy with the results, they even felt sorry for Hilary, well, just a tiny bit. Having bumped into Hilary at the dining hall, she said, "I can't study with all this bombing nearly every night, no sleep." And with that had walked off in a huff.

The others just stood there looking after her and feeling bewildered. "What about us! We had to suffer the same."

Four-thirty, Lizzie was sent back to the board in the corridor and again came back with where they were being allocated to once they got back from holiday. Daisy and Lizzie were together in theatre, Jenny got her worst fear, maternity and Claire got casualty.

"How am I going to deliver babies?" she cried out. "They are little humans!"

"You will be fine," they all chorused together.

"Huff!" she went.

"We are together," said Lizzie, excited to be with her friend.

"Yes," replied Daisy. "Theatres will be very busy, especially at the moment with all these injuries that are coming in. I hope the sister is nice because we will be learning as we go."

Finally, Claire piped up, "I've got casualty department, and already I feel sick with nerves."

"You will be fine," came the reply.

She looked over at her friends with some trepidation. Their holiday this time covered Christmas Eve, Christmas Day and Boxing Day, and back the day after, due to the hospital needing as many nurses as possible at the moment due to some qualified nurses leaving to join the forces.

This left the hospital short of nurses. Many of the young doctors had also left to join up, which meant they were left with older doctors who had come out of retirement to help.

Hilary had caught them later, looking very relieved that Matron had been lenient, and she had been allowed to stay as they needed nurses. She had said she was a good nurse, besides this result, but "I have no more chances," she said.

The others had said well done to her, as they headed off in different directions.

Chapter 22

Daisy stood by the door and was waiting patiently for Lizzie to finish packing.

"Just a few more things to pack and I'm ready," she said cheerily. A few minutes later she was finally ready; both girls looked back at their room, happy they hadn't forgotten anything. Picking up their handbags, gas masks and suitcases, they both popped next door to collect their friends.

"Are you two ready?"

They both said, "Yes" together.

All four headed down the now familiar stairs to be met by Home Sister.

"Have a lovely Christmas and come back refreshed and ready for work."

With that they picked up their cases and walked out into the bitterly cold December day. They were starting to have a soft spot for the stern older nurse.

Saying 'goodbye' to Claire, hugging each other and then Jenny the same, the other two hugged at the underground. On the platform as Daisy waited for the train, she noticed the beds left to the side, where at night the families of the East End would be back and calling the tube station their home. On arrival to St Pancras, it looked different this time she pondered, it was badly damaged from the bombing. The only thing so far not damaged was St Paul's Cathedral.

St Pancras was also looking war-weary, and it was busy with service personnel. All trains were delayed because of the bomb damage from last night, it had been a particularly heavy raid, so Daisy found a space on the floor, made herself comfortable and sat down to wait. Five hours later, her train was ready, and with all the other frustrated, tired passengers, they climbed aboard.

Another four hours and she finally reached Luton. Leaving the station, walking through the streets towards home, she noticed all the bomb-damage, rubble and ruins. She prayed her family home was still standing and that they were all safe. In the last letter her mum had sent, it was still okay, but last night's raids could have changed that in an instant.

She shivered but not from the December cold and put it behind her, pulling her winter coat closer to her, she headed towards home picking up the pace. Turning the corner into her familiar street, she held her breath, took a look and breathed a sigh of relief, her home was still standing, some of the others in the street had taken a battering. She noticed some of the windows were cracked even with the recommended anti-blast tape on them to stop bomb damage.

Daisy hurried up the entry and pushed open the back gate, pushing the back door open with her hand she said a cheery "hello."

Her mum, surprised on hearing her daughter's voice, came to the door, stood and inspected her daughter very closely and took her in her arms and hugged her tight.

"Welcome home, how long are you here for?" she said tenderly. Before Daisy could answer Hannah said, "Let's have a cup of tea and a catch up." Daisy watched as her mother took her suitcase and put it to one side. Putting the kettle on, she then got the teacups and Daisy took her coat off, put it behind her chair and sat down.

Hannah seized her daughter's hand and lovingly rubbed it; "It's nice to have you home for Christmas love."

"It's only for a couple of days," Daisy replied.

"It's just lovely to have you home and safe," said Hannah, sincerely. "Now run your case up to your bedroom, and wake Mark as he had a sleep this afternoon. We haven't slept well due to the bombing."

"Has it been bad?" asked Daisy, concerned.

"Yes," Hannah said, looking over at her daughter. "Have you had it bad as well?" Hannah inquired.

"Yes, they are after the docks," replied her daughter.

'When would this war be over?' They both thought.

Her mother was looking tired, older, and had bags under her eyes. "When was the last time you slept?" asked Daisy lovingly.

"It's been days," replied her mother sincerely.

"Do you want to go and have a rest while I start the tea?" Daisy offered.

"Thank you, darling, but really, I am fine. I want to spend time with you." Hannah took a long look at the daughter now they were standing in the kitchen and thought how grown up she was becoming and noticed the difference between her and Mary.

"There's not much food in the shops, so I went out early and queued and got as much as I could for Christmas dinner tomorrow," Hannah said.

"I have presents for all of you, it's been hard due to the rationing, and the shops' shelves are empty, or you have to pay the earth through the black market," Daisy said, full of Christmas cheer.

"You haven't?" asked her mother seriously.

"Did you get a Christmas tree?" enquired Daisy with some excitement in. her voice.

"Yes, a small one," replied her mother. "We were lucky, Mark is so disappointed it's not bigger, but we will make it up to him. We have made paper chains. Your father and brother will be home soon, I can't believe your brother will be eighteen next year. Where has the time gone?" her mother contemplated. "When Mary gets back, about six o'clock, we will have tea. Go and wake up Mark, he will be pleased to see you."

Up the stairs she went warily, leaving the warmth of the kitchen, up at the top she paused outside her brother's room and looked inside, Mark was snoring gently, he looked so peaceful, Daisy didn't want to wake him. She went over to him and gently shook him awake. Once awake, he looked up and wiped his eyes and couldn't believe who he saw standing there.

"Daisy," he called. "Daisy."

"Yes, I'm home for a few days holiday," as if to answer his question.

"Are you home for Christmas?"

"Yes," she replied with a smile on her tired face. He gave her a big hug, and his older sister hugged him right back.

Both went back to the warmth of the kitchen and waited for the rest of the family to arrive home, then Christmas could begin in the Peter's home. By six-thirty, everyone was home, and tea served. The talk was mainly about the war, the bombing and rationing. Daisy asked about Bobby, who was still abroad somewhere hot.

"I had a letter from him the other week," Mary answered.

"Have you got someone special?" she asked her sister seriously.

"No one at present, I am too busy with studying," she said, not looking at her twin sister; otherwise, she may have noticed the slight blush to her cheeks.

The evening went quickly and turning the wireless on they listened to the news, which was not good. The bombing was carrying on relentlessly, destroying towns and cities all over Britain. Killing thousands of innocent people. The battle of Britain was over, with many pilots having been killed or badly injured.

Her thoughts turned to Eddie, Lizzie's brother. He had been lucky, shot down but had parachuted into a field, no injuries and was back fighting the next day, but the German Luftwaffe had sustained heavy losses. Hence, the news stated, news coming from Germany was that Britain was bombing them very heavily.

Jack sat smoking a cigarette and looking at his eldest daughter; he was smoking more; he observed how grown up she was becoming. Mark had at last gone to bed; he was tired and so excited for Father Christmas to come. The rest of the family prayed that there would be no bombing tonight or tomorrow. About ten Daisy and Mary went up to bed, having wished their mum and dad a goodnight.

"See you tomorrow," they both replied.

Once up in their shared room, they quickly got changed and jumped into a warm bed, Mum had put a hot stone bottle at the bottom to get it warm for them. For the first time in a long time, Mary hugged her sister, and they fell asleep close together, they didn't hear their parents come to bed.

Daisy had already given her presents to her mother for Christmas Day to hide with hers. They were lucky that night, no bombers came, and they all slept well.

Christmas Day had arrived; Mark got up early and was told to go back to bed by his father. At seven he was allowed to get up, the rest of the household was up as well, dressed in their dressing gowns and slippers. The wrapped presents were all placed under the small tree which was sparkling in the corner of the front room. Mum was already in the kitchen, getting breakfast so she could start getting dinner ready, the chicken was already in the range.

Daisy had managed to get her sister a bottle of perfume that she liked, her brother George a torch, Mark some toy soldiers, Mum a scarf and Dad some cigarettes.

They opened the rest of the presents, the wrapping paper left discarded on the floor to be picked up later, and then the whole family got dressed and ready to help Mum prepare dinner, the boys playing with Mark's toys. The wireless was on in the background playing Christmas Carols.

The rest of the day went too quickly, and soon it was bedtime for Mark. "I've had a lovely day," he said sleepily. Daisy took him up to bed and read him a story, soon he was fast asleep.

As she walked down the stairs, she hoped that the bombers would keep away and let them have a peaceful night. Again, they did not come, and they had a lovely Boxing Day.

The next day Daisy was up early. "I had better go after breakfast," she said to her mother, "as the trains could be running late."

Her mother and Mark were the only ones at home. "Do you want me to walk to the station with you?" asked Hannah.

"No, thank you, keep in the warm with Mark. I will say goodbye here."

All packed, coat and scarf on, ready to go, she hugged her brother and then her mother.

"Take care and come home soon."

Leaving the warm house was a wrench, but she wanted to get back to her friends, she wanted to know how Lizzie had got on with her family. At the station, the trains weren't running too badly, and by lunchtime, Daisy had arrived back in London and stood waiting for the underground train to arrive. Daisy made it back to the nurse's home by one p.m. and then waited for her friends to arrive back.

Chapter 23

Lizzie had left Daisy and made it to Marylebone Station with some difficulty. Looking at the devastation all around her, she noticed, people were looking weary, but they were still walking with a determination that they wouldn't be beaten. As for Daisy the trains were running late due to the horrific bombing the night before. It was after lunch that she arrived at Warwick station and that too had some damage. She felt the December cold as she alighted from the train.

Picking up her suitcase and putting the gas mask securely on her shoulder, she looked around for Geoffrey. She spotted him waiting for her in the Rolls Royce. 'How did her father get the petrol?' She thought but wouldn't ask. Maybe for the best, she didn't know. Once inside she gave her congratulations to him and Edna, affectionately known as cook, and asked when the wedding was going to take place?

"Not yet," he replied, "but very soon, if I get my way. We are not getting any younger," he said, laughing to himself.

Lizzie couldn't help but smile. "You will notice a big difference to the house miss," he said, and he was right.

As they drove up to the house the amount of movement was incredible. Lizzie wanted to know how her mother was coping with all these changes? But it was too late, Geoffrey couldn't continue as Lady Margo, hearing the car tyres on the gravel, came to the entrance to greet her daughter.

"Darling, you are home!" She heard her mother through the closed window.

"Hello, Mother." As she got out and gave her mother a kiss on the cheeks.

"Welcome home, and Merry Christmas," she said jovially.

Lizzie was taken aback by her mother's manner, yet she did seem different. Entering the house via the kitchen, she gave cook a hug and congratulated her on her forthcoming wedding to Geoffrey. Cook said she had heard from Geoffrey that Lizzie had offered to help him to propose, but he had managed it himself with a bit of encouragement from Edna.

While this was going on her mother was looking with keen interest, not saying anything. Lizzie followed her mother through the kitchen, and she heard cook shout over her shoulder. "Come down later for tea and biscuits, they are freshly made today."

Lizzie turned and said, "Yes, that will be lovely, thank you."

Her mother carried on walking up the back stairs to the west wing. Her mother had made the rooms quite cosy she thought, looking around.

"I have put you in the one of the guest rooms, yours is being used by the injured men." On reflection she said, "I knew you wouldn't mind. Let's have tea and a catch up," said Lady Margo. Aunt Lynn and her husband Edward are helping downstairs, they are still staying until they are re-housed, realistically that could be a long time," her mother said.

"It will be nice to catch up with them," Lizzie said as she made her way into her new room, it was a lot smaller by comparison to her bedroom, bland looking with a single bed, bedside table, wardrobe and a small window looking out onto the grounds.

"The bathroom is down the corridor, we have to share," her mother pointed out, "but you are used to that," she said looking directly at her daughter, Lizzie nodded her head.

"Your aunt and uncle are in the next room."

"Father and myself are down the corridor, and Eddie is the other side of you. I will let you get settled, come and find me in the sitting room later and we will have tea, or we could join cook in the kitchen if you wish."

Lizzie couldn't believe what she was hearing, her mother sitting in the kitchen and actually eating there too! Wonders would never cease to amaze her.

"The kitchen will be fine, thank you." As she headed for her room to unpack.

Maybe her mother might change her mind and let her not marry Charles. 'I will have to hope and pray that happens' she thought as she took off her coat and gas mask and put it on the hook at the back of the door. What she had noticed the most was the peace and quiet, it was so peaceful here you wouldn't know there was a war on, apart from when you were downstairs. Having a quick glance around the room she noticed it wasn't very big. Lizzie didn't mind, she picked up her case and dropped it on the bed, taking her time, she placed her few clothes in the small wardrobe, she couldn't wait to go down and see what was happening to her former home. First, she was hungry, and those biscuits did smell delicious!

Once ready, she met her mother in the corridor and they made their way back towards the warm kitchen. Cook got them seated at the large table, picking up the plate of biscuits and placing two cups of tea in front of them.

Her mother said, "Please join us, Edna."

"Well, thank you your ladyship." All three sat down, the conversation was slightly stilted, but Lizzie began by talking about the wedding and asked if they would both still be working here?

"The wedding would be in summer and yes, they would like to stay until they both retired," answered a happy cook.

The relief on the face of her mother was there for all to see. They heard voices and then they saw her aunt and uncle, followed by her father with Dinky. The dog ran up to her and she gave it an affectionate rub.

"Welcome home, Lizzie," all three chorused together.

She got up and gave her aunt and uncle a warm hug and then she went to her father. She felt a bit strange, following what she had learnt from her aunt on her last visit home. He gave her a warm loving smile and she gave him a big hug in return; he was still her father. She noticed he was looking tired and much older.

Having finished more tea, all four left the warmth of the kitchen and headed up the stairs to where the hall was. Pushing the door open, Lizzie stepped out into bedlam.

Doctors were running about and so were the nurses too, there were beds all over the place as no space was left. Servicemen were either sitting on their beds or by their beds in chairs, some were playing cards and listening to the wireless. Her father and uncle had put Christmas decorations around, they had even managed to get a tree which they put up and decorated that as well. Some of the men had helped apparently. The dining room was made so that the servicemen who could, doctors and nurses, ate their meals in there, while her parents, aunt and uncle, had their meals in the kitchen.

Tomorrow being Christmas Day, the family had been invited to join the doctors and nurses for dinner, and her parents had agreed as long as it didn't inconvenience them. Lizzie continued the tour, and headed to the drawing room and library, these were also made into makeshift wards. Upstairs, was where the officers slept, and stayed, until fit to either go home or back to their regiments. Due to the weather being bitterly cold and a chance of snow, no one could go outside until it warmed up.

Her parents introduced their daughter to the injured men, and they all thought the young lady was charming. The afternoon went very quickly, and Lizzie sat on her bed a little later, wishing her brother was here, he had been lucky, he had survived the Battle of Britain. He had lost a lot of friends and colleagues which had affected him quite badly, the losses had been many but the Luftwaffe had lost a lot more accordingly to the news. He was still stationed in Kent but now by the coast and had been promoted to Squadron Leader. He had accepted the promotion reluctantly.

Dinner was rabbit stew served in the kitchen before cook had gone home, she lived in the nearby village and cycled in every morning. The family sat around the big table, tucking in to the stew, which was delicious, cook had made a trifle for dessert, which also went down a treat. They washed up and cleaned away, leaving the kitchen clean for cook in the morning, her mother had let her aunt and Lizzie do the washing up, so some things hadn't changed.

Lizzie stood yawning, made her excuses and kissing everyone, said good night, and headed up for a bath, and then bed. As she sunk into the hot water and she let the warmth soak into her weary bones, she had to smile at the change in her mother. They hadn't talked about Charles today, but she would be sure to bring it up tomorrow. Having dried herself off, letting the water get cold, she entered her bedroom and found that her mother had lit a fire and the room was nice and warm.

Feeling very drained she climbed into bed and snuggled down, pulling the sheets and eiderdown up around her. Tomorrow would be Christmas Day and next week a New Year, 1941. The house was quiet and she soon drifted off to sleep as it was nice not to be woken up with hearing the siren. She prayed no bombs would be dropped tonight and that her brother, Daisy and her family were safe too.

Morning came and Lizzie was up early. She heard the Nurses running around downstairs, she was used to waking up early now, it was becoming a habit.

Her routine at Christmas would be to quickly get dressed and run down to see cook and wish her a Happy Christmas, before going to see her parents in the drawing room, where they would exchange presents later that morning, but not today.

She headed straight for the kitchen and that's where she found all her family and Eddie sitting at the table looking tired. Gazing over at her brother, she did a double take and ran over to him, he stood up and took her in his arms and hugged her.

"Hello Sis, Merry Christmas," he said.

Lady Margo glared at her son. "Will you speak correctly and call your sister by her name?"

This made Eddie and Lizzie laugh. Lady Margo turned a shade of purple and shook her head in dismay, she was just about to say something but thought better of it. Lizzie had prayed for her brother to come home, and her prayers had been answered.

"Let me look at you?" scrutinising her brother all over she was happy to see he had put some weight on, the last time she had seen him he had looked gaunt.

Her mother recovered and told her daughter to sit by her brother and she was given a bowl of hot porridge. Lizzie put a dollop of jam on to a spoon and stirred round, licking her lips, eating it up very hastily.

The family exchanged presents which were only a token, like a lipstick, hankies and for the men cigarettes and some booze as it was a struggle to get items, apart from on the black market which was a criminal offence and carried a hefty sentence if caught.

Lizzie knew her father, if he wanted, could get certain items through his contacts, so she wasn't about to ask when her parents pulled out a pair of new shoes her size. They fitted perfectly and she accepted them, hugging her parents. Her brother got a part for his car that he urgently needed, her aunt and uncle were given a bottle of wine from her father's cellar, which they were happy with.

Later, they all visited the injured men and wished them all Merry Christmas. They had enjoyed that immensely. Her brother spent time talking to them and they exchanged stories.

Lizzie went to see cook and gave her a present of a bottle of perfume she had bought back in London before the shelves had gotten low. Cook was so overwhelmed she started to cry, and Lizzie held her and wished her a Happy Christmas. For Geoffrey she had got a pair of new driving gloves, he was so pleased he couldn't contain himself, he hugged her tight. "Thank you, miss," he said.

"Please call me Lizzie," she sighed. "The war is changing people's attitudes towards the wealthy," said Lizzie. "The world we live in is changing. We will soon all be equal; you mark my words," she reflected.

Cook had mostly prepared the meal the night before and she only had to cook the chickens, and they were in the oven since first thing, and the vegetables were also cooking away nicely.

"Do you need any help?" Lizzie offered Edna.

"No, thank you, your mother and aunt have been helping."

Lizzie couldn't believe her ears! Yes, her aunt but her mother, never. 'Does a leopard change its spots?' She wondered.

Christmas Dinner was a great success, everyone had enjoyed the food and the doctors and nurses were full of Christmas Pudding that cook had made the other year. Her father had shared the sherry, and everyone was sitting round the wireless, listening to carols.

Lady Margaret had sent cook home early, saying she and Aunt Lynn would serve a cold tea, and the rest of the family would help.

Eddie finally caught up with his sister during the afternoon, she was up in her room resting, Eddie was next door, he knocked, and she said, "Enter, oh, hello!" she said warmly when she spotted her brother entering.

Eddie sat down on her bed by her side. "How have you been?" he asked, and they chatted away about what they had both been up to recently.

She talked about her training and said now she would be going into theatres for eight weeks or so. She was both excited but also very apprehensive, but at least Daisy was with her. She couldn't believe she was in her second year of training and in a year's time, would be a qualified nurse. This led onto the subject of Charles. Lizzie enlightened her brother of the time they met up at the station, and how he was still on about getting married but living separate lives, once the deed was done.

"I still don't want to marry him," she said most defiantly.

"Have you talked to Mother yet?" Eddie enquired, knowing full well that she hadn't.

"I hoped to later today or tomorrow, before I have to go back, and hopefully catching her in a good mood." Lizzie didn't tell her brother about the hotel room as he would have killed Charles and her brother had enough on his mind at present.

"How is Chris?" he asked carefully.

"All right from his last letter, all I know is he is in the heat somewhere." She opened her heart and told her brother that she loved him and couldn't wait for him to meet him, when it was possible.

Switching the subject, she began by asking, "How have you been, and how is Glenda?"

With a long sigh, he replied by telling her about all of his friends that had been killed, and how he missed them very much, they had all trained together at the start of the war. There were only three original friends left, and he made sure they were still in his squadron, where he could personally keep an eye on them as he felt protective towards them. He told of the letters he had to write to their parents, explaining how they each died. He told of the heart-breaking letter he received back thanking him for his kind words. He never wanted to do that again, but he knew in his heart he may still have to, it came with the job.

When he mentioned Glenda, his face lit up. "She is wonderful, she really did keep me sane during the worst of the fighting, and between you and me, I want to ask her to marry me, as soon as we can."

Lizzie looked her brother straight in the eyes. "Seriously," she said, "you need to tell her about your title as soon as possible, it shouldn't make a difference if she truly loves you. Telling our parents, especially our mother, is a different story."

"Next leave I have, I will bring Glenda home with me to meet the parents, show her the house and I want to meet her parents and her family. I want to ask her father for his daughter's hand in marriage. I would like her to meet you, we will come up to London next time we have some free time, and you can meet her."

"Yes, I would like that very much," said Lizzie.

"I have told her all about you, and she's really keen to meet you," he said.

It was getting late, and they had promised their mother to help with distributing out tea.

"Come on, or she will be sending out the search party looking for us," he said, pulling his sister off the bed.

Before they left the bedroom, Eddie said, "Thank you for listening, and for just being you."

Lizzie gave her brother a hug and a peck on the cheek, this had been very difficult for her brother, she knew he carried a big burden, and she hoped she had lightened the load for him just for a little while.

They ran down the back stairs, laughing as they went like they used to and found their mother and aunt organising the tea, with the help of a merry Uncle Eddie, their father was nowhere to be seen. Once tea was completed, they had a free evening and they both thought it was the right time to speak with their mother, they found her in her sitting room with the wireless on in the background.

Margaret looked up as her two children walked in, she knew by their faces they wanted to talk with her. Eddie took a deep breath and went first, so he told her all about Glenda and that he wanted to marry her, he waited, he was holding his breath, as his mother had been very quiet the whole time, and then she spoke.

"Over the last few months, I have had to make drastic changes to my life which I hopefully have embraced, but when it comes to marriage, you both will marry a certain type of person with breeding, it is a privilege to have this, and you hold a title."

Both looked back at her, stunned. Eddie turned around, anger was rising in him. "I will marry her, and you will not stop me," he shouted. "I will be twenty-one next year, then I am free to get married to who I want."

"I have already chosen Francesca for you, nice girl, good breeding, she is in the army."

"Somehow I don't think she is the marrying type," said Eddie laughing.

"Why?" asked his mother seriously.

"Oh, you will understand some day."

Lizzie was grinning.

"Do tell me!" she said again.

"No, Mother, I am going to pack and go back to my base first thing in the morning, Sis, I will talk to you soon, if we don't see each other in the morning."

With that he was gone, slamming the door as he went.

Lady Margo was shocked and looked at the closed door. Lizzie was just about to go after him, when her mother told her to stay.

"You will still be marrying Charles, nothing has changed young Lady." Her daughter just stood glued to the floor, she wanted to tell her about Christopher, but thought better of it at this time.

"I'm tired," she said and excused herself to go to bed, she couldn't stay in the same room as her mother at this time. Lizzie ran back to her room, she really wanted to check on Eddie and she was just about to tap on his door when she decided to leave him to cool down. Lizzie slept very badly all night, tossing and turning, glad there were no raids again, the Germans must be celebrating Christmas, she thought. She would have a quiet word with her aunt tomorrow, before going back the following day.

Boxing Day was dreary and dull with a light wind, just like her mood. Eddie had made his escape early.

Her father asked why his son had gone back a day early?

Lizzie said mockingly, "Ask your wife, my mother," she carried on. "He wants to marry a commoner, a girl he has met at the base."

"We'll let him, he is a grown man," said her father firmly.

Looking at him, she wasn't sure if she had heard right. Her mother was glaring at him and her aunt just looked at her sister with pity.

"Can I speak with you Aunt Lynn, after breakfast?" Lizzie asked.

All the while cook had been listening, she really thought that her Ladyship had changed but realised she had been very wrong!

Breakfast was unbearable, and Lizzie couldn't wait to get away, she found her aunt getting her coat on to take the dog for a walk.

"Can I join you?" she asked in desperation.

"Yes, come on."

Lizzie got her coat, scarf and wellington boots, and they headed outside. They walked in comfortable silence until they got to the lake.

She turned to her niece. "What's the matter? You look so sad today?"

"I have met someone, a captain called Christopher Jameson at the hospital while he was visiting his injured men. He is in the Scots Guards. He is lovely, so different from Charles, and I've fallen head over heels in love with him. I really don't want to marry Charles, and he is so unstable, he wants me to sleep with him the next time I see him. Oh, Aunt, what do I do? Mother won't change her mind."

Seeing how forlorn her niece was. "Leave your mother to me!" her aunt said with a defiant tone, and with that they turned around and walked back to the house and warmth.

Lizzie didn't know if to believe her aunt but she had no choice, at this precise moment her future was looking very bleak, but she did feel a bit brighter, she kept out the way of her mother as much as she could, packed her case, trying not to cry and stayed in her room, only coming down for meals.

The evening dragged and her aunt popped in to see her niece to see if she was all right.

"Don't worry, I will see you soon," she said. "Keep your chin up."

Lizzie slept badly again, she got up early and got Geoffrey to take her to the station as soon as he possibly could. She said her goodbyes, promised to see them all soon, and left, only glaring at her mother.

"Darling, I'm only thinking of your future," was her mother's parting shot at her daughter.

She kissed her father, aunt and uncle at the door. Geoffrey got her to the station, the first train left in about an hour's time. She stood waiting, trying to keep warm, still fuming at her mother. Geoffrey had said she will come round, cook had told him all about it, he hoped she didn't mind.

"No," she said, "it's nice to have someone on my side."

He had given her a kiss and a hug and left her standing on the station platform, the train pulled in on time and she made it back to London in good time. She was glad she was on her own because she wasn't much company today, she wanted to speak with Daisy.

The underground was busy and as soon as she saw the hospital ahead, she quickened her pace, she really wanted to break down and cry, she kept strong for a long as possible and would save that for Daisy and in the privacy of their room.

Lizzie walked quickly to the nurse's home raising her hand to Tom in his hut, she really hoped Daisy was back. Luckily, she saw no one coming up the stairs, standing by the door to their room, she took a deep breath and opened it. Daisy looked round at her friend with a big welcoming smile on her face and Lizzie took one look at her friend being friendly and loving, and she burst into tears. The floodgates opened. Daisy rushed over to her distressed friend, gently she took her in her arms, rubbing her back soothingly, asking her what on earth had happened?

First, she thought something had happened to Eddie, but then she thought no, it was probably Lizzie's mother being unreasonable. Waiting for Lizzie to settle, she led her to the bed and they sat down together. Taking her hands in hers, rubbing the knuckles gently, she spoke softly.

"Tell me in your own words what happened, only if you want to, mind."

Lizzie had stopped crying, wiping her nose with her hanky, she began, "My mother still wants me to go ahead and marry Charles." Not catching Daisy's eyes, looking at her hands. "I really thought she had changed, how wrong I was," she said in a distraught voice, 'a bit of me wanted to tell her about Chris, but I'm glad I just stopped myself, but she's adamant that the wedding will still go ahead.

"Eddie was brave, he told her about Glenda and that he wants to marry her. Again, she went mad at him, told him in no uncertain terms he has to marry a titled girl of her choosing. Well, you can imagine what Eddie's response was to that, he was fuming, he left the next morning early, back to his base."

Daisy really felt for her friend. "What are you going to do now?" she asked sincerely.

"Well, my aunt says not to worry, she is going to try and help."

"Well, there you are then, it's not all doom and gloom!" Encouraged Daisy.

"I so wanted to tell her, as it was all going really well up till that point. The first thing I need to do is telephone Eddie, as he left in such a state, and check he got back okay, see what he plans to do now. He can legally marry without permission next year, that's not too long," she said.

"Where was your father while this was going on?" Daisy queried.

"Nowhere to be seen, he is a coward when it comes to my mother." Lizzie wanted to get off the subject.

"How was your Christmas?" enquired Lizzie with affection.

"It was lovely, but not long enough and not eventful like yours," Daisy said.

"Well, we start in theatres tomorrow, at least we will be together, so we had better go through the textbook tonight to refresh our memory," offers Daisy opening the book.

"Let's get unpacked and get the room sorted, as the coats are thrown on the bed, and suitcases need unpacking, then see if Jenny and Claire are back. We can all study together," says Lizzie looking encouragingly at her friend."

Chapter 24

They worked together to tidy the room and Lizzie's mood had lifted by the time they had finished. She actually smiled when Daisy pulled out a dress from her case her mother had amended for Lizzie as a late present.

Knocking on their neighbours' door they heard that someone was in. Claire opened the door and she hugged both girls in a warm welcome. Jenny arrived back much later because of the trains being delayed near Brighton, due to the bomb damage. The south coast had been badly targeted by the Luftwaffe.

Lizzie, on hearing this, was still worried about her brother being based along the Kent coast.

The rest of the day was spent studying, Jenny was still petrified about maternity and hurting the little babies, saying she had never touched a baby. Nothing the girls could do would calm her nerves. The apprehension was rubbing off on Claire as well, she was getting worked up about casualty, hoping she would cope.

"Pull yourselves together, both of you," Daisy said.

"It's all right for you, you're with Lizzie," replied Jenny.

The girls spent the afternoon with their noses in nursing books, only stopping for tea. By the evening they were all feeling a bit more confident than they had earlier.

"Right, who's ready for a nightcap? Go get your glasses and we will have a drink to help us sleep." Lizzie poured larger measures to celebrate their second year and the girls all went to bed slightly merry.

Monday morning the girls were up at different times, Jenny and Claire had gone off early for their shift, carrying niggling headaches, both girls taking aspirin upon getting up. The other two were up a bit later as theatres didn't start till nine unless there was an emergency, mainly because the consultants never got there any earlier.

When you work in theatres, they were informed by Theatre Sister when they had gone to get their shifts, you are allowed to wear your own clothes to the hospital, as you have to change into a cotton green theatre dress. Both girls were told to eat well as it may help them not to faint and it's a long day standing on your feet underneath the bright lights and warmth. As neither had ever been in an operating room they couldn't tell if either of them would embarrass themselves, by fainting. Sister Robinson was waiting in reception to greet them, cheerfully saying, "Good morning girls, let's get you into your dresses, find your sizes and wellington Boots."

Once changed, Sister Robinson showed them around the operating room, it was very clean, and they could smell the carbolic. It was very basic with a long black table in the middle, it had a big round light that once on, shone very bright and warm, situated over it and at the head of the table. All the equipment that the anaesthetist used was in the room where the patient was asleep.

"We have a busy morning due to the constant bombing; the injuries people are sustaining are very severe." Mr Hughes was an orthopaedic doctor brought out of retirement and doing a few amputations this morning. "This afternoon, we have an appendix and gall bladder removal."

By nine the first patient, a young woman in her twenties was wheeled in on a trolley. With a help of a porter, they placed the patient on the operating table.

Daisy and Lizzie scrubbed their hands with soap until they were raw and then placed surgical gloves on their hands. The surgeon and his registrar had washed their hands and had gowned up and had face masks on.

Sister Robinson was already gowned up and was busy setting out the surgical instruments in order. The anaesthetist put a black mask on the patient's face and within a few moments she was fast asleep.

The surgeon took his knife and began, Daisy and Lizzie were watching with total interest taking it all in, asking questions as the surgeon worked. Sister Robinson answered them all, and it was getting very warm in the room with the big light beaming down on them.

Lizzie stood and felt herself getting dizzy with sweat dripping down her neck. She wanted to sit down but there was nowhere in this sterile environment, she was really trying to fight it. Daisy gave her friend a concerned sidewards look as she had gone very pale, but Lizzie didn't acknowledge her. It was getting warmer and warmer, and with the smells, and there was plenty of blood, before she knew it she'd blacked out and went down on the floor with a bang.

Luckily avoiding anything. Lizzie soon came around with Daisy taking care of her.

Sister Robinson said in a soft calm voice, "Don't worry, it happens all the time, you'll get used to it."

Lizzie felt so embarrassed! Sister Robinson gave her cooling drink of water, and told them when Lizzie was recovered enough, they could wash down the operating room ready for the next patient. She soon felt better and was even pleased as she reacted better to the next operation. Following lunch, the next two cases went fine.

By Late afternoon, all cleaning finished, the two women were released by Sister Robinson who said they had done well for their first day, as they headed for the exit. They both left with big smiles on their faces, sore hands from the disinfectant and headed back to the nurse's home, and meeting up with the other two girls for supper.

They all exchanged notes on how their days had gone. Lizzie told them that she had fainted, and the others couldn't help but laugh at their friend's misfortune. Jenny had helped in one baby delivery, which had taken all shift. When the baby had finally arrived, it was a little girl. Claire had been busy, a bus had hit a crater in the road caused by a bomb and had turned over on its side, there many injuries, ranging from small cuts and bruises, severe cuts that needed stitches, to broken arms and legs. Claire had been run ragged, but she had really enjoyed it.

It sounded like all four nurses had been thrown into the deep end, they blamed it on the war, but all had surpassed themselves. Sitting on Lizzie and Daisy's beds, none of the girls were drinking tonight as they were still recovering from last night. There was relief at feeling normal and not nervous as they were this time last night.

At least they had an understanding of what to expect from now on, and all four nurses felt the weeks would go by very quickly.

Lizzie, excused herself, put on her winter coat and scarf, and she made her way out into the bitterly cold December night. It was dark and the moon sat large in the night sky, it was a bomber's moon as the

Londoners called it. A chill went through her body, the Luftwaffe would be coming tonight for sure, it made her hurry along to the telephone box.

The operator put the call through to her brother's base, and she waited patiently for him to come to the phone. She heard Eddie's voice, it never sounded so good.

"Hello, sis," he said jovially, "how are you?"

Then he heard the sobs, Lizzie was trying not to cry but a loose tear trickled down her face, she brushed it away with her gloved hand as she explained what their mother had said once Eddie had gone.

He couldn't understand how their mother could be so heartless and cold. She was acting like it was a business arrangement rather than a romantic marriage proposal.

Lizzie was adamant she was never marrying Charles. Eddie was actually okay with what their mother had said in the heat of the moment, he said, "that he would indeed be twenty-one in March and then could get married if he chose too."

He knew the consequences if he did, he would be cut out of the will and disinherited, but he really did love Glenda, she was his world and if he survived the war, could get work flying.

Then she told him about what Aunt Lynn had said, that she would help to sort out their mother and not worry.

"What will she do?" he asked, his interest piqued.

"I really don't know," said his sister truthfully, "but I hope whatever she does works." Crossing her fingers.

They spoke for a few minutes more and then were told the call had to end, they said their goodbyes and in the last breath she told her brother to stay safe. On replacing the receiver, she wrapped up warm and headed out into the cool air back to the warmth of her room.

Walking back, it gave her a chance to think, would her brother really go ahead and get married without permission? Deep in thought for a moment, she believed he would, the war was changing people, changing their views, values and what was important to them as life was so precious.

Back in the room, she was glad that Jenny and Claire had gone to bed, she discarded her coat, hung it on the hook and sat down on her bed.

She explained it all to Daisy, that her brother was okay, and he would

194

wait and see what their aunt had planned and wouldn't do anything hasty, at which she was grateful. Both girls were mentally exhausted and so they decided to have a hot bath and then get an early night, hopefully with no bombers, Lizzie wasn't so sure.

The minute the girls were back in the room, the air raid siren went off. Getting quickly dressed in warm clothes, wrapping up in warm coats and not forgetting gasmasks and tin hats, they knocked for the others and made their way to the basement — probably for the duration of the night.

All the other off duty student nurses made their way in an orderly manner, it was becoming a regular routine but not one they relished, the basement was cold, damp and very dark as it was barely lit. Once settled everyone could hear in the distance bombs dropping all around them, some even getting too near the hospital for everyone's liking.

"They must be attacking the docks again," said Daisy with her voice quivering slightly.

They could hear British guns, which were placed in the park, firing back at the bombers. All through the night the bombs and incendiary devices kept raining down around them, keeping the girls awake. The walls shook, some brick dust making them cough and their mouths dry, all four could do with a drink of water. The all-clear sounded at five o'clock and all four trudged wearily up to their rooms to get changed. Lizzie and Daisy knew they would be working flat out in theatres all day, so did the other two, especially Claire in the casualty department, all dealing with the aftermath of the night's attacks.

Jenny hoped with all her heart, wishing that the babies would be born in a safer, happier time, not during a war that could go on for years.

Chapter 25

The day did go undeniably very fast. By the time Daisy and Lizzie had returned to their room, stopping off in the dining hall for tea, they had collapsed on their beds.

"I could sleep for a week" said a tired sounding Lizzie, she was standing by the open window in the dark, smoking a cigarette. Daisy agreed, they had a quick strip wash in the bathrooms, trying to wash the smell of bleach from their skin and then waited in their room for the others. Both hoped and prayed that the bombers would not return tonight, as they were so fatigued, little did they know that in a few hours they would be back. The attack began about nine and the siren commenced wailing, the girls repeated the routine from the previous night, making the basement their bed for another night. Sitting in the hard deckchairs they tried to sleep or doze as much as they could. The bombs kept falling, some extremely close, everyone hoped that the hospital was safe.

Both girls had received letters from their families and were reading them during the night. Daisy's parents and siblings were all right and Luton was still being bombed, as was the rest of Britain. Lizzie's parents were both fine, her mother had not relented and was still on about the engagement and wedding. Lizzie glanced over that part, reading the rest, her father was good and was working with the doctors and nurses, really enjoying it, and more importantly getting fulfilment from it.

Her brother had written a brief note, saying he was all right and was coming up to the city at the weekend and wanted her to meet Glenda as he had some leave.

The girls decided to reply to the letters that evening, hopefully without any interruption. In the morning the girls, once the all-clear sounded, went up to their room and got ready to go onto their shift. First, they stopped in the dining hall for breakfast and caught up with the latest update of bomb destruction in the area, they were all shocked at the actual damage they saw on their way. Walking into the hospital they could smell the cordite in the air and saw the destruction for themselves, it was everywhere, bomb damage and ruins where buildings once stood. The hospital was still standing but had slight damage, the windows were cracked even with the anti-blast tape on them and some of them would need replacing but nothing too serious.

Again, the day flew by, but it was very tiring and wearing, people were getting agitated and had short tempers, due to the extreme tiredness they were experiencing, they were wondering how long their bodies could take this lack of sleep. Following tea, the girls wanted to relax and reply to their letters, again they prayed that the bombers would be quiet tonight. Yet again the Luftwaffe came, the two girls managed to write their letters and left them in their room ready to post when they had a chance to get to the post box. On a rare day off, one or if more if they were off the same time, would go shopping. The streets were full of craters, where shops and houses once would have stood, now there were just ruins.

It was January 1941 and the people of London were all tired and fed up but they had an inner fighting spirit to keep on going even when times were hard. Daisy noticed the day she had gone shopping, that the docks were still on fire, the fires blazing into the sky. The London Fire Brigade were struggling to put the fires out, hose pipes everywhere. The firemen looked weary, but Daisy was impressed how they kept on going, some of the buildings were dangerous so they had to be bulldozed for people's safety.

On Saturday night, Lizzie got the bus and travelled to Leicester Square to meet her brother and to finally meet Glenda, she couldn't wait, she was excited, Lizzie was early and stood wrapping her coat tighter to her, protecting herself from the bitter cold January evening. So far, she had been lucky, no sirens had gone off yet, she felt a hand on her arm and her name being called, she turned and saw her brother with a pretty young woman in RAF uniform wearing their greatcoats over their uniforms.

Eddie made the introductions and both women shook hands. They all agreed they wanted to get out of the cold, so they all headed to the local Lyon's corner house and got a hot cup of tea. It was really busy when they entered but they were lucky and found an empty table. A waitress soon came, took their order and left them alone to talk.

Eddie began by saying his sister looked tired, she laughed and said, "So does half of London." All three laughed.

Lizzie asked Glenda, "Where do you come from?"

"Barnstable, in Devon," she replied, she loved growing up living by the sea.

The two women kept talking, each getting to know each other better, Eddie joined in when he had a comment to make. The food and tea came and they tucked in, it was really tasty. Lizzie wanted to know how her brother was? She sat back and took a good look at him, studying him intently, he looked better than the last time she had seen him, he seemed happy and had lost the haunted look.

Eddie seemed nervous all of a sudden, as if he had something on his mind, his sister said bluntly, "Spit it out."

Eddie took a deep breath and blurted it straight out, "We are getting married as soon as we can."

Lizzie was shocked but not surprised, looking at her brother and his bride to be she said, "Congratulations. The only one problem is Mother!"

Turning and talking to Glenda, "Has he told you who we are?"

"Yes," Glenda replied, "a few weeks ago.

"He explained everything, and you still want to marry him? It must be love, or you're mad to join our family," Lizzie said laughing.

The mood was light. "I think if you are serious then you need to speak with Aunt Lynn and get her advice and help, as she is on our side and she may soften the blow when you tell Mother."

"I was going to her," her brother replied.

"When is the date?"

"We haven't decided, I was waiting to get Lynn on our side to help."

"Give me plenty of notice and I will get the time off to come," she said.

"May I see the ring"? asked an excited Lizzie. Glenda offered her left hand and rested it on the table. Lizzie held her fingers, taking in the beautiful solitaire diamond ring which sparkled in the light. Her brother had chosen well. "Welcome to the family" said Lizzie smiling at her future sister -in -law. Lizzie couldn't help the slight pang of jealousy towards her brother and his fiancée, how she wished it was Chris and herself announcing their engagement, one day she hoped.

By nine she was ready to head back to the hospital as she was very tired from lack of sleep.

With a warning, "Don't leave it too long to speak with Aunt Lynn and let me know the outcome." She put her coat on to brace herself for going out into the cold and picked up her gas mask case, putting it on her shoulder with her handbag. She kissed both of them goodbye and hugged them both tightly. "Stay safe," she said, and headed out into the night.

Still she was lucky, no planes so far and she took the tube back to Whitechapel. Her thoughts were about her brother and his plans to get married. Glenda was nice and she wished Eddie well, but the trouble was their mother and how she would react to the news. Aunt Lynn had better come up with a plan and quick she sighed.

Eight weeks flew by, both girls had enjoyed theatres after that first mishap with Lizzie fainting on the first day. Sister Robinson had been pleased with their progress, and work rate and was sorry to see them both move on, but they were both excited to be going to the casualty department.

Claire had really enjoyed her time and she said that they would to, it was busy, and hard work! Nevertheless, very rewarding. Both girls observed their friend with fondness and agreed with her comments.

Claire was going to maternity and Jenny to theatres. "You will be fine with Sister Robinson, she is very fair, and will teach you a lot."

Jenny had done surprisingly really well in maternity and had excelled herself more than she thought she would. After a panicky beginning Jenny had settled, and had enjoyed maternity enormously, Sister McKenna had been exceptionally helpful, and kind with her nervous student. Seeing a baby born was moving, you couldn't help falling in love with it and handing it over to its mother was very gratifying. There were some upsetting moments, when the baby you had delivered was in fact dead, and you had the distraught mother crying when her baby was taken away.

It was your job to comfort her and let her grieve in peace. On one occasion the baby had been born quickly, the head was soon engaged and very soon the baby was born, in a hurry to meet its mother. Gazing at her friend fondly, she knew that Claire would be fine in maternity and would settle quickly.

There was no stopping for school as the hospital was low on nurses and needed new ones as soon as possible. So they would be going straight into their next rotation.

Monday morning found the two girls arriving at the entrance of the casualty department, they were met by a severe looking Sister Kinley.

"Well, what do we have here?" Were the first words she spoke.

Sister Kinley was tall, very thin and had a beak nose which was long, her blue uniform hung off her. The two student nurses regarded their peer with fascination, trying not to look at the nose, at the same time trying to work out the tall Sister. They introduced themselves, Daisy going first, followed by Lizzie. Apparently, everyone knew who Lizzie was as her title had quickly gotten around the hospital.

Once introductions were made, the two nervous-looking student nurses were shown around the department by Sister. Out the front was a large room with benches in it, this is where people sat waiting to be called to see the doctor, who today was Doctor Gregg, helped by Staff Nurse Perkins. Both Nurses found the locker room, put on their cuffs and clean white aprons and set to work helping to clear the room. They worked mechanically and only stopped when told to.

A few ambulances had arrived during the morning, bringing the injured and dead. The ambulance drivers were friendly, some of them even being women. The young girls admired them massively, especially what they saw and had to deal with on a daily basis.

The morning had gone swiftly, Daisy and Lizzie had only stopped for a break once when the room was nearly empty, then Sister had told them to hurry to lunch and be back in thirty minutes, just enough time to eat hurriedly. The girls got to the dining hall, collected their food and sat down, then they took a breath.

"What a morning!" They both said in unison.

"I thought the ward was busy, but this is a different kind of busy, and you never know what is going to arrive," Daisy said.

Rapidly finishing their food and having a quick drink of water, the two girls headed back to the casualty department and the afternoon. It soared by; an ambulance had arrived bringing four casualties, who had been pulled out of a building alive. The team got working and the victims were dispensed to the right department or ward. Two went to the ward, to await theatre, another went straight to theatre as they could not wait and the last, after being treated, could go home.

The rest of the shift went on satisfactorily, especially for the first day, by five the two student nurses where dead on their feet, both physically and mentally, they slowly made their way to the nurse's home, only stopping at the dining hall for tea.

Jenny and Claire were already seated in the hall, tucking into their food as the others found them and came over. The two girls sat down and ate their food in silence. Once finished, they spoke to their colleagues about their day. All four had a busy day, if not an excellent day, all had learnt a lot and were looking forward to going back which was always a good sign. Jenny had liked Sister Robinson as soon as she had met her, and unlike Lizzie, hadn't fainted.

Lizzie gazed at her and said, "Well, there is a first time for everything."

Laughing, the others joined in, they wouldn't let her forget it, but she didn't mind one bit. Claire had enjoyed maternity, helping to deliver a healthy little boy nine pounds six ounces. She had a big grin on her face for the rest of the evening and Sister McKenna had been pleased with her new student. They cleared away their plates putting the trays on the rack provided and headed to their room, as Lizzie was desperate for a cigarette. Once in the darkened room, she opened the window and lit up, took a puff and blew the smoke out of the window into the February night air.

Jenny soon joined her, and both were standing there in the dark, it was quite a picture with just the tip of the cigarettes for light. Once satisfied, they closed the window, pulled the blackout blind back in place and turned the light on.

"I hope the bombers don't come tonight?" said Jenny in an anxious voice.

All three agreed in earnest and put the worry to one side, heading for early baths as they hoped the hot water would ease the pain in their feet, legs and give them a chance to relax after a hectic day. Once all settled in their pyjamas, they congregated back in Lizzie and Daisy's room, where they had a nightcap. By seven-thirty, the thing they dreaded the most happened, the siren went off making a racket in the quiet night sky, you wouldn't believe that in a few minutes the peace would be shattered by the enemy planes flying over.

They got ready, they were already dressed, just in case, Jenny and

Claire went back to their room to get their winter coats to combat the cold while they were down in the basement and to pick up their gas masks and tin hats, automatically, coming out of the door, they met the others, and swiftly made their way to the basement for another night of discomfort and trepidation.

By early morning the all-clear sounded, it was getting light, but you could smell the aftermath of all the bombs being dropped, the docks had taken a pounding again. The girls didn't have time to look outside, beyond the hospital at the destruction, as they made their way back up to the nurse's home to get ready for work. Lizzie was the only one on a late shift, she could easily go back to bed to get a few hours' sleep, but she knew her conscience wouldn't let her. The casualty department would be busy, so she like the others got ready into their uniforms and quickly, forfeiting breakfast, made their way into the main block. The ambulances were arriving one after the other, you could hear the bells ringing in the distance.

Lizzie and Daisy got straight to work helping the doctors and nurses already there, trying to patch up the walking wounded and attending to the more serious in a professional manner. The morning passed in a blur, one after another the people were patched up and either sent home, if they were lucky, and if unlucky, then patients were kept in if more severe, hospital beds were scarce so only the severe were admitted. Both girls managed to have a quick break, grabbing something to eat hurriedly as they were both starving, and Sister Kinley had only given them twenty minutes before heading back to carry on.

By late afternoon the casualty department was back to being nearly empty, the girls were scrubbing down the benches and tables that had been used earlier with carbolic soap, wiping the dried blood and excrement away, ready for the next time. Sister Kinley told them to get cleaned up and make sure to put clean aprons on as they were dirty.

Lizzie was allowed to have a break before continuing her shift into the evening and Daisy was sent home for the evening. She felt guilty leaving Lizzie but at least one needed to rest. The bombing was also happening during the day as well now, Hitler and the German Luftwaffe was coming onto Britain, full on, and on many occasions the patients who could, were taken down to the basement of the hospital while the bombs rained down all around them.

The weather had improved by the beginning of March, the nights were getting longer, but the bombs were still being dropped day and night, it was relentless. London was looking tired and weary; the people of Britain were worn out, but they had an inner strength to keep fighting, to win this war. All around the buildings and shops were badly damaged or completely destroyed, it would take years to repair or rebuild.

The hospital had been hit but not so badly that it would have to close. Lizzie and Daisy had been told, because of the amount of injured people still being treated on a daily basis they would have to stay in the casualty department longer than normal. Neither girl minded, but they were looking forward to doing maternity, when the time was right.

Daisy was to go onto nights for a week starting tonight as another student nurse had gone down with the flu. She tried to catch a few hours' sleep during her afternoon off, she had managed about two hours before getting up and laid reading a book on her bed for another hour.

Lizzie came off shift at five, got herself changed and both girls headed down to the dining hall for tea, they didn't bother to knock for Jenny and Claire as they were on late shift today. While heading down the stairs Lizzie was carping that her feet were sore from standing all day.

"I'm going to get varicose veins!" she said moaning, trying to get a look at them as they descended the stairs.

Both women devoured their food quickly as Lizzie wanted a cigarette. The days were warmer, and it was only raining slightly. They stood milling around outside while she had her cigarette, they looked across at where the docks were situated, they were still burning, the fires lighting up the sky.

Once her craving had been satisfied, and both were only a tad damp, they proceeded to head back to their room. It was nice to get back inside, the air outside was rank with the smell of burning. Back in the room, they were both lounging on their beds, talking about the day they both had, a bit later Daisy went and had a bath, she wanted to relax, and she thought the warm water would help calm her nerves as she felt nervous going onto her first night shift.

Due to the bombing, she didn't know what to expect during the night and so she came back to their room, hung her dressing gown on the back of the door, dried her hair with a towel and changed into her uniform, making sure her hair was in a tidy bun held by Kirby clips.

Once in her uniform it always gave her an air off reassurance that she didn't feel on the inside. She prayed that it would be a quiet night, because they usually only had a small team of doctors and nurses on duty during the night, but due to it being war time that had completely changed.

Chapter 26

At six forty-five she said "goodnight" to her roommate, who sat reading a book. Lizzie put the book down, jumped up off the bed and hugged her friend tightly, wishing her well for the night. "See you in the morning, stay safe," they both said. With that, she opened their room door by the handle and ran down the stairs, said "goodnight" to Home Sister who passed her going up the stairs.

On crossing over the grounds, avoiding the massive hole in the ground caused by a stray bomb that luckily hadn't gone off, the bomb disposal team had come and cordoned off the site while they dealt with the bomb. On her way to the main building, she noticed it had stopped raining and she spotted other nurses all going in the same direction, they must be all going onto nights she thought.

Making her way along the long corridors towards the casualty department, she passed a lot of military people heading in different directions around the hospital, they must be visiting she assumed. Stopping at the entrance she took one look around and, on entering, she proceeded to the locker room, put the cuffs and clean apron on, which were in her locker, taking her time to look over her appearance in the mirror and then she took a deep breath, pulling the door open.

What she found on the other side was a waiting room half full. Sister Kinley was dealing with a poorly child and trying to calm the mother, Staff Nurse Albone had just come on shift, like Daisy, and was to be in charge under Night Sister. Night Sister, once happy the department was running smoothly, spoke to Staff Nurse Albone saying only call her if it was an emergency, with that she disappeared into Sister's warm and cosy office.

The Staff Nurse stood looking back at the disappearing Night Sister. "Well, would you believe that!" she mumbled under her breath.

Turning back to Daisy and another nurse, who was a third year, and who had arrived just in time to witness the exchange between the two members of qualified staff.

"Right," came the assertive tone of Staff Nurse Albone. "Let's get cracking."

She gave out her orders and both girls got to work at a quick pace. Another Staff Nurse would be on later, she would be on duty at nine, as she had only gone home late afternoon to sleep.

Daisy was placed in the waiting room and her first patient was an elderly gentleman who had a gash on his head from falling down on an uneven pavement. She led him into a room with a couch, making sure he was safe, she went off to find the on-call doctor. Doctor Carmichael was in his fifties and was very caring, she took him to her patient. Once the examination was over; the patient luckily didn't need stiches and Daisy only had to bandage his head. Once he was patched up, she was able to discharge him home before the bombs began to fall.

It was a thick cloudy night, so fortunately the bombers wouldn't be coming. Working in an orderly manner they cleared the waiting room by midnight, and Daisy was allowed to go for her break. The dining hall was quiet, and there was not much to eat, just tea and toast. Once she finished, she sat writing her letter home to her parents. She had it written by the time her break was finished, she had asked if they were okay and staying safe? And that her brothers and sister were doing all right? She would be home when they were allowed annual leave, but she wasn't sure when that would be. She asked about Bobby and had they heard from him, she knew Mary would have, and if they had, was he okay? Daisy sat back in her chair, a wave of tiredness came over her, and she had to fight to keep her eyes open, her mind turned to Dr Reynolds and where was he, she hoped he was safe.

It was good to walk back through the deserted corridors, the letter was placed in her locker till the morning, when it could be posted before she went to bed. The rest of the night went quickly, they had a lady brought in, mid-labour and she was rushed off to the maternity ward. Daisy stopped and spoke with the girls who drove the ambulance and helped them clear up before they got called out again. By seven, the early shift arrived, and Daisy and the rest of the night shift was dismissed, she slowly walked her tired body to the dining hall for a cooked breakfast, the greasy egg was just what she needed before bed. Once finished she made her way to the nurse's home and a comfy bed, stopping at the post box to post her letter. On entering her room, she crept in as Lizzie was still asleep as she was on a late shift. Normally the nurses on nights would be put on a floor to themselves but because of the war it was changed. Daisy got changed as quietly as she could, hanging her uniform up, she got into her pyjamas and got into bed. Lizzie had stirred, noticed her friend was back and wished her well.

"See you tomorrow," she said.

Daisy said "goodnight" back and as soon as her head touched that pillow, she was gone.

Lizzie woke up just after nine, got herself dressed quietly not waking her friend and went for breakfast, making sure she closed the door slowly. As she was walking back from the main block, she thought she had better write to her parents, especially her mother as they have left on bad terms, she would also write to her brother. A letter had arrived a week ago from Charles and she had been deliberately putting off to reply. With Daisy fast asleep and she didn't want to go shopping, it was the right time to reply to her letters. Sitting down at the desk they shared, she pulled out her sheets of paper and found a pen and began.

Firstly, she wrote to her parents, she began by quickly re-reading her parents' letter. Her mother had written that she was sad that she had left on bad terms, and she was told by her mother in no uncertain terms that she still had to marry Charles as soon as her training was over. Lizzie still hoped that the war would keep Charles away for a very long time and give her aunt enough time to help her. Lizzie put her mother's letter to one side and so began her letter. She wrote that she was fine, and her training was still going very well. She hoped that they were both keeping well? She would try and get home when she next had leave. Lizzie asked when the wedding of Geoffrey and Edna was taking place. She would try and get home to attend as she thought the world of both of them. Lizzie didn't mention Charles at all, as she wanted to keep the letter short and to the point, she signed off Elizabeth and would now wait for a reply.

Her brothers' letter was totally different, she first asked how he was? and how was Glenda? Next, she asked when they were next free to meet up again in London, and finally she mentioned that her mother hadn't changed her mind and that she had to still marry Charles, so she didn't think she would change her mind about her brother marrying Glenda.

Her final letter was to Chris, the Air mail letter had arrived two days ago, and it said he was all right, watching over his men, keeping them safe. She re-read it and she fell more in love with this caring man and knew that her future lay with Chris, if he would have her. He couldn't say much more because of the censors blacking out what you couldn't say but he said he cared for her. She answered she was well, and her training was keeping her busy. Loving her job more with every day that passed, and she hoped she would see him soon, as she missed him dreadfully and signed off 'affectionately yours, Lizzie'.

Lizzie sealed the three letters, placed stamps on them and looked at Charles' letter, it was very short, and it basically said that he was thinking of her and couldn't wait to get back to Britain, to meet up. She knew what that meant, a hotel room and sex, but that was definitely not going to happen as long as she had breath in her body.

Again, she got a sheet of paper and began, asking was he well, and his parents too? She really didn't know what else to write because she wasn't going to mention the hotel room. Oh! how she wished he would be kept abroad for as long as possible, crossing her fingers. She sealed up the envelope and picked up the four letters and grabbed her coat. Even though it was March it was still very cold. Keeping quiet she opened the door and closed it behind her, she ran down the stairs to the nearest post box and pushed them into the slit. Once done she looked at the time, she had an hour till she needed to get ready, so she decided to pop to the shops, even though there was barely anything in them to buy.

Lizzie bought what she needed and could get, with her shopping placed in her bag she made her way back to her room, keeping as quiet as she could, she got changed, feeling for her things in the dark. Before she left, she whispered to her sleeping friend, see you tomorrow. With that, she headed for the door and lunch in the dining hall. Instead of going back to the room, she made her way to the casualty department and the locker room, where she finished getting ready by putting her hair up into a tight bun. It would be the one day that she hadn't done it tight, and a hair would stray, and Matron would see her, but since Dunkirk she had been kept busy and had other priorities. Lizzie looked at herself in the mirror, happy with what she saw, made her way into the department and her shift. As it was a cloudy, damp day, again no bombs had been dropped for the second day in a row, but everyone knew the bombers would be back once they had a clear sky.

Daisy had slept well; she had been tired from the night before having very little sleep. Once up and washed, she made her bed and lay on it reading a book. She looked at the time, it was five, so she finished her page, and got ready to head to the dining hall for tea, she was so hungry that her tummy rumbled. In the dining hall she had a chance to catch up with her friend. Jenny was in there having her tea, having just finished her shift in theatres.

"How was it today?" asked Daisy.

"Fine, very busy but at least we have a couple of days rest from the Luftwaffe," she replied.

They sat talking for a while until Daisy said she needed to head back to her room to get ready, she stopped outside with Jenny, while she lit up a cigarette and puffed away on it. When finished, the two friends made their way to the nurse's home, the big crater had been filled in once the bomb had been sorted out and taken away.

Once at Daisy's door they said their goodbyes, and Daisy unlocked her door and twisted the handle to open it, once inside she felt a bit lonely, she missed Lizzie. Daisy gave herself a stiff talking to, she told herself to get it together, she would see Lizzie swapping over shifts. Once in her uniform, she sat on her bed, tied up her shoes, straightened her uniform, picked up her coat and gas mask.

Checking the time on her fob watch she saw it was time to get to work, running down the stairs she raced across to the main block. Daisy made it just in time, she got herself ready and out she went. She just had time to speak to Lizzie who was going off shift, they both hoped that they had a good night, and could have more time to chat tomorrow afternoon when Daisy had woken up.

Watching Lizzie gather her belongings and head off, Daisy was called to the waiting room, where Staff Nurse Albone was already with a patient who was brought in by the auxiliary ambulance crew and needed help. The early evening went off fine but by nine the siren went off, Night Sister appeared and told them to get as many patients as they could to the basement, then come back as they would be busy. They worked quietly and quickly, once the patients who could get to the basement were safely installed, they prepared the department for casualties and then they waited in silence.

Daisy looked around at the others, who all looked scared like her, she felt physically sick, and she was shaking slightly but she tried not to show it. They could hear the bombers overhead, and then the bombs whistling down, exploding when hitting their target. Daisy was praying that they missed the hospital and for her family at this time, for what seemed like forever the ambulances could be heard in the distance starting to bring the injured and dead. Daisy nervously stood, saying a quiet prayer with Staff Nurse Albone.

She looked at her tense student. "You will be fine," she said, squeezing her shoulder.

Daisy looked at her superior, giving a weak smile, unable to speak through fear, as the first ambulance arrived at the door. The air around them was full of dense smoke and soot, and Daisy looked over to where the docks were situated and buildings were on fire, the flames raging high in the night sky, which left a redness. A fire engine went speeding past, bells blaring, towards the fires, as the nurses got to work ushering the first of the wounded into the casualty department, giving their attention to the most serious first.

Within the first hour, it was chaotic, nurses and doctors running back and forward as the injured were being treated and the porters were wheeling the ones already treated out to the correct ward or department. The dead were sent to the mortuary, and their families could deal with the formalities, paperwork the next day. Some of the less severe casualties could be patched up and sent home.

Matron had arrived, as she did every night, and was organising her staff with military precision, keeping the department running smoothly like a well-oiled clog and morale high. As the bombs were falling nearby, the walls of the hospital were shaking and Daisy just kept working, even though she was very scared, she had never prayed so much in all her life.

By five in the morning, it had begun to quieten down, the enemy bombers had headed back across the channel, the all-clear sounded. Matron sensing her staff were dead on their feet, sent her tired and worn-out staff to have a fifteen-minute break, two at a time. Daisy hadn't stopped and her feet ached terribly, her mouth was parched, and she was dying for a drink. Once she got to the dining hall with another student nurse, the kitchen staff had laid on tea and coffee, and plenty of toast. Daisy took the coffee which was Camp, this tasted like chicory, which she wasn't over-keen on but it would keep her awake till she went off, and she picked up her toast, sat down in the nearest chair, taking a sip of the hot liquid, tasting the sugar, her shoulders dropped in relief that she had survived the night.

It gave her time to consider the sights she had just witnessed, at her young age. Once full from eating and her thirst satisfied, she took a look at herself. She did look a state, she hadn't even stopped and taken off her apron she was that tired, if Matron had caught her, she would have pulled her up, even given her an official warning.

Walking back to the casualty department, she stopped in the nearest toilet and tidied herself up, as best she could, looking in the mirror. What she saw glancing back was a visibly tired and unkempt young nurse, she hoped Matron was too busy to notice, because as soon as she could, she dived unseen into the locker room and quickly changed her apron, luckily, she kept a spare in the locker, she would need to put the dirty one into the laundry for washing.

Good job she had, as Matron, as luck would have it, walked past as she came out the door. Daisy pulled back her shoulders, held her head high and walked past her.

Halfway down the corridor she believed she had gotten away with it, but then she heard, "Oh, Student Nurse Peters!" She turned to face the stern woman. "Next time remember to change your dirty apron prior to going to break, remember the rules of hygiene and we have standards here at The London, I will overlook it tonight, due to the unusual circumstances we are facing. Well done for tonight! You handled yourself very well, soon it will be time to go off and do try to get some sleep, you have earned it." With that she was gone.

The young student nurse stood, looking bewildered, peering back as the mature woman walked away. Had she actually just praised her?

"Thank you, Matron," was her modest reply, Matron had already gone. She found Staff Nurse Albone in the now nearly empty waiting room.

"Let's get the room tidied up, and then the early staff will be here." Looking down at her fob watch on her now dirty uniform. "And we can get off to bed."

The last few patients were dealt with swiftly, and by the time they had finished, the early staff were ready for hand-over. Staff Nurse Albone took the hand-over to her colleagues who looked like they were all sleep-deprived themselves.

Lizzie caught up with her friend before she left, taking a look at her, she asked compassionately. "How, was it?"

Daisy answered truthfully. "It was bad and very scary, did you get down to the basement?" she asked Lizzie.

"Yes," replied a very weary Lizzie.

Seeing her friend was worn out they said their goodbyes. "See you later." Lizzie squeezed her friend's hand and they went in different directions, one into the waiting room to commence her shift and the other to the nurse's home and a comfy bed and long overdue sleep.

Daisy collected her cape and gas mask from the locker room, she still had her tin hat on her head and made her way along the now familiar corridors to the nurse's home, only stopping to talk to some of the other nurses from her set. Picking up her mail from the pigeon hole, she tucked her two letters into her cape pocket, ready to read later once she'd had some sleep. Climbing the stairs to her room felt like climbing a mountain this morning, heavier than normal. Both legs ached and she really wanted a bath to wash the grime off her, then she hoped she would at least feel human again.

Leaving the bath to run, she went into her room and collected her wash things, pyjamas and dressing gown. Once sitting in the warm water, she let her tired mind wander back to the night before. It had been one of the worst nights of bombing and the injuries and destruction she had witnessed would leave a lasting impression on her. Her legs began to feel better by soaking them. After a while the water was getting cold, so she got out and dried off quickly. Walking back to her room she couldn't wait to get into bed, hanging her dressing gown behind the door, walking over to her bed, climbing in between the clean sheets, her head lightly touched the soft pillow and soon she went into a deep sleep, hoping no bombs would be dropped during this day.

The day did pass with no interruptions, and Daisy slept very well, only waking late afternoon when Lizzie entered the room marking the end of her shift. Rushing off to use the toilet, she left her roommate to get changed out of her uniform.

Returning, Daisy sat on her bed and listened to Lizzie tell her about her day. More casualties had been brought in throughout the day, Jenny had been kept busy in theatres, and Lizzie's day had gone exceptional fast, and both the girls agreed they had learnt so much these last few days, more than any textbook would teach them.

Daisy changed into a clean uniform that she had picked up from the laundry, collecting a couple of clean aprons and got ready to go to work. Looking over at her desk she saw her unopened letters and would read them later before she went. Both women walked to the dining hall, where they had tea, cheese on toast, and sat chatting for a while. Daisy was enjoying night duty but was ready to get back to normal. Lizzie had picked up her mail on the way up to their room following her shift. She would read them while Daisy was reading hers. She had one from Christopher which she was really looking forward to reading on her own, the other from her parents, not so. She recognised her brother's handwriting, which made her smile and finally one from Charles, at least he wrote, she thought, but it left an uneasiness, and she would leave that to last.

Daisy on getting back to their room, made her bed and then sat down to read her letters. Ripping the first envelope open, she took out the letter and read through it, her parents were fine, only slight damage to the house so far. Her brothers were doing all right, Mark's growing and Mum's worried she should have sent him away to the country, her parents had decided against it at the beginning of the war. George was working hard, and one morning had gone to the recruitment office and, against his parents' wishes, had joined up, both her parents were furious, and her mother had cried for days. Her father had wanted to go down to the recruiting office to argue that his son was too young, but it would be to no avail as it was the law, George officially was now in the navy.

"He's joining the navy!" Daisy said in a shocked voice, she had to re-read the letter twice. "He is too young!" She looked over to Lizzie.

Lizzie looked back over, seeing the concerned look on her friend's face. "He is eighteen now?" queried Lizzie.

"Yes," replied Daisy.

Lizzie asked if Daisy was all right?

"Yes, I will be, but I'm in shock at the moment," she said, glancing down at the letter. "My brother George has enlisted in the navy," she said again to confirm.

"I will write to my parents as soon as I can." She carried on reading.

Lizzie didn't say anything else, she just let her friend read on.

Mary was doing really well, missing Bobby, they were officially going out together now, she knew in her heart this would happen, so it wasn't a big surprise, it still hurt slightly but she was pleased for them both, if they were happy, she thought. Maybe her sister wouldn't be so nasty to her when she came home next? She thought.

Her mind drifted to Dr Reynolds and again was he all right and, more importantly, where was he? She finished her parents' letter still in shock, Daisy was now worried for her brother who would soon be going off to war. Mary's letter basically told her about Bobby and that she was happy with him and as soon as they could, they would get married, when he was next on leave. Picking up the read letters, Daisy, left them in a neat pile on the desk, got her cape from behind the door to put on, ready for her night shift, three down two to go then back on days she thought.

Saying goodnight to her friend and telling Lizzie not to worry about her, she headed out the door, and towards another uncertain night. Lizzie watched the back of her friend as she closed the room's door, turning to her bed she sat down and pulled her letters out leaving the blue and red striped one till last. She wondered what was in store for her. First, she opened her parents' letter, it was full of the usual stuff, hoping she was staying safe, and they were both well, and working hard at their home, helping to tend to the injured. Her mother was helping cook, down in the kitchen, and they were becoming firm friends, according to her mother, she couldn't believe what she was reading, her snobby mother, cooking and being nice to Edna! Her Mother mentioned the wedding, it was going to be held at the hall on a Saturday in August. Lizzie checked her calendar, and promised to herself she would do all she could to attend. Then she got to the part she was dreading, Charles. Her mother kept on about the engagement and asked had she heard from her fiancé, she deliberately ignored them questions and continued reading, finally her mother asked when she would be home again.

Folding the letter, Lizzie sat back, and she wondered could her ice queen mother, actually be changing. She really wanted to believe it with all her heart, but something kept holding her back, only if she saw it face to face, then it could be true. If her mother had changed, then maybe she could change her mind about Charles and accept that Lizzie wanted to be with Christopher. Lizzie looked at the air mail letter sitting on the bed unopened, she couldn't believe that you could love someone so much, and know nothing really about them. She hated this blasted war, but then felt remorse for saying it, thinking of all the young men fighting across the world for peace.

Next, she picked up the letter from her brother, Eddie, he was doing all right, now the Luftwaffe had turned its attention to the cities, he and Glenda would be up in London in a few weeks and promised to meet up. They were doing well and planning the wedding which was going to be low key. Eddie wanted to set up a date with Aunt Lynn to talk about how to deal with their mother, and soon. Lizzie would write to their aunt as soon as she could, as she wanted this sorted out as well. Feeling more relieved and picking up the airmail letter, she opened it with some trepidation, reading it between the blacked out censored parts. Christopher was working hard to keep his men in order, which was hard in the intense heat, they must be in India, Egypt or Italy? She thought. He talked of love and finding his soulmate, even though they had only just met. The dance seamed a distant memory now but left a warm feeling inside of her. Now she had the job of replying to all the letters, before bed. She hoped tonight that bombers would give them a night off and that Daisy kept safe while working.

Daisy finished on nights, the last two were not too bad, as it was cloudy and the bombers had no choice but to stay away, she was glad to get her body clock back to normal and to eat at regular times and to see her friends, she had missed their chats. Lizzie was pleased to have her roommate back and she wanted to celebrate, so with the others, they all gathered in their room and broke the whisky out.

Chapter 27

During the month of May the weather had improved dramatically, and the bombing had slowed, the country was reeling from the news that the British ship Hood had been sunk by the German ship Bismarck, now the chase was on to sink it.

A few days later, the girls are listening to the wireless, and hear that good news, the Bismarck had been sunk! That was a cause for great joy to the population of Britain, but with it a tinge of sadness for all those lives lost, 'that was the cost of war' all the girls thought.

Daisy's mind travelled back to her recent letter, and that it could soon be her brother George fighting the war on the waves, it made her shiver, she had written to her parents saying how shocked she had been at first but once she had gotten over the initial shock, she was pleased for him if it was what he really wanted, and she hoped her parents would understand that it would be good for him.

Lizzie and Daisy were going onto maternity, and that would take them up to some holiday and then school for a week after which the girls had exams at the end of the week. Then they would commence the final year of training in September.

They then had to make the decision, what they wanted to do as qualified nurses? Daisy and Lizzie had discussed this at length, and both wanted to go into the army together and see the world, Lizzie secretly hoping the little problem of Charles would have been dealt with by then. Lizzie was happy because their holiday had in fact coexisted with the wedding of Edna and Geoffrey, so she could attend. She was excited and would now have to look at the dresses in her wardrobe she had brought with her and decide which one to wear for the ceremony.

The little church was situated in the grounds of the family home, and it turned out her father was going to give the bride away; Lizzie was pleased for her friend.

On a Monday morning at the beginning of June and with a spring in their step, very nervous and a little apprehensive, the two student nurses walked into the maternity ward to begin their first shift. It was getting easier as they were growing in confidence with every ward and department they went to, but it was always nerve wracking to meet the new ward sister.

Sister McKenna was there to greet them, she was small and bubbly but could be fierce when called upon, just right for the maternity ward and, once introductions were made, they headed to the locker room. All the wards were a similar layout, which made life easy. By late afternoon two babies had been born, both boys and both well and at this very moment in the nursery awaiting feeding. Daisy stood at the door looking in awe at the little bundles, all wrapped up, and she wondered would she feel so much love, if and when she had children? After much thought, yes, she would, unconditionally, and with that the third-year student nurse came in to take over, as it was time to go off shift. She made her way to the locker room, where she found Lizzie getting herself changed. As the girls headed down the ward they said 'bye' to the mothers of the two babies born today, who sat feeding their little boys. There would be no visits from their husbands, as they were both fighting somewhere abroad at present, and the only way the men could be told of the happy news was via letters.

The friends walked back to the nurse's home in a happy mood, it was a nice feeling, especially after some bad nights of bombing. They went to the dining hall for tea.

Eddie had replied back quite quickly to Lizzie, he would be up in London on the following Saturday evening with Glenda and he really wanted to meet up with her, if she was available. As luck would have it, she was off that weekend, so she replied straight away and plans were made. She really missed her brother's company and was looking forward to catching up with him and getting to know Glenda better.

The Saturday in question soon came around, it was a warm evening as Lizzie hopped on a bus up to Leicester Square, when she arrived it was full of activity, full of military personnel milling around enjoying the summer evening, her brother had already arrived with Glenda. Lizzie ran up to Eddie and threw her arms around him, kissing him on both cheeks, standing back to take a look at her brother, he looked tired but very happy.

Turning to Glenda, she gave her future sister-in-law a warm hug and the once over. Glenda was a pretty girl with beautiful brown eyes, she could see why her brother had fallen for the girl.

There had been less raids lately, as the rumour was that the Luftwaffe had sustained heavy losses in the Battle of Britain, so all three hoped tonight would be quiet. Eddie crossed his fingers behind his back. All three made their way to Lyons Corner House for supper and a catch up. It turned into a lovely evening, Lizzie genuinely liked the girl the more she got to know her, and made a silent promise that she would help her brother get his wish to marry this girl when the time was right. He had been to meet her parents, driving down to Devon when he had some leave because he didn't want to go home to see his own parents, not the way their mother was behaving. They had all got on well, and Glenda's parents had taken to the brave Squadron Leader. Plans were started for the wedding, and Lizzie asked if Eddie had heard back from Aunt Lynn?

"Not yet," he said, her mind must be on other more important things, like sorting out somewhere to live as she had lost her house with the bombing in Coventry, he explained to Glenda.

"Right, let's get out of here. Let's get tickets for a west end show if we can?" Her brother and Glenda were travelling back down south in the morning. Luckily, they managed to get three tickets and made their way to the theatre, it was a welcome release for all of them, for a few hours they could escape the horrors of the war.

Once the show had finished and Lizzie was recovering from laughing so much that her sides ached. Kissing both her brother and his fiancé goodbye, they went off in different directions. Sitting on the bus travelling towards the hospital, it gave Lizzie time to think, her Aunt Lynn had better come up with a good solution to her mother's interference. She really did like Glenda, and it didn't bother her she didn't have a title, or wasn't even a lady, the fact of the matter was Glenda made her brother very contented and most importantly loved.

Sitting back in her seat, Lizzie hoped that would be the same for her and Christopher once he found out who she really was because she was growing to love him more as the days went by, even though he was thousands of miles away, fighting this war. In his letter he had written of the love he had felt as soon as they had met, and he wanted to spend the rest of his life with her, if she would have him? Well, she knew the answer to that straight away. This was why she had chosen the army once she qualified as she hoped she would be posted near him, she knew in her heart is was not likely to happen, but she was prepared to take that risk, part of her was a tiny bit jealous of her brother, he got to spend time with Glenda, even share a hotel room.

Lizzie knew that if Chris asked her, she wouldn't hesitate saying yes, even though it was morally wrong. God, she could be dead any day but when Charles suggested it, it made her feel physically sick. Pushing the cord for her stop, she waited for the bus to brake, saying 'thank you' to the conductor, stepping off and walking towards the hospital, she felt contented as well, her boyfriend may be a long way from home, but she had good friends and a job she loved, the only problem in the way was her obnoxious mother!

Lizzie hoped that when she went home for the wedding, then just maybe she could try again and talk some sense into her. If that failed then she made a vow that she would not return home again. It made her heart ache, as she would miss her beloved father, Edna and Geoffrey because they had become like her family to her, not like her mother, the ice queen. Lizzie actually wondered if her mother could ever show her true feelings or even love someone or something, because at the precise moment Lizzie, with a heavy heart, didn't really think so.

Standing outside her room, she fixed her happy smile in place and entered saying, "I'm back." Daisy was sitting up in bed, reading a textbook on childbirth.

"Interesting reading you have there," said Lizzie, raising an eyebrow as she spoke.

Her roommate laughed. "Have to keep up to date as it may come up in our finals."

"Let me get changed, then we can look at it together, and test each other till lights out."

While Lizzie put her night clothes on, she opened the window, making sure the blackout curtain was in place. "Thank you," said her friend as the next thing she did was light up a cigarette, standing by the open window in the dark, she explained how her evening had progressed, and she talked about the show they had seen.

One thing she wanted the most to mention to her close friend was her brother sleeping with Glenda. It had revealed very different feelings and she wanted to talk about them, shyly she finished her cigarette and turned the room light back on and sat down by Daisy on her bed.

"Budge up," she said, sitting comfortably. "Daisy, can I ask you something?"

Daisy looked at her best friend. "Of course, anything." Trying to work out why her friend was so serious at that precise moment.

"I was thinking if Chris asked me to share a room, I would say yes, no hesitation, does that make me a bad person?"

"Oh god, no," replied her close friend, who took her hands. "If you love someone with all your heart, and it feels right then do it. My only advice to you would be, blushing like a beetroot she said, use a French Letter if you can get one."

Lizzie, seeing the state her friend was in, laughed at her, both girls hugged and carried on testing each other. Now it was Daisy's turn to wonder. If the lovely Michael, Dr Reynolds, asked her the same question, how would she answer? Taking her time to think and trying not to blush again, she would most definitely say yes.

Seeing the slight blush on her friend's cheeks, Lizzie asked, "Are you okay, not coming down with anything?" She eyed her friend suspiciously, laughing.

It did both women good, after so many weeks of seeing and dealing with death and devastation, the room felt lighter, and both slept well that night. Over the course of the weeks the women settled into a routine of early and late shifts, many of the births they dealt with were problem ones, as most of the ladies of the East End had home births with only a midwife and family member present.

One late shift, Daisy was dealing with a woman by the name of Alice, her husband, like most, was away in the navy, in the convoys. She had arrived this morning with some unexplained bleeding, on examination the doctors had decided to keep her in, as this was her first baby. Alice was placed on bed-rest and Daisy was told to keep an eye on her, during the afternoon Alice started to experience terrible pains and went into premature labour, by the late evening her baby girl had be delivered dead.

Alice was devastated, and she kept on crying. Daisy was at a loss with how to comfort her, she wanted her husband, but he was miles away. Luckily her mother arrived and held her daughter while she cried, her heart went out for her little girl. Daisy couldn't wait to get off, she was so upset that she felt relief once the night shift turned up. She raced back to the nurse's home, her heart pumping fast, nearly breaking the door down. She was relieved when she saw Lizzie was there, she fell into her arms, sobbing her heart out. Lizzie was extremely concerned as to why her friend had entered the room at the race of knots. Once the sobbing had subsided, she pulled her over to the bed, giving her a cuddle.

"What's the matter?" she asked, concerned.

Daisy then went on to explain to her roommate the events of the shift. "I held this dead baby in my arms, she looked so peaceful as if she was asleep, but I felt so helpless." Lizzie really felt for her friend, they had only read about this the other day, but to actually see and deal with it was totally different.

Sitting and talking to each other helped and they both agreed that they couldn't save everyone, it was a hard learning curve for both. Over the last few months, they had learned to toughen up and be strong even though they didn't feel or believe it. The rest of their shifts passed with few incidents, and their time on maternity came to an end. It was the end of July, the weather was hot and all the girls were looking forward to a few days annual leave. Daisy was going home to hear about her brother George joining the navy and Mary's engagement to Bobby. For Elizabeth going home always held some dread, but this time at least she had the wedding to look forward to. She had found a pretty summer's dress to wear in her wardrobe. Jenny and Claire were both glad to be going home for a few days' rest after their time in theatres and the casualty department. Both had admitted it had been tough going through a difficult period of the war.

On a Friday evening at the start of August, the four girls found themselves packing to start their leave the following day, the worst part for each of them was the journey, as it could take forever. Once all their suitcases were ready and placed by the door, Jenny and Lizzie were standing by the open window, it was still very hot and there was little or no breeze that evening. Both had lit cigarettes in their fingers, turning to face the open window, Lizzie blew smoke out through it, this was becoming a habit as they couldn't be bothered to walk outside or go down to the common room. Hilary would probably be in there with her group of followers.

"I think early to bed tonight, as we all have long journeys ahead of us." Apart from Claire, who only had a short distance to travel, to Woolwich. Lucky for her and her family, her home having been hit but only sustaining slight structural damage which could be repaired, the houses across the road had been totally destroyed.

Claire hadn't said much but she wished her parents would move out of London to the country, but her father being stubborn wouldn't hear of it. Well, it was his decision and she couldn't make him change his mind, so like everyone else she got on with it. Jenny's family had been hit as well, as the Luftwaffe liked to drop their bombs on the south coast, she had watched every night, her roommate kneeling by her bed, praying that her family stayed safe.

Each one knew that so far, they had been fortunate as they had not lost anyone close, apart from Lizzie losing her cousin at Dunkirk. Having said "goodnight" to their two colleagues, they were left in their room alone, and once ready for bed they both lay there. Sleep was very difficult to come by, as the room was extremely hot and sticky, even laying on top of the sheets couldn't cool the girls down. Both girls tossed and turned, it could also be the feeling of slight apprehension about going home after this length of time, both women had grown up in the last seven months and were no longer the naive girls that had left to start their training. They had witnessed and dealt with situations and incidents, that unless you had seen it with your own eyes, you would not believe.

Morning took forever to arrive, but it was still very hot, they got themselves ready to leave. Following breakfast, the women finished off getting ready, picking up their suitcases, gas mask and handbags, they both took one more look around the room, and once happy Lizzie closed the door, locking it. Living with so many different types of women, you could never really trust them completely, some would steal from you, others, well you wouldn't want to make their acquaintance.

At the bottom of the stairs was Home Sister, waiting by the door to see her flock off, saying, "Goodbye and see you in a few days. Have a safe journey," she called as the women made their way out into the bright sunlight, stopping as the hot air hit them.

Stopping to talk to Tom in his hut. "Have a lovely, leave you have earned it," he said to them all, he knew what pressures these young women had all been under the last few months, and he was proud of every one of them as if they were his own daughters. In fact, his daughter was working in an ammunition factory in Woolwich, and was enjoying it, at least she was still living at home. His son was in the army fighting with his regiment somewhere hot, he prayed every night to keep him safe and bring him home to his wife and son who lived not too far from Tom and his wife.

The journey to the underground was busy with each carriage full with service personnel. Both girls noticed that more women were in uniform, the Prime Minister was hoping that America would soon enter the war, which would mean more men around.

The president of America, Franklin D Roosevelt, didn't want to get involved, which didn't please Winston Churchill. It had been a few months since Germany had invaded the Soviet Union back in June, and people felt Hitler had made his first wrong move.

The girls changed trains at the station, where they said, "Goodbye, see you in a few days." Daisy knew her friend would be back before her if the problems at home hadn't settled down.

Daisy found her platform and waited for the arrival of the train, she observed the bedding which was laid out ready for the night, and she suddenly felt a pang of sympathy for these people, but she knew they were tough. Having met a lot of East Enders, she knew they wouldn't want sympathy; they were proud people, and they would beat Hitler and the Nazis. It was busy at St Pancras Station, filled with service personnel rushing to either get a train or connection.

Some people were looking at her for not being in uniform, but she ignored them, walking along to find her train to Luton and her family. It felt like ages since she had been home, she had changed in lots of different ways and so probably had her family, war did this.

Chapter 28

The train was in the station and she found a carriage, luckily, she got herself a seat, placed her suitcase in the above rack, keeping her handbag and gas mask by her side, she carried a light rain coat, as you never knew with the British weather, she finally made herself comfortable for the journey home. Daisy sat chatting to her fellow travellers as she waited for the train to get under way, it was very hot in the carriage. All the windows were open to get a flow of air into them. Looking down at her watch on her wrist, she noticed it was ten o'clock, the train started to build up steam, ready to pull out of the station, and Daisy heard the station master blow his whistle. Slowly the train began to move, Daisy felt on cloud nine, she was going home. Once it had built up enough steam, they left the dreary city behind and the bomb-damaged buildings They were rushing through the green countryside and making good time, there was still some damage to the railway tracks, but the workmen had worked hard to repair them very quickly and the train hadn't had to stop. As they approached Luton, the train started to slow, what she noticed first was the damage to buildings and houses, she hoped with all her heart, that her family home was in one piece, her mother hadn't mentioned in her letters, of the house sustaining any significant damage, but she might have decided to do that to keep the truth from her eldest daughter. Daisy stood, waited for the other passengers to disembark and she collected her belongings. Once off the train, she walked to the ticket collector who took it from her. Making her way to the main entrance, the heat hit her, it was boiling hot, but she still decided to walk home. She had written to tell her family telling them she was coming, so they shouldn't be surprised with her arrival.

The warm weather made her feel cheery, but her surroundings told a different story. Luton had been hit hard and most of the buildings were in ruins, the bomb damage was everywhere, and some were completely gone. As the streets got familiar to her, her heart was pounding hard against her chest, feeling nauseous, she took deep breaths and prayed her home was still there, what would she do if it wasn't? There was no time to think about that, as she turned the corner, she saw with instant relief, her home was still standing! Okay, she looked, she noticed there was some damage to the windows but everything else looked fine, no structural damage that she could see. She stood waiting for her heart rate to go back to normal, before walking up the entry at the side of the house.

Turning the door handle she pushed it open. "Hello, I'm home," she called out, walking onto the warm kitchen, putting down her case, hanging up her gas mask and handbag on the peg behind the door. Daisy looked around the familiar kitchen, it smelt and looked like home. Her mother came through the door into the room wearing her apron over a summer dress, the window was open fully to let some air in.

"Daisy love, you're home." Hugging her eldest daughter tightly, and Daisy holding on to her mother in return.

Daisy let the tears she was holding in, fall. "Why are you crying?" asked her mother softly, she wiped a tear from her daughter's cheek.

Daisy dried the remaining tears from her eyes, on a crisp white hankie her mother passed to her, answering her mother by saying "I got it into my head that our house had been destroyed and was no longer standing." Her mother tenderly took her daughters hands.

"Daisy love, I would have written and told you." Daisy knew she was being silly but the last few weeks at the hospital had played with her emotions, not realising just how much until now, being here with her mum.

"Take your coat and hang it up," said her mum, which she did. "I'll put the kettle on, then we can have a cup of tea and a catch up." Hannah went over and filled the kettle.

Helping to set the kitchen table, she chatted away to her mum as if she hadn't been away, she took time to scrutinise her as they talked. Daisy was concerned, what she saw was how much older looking her mum was, she had more lines around the eyes. Before she could say something, they were interrupted by her brother. Mark had come in from playing out with his friends, it was the summer holidays.

"Shall we go to the park after lunch?" he asked his mother.

"Don't you have work today?" Daisy asked her mother.

"No love," came the reply, "since rationing, clothing has been short and there's not much call for dressmaking at the moment, just make do and mend."

"Yes, I would like that very much," she said, trying to keep the worry from her voice and not to worry her daughter.

"Are you and Dad okay for money?" she asked, embarrassed.

"Don't worry, we are fine."

"But you have lost George's rent money now he has gone." Daisy offered. "I could send you some if you are short?"

"No love, but thank you, we are okay, your father has plenty of overtime and I have work, just not as much as before the war, Also I put plenty away at the start of the war for a rainy day."

"What about Mary? Now she is full time at Woolworths does she help?" asked Daisy, thinking her sister should help now she was earning.

"Yes, but your sister is saving up to get married, when Bobby is next home on leave."

"But they have only just begun to go out together?" Questioned Daisy. Daisy always knew her twin was selfish and always looked after number one, being herself.

"Let's have a sandwich and a cold drink of lemonade for lunch, then we can get you settled and then we can head out."

Mark so was excited to have his sister home, letting him sit on her lap even though he was getting heavy.

"Tell me about George," asked Daisy hesitantly.

Her mother's voice began to break. "As you know he always couldn't wait to join up, and as soon as he was eighteen, he was at the recruiting office, and they signed him up straight away. There was nothing your father could do to stop it. He came home so happy with the news, but it broke my heart." She was crying gently. "I knew he would have to go, just not yet! At present he is doing basic training, down near Portsmouth, and I worry all the time because of the bombing of the docks down there."

Dabbing her eyes, her mum went to the front room to the sideboard and picked up a photo frame of her brother, looking at it, he looked so smart in his uniform but so very young, she came over feeling so proud of her sibling. Handing it back to her mother, who proudly placed it back on the side. The three of them spent the afternoon walking around the park, avoiding the gun placement, and sandbags placed around. Once home Daisy helped her mother start tea and they waited for her father and sister to come in from work. Her father was over the moon to see his daughter and was full of questions. She tried to answer them but some of the things she had witnessed she couldn't explain to her family, maybe to her dad when he was on his own.

Mary was excited about her engagement which was understandable, she didn't have a ring yet as she didn't want the same one Bobby was going to give to Daisy, so he had promised to pawn that ring and buy her another when he was next home. Daisy didn't feel uncomfortable that her sister was engaged and going to marry Bobby, she felt like she'd had a lucky escape, it wouldn't have worked between them.

She kept thinking of Michael, whether their paths would ever cross again, and most importantly would he like her, like she liked him? He was a doctor, she came from a working-class family from Luton, she sighed, she would hopefully find out one day.

Later, as she got ready for bed, her sister was already in it as she had to be up early to go to work. The room was still hot, and the windows were fully open, the black-out blind pulled over to keep the light from shining. Daisy had just climbed into bed when the siren went off, and her father called up. Daisy woke Mary and then got Mark and all five of them made their way out into the Anderson shelter in the garden, Dad leading the way with a torch, the beam was filtered. Daisy had never been inside, so it was a novelty for her, she found a seat on the bench and sat by her sister, Mark had climbed on her lap, he cuddled into her.

She wrapped her arms around him, keeping him safe, her mother and father sat on the other bench, all the family waiting for the bombs to drop, you could feel the apprehension in the shelter. They didn't have to wait long, and you could hear the drone of the engines in the distance, as they approached their targets, moments later they heard the explosions as the bombs hit, it was still scary, even though it had been going on for a long time now. They could feel the shaking of the houses nearby and they all prayed that their home would be saved tonight. The only consolation was the fact it was a very warm night, the heat hadn't really gone, and so it was not uncomfortable to sit in the shelter, Hannah had made up a flask of tea and brought biscuits in, so she shared them out amongst her family. At five the all-clear sounded, her father having not been on ARP duty tonight, spoke to his wife and told her he was going off to help with the people buried or injured, telling her he would be back later.

"Stay safe," she called after him. Jack opened the door to the shelter, you could smell the cordite and the clear sky was bright red with fires burning in the distance, they had tried to target the tank factory said her departing father. A few moments later he popped his head back inside. "The house is all okay, but there is the smell of gas so don't put the gas on," he said to Hannah.

Hannah looked at her children and took a sleeping Mark in her arms. "Right, let's get you to bed for a few hours' sleep, I will be downstairs if you need me." Hannah carried Mark up the stairs to bed, closely followed by Mary.

Daisy knew she wouldn't be able to sleep; "I will see if they need help with the casualties." And with that she hurriedly went back inside and got changed, she was off to the bottom of the street to the nearest ARP post.

Hoping her father was still there and she could go with him and help. Luckily, he was, he was startled to see her, but he knew she would be invaluable to them. He gave her a hard hat with ARP on it and luckily, she had put her trousers on that morning that her mother had made. They were given their orders and they set off. It was nice to spend some alone time with her father, and they talked as they walked to the road that had been badly hit and needed them to help dig people out of the rubble. The ambulances had already arrived, the four women auxiliary ambulance crews were waiting patiently, Daisy and her father got to work, moving piece by piece slowly, every so often they were told to be quiet, as they listened for any noise. Then. They heard it, a baby crying, they dug again, slowly and there he was, protected by his mother who had taken the full force of the blast. Once they were both rescued, Daisy checked the mother over, she found a slight pulse and the little boy seemed fine.

The ambulance crew got to work, and both were quickly dispatched off to hospital for a check-up and to get the mother the medical help she needed urgently. Daisy listened to the bells of the ambulance as they disappeared into the distance, and they carried on all morning, pulling people out of the rubble.

Her father had to go to work, but Daisy stayed and kept on going. By lunchtime the dead or injured had been found and taken off to hospital or the mortuary, a weary Daisy made her way home to get cleaned up, and get something to eat and drink. Once she entered her street, she felt a tired relief wash over her, and she walked up the entry and entered the kitchen. The door was open, and she called to her mother, who came rushing to see her daughter, taking one look at her, she gave her a loving hug.

"You have done well." She was very proud of her daughter and sat her down at the table. Once she was fed, Daisy asked for a wash, she couldn't use the bath as the water pipe had been damaged. She wanted to wash the grime of the morning away, she stripped off her clothes and stood in the kitchen at the sink, having her wash, her clean clothes by her side on a chair.

Hannah looked at the dirty blood-stained clothes on a pile on the floor, she would clean her daughters' clothes before she had to return to the hospital.

Once washed she felt clean, almost human again, she now wanted to sleep for a while, so she made her way up to bed and slept. It felt strange lying in her old bed, but she was so exhausted she rolled on her side and fell into a deep sleep.

Hannah woke her up in time for tea, and she made her way down the stairs through to the kitchen. She hoped tonight, no she changed that, she prayed that tonight the Luftwaffe would not come. The family sat round the table, eating their tea and she looked around, she felt so much love for her family and that they stayed safe. Yes, that night, Daisy got her wish, the Luftwaffe also stayed away the next night, and the next morning she was up early to go back to London.

Finally packed, she took her suitcase carefully down the small stairs into the kitchen, the weather was still hot with a chance of thunderstorms later in the day, hopefully, she thought, she would miss them, if she left soon. Daisy had said her goodbyes to her father and sister the night before, only Mark and her mother were left. Hannah had made her egg and bacon which she tucked into with relish, how she would miss this. The food at the hospital was all right, but you couldn't beat her mum's cooking.

"I'll walk you to the station," Hannah offered as they stood washing up the breakfast things.

"That would be nice Mum, but don't you have a client?"

"Not yet," came the reply.

"Thank you," said her daughter with gratitude.

"Right, let's get your things together so we can make tracks."

Mark got himself ready, he sat on the bottom stair putting on his worn looking shoes.

"Do you want some help?" she asked.

"No," came the reply. "I'm a big boy now!"

She had to laugh at her little brother, oh, how she loved him. Daisy stood at the door of the kitchen, she took one more look around, and felt a pang of sadness come over her. She would miss her family terribly, but she knew in her heart she had to go back and qualify as a nurse, she had worked hard to achieve it, and the end was in sight.

Her mother locked the back door and all three walked through the entry out into the bright sunshine, the heat hitting them as they walked along the street. They could still smell the cordite from the previous raid. The last raid had caused a lot of destruction, the workmen were already trying to repair the buildings that were dangerously hanging and could cause injury to people, if they fell. Daisy, her mother and Mark kept clear of these and were chatting in an easy free-flowing manner, Daisy as she had gotten older, had begun to enjoy this time with her mother, their relationship had improved, and she knew they were very proud of her achievements so far.

As the station came into view, the three of them crossed the road to the entrance, her mother and her brother stood in the centre of the concourse with Daisy's suitcase, while she went off to buy her ticket and find what platform her train was arriving on.

"I need platform two," said Daisy.

Her mother picked up her suitcase and walked her to the platform.

"You will be careful?" her mother said seriously.

"Yes, I promise," she replied with emotion.

"And write to George, he will be joining a ship soon."

"You gave me his address. I have the paper, it's safely in my case, I

230

promise I will do that tonight."

They stood there quietly, observing their surroundings, they both heard the train in the distance, and it slowly arrived, the steam bellowing out through the funnel.

Hannah hugged her daughter tightly, Mark wanted in on the action and Daisy scooped down to hug her little brother.

"Look after Mum?" she whispered, "you're the only son left."

"Yes, I'm a big boy now," he said, puffing his chest out.

Daisy couldn't help but smile at that action. The train pulled to a stop, Daisy climbed aboard turned and waved, she walked along the carriage found an empty space, as all the seats were taken, she made herself comfortable, and waited for the train to pull away.

The whistle blew, the train jerked, and it picked up steam, she tried to see her mother and brother, but they were out of view. 'I will see you soon' she promised, her heart aching just a little bit. She felt a tear at the back of her eye. Trying to think nice thoughts, they turned to her friend Lizzie and how had she faired at home.

Chapter 29

Lizzie had crossed London on the underground to Marylebone Station, like most when she had arrived it was full of service personnel, rushing to and from trains on the concourse, she could feel the heat as she waited. Lizzie bought her ticket; her train was running late, so it gave her time to get a drink at the buffet.

Entering the dreary building, it was full of people, she joined the end of the queue and waited her turn, finally, the waitress got to her and asked what she wanted.

"I'll have a tea and a piece of Victoria sponge, please?" Glancing at the cake on a large plate on the counter. Looking around for a seat, she found one near a table that had just been vacated, the waitress, when free came over and took the dirty plates and cutlery away, wiping the table down. Lizzie took her seat and studied her surroundings, as she drank her tea, tasting the cake, it was edible but slightly dry, she understood, it was difficult to get the ingredients with rationing.

Forty-five minutes later, Lizzie heard her train being called, she collected her belongings and headed for the door. Making her way towards platform one; the train was in, she found a seat and got comfy, making sure the windows were all open to let some cool air in as the carriage felt very warm. Four airmen soon joined her, and they spent the journey chatting together. It made her think of Eddie, her brother; it brought a small smile to her face, she drifted off, wondering if he was all right, and she wondered how would these few days, work out with their mother.

The journey was pleasant with no more delays, and they arrived in Warwick by lunchtime, the airmen helped Lizzie off the train with her suitcase, placing it on the platform. Thanking them and wishing them well, they climbed back on board to carry on with their journey. As Lizzie left the station, turning to her left she spotted Geoffrey, he still was driving the Rolls Royce. How her father still got petrol was a mystery to her, but she wouldn't ask. Greeting Geoffrey with a big smile, he grabbed her suitcase, placing it in the boot, Lizzie got herself into the back of the car, placing her handbag and gas mask on the seat beside her, he had all the windows open. Sitting back, she took a deep breath and waited till Geoffrey was installed behind the steering wheel.

Firstly, she asked, "How are the wedding plans coming along and are you ready for tomorrow?"

"Yes, everything is in place," Geoffrey answered. Apparently, her mother had been a big help. How Lizzie wished she was like that with her, but she saw a different side to her mother, she still prayed she would change in time.

Then she asked, "How are my parents?"

The chauffeur replied, "They were both doing well." Her mother was helping the injured soldiers in the Hall. Her father was working around the grounds as some of the younger gardeners had been called up.

With some apprehension, they arrived at the Hall, driving down the long sweeping driveway, the green lawns were looking brownish from lack of rain she observed, some soldiers were sitting in the shade under the big trees.

Lizzie felt nervous, she surveyed her home, she really didn't want to argue with her mother, but she just couldn't help it. Arriving at the back of the Hall, she felt slightly better, she climbed out and waited for Geoffrey to get her suitcase. Edna, the cook, was waiting by the door, Lizzie turned, she gave her a warm hug, and she relaxed into it. "Welcome home," Lady Elizabeth said.

Lizzie said, "Remember, please call me Lizzie," she said, releasing her hold on the elderly cook, standing back she scrutinised the bride to be, who looked older but well.

"I'm glad you could make the wedding."

"I wasn't going to miss it if I could help it," said Lizzie.

They went inside, out of the heat. "I made you some biscuits, and there is cold lemonade as we didn't know what time you would be coming."

"That would be lovely, thank you." They all sat around the large table, Geoffrey joined them once the Rolls was put away.

"What time is the ceremony tomorrow?" Lizzie asked.

"Eleven o'clock," Edna replied.

Edna brought the biscuits out and poured the lemonade into glasses, they sat drinking and whispering when they heard her mother's voice coming down the back stairs.

She entered the kitchen, stopped and gazed over at her daughter.

"You're back then!"

Lizzie stopped eating and considered what her reply would be. "Yes, only for a few days, then I have to be back."

"Have you heard from Charles?"

"Yes, he has written a couple of times."

"When are you meeting up?" she asked.

"We can't at the moment, he is still away."

"Well, just make sure that you keep your promise." It was the only reply she got.

Her mother turned and walked back up the stairs, not glancing at her daughter. Lizzie just stood watching the back of her mother as she left.

"Did that just happen?" she asked to the rest of the room.

Edna went over to Lizzie and held the poor girl, as the tears came. The tears wouldn't stop, Edna gave her a hanky.

"I don't love him," she cried.

"I know, but your aunt will come good," said cook.

"I hope so because I don't know how much more I can take," cried Lizzie.

Keeping out the way of her mother would be easy in this big house, her father came in via the back door, seeing his daughter in such a state, he guessed who had caused these tears.

He went over to her and gave her a hug. "What has she done now?" he asked angrily.

Lizzie explained to him, and he shook his head in disbelief. Clifford tried to comfort her, but he wasn't used to it.

"Thank you," his daughter said when her father let her go, it was nice to feel his strong arms around her. Drying her eyes, she picked up her case and made her way to her room. Lunch would be at one, to be honest, she wasn't looking forward to it, but she knew she would have to face her mother again at some time. Lizzie got to work on unpacking her dresses; she had chosen one for the wedding, a pretty yellow one with white sandals, that she hung up in the wardrobe for tomorrow. The rest of her clothes were placed in the drawers of the cabinet, and shoes placed on the floor. Sitting on the bed, the mattress was soft under her, she wanted to cry again, but she knew she was stronger than that, she would fight for the right to love Christopher. Just before one, she headed down the back stairs to the kitchen, and with apprehension she entered.

Her mother hadn't arrived yet, Edna sat her down at the table, waiting for the food to be brought out of the oven. "It's rabbit pie and mash, shot by your father yesterday."

"That will be lovely." Licking her lips with anticipation, she had always loved cook's cooking. Her father arrived and sat by his daughter, squeezing her hand as reassurance, he smiled, she smiled back nervously, then what she had been dreading, her mother entered the room, still strikingly beautiful but now with more lines around the eyes.

She noticed her hands were ageing. Not observing her daughter, she sat down and cook dished up the meal. They ate in silence. Lizzie was glad when it was over, and she could go off and have a walk around the grounds, maybe talk to some of the wounded soldiers and Army nurses. Before leaving, she helped cook wash up and dry, she mentioned her training and how well she was doing, she omitted she loved it. Lizzie told her about her friend Daisy and how she wished she could bring her here, but she knew the reaction her mother would have, with Daisy being working class!

"My mother is a snob; she will never change." She held her hands up in desperation. Then Lizzie told Edna about Chris, how they met and what he meant to her, she even admitted he was the man she was going to marry. Edna didn't say anything, she just listened, she could see the joy this young man brought to Lizzie,

When the time was right, Edna glanced at Lizzie and said: "Your mother at present is scared of the changes going on in the world, once she realises that all people are equal, she will have to change for the better."

The young Lady viewed the cook, with much adoration. After a few moments and with great thought, maybe the older lady was right, with renewed optimism she went out into the afternoon heat, with a spring in her step and her heart a little lighter. Binky arrived by her feet just as she was setting off on her walk; she walked by her side, Lizzie was talking to the dog as if it could understand everything she said. When they got to the lake, she stood watching the swans gliding elegantly across the calm water, how she wished she could go for a swim in the cool water.

Under a tree she met a young woman. "Hello," she greeted. "Enjoying this heat?"

"Hello," the woman replied cheerfully back.

Lizzie walked over to her with Binky at her side, Binky laid down in the shade.

"I'm Lizzie," she introduced herself.

"I'm Agnes," replied the woman under the tree.

Lizzie asked if she could sit down?

"Please do." Lizzie sat down by Agnes.

"What do you do here?" she asked interested.

"I'm a nurse in the Queen Alexandra's Royal Army Nursing Service, stationed here treating the injured and helping with rehabilitation."

"Do you enjoy it and where will you go next?" Lizzie was interested, she waited for Agnes answer.

"Yes, the young soldiers are friendly, courageous dealing with their injuries, and they work very hard to get as fit as they can, and I love the Hall," and as an afterthought, she said, "Lady Margo and Sir Clifford are very nice. I don't know where I will be posted next, but it could be abroad at any time."

That little bit of news piqued Lizzie's interest; she would talk to Daisy when she got back.

"I see you have met Binky," Agnes mentioned.

"Yes, she is my dog."

"Oh!" said Agnes, "then you must be Lady Elizabeth." Blushing with embarrassment. "I'm so sorry your Ladyship," she said, trying to get up.

Lizzie, seeing her nervousness and discomfort, stopped her. "Please stay seated."

She wanted to put the young nurse at ease, so Lizzie explained that she was at The London training to be a nurse and she would like to join the army once she qualified. The two women sat talking for ages, until Lizzie said, "She had better get Binky back for a drink and something to eat."

"I too better be getting back, or I will be in trouble with Matron, I'm on duty later."

It was lovely to meet Agnes, and she wished her well. "Our paths may cross again," she laughed.

"Maybe," came the reply. "Can I walk back with you?" Agnes asked shyly.

"Of course, you can," replied Lizzie cheerfully. "I would enjoy your company on the walk back."

Binky jumped up, and the two women followed, and they headed back through the grounds towards the Hall. When they reached the entrance, Agnes went through the front door.

At the same time, Lizzie took the side route to the kitchen, and she turned around quickly before Agnes disappeared and called out, "Can we meet up again before I go back?"

"Yes, come and find me," Agnes called back.

Lizzie spent the rest of the day and evening helping prepare for the wedding, she kept out the way of her mother, who was talking to the vicar and sorting the church out. By ten she was worn out and decided to head for bed. She said "goodnight" to Edna. Geoffrey, had already left to get an early night.

"I'll see you in the morning, try and sleep," said the cook, she hugged the young girl, who she treated like a daughter, Lizzie kissed the cook on the cheek, then turned around and headed up the stairs.

Once alone, Lizzie pulled out a solid silver photo frame that she bought for Edna and Geoffrey as their wedding present.

Placing it to one side, she went and ran a bath, filling it up to the regulation line drawn around the rim, she undressed and climbed in. She thought of Agnes and remembered all that she said, she couldn't wait to mention it all to Daisy, this was their chance to see the world.

Laying back in hot water, she washed the dirt off and shampooed her hair; it was nice not to rush. Once the water had cooled, she got out. Pulling the towel off the chair, she dried herself quickly, leaving her hair to dry and made sure the window was fully opened in the room. Lizzie flopped on the bed and regarded the dress hanging from the front of the wardrobe, she hoped that Edna and Geoffrey had a beautiful day.

She must have been tired because as soon as her head touched the pillow, she had fallen fast asleep. Lizzie was woken by the noise of the birds in the garden and clattering coming from the kitchen, she quickly changed into something easy, and pulling back her hair, and she ran down the back stairs.

Her mother was there, Lizzie stopped in her tracks, she was going to turn around and quietly go back upstairs, but her mother heard her and said, "Stay, I could do with the help today."

Her daughter hesitated for a second. She remembered the wedding; "I'm doing this for Edna and Geoffrey."

"Fine, we will call a truce."

"All right what do you want me to do?"

After that they both worked together to prepare the food for after the wedding. By the time Edna turned up, most of it was ready, they had saved all their ration coupons and food, and it looked good.

Edna had made a cake with help from friends and family. It sat at the head of the table. Just for today, one of the rooms in the Hall had been made ready for the wedding and they took all the food up into the room. Lizzie was surprised how well she had got on with her mother; no cross words were exchanged, it felt nice, it made Lizzie smile. Once Edna was satisfied, with Lady Margo casting her eye over it, Lizzie was allowed to get ready. Rushing up to her room, she first put some makeup on and then climbed into her dress, finally putting on her sandals. Taking one more look in the mirror, she was happy with the results, picked up her present and headed downstairs.

Waiting in the kitchen was her mother, Edna and her father, who was looking very smart in a black morning suit. The bride was wearing a matching skirt and jacket in light blue, topping it off was a pretty hat that she had purchased especially for today and her mother was dressed in a delightful dress, with an enormous hat.

Lady Margo regarded her daughter, casting her beady eye over every inch of her and said, "Darling, you look divine."

"Thank you, Mother," replied Lizzie, taken by surprise at the compliment. Perhaps her mother was ill? Edna's flowers came from the garden, and one of the patients had tied it together to make a bouquet.

Today her father was driving the Rolls, they all walked to the front

238

of the Hall, and some of the patients had come to watch the bridal party leave for the church. Mother sat in the front beside Father and Edna and Lizzie sat in the back. Lizzie, seeing how nervous Edna was, took her hand and gave her a reassuring smile, Edna gratefully returned it.

The sun was out, and it was warm again, some of the soldiers were watching from the grounds as they sat in the shade out of the sun. The church was just a mile up the lane, and they were there in no time. Father stopped the car outside the church; he jumped out, helped his wife out, ran around the side and helped Edna out too. Lizzie opened her door and climbed out into the bright sunshine.

Lady Margo and Elizabeth entered the church first, Lizzie insisting that her mother went in before her. It was cool inside the church and eerily quiet, Lizzie noticed Geoffrey was standing at the front with his brother, the best man, they both looked very dapper in their suits. Both women took their seats at the front to await the bride, soon everyone stood, and the organ began to play, the doors of the church opened, and Edna and her father began their slow walk down the aisle.

Lizzie watched with love; she saw two very happy people become one. Geoffrey, when he saw his bride, was beaming, they stood together at the altar and the service began. Forty-five minutes later they were pronounced husband and wife, they were allowed two photographs, and then her father drove the happy couple back to the Hall, where the reception was to be held.

Lizzie walked with the other guests, including her mother, along the path back to the Hall. Lizzie could smell the lovely scent of the flowers as she passed. They walked side by side; they had to talk Lizzie thought because the silence was unbearable, Lizzie did a nervous cough. her mother regarded her with an unyielding look. Her mother shocked Lizzie by being the first to speak.

"The service was delightful, and didn't the bride look lovely?"

Lizzie gazed at her mother, agreeing with her, she said, "They make a lovely couple."

"I'm pleased they finally got together." Lady Margo knew her daughter was trying to keep the conversation light, as it was not the right place or time to start an argument.

Walking along, both of them kept a comfortable distance between themselves, Lizzie wanted to talk about her engagement to Charles, but she knew this was not the right time.

Lady Margo showed her daughter the work her father had done to the grounds since losing the gardener, she talked as if she was proud of him.

"Mother, can I ask you a question?" asked Lizzie in a serious voice.

Her mother stopped walking, turning to her daughter she surveyed her. "I suppose so," came back the reply, she feeling she had little choice.

Lizzie stared right into her mother's eyes as if burning into her soul, she took a deep breath. "Do you love Father?" she asked seriously.

Her mother didn't reply straight away and took a moment to consider her answer. "Not in the beginning, if I am honest, I'm sure your aunt told you with great joy that we had to get married, as I was expecting Edward," Lady Margo said with a blush to her cheeks. "Your grandfather was livid but I was happy because your father's family was rich, and I wanted to give myself a better life than the one I was born into."

Lizzie looked over at her mother.

"At the start, it was hard, as we didn't know each other well and we were very young. Once Edward was born, it was much harder as we had a young child to care for, yes, I got a nanny, but we were strangers, and I didn't bond with the baby, not like my sister."

Lizzie wanted to tell her mother she still cold and hard even now. Still, she bit her tongue, best to keep quiet she thought. "Please keep going?" Gazing at her mother encouragingly.

"Well, our life improved dramatically once your father's parents died and your father took over the business," Lady Margo continued. "They didn't like me, as they knew I had trapped their son and then you came along soon after Edward. I think we grew to love each other once we got to know one another as we got older. That is why I'm certain you will be the same with Charles."

Lizzie stared at her mother. "I don't think so." And left it like that. She walked off towards the Hall and the wedding reception.

Her mother stood for a moment, watching her daughter go and then followed her. Lizzie's mind was reeling from the statement her mother had just made, she was adamant in her heart that she didn't like Charles or even loved him, she knew her heart belonged to Christopher. Walking at a quickened pace, she reached the front of the Hall and caught up with the wedding party who were just about to go inside. She put on a happy face and went over to stand by her father, who was talking to some of the doctors.

Seeing the state of his daughter he held her arm, asking in a concerned voice, "What's wrong?"

Lizzie didn't want to spoil the day, so she said, "Can we talk later?" Glancing at her father.

"Yes," he replied in a gentle voice.

Sir Clifford gathered the guests and led everyone into the Hall, it was nice to get out of the heat, and walked into the room they were to use, it looked beautiful. Her mother had worked hard decorating it, she thought. The tables were laid out in two rows with lovely tablecloths on them, all the plates were placed in order, and everyone took their seats, the meal was divine. Cook and her mother had done a brilliant job with rationing, and her father had caught some rabbits, a couple of girls from the village had been asked to help to serve the food.

Once the plates had been cleared away, the speeches were done, and then the band played, some of the wounded soldiers and off duty nurses were invited to join the celebration. Lizzie was not short of dancing partners, she was twirled around the dance floor by eager soldiers, bringing back memories of her and Chris dancing all that time ago, she tried to stop the tears, but they fell. What she didn't notice was that her father had been watching her.

Her father danced with the bride, and then he danced with her mother. They made a striking couple, he looked at her mother with affection, she hadn't noticed that before. Her mother was smiling back at her husband; what she saw was love. Lizzie needed some fresh air and made for the open French window which led into the rose garden, it smelt and looked wonderful she thought.

She didn't hear her father come up behind her, he touched her arm and led her to the seat. "Sit." Her father gazed at his daughter and began, "My darling girl, why are you so sad?"

Lizzie wasn't about to lie, so she said, "I've met someone special," looking at her father.

"Go on," he encouraged, looking at his daughter with love. "I take it, it's not Charles?"

"No, Father, he is an officer in the army Scotch Guards and is stationed abroad at the moment. We met at the hospital following Dunkirk, he was visiting his men." Looking seriously at her father she said, "I've fallen in love, and I can't marry Charles as I don't love him."

She felt relief saying it out loud, her father held his daughter's hands in his, and after a pause and some consideration he said: "You won't have to marry Charles, I will sort your mother out, with the help of Aunt Lynn, so don't you worry."

Lizzie mentioned what Aunt Lynn had said to her about sorting things with her mother.

"Well, we will work together," he said smiling at his only daughter. Reluctantly letting go of her hands, he pulled her up into a hug, Lizzie melted into her father's chest, she could smell his cologne.

Now she had tears of happiness sliding down her face, she wiped them with her hanky as she went back inside, she felt as if a heavy weight had been lifted from her shoulders.

The rest of the evening flew by, she sat talking to the soldiers who had stayed for the band, she even saw Agnes who had popped her head in. They had to close the French window and place the blackout blinds back once it had got dark, the dancing went on till ten. Dead on ten, the band stopped, and Edna and Geoffrey said their "goodbyes" and headed home for the night, they were going to stay in the country for a couple of days for their honeymoon, going by train tomorrow.

Lizzie went up to the happy couple, she hugged each one and gave them their present, they opened it together. The photo frame was a hit, the couple were both taken aback with the gift. "Thank you," they said in unison. Both kissed Lizzie goodbye and said, "We will see you next time you are home?"

"Yes," she replied.

Once the happy couple had left, her father dropping them home in the Rolls Royce, she went up to her mother and said: "I'm tired, I'm off to bed. I promise I will help you tomorrow to clean up."

Her mother said, "Of course, it's been a long day, we will all muck in and sort it out in the morning."

Lizzie said her "goodnights" and headed up the back stairs to her room, as a soon as she closed her door, she sunk on the bed and reviewed the day. It was the first time in her young life that her mother had been honest with her and she did believe what she had just witnessed, that her mother now loved her father very much. She hoped and prayed that both her father and her aunt came through with their promise to deal with her mother, and she would be able to be with Chris, once this war was over. But Lizzie knew in her heart it was still going to be a long way off.

She got undressed by the moonlight as she had left the bedroom window open, as it was a hot night again and once ready for bed, Lizzie lay on the top reading, as her mind was whirling around with the day's events. Once she got to sleep, she slept well, as it was nice to get her problems off her chest by talking to her father. He had listened to what she had to say, and Lizzie woke in the morning ready to help her mother when she finally came downstairs.

Her mother had cooked breakfast and was sitting at the large table, pouring herself a coffee. Lizzie sat on the other side of the table, her mother handed her a plate of bacon and eggs. Lizzie didn't notice how hungry she was, until smelling the food being cooked in the large frying pan. Eating it all with bread and butter she then helped her mother wash up, and they made their way into the room which had been used the day before. They got to work tidying the room, in comfortable silence, only speaking when Lizzie needed to know where to put things away.

Between them, they finished just before lunch, and Margo said: "Darling, I need to organise some lunch for everyone, I don't know about you, but I have built up an appetite?"

Her daughter looked at her and agreed as she did feel hungry, they walked together down into the kitchen. Her mother found what she needed as Edna had left everything ready. Lizzie thought she definitely knew her way around the kitchen, she had been taught well by the cook. Lizzie wondered if Edna and Geoffrey had set off on their honeymoon this morning in the country. She hoped they had a lovely time, as they deserved it, it was a shame she would not see them when they got back. Her mother brought her back from her daydreams, and they got to work preparing the meal for the patients and staff. It would be sandwiches and cake for lunch and then for tea rabbit stew, which they would prepare after lunch.

Everyone enjoyed the sandwiches, and they finished the wedding cake off, with cold lemonade to drink. As soon as lunch was finished, Margo asked her daughter to stay and help prepare the stew; the rabbits were ready as Sir Clifford had prepared them when they were caught. Lizzie peeled the potatoes, and her father came down and helped with the vegetables.

They all worked well together in synchronisation, Lizzie genuinely hoped that the army taking over their home would bring her family closer together. Maybe, she wished, that in the end her mother would let her choose who she wanted to marry. If Margo met Christopher, then she would certainly change her mind and like him. Time to get in contact with her aunt, now she found out from her parents that her aunt had a new home on the outskirts of Coventry, purchased with the help of her and Edward's parents.

The three of them were chatting while preparing the stew, and Lizzie was getting to see another side to her parents, which she had never seen, they were helping each other, and it seemed they were truly enjoying each other's company. The afternoon went very quickly, and the three carried the stew up into the dining room, where they served it to the soldiers who could sit at the table, the nurses taking the stew to the patients in the beds. Agnes came into the room and took some in a bowl to a soldier she was nursing, and then asked to have hers when she got her break. Lizzie stood admiring Agnes's smart uniform her grey dress and scarlet-trimmed cape looked distinctive.

Lizzie was going back to The London tomorrow, she felt slightly disappointed because she really would miss her parents for the first time since she went away to boarding school.

"I will help to wash up now all the stew has gone, and then I need to pack my clothes. Can I take Binky for a walk as it is still warm outside, and we haven't had a raid for a few days?"

Sir Clifford looked at his daughter lovingly and said, "Certainly." So they took the pots and carried them to the kitchen and got to work washing up in the big sink. Between the three of them, the job was completed in quick time, Lizzie excused herself and went off to do her packing. Binky followed her up to her room; she had been sitting in her bed in the kitchen all afternoon, as it had been another hot day, they could do with a thunderstorm to bring the heat down.

Packing didn't take long, as Lizzie had the art of it down to perfection. Binky had climbed onto her bed, watching her mistress while she worked. Once finished, Lizzie called Binky, and the dog jumped off the bed and followed her out the open door down to the kitchen.

Her parents were still in there, drinking coffee together, she heard laughter as she entered the room. It made her feel warm inside as she could see that they were so happy in each other's company. Lizzie and Binky headed out the back door and proceeded towards the lake; it was nice to be out in the cool of the evening. Looking up at the sky, she could see dark clouds rolling in. "Come on girl, we had better be quick." Looking down at the dog who had been her companion for a long time; "otherwise, we are going to get very wet."

Walking briskly, they made it to the lake, as they turned around, the first few heavy drops of rain begun to fall, Lizzie said, "Come on girl, lets go!" And with that she began to sprint. They made it back in record time, but she was soaked, and Binky ran into the kitchen once Lizzie had opened the door, and she shook herself in the kitchen, which made her mother shout at the dog.

Her father got an old towel and rubbed the dog dry, who was enjoying the attention. Her mother got Lizzie a towel and told her to run a bath and not get cold. Lady Margo got to work cleaning the kitchen where the dog had just been; Binky climbed into her bed.

Lizzie did as she was told and quickly went upstairs and into the bathroom. Running the bath, she got out of the wet clothes and climbed into a hot bath, relaxing into the warmth, she could go to sleep. Twenty minutes later she climbed out, emptied the tub and cleaned it, put on her pyjamas; sitting on the bed reading listening to the rain against the now-closed window. Lizzie read for a while, till she felt her eyelids droop with tiredness, she climbed into bed, it was cooler thanks to the rain and soon fell asleep.

It was still raining as Lizzie woke up, she dressed for the journey, took a look in the mirror, and happy with what she saw, ran down the stairs for breakfast. Lady Margo was already up and had again made breakfast.

"Do you do this every day?" her daughter asked.

"Yes," came the reply.

Again, she was taken by surprise, her mother pointed to the table.

"Sit," she said. Lizzie did as she was asked and was handed a plate. She didn't realise how hungry she was and tucked in, once finished she helped her mother to clear up and wash the plates and cutlery, ready for cook's return in the afternoon. Her father was driving her to the station, she brought her suitcase down and collected her belongings.

With great sadness she said her goodbyes and gave her mother a warm hug which was a first, her mother hugged her back with warmth. It was still raining as Lizzie climbed into the Rolls, and felt her tears fall as her father drove away from the Hall. Sitting in the front, her father noticed the tears and took one hand off the steering wheel, rubbing her hand with tenderness, which made the tears fall freely, she took out her hanky and wiped them. Glancing at her father she felt foolish, she was turning into a soppy mess, but she had to admit, it was a nice feeling having a close family, if only Eddie had been home to witness it. When she got back, she would write to him and tell of the events that had transpired these last few days.

"I'm sorry," was about all she could say to him, as they approached the station.

"Don't be daft," he said.

"Do you think Mother is mellowing?" she asked hesitantly.

"Honestly, who knows," was his reply. "This may be just a one-off, or truly something to last a lot longer. Be patient," her father offered as advice. "If this young man is worth it, then he will wait for you as long as it takes, and with this war, it may be a long time."

Lizzie absorbed what her father had said and got out of the car, he ran around to get her suitcase, while she collected her handbag and gas mask, from the front seat. Stopping in front of him, he held out his arms, and she went into them, and he held his daughter tight.

"Promise me you will stay safe, they are still bombing?"

Before she could answer, she heard the train to London approaching, and her father carried her suitcase onto the platform, the train slowed and came to a stop. Lizzie hurried to buy her ticket luckily there wasn't a long queue, rushing back out onto the platform to the awaiting train. Lizzie opened the carriage door and put her case in and then climbed in, she turned to have one more look at her father, who then closed the door behind her, she lowered the window and stuck her head out.

"Promise me you will stay safe?" he said again.

"Yes, I promise," she called out as the train pulled out of the station.

The journey back to the hospital was uneventful, and she arrived back by mid-afternoon.

Chapter 30

Daisy had arrived back first, she knew her friend was not back, because as she entered the grounds of The London, Tom, the head porter had told her that nobody else had arrived yet. Heading towards the nurse's home, her mind travelled back to her home and what had occurred yesterday, she would be able to talk to Lizzie about what she had witnessed, she would understand.

She also wanted to know how her friend had managed at home, especially dealing with her mother. Walking up the stairs to her room trying to balance her suitcase, looking around, it really was feeling familiar now and like home. Stopping at the door she put her suitcase by her leg, she found her key in her handbag and unlocked her door, entering, she headed over to her bed, dropped her suitcase on it ready to unpack. Placing her coat on the peg, hanging her handbag and gas mask she turned and got on with unpacking. It didn't take too long, and at last all her clothes were hanging back in her wardrobe, her mother had managed to get them clean and she came over nostalgic and prayed her family would be safe.

Daisy looked down at the watch on her wrist, checking the time for lunch, if she hurried, she would just about make it. Locking the door, she raced down the stairs, pushing the door out into the sunshine, running across to the main block, she carried on down the corridor to the dining hall. Choosing a sandwich and drink, she found an empty space and quickly ate it, and with a flourish cleared away her rubbish, and walked back to her room, saying hello to her fellow nurses as they passed in the corridor.

Once outside her room she heard someone inside, she slowly turned the knob and entered. Relief washed over her when she saw Lizzie, unpacking her clothes.

"Welcome back," she said and reached out and hugged her friend in a tight hug.

Both girls burst into laughter. "Come and sit on the bed, so we can catch up." Lizzie patted the bed. "I have so much to tell, but you go first," she said looking at Daisy.

Sitting on her bed she explained about her brother and that he was now in Portsmouth training before joining his ship. Then she told her about the air raid and helping to find the baby that had survived and her mother barely alive. Daisy started to cry and her friend held her tight as the tears fell.

"I'm so sorry," she said in a low voice once she had settled. "My emotions got the better of me, I knew you would understand," smiling at her roommate. "Now tell me of your time away."

Lizzie explained how her mother had helped in the kitchen, prepared the house for the wedding and really looked as if she loved her father.

"I have never seen her show any affection before."

Daisy asked, "What has changed her?"

Lizzie said, "I honestly don't know, but having the injured soldiers there has helped my mother show some compassion."

Lizzie told her friend about Agnes and being a nurse in the army. "We should really look into that once we are qualified," said Lizzie.

Daisy eagerly agreed. Then Lizzie told her, she had opened up to her father and had explained to him her love for Christopher and how her father had been so supportive and offered to help sort it out with the help of Aunt Lynn.

"I really hope it works out well for you," Daisy said, but she knew her friend had a long way to go, as once Lady Margo had a plan or idea, she didn't give up easily, but at that precise time she would let her friend enjoy the moment.

Jenny and Claire arrived back during the afternoon; Jenny had said the bombing had been exceptionally bad down in Brighton, and her mother and uncle and his family were lucky to not be hurt, the home had slight damage, mainly the windows. Her brother Freddy had joined the army and was somewhere abroad fighting at present.

Claire's family had been lucky as well, and they were all okay. Her sister had just turned eighteen and was joining the Wrens and going down to Portsmouth to start her training. Her brother had another year before he could join the navy unless he lied about his age.

For all four, it was nice to be back, to catch up with each other's news and get ready to finish the second year and to go into their final year with a flourish and optimism. They all hoped that at the end, they would come out as qualified nurses.

Lizzie didn't tell the other two what had gone on at home, as Daisy was the only person she confided in. It was still hot and the rain from last night had long gone, it had cooled the air slightly, but the heat had returned during the day, especially in the city.

After tea, they all sat outside on a patch of grass which had dried in the heat, letting the late afternoon sun beat down to warm their faces, they all listened to the birds sitting in the tree above singing, while Lizzie and Jenny had a cigarette or two.

"Have you heard from Eddie?" asked Daisy, making conversation.

"No, I need to write to him. I was hoping to do that tonight and I desperately need to write to Aunt Lynn now she has moved into her new home. I have received a letter from Christopher, which was waiting for me when I arrived back." She hadn't opened it and was itching to read it as soon as possible, it was sitting on their shared desk, where she had left it.

Once the girls had finished their cigarettes, they decided to have a walk as it was a nice early evening, they walked along Whitechapel Road and down by the docks as far as they could go, it was full of ships unpacking their goods. The steel cranes stood tall, swaying against the back drop of the ships all lined up to be unloaded. The noise from the docks were deafening. Walking back, they looked around at all the bomb damage and destruction, it was everywhere, they all prayed that the worst was over.

They walked in the entrance to the hospital and proceeded up to the nurse's home where Lizzie offered them all a night cap. By eight the girls went their separate ways to get ready for the morning, uniforms were prepared and Jenny and Claire both went off to have baths.

This gave Lizzie the chance to read her letter from Christopher, she sat on her bed as she opened the envelope without damaging the sheet inside. It never said much as the censor blocked out a lot but as she read, it was full of love and of hope, he couldn't say where he was but she guessed, and hoped their paths would cross again before the end of the war. He wanted her to meet his family. And she felt she couldn't write that back just yet as she had to pave the way with her mother.

Daisy sat reading but was observing her friend as she read the letter, her expression was full of love, and it gave Daisy a warm glow to see her friend happy. Daisy hoped she would find this kind of love someday, and her mind slipped to a certain Dr Michael Reynolds, and she wondered where he was. She hoped he was safe and well, and it put a smile on her face which didn't go unnoticed by Lizzie.

Finishing the letter, she placed it back in the envelope and popped it in her drawer with all her others, keeping them safe for if she wanted to read them again. She had numbered them and kept them in order. Pulling out her sheets of writing paper she went back to sit at the desk.

Her first letter was the most urgent, as it was to her aunt Lyn asking for help. Sorting out this situation for her brother and herself, and adding her father was now willing to assist as well. She really hoped that her aunt answered soon as Lizzie was worried that Charles would be back and make her meet up in a hotel room, she knew she wasn't strong enough to fight him and she wanted her first time to be with someone she truly loved, and there was the possibility of her getting pregnant, which she didn't want.

She had heard during their training, of men using a French Letter which they had been given, and she would make sure that if it was Charles, he would use one! Before that actually happened, she would try and keep Charles out of the way and she secretly hoped he stayed abroad and that their paths didn't cross. Her next letter was to Eddie updating him on all the news of home, he would be surprised about their father and even more at how their mother had changed. Once these two were sealed she stuck stamps on them to post them in the morning.

Daisy had to write to her brother, George and she would do that the next evening, finding she was tired from travelling. By ten it was lights out, it felt nice being back in their beds and they lay talking quietly, until sleep took them, they both did hope the bombers would keep away tonight.

They did in fact have a peaceful night with no interruptions; they were both up early and ready for breakfast, knocking for Jenny and Claire. Hilary was up and boasting as usual, the girls ignored her, and walked down to the dining hall. Breakfast was a noisy affair and once finished the girls headed off to their rooms to finish getting ready, they picked up their notebooks and textbooks and set out to the Preliminary Training School. In the classroom the girls sat down, chatting quietly and waited for the lecture to commence. Dead on nine Sister Tutor entered the room, which went silent, and they began. Lunch time soon came around and they advanced to the dining hall, all four talking about what they had learnt that morning, lunch finished and they made their way back for an afternoon of more lectures and practical lessons.

By the end of the day, they were all tired and after tea they met in Lizzie and Daisy's room, to go over their notes, ready for the test.

Daisy managed to write to her brother, saying he was foolish but very brave and how proud she was of him, and to keep his head down and stay safe. The rest of the time flew by, and Friday was soon approaching. Exam day and the girls were feeling the pressure and the nerves were playing havoc.

"Remember, we know it," Lizzie said to her friends as they entered the classroom. Taking their places, they were told to start, and they turned the paper over and began. Their results would be up on Sunday morning and their new ward placements later the same day, most of the wards were filled with injured service men, and some civilians who had been caught up in the bombings.

They had found out that in their final year they would be nursing on a ward filled with German soldiers who had been shot down and injured. Daisy and Lizzie had talked about how they would feel, could they control their emotions, as a German had killed a cousin of Lizzie's? Both had agreed that they could be professional and just do the job they were trained for. These men were only fighting because of one man, Hitler. If they refused; they would be in great trouble.

The exam was over quickly, and the girls were released once they had finished, they had been given the rest of the day off, so they decided to make the most of the sunshine and sat out on a blanket on the grass. The Luftwaffe had only come over one night this week and the raid did not last long, there was still some damage to the docks but the hospital was missed. Day time raids were becoming less, it was good, but people still couldn't believe they were truly over the worst. Saturday night as usual the girls were agitated and couldn't settle, tomorrow the results came out; the nerves were playing games. None of them could eat much, as they felt sick, and they all hoped they would sleep well. Lizzie got the scotch out and gave a bigger measure than normal, to settle every one down. By ten they were all sleepy and went off to bed. It was decided between them that Lizzie would check the board in the morning.

They gathered together wishing each other a good morning and all advanced to the dining hall for a cooked breakfast, they ate it in silence as they all felt sick with nerves, they got like this every time. It would be all over just after ten when that list got pinned to the notice board, and the girls were put out of their misery. Lizzie being the confident one, knew they had all done well, in particular Daisy who always shone in the exams, the other two really had nothing to worry about and neither did she.

Walking back to the nurse's home, they stopped outside so Lizzie and Jenny could smoke, it was another beautiful day, the weatherman had stated on the wireless the other night that the weather was going to break in a couple of days and would become more unsettled but still warm. Having both finished their cigarettes, they stamped them out and all four went back to their rooms to finish getting ready. Dead on ten they pushed Lizzie out through their door, Jenny and Claire had joined them for their nervous wait. Lizzie had peeped out, to witness Sister Tutor pinning the list up. A group of girls had already gathered round the board and were scanning the list, there were squeals of excitement, Lizzie finally got to the front after patiently waiting her turn, she too scanned. Daisy was, as she thought, at the top, herself second, Jenny and Claire not far behind, but with some relief they had all had passed. She basically skipped a few steps back to her room, noticing the girls had their heads sticking out watching her mannerisms the whole time. They had hurried back into the room on seeing her return. Lizzie tried her hardest to conceal her happiness, but once she faced all three, she couldn't keep it going, she let out a whoop.

"Well?" They all cried in unison, looking directly at Lizzie. She smiled and recited what she had seen, all three beamed with pride.

"What did Hilary get?"

"Way down, she has just passed."

"She won't be pleased with that," they all cried.

The rest of the morning flew by, the girls spent the morning relaxing in the room, talking about where they would be placed. Soon it was lunchtime, the dining hall was busy for a Sunday, and the girls had to join the end of the queue, chatting away to each other as the line moved forward slowly. Reaching the hatch, they chose their food, which was hot, bland but edible looking. They took it to an empty table and sat down, picking up the cutlery they all tucked in. With lunch finished, they had the afternoon free, clearing away their dirty plates and cutlery, the four went outside to get some fresh air and to have the customary smoke.

By late afternoon, the four had red faces from the heat of the sun beating down on them, they made their way back inside to look at the list for their upcoming placements. By four, the list was in place, put there by Sister Tutor, Lizzie again was designated checker. Looking up at the board, all four were to work together on wards mainly filled with injured servicemen. They were to cover between one floor working on either ward, it wasn't perfect, but it was war time.

The girls were excited to all be working together for the first time, the day so far had gone exceedingly well, they were all excited for the next day. After tea, the girls sat around in the common room listening to the news on the wireless.

"We need the Americans to enter the war," said Lizzie seriously, then we have a chance of winning it." The others agreed and they hoped that soon it would happen but more unlikely it wouldn't happen, not in the near future. The president was against it, but Churchill still hoped.

Turning off the wireless, they walked up the stairs to bed, saying "goodnight, see you tomorrow." Daisy and Lizzie headed into their room, and they got into their night clothes, ready for bed. Like every night, when they were on the same shift, they talked until sleep took them, it had been an emotional day. It was common that on the first morning of a new ward, it was always an early shift, late shifts would come later in the week once they got their 'off duty' notifications. Lizzie and Daisy entered ward three, walking straight to the locker room they got ready. Once they were happy in their appearance they went and joined morning hand-over.

Sister Williams motioned them to join the other nurses. "So, we meet again Student Nurses Peters and Fenton, nice to see you are on time and dressed appropriately," she said with a slight glint in her eye, glancing down at the watch on her breast and then looking back at the two young women. "Right, as you can see, we have a full ward mainly consisting of young, wounded soldiers and a few civilians caught up in the bombing. Bed baths have been completed by the night shift and it's just a few washes left, then dressing round and TPR and blood pressure round."

At eleven Lizzie was sent to her break, Daisy had gone before and carried on taking temperatures, pulses and respirations. On completion she was told to do blood pressure checks on the men needing it. Daisy placed the cuff on the young soldier's arm, pumping it up till the cuff ballooned and then released it slowly, listening to pulse through the stethoscope. Recording the details on a chart, she happily chatted to the young man, and having a discrete laugh with him. If she was caught by Sister Williams, she would be angry, and Daisy would be sent to Matron's Office. Not wanting that to happen, Daisy had learnt to hide bantering with the young brave soldiers. Lizzie felt right at home on this ward too, and both girls knew they would enjoy their time on the ward.

By five they were both tired and happy to be sent off. Leaving the locker room they walked through the ward to the door, the soldiers were watching their movements and the fit ones were whistling at the two girls. Sister heard, came out of her office and shouted at the men. Both girls nearly ran through the door laughing, with Sister Williams' voice still in the background they headed off down the corridor and back to the nurse's home, tired feet forgotten. The girls had found out they were to stay on this ward longer than normal due to staff shortages, and so they went into their final year on this ward.

Two years had passed since the start of the war and so much had happened, Lizzie had got a reply from her Aunt Lynn at last, the letter was waiting for her after a shift a few weeks later. She recognised the handwriting on the envelope, and ran up to her room, hearing Home Sister telling her to slow down in the background. Up in her room, she got changed very quickly and laid on the clean bed, she was fascinated to read it.

Opening in a flurry, she nearly ripped the sheet inside, so she carefully pulled out the sheet and opened it. Scanning over the writing, then reading it again once she had taken in what it had actually said. Basically, she liked her new home, thanking Lizzie's mother for the donation towards it, she was happy that her aunt was at last settled. Reading on her aunt thought that in time her mother would probably change her mind on her own and once she had met Christopher it would all go smoothly along. Lizzie was a little upset at this comment, she wasn't so sure that her mother would change that quickly, so she read on and her aunt continued, if her sister didn't change, then her aunt and father would step in.

Well, she had better hurry for the sake of her brother and Glenda, she had mentioned this in the letter. Well in the meantime, she and her brother would have to meet up and take Glenda home with them next leave they had together and work on their mother from that angle. If she was to meet Glenda face to face, as her aunt suggested, then hopefully she could see what a pleasant and delightful girl she actually was, and that they loved one another very much. It may, just work she thought, she would contact her brother and set the plan in motion, if on the off chance it failed then she would have to rethink with the help of her aunt and father, at that moment she felt like crossing her fingers.

Sitting on her bed, she laid back and thought she would run the plan through with Daisy when she returned from her shift, and gauge her reaction, she might have an idea too.

Much later an exhausted Daisy walked in having finished late. "We had an emergency," she stated. "But it got all sorted." Rubbing her tired feet, once taking her shoes off, she sat on her bed to slowly unwind from her day.

Lizzie dived in explaining about the contents of her aunt's letter and her advice. "So what do you think," she sat back patiently waiting for her friend to answer.

After what seemed like a long time Daisy spoke. "I think it may work, your mother, if she was to meet Glenda, could see what the girl is like in the flesh."

"Yes," agreed Lizzie. "But she is very stubborn.

"Then you have to convince her more. Between the three of you and don't forget your father, once he knows he will help."

"It may just work," Lizzie thought.

"Now I'm actually shattered," said Daisy.

"What happened," asked Lizzie, concerned for her friend.

"Well, a building collapsed and trapped people walking by a young boy got caught and he had to have his leg amputated, another man died."

Her emotions were all over the place, so Lizzie pulled out the bottle from under the floorboards and poured her friend a large drink, her heart ached for her.

Lizzie's thoughts turned to the little boy whose life had been turned upside down today due to this war, shaking her head she carried on talking to Daisy.

Chapter 31

The weeks were flying by, Lizzie did in fact write again to her brother, who wrote back when he could. Yes, he agreed to give the plan a go, as he hadn't been home since the last time, just before Christmas, when he had fallen out with their mother.

In the meantime, she had also heard from Charles who would soon be back in the country, and he wanted to meet up with her in London and at a hotel, which he would sort out. She really didn't want to go, her heart wasn't in it, but what choice at that moment did she have. If she didn't go, he would inflict more mental pain on her until she did agree, she was torn.

Lizzie sort of had a plan, she had a thought if she plied him with lots of alcohol, maybe he would just pass out on the bed and she would be gone before the morning when he woke up hopefully with a sore head, she knew it was a weak but at that very moment it was the only one she had.

On the Saturday in question, she got her pass to be away from the nurse's home for twenty-four hours. Daisy was worried for her friend, she had explained her plan and Daisy didn't like it, she tried to get her to cancel but Lizzie was adamant she was going.

Finding a dress that was comfortable and not sexy, she wrapped up warm in her coat as it was October and the weather was changing, summer had turned to Autumn, she said a nervous goodnight to her roommate and hugged her tight.

Daisy said in a very apprehensive voice to please be careful, she was nearly begging her to change her mind and not go but her friend was adamant she was going whatever the consequences. All the way there she felt sick, at one stage she nearly turned around but drew some strength from inside her. As she arrived at the hotel she physically shook and pulled her coat up around her and she took a deep breath and entered.

Charles was already sitting in the bar, drink in hand. He spotted her and waved his hand, and she walked over. He seemed surprised she had turned up.

"I really didn't think you would come?" he sneered.

"Did I really have a choice?" she asked, her voice shaking.

"No, not really, as I would have made your life hell, before and when we are married," he snarled callously. "You are going to sleep with me and enjoy it, understand."

She nodded her head. Unable to speak, she felt the goose bumps on her arms.

"Here, have a drink." He passed her a whiskey and she downed it in one, he smiled. They sat for a while in silence, Charles kept the drinks coming and all Lizzie could do was keep drinking them, she didn't want to make conversation with him.

"Please, let's get this out the way," she mumbled.

"What's the hurry?" he asked. "We have all night," he said laughing.

They talked about his time away and he how would be off again soon, which couldn't come quick enough for Lizzie. He was going to see his parent's tomorrow and then they could start to plan the wedding.

Lizzie thought she was going to be sick. "I need the toilet," she said, and rushed off. Once inside to room she splashed her face with cold water.

She tried to calm her nerves and said, "I can do this." Walking back to the hotel bar, Charles was already standing, so her plan had gone out the window.

"I have the room key." He waved it at her, and he led her up the stairs, gripping her arm tightly so she couldn't get away, she swayed a little, she spent the time looking around trying to forget the pain in her arm. It was okay she thought but not plush, well, what did she expect, the Ritz!

The room was on the second floor, he put the key in the lock and turned it, the door opened, and they entered. The room was dark, especially with the blackout blinds pulled and the curtains closed. Charles found the light switch and he put the light on. Lizzie took a couple of moments for her eyes to adjust, there was a double bed, the sheets looked worn and outdated but clean and it had a bathroom with worn looking towels on the rail, she looked around trying to stall for time.

Her arm throbbed, she rubbed it. He took his jacket off and he sat on the edge of the bed, he calmly asked her to join him. She went over and sat down as her head was reeling with pain.

"Take your dress off," he ordered, which she did, it took longer as her hands were shaking. Now standing in only her underwear, Charles looked her up and down his lips salivating. "Now your underwear." So she did as he asked and removed her bra and knickers. As she did so she shivered, she felt exposed, she rolled down her stockings.

He looked her up and down taking her in, he licked his lips with anticipation, dribbling he wiped his mouth with the back of his hand. She wanted to cry, her emotions were all over the place, she tried to calm her nerves, she had drunk too much.

He got himself undressed in a hurry. "Lay down he ordered."

"Before we do this, have you got a French Letter?" she asked as calm as she could, her voice was dry.

He laughed. "How on earth do you know about them?" So Lizzie was not as naive as he first thought

"I'm not that naïve," she replied angrily, as if reading his mind.

"No," he snarled, nearly shouting.

"Then we are not doing this, I have changed my mind," she answered calmly. She went to get up and put her clothes back on, her hands shaking again.

He grabbed her, pushed her back on the bed with some force and slapped her face hard, she reeled back on the bed, tears pricking her eyes, she wanted to rub her face, but he pinned her down with some force. She could feel he was aroused; his penis was erect and against her. He grabbed her arms and held her down as he got on top of her, she tried to fight but he was just too strong, he kept pressing his penis against her, he positioned his hand and guided himself in with some force, Lizzie cried out in pain, as he entered, he thrust in and out, pounding against her, she was crying as he came.

He was incensed as he had come quicker than he would have liked. Once spent, he rolled off her and once he got his breath back, he said, "Well, my little fiancé was a virgin? And I'm sorry to say it was not very good. I've had better, you had better sort yourself out!" Laughing he got up and dressed and said, "I will be in contact, be good." With that he left the room.

Lizzie laid still, controlling her shaking and taking deep breaths, she tried to get up. She was so sore, she looked down and saw blood between her legs, she retched and just made it to the bathroom and vomited into the toilet. Once finished she felt better, wiping her hand across her mouth. She had a drink of water, and she looked at herself in the bathroom mirror and saw the red mark on her face where he had slapped her, and her make-up had run. Lizzie thought she could hide it with some powder.

Slowly she walked unsteadily back to the bedroom and she got dressed slowly, feeling disgusted with herself and feeling as if it was her fault, well she did let it happen. When ready she checked her appearance, once happy, locking the room, she walked down the stairs and handed the key back.

"Do I need to pay," she choked, trying not to cry.

"No," the elderly receptionist replied, the gentleman paid in full.

"He is no gentleman," she said to herself.

"Can you get me a taxi, please?" she asked.

"Certainly," he said looking concerned at the young lady stood in front of him. "Are you all right miss?" he asked.

"Yes, thank you." Lizzie replied shaking.

The taxi arrived, she got in carefully and told the driver where to go, and she prayed Home Sister didn't see her in this state as she didn't want to answer any questions. All she wanted was a hot bath, Daisy and her bed.

On arrival at the hospital, it was late, and she paid the driver. Walking over to the nurse's home she knew the door would be locked, she waited till Home Sister was in her room and she found the spare key, that was hidden. Unlocking the door, she crept in and took the stairs tentatively up to her room. Daisy hadn't locked it, she opened it and she saw her friend asleep; she walked over and shook her awake.

"Daisy, Daisy, please wake up," she cried.

Daisy opened her eyes, still full of sleep. She took one look and knew something bad had happened, she sat bolt upright and rubbed the sleep from her eyes, then she got up and her friend starting crying.

The tears kept falling, Daisy just held her tightly until there were no more tears left for her to cry. Once she was feeling better, Daisy gently led her to the bed.

"Come sit." Lizzie was grateful as she felt her legs were about to give way. She began to explain what had happened earlier and Daisy just sat rubbing her back and listened, not judging her at all.

"Do you want to tell the police or go to casualty?" she asked attentively.

"No, they will say it was my fault, that I led him on. Even encouraged him."

"Let's get you into a hot bath and bed." So Daisy helped her distressed friend to the bathroom, hoping that the running water wouldn't wake anyone up, or bring Home Sister up the stairs enquiring what was going on. In the light of the bathroom Daisy saw the red angry mark on her friends face but decided not to say anything at present. "I am right outside the door, shout if you need me."

Closing the door behind her, Lizzie climbed in the hot water, a warm comforting feeling washed over her as she laid down in the hot water. She wanted to wash the events of the last few hours away from her memory forever, but she knew in her heart that the events would be there for a long time. She noticed the hand marks on her arm where Charles had gripped her really hard, she would try and hide them till they healed up.

Daisy stood outside the door the whole time, waiting till she heard the water go down the plug hole. Lizzie got dressed into her pyjamas.

The door opened, and Daisy took her friend and led her to their room. "Come on, get into bed and we will talk in the morning, lucky we are both off tomorrow."

Neither of them could sleep, Daisy kept an eye on her friend all night. She heard the crying and didn't hesitate, she got out of her bed, walked over to Lizzie's bed and got in with her and held her tight the rest of the night.

Sunday morning arrived, both girls woke up together, Lizzie was aching all over, her eyes sore from all the crying, her first words to Daisy were, "Thank you, for last night."

Daisy just held her friend again. "I'm here for you, don't you forget it." Lizzie, now she had time to think, said seriously. "What happens if I am pregnant?"

Daisy said, "Let's cross that bridge if it happens, when are you due another period?"

"Around four weeks, I have just had one."

"You may be fine," Daisy said encouragingly.

"It's going to be the longest four weeks of my life," replied Lizzie.

Her friend hugged her tight. "Are you up for some breakfast or do you want me to say you are sick?"

"No, I have to act as normally as possible, otherwise he has beaten me, and that won't happen."

Daisy heard the determination in her friend's voice and in her actions. "Right, let's get dressed and go and get breakfast, and spend the day together, are you going to tell your mother?" asked Daisy.

"No, I'm going to tell no one apart from you and I will write to my aunt and explain to her. My only concern now is how Christopher will cope with the news, when I tell him I was raped."

There, she had actually said it out loud, and now she could start to rebuild her life, hopefully. Oh! how she wished she hadn't gone to meet him, but she knew in her heart he would do cruel things to her if she hadn't gone and would have made her life hell. Now she understood what could have happened a few years ago, she would ask her brother again and get him to find out why it was brushed under the carpet and kept quiet, then she could use that against the evil man. Maybe if her mother knew the truth, then she would let her daughter marry the man she loves.

Luckily it was only the two of them to go for breakfast this morning, so with a slower pace than normal the two girls walked down to the dining hall. As they passed Home Sister's office, they heard her.

"Student Nurse Fenton, stop right there." Both girls looked at each other startled and stopped in their tracks.

Home Sister came out of her room. "Why are you back early, and how did you get in?" Home Sister stared directly at the young student nurse awaiting an answer. She wanted to know, her voice coming across angry.

"I was not well, and the door was open," she lied, hoping she was believed.

"Well, I can see you don't look well, do you need to go to sick bay?" asked the concerned woman.

"No, I will feel better this morning."

"All right then, I will look into the door being left open, with that you are free to carry on."

The girls couldn't get away quick enough, and hurried across to the main block. "I'm not telling her about the key, as it saved me last night. I hope she doesn't find it, we will move it to a new hiding place later, and then move it back when it's safe, letting everyone know what's going on."

The dining hall was quiet for a Sunday morning, breakfast was a very tense time as Daisy didn't want to say the wrong thing, so she was glad to leave and get back to their room. Lizzie got some strange looks as she moved gingerly but ignored the stares.

They finally got back to the room. "Please take it easy today and will you be okay to work tomorrow?" Daisy asked concerned.

"Yes, I promise, I will fine tomorrow and fit to work," promised an unsure Lizzie.

"Now get back into bed get some sleep," said Daisy.

As Lizzie got undressed, Daisy noticed the red finger marks on her friend's arm, but she didn't say anything.

"I will be here if you need anything," offered Daisy.

"Yes nurse," came Lizzie's reply, laughing for the first time today.

She did feel exhausted. Lizzie fell asleep as soon as her head touched the pillow and she didn't wake up till late afternoon. Daisy had kept her promise and had been there the whole time reading her book, all the time she was feeling angry at her friend's recent ordeal.

"Wow! You look a bit better!" she said with gusto.

"I feel it, the sleep did me good, let's go to get tea, I'm starving, and don't forget, not a word to anyone."

"I promise," Daisy replied solemnly.

Jenny was coming out of her room and joined them for tea, she could tell that her friend was out of sorts and would quiz Daisy later. Daisy, once she got into bed after sorting her friend out, looked back at the last twenty-four hours and felt the tension escape from her body. As she relaxed; she knew it would take time for her friend's pain to heal. The next hurdle to cross was if she was pregnant. Daisy crossed her fingers and prayed a lot. In fact, she hoped and prayed over the next four weeks.

Lizzie's mind was not on the job, and she was pulled up many times. She was even sent to Matron's office and given a warning to get her act together or she would be put on a verbal warning. That night Daisy gave her a good talking to. Over the next week, Lizzie slowly started to be her old self, not a hundred percent but her work improved, but her mind still kept wandering and she worried whether she was pregnant. If so, would she keep the baby? She knew she couldn't get rid of it, so she would have to leave.

On roughly the fourth week her question was answered, one morning she was on the ward having the usual stomach ache all morning, she came rushing over to Daisy. "I need to go back to the nurse's home to put on some sanitary wear. These were made of old sheets which were mainly washed or sometimes disposed of. I have started my period. I'm not pregnant." She was on cloud nine.

Lizzie nearly skipped with joy down the ward, and Daisy, well she was really delighted for her friend, now Lizzie could start to heal. Lizzie had written to her aunt and to her brother, she now had to wait for their replies. Aunt Lynn was the first to answer, she was shocked at the news but relieved her niece was not in the family way. Her Aunt Lynn was more determined to stop this wedding happening than ever before. Eddie's letter took a bit longer to reach her, he promised to look into that small matter that happened while at school, he would get to the bottom of it. He was concerned for his sister, as he had read between the lines of her letter that something bad had happened involving Charles.

Putting the letter away she was glad her brother hadn't pried further and maybe in time she would be able to tell him what happened, but she knew he would kill Charles if he did find out. Her biggest worry was what Chris would do if and when she told him, as she didn't want to lose him. She knew she would have to tell him sometime as she wanted no secrets between them.

Things after that sort of settled down and the four girls got into a regular routine. Jenny, concerned for her friend did ask Daisy but all she said was she had been unwell and was now better. Jenny knew to leave it at that, but she knew there was more to it. If the two girls wanted her to know then it would come out in time.

By the end of November, everyone was building up to Christmas and the start of 1942, and both Daisy and Lizzie were going on nights for two months at least. They both looked forlorn when they were informed, but to cheer them up, they would both be on nights over Christmas and New Year on opposite wards, with one staff nurse scheduled with them. Night Sister would be around if there was a problem. This was a big responsibility for both of them and they knew it, as they were entering their management experience. On the first week of December events changed, on seventh December the Japanese launched a sneak attack on Pearl Harbour, a big American naval base in Hawaii.

Lizzie and Daisy had settled on to nights and had the news on the wireless one evening before they had gone on shift. Lizzie said that would bring America into the war for sure now, and she knew the tide was turning in their favour. On December eleventh, Germany and Italy declared war on the United States and then the United States declared war on Germany and Italy. For Britain it meant that they had America as an ally and it gave hope to Britain. This was what Churchill had wanted for a long time, now it was really happening.

The week leading up to Christmas the wards tried to get into the Christmas spirit, but it was hard, as many people were still suffering. Rationing was bad and there were long queues everywhere you went for food and no shops had anything stocked now for days. If you wanted something special you had to get it on the black market and then you paid a bigger price for it. It was also a criminal offence and if caught, it meant a prison sentence.

Both girls were working Christmas Night and had arrived on the wards ready to start their shifts. Daisy was on Ward four and Lizzie across the way on Ward three, the layout was the same, some of the older medical students had been called in to help as some doctors had been called up for the services.

Tonight, they wanted some fun, they had taken the skeleton from the medical school and placed it in an empty bed, putting pyjamas on it, and pulling the sheets up around it, in the dark it looked real. They then put a screen round and left, they got busy, and completely forgot it was there. Daisy had watched as this was taking place, laughing quietly to herself, but she wasn't laughing when Night Sister had pulled the screen back, looking down at the bed, blinking twice she did a double take and then went a red colour.

Daisy thought she was going to burst a blood vessel, she tried to look busy, but she caught the eye of Night Sister, who stared at her intensely.

"Who did this?" she cried carrying on looking directly at Daisy.

"I don't know," replied the nervous Daisy.

"Well, if you don't tell me, I am sending you to Matron first thing in the morning."

Daisy's face went white. "But it wasn't me."

"So, tell who it was?"

Glaring at Night Sister. "I don't know!"

"Don't lie, girl."

Daisy wasn't going to tell on the medical students, but she didn't want to get a black mark against her name.

"First thing, before going off duty, report to Matron's office. Eight a.m. Get it cleared away," Night Sister said as she walked down the ward, and with that she was off out through the doors.

She hadn't realised the medical students had been watching from the locker room laughing at Daisy's misfortune. They approached the desk sheepishly and Jack the ringleader came up to Daisy and apologised and spoke to the young nurse, "Happy Christmas," he said cheerily. "Thank you for not giving the game away."

"She knows!" Was Daisy's reply. "She is not stupid."

"But we will take that chance, after all it is Christmas," he kissed Daisy's cheek and she blushed, he laughed.

They took the skeleton and left the ward with it tucked under Jack's arm, unbeknown to them some of the patients had also seen and watched the antics, they were also laughing and saying Night Sister had it coming. With that Daisy started laughing again with tears rolling down her face, she spotted Lizzie watching from the entrance to the ward, she too was laughing.

"Did you see?" she asked.

"Yes!" Was her only answer.

"Well, I'm glad you find it funny! I'm in trouble tomorrow morning with Matron."

"Oh, come on Daisy." Taking her arm. "Matron will know who the culprits are, you will be fine, let's go to our break." And with that the two friends headed towards the kitchen.

They sat in the quiet kitchen with the medical students and chatted with them about America entering the war and what that would mean for Britain, they all agreed it was for the best. Lizzie and Daisy finished their break, and Lizzie headed back to her ward. Daisy thought of Dr Reynolds and hoped he was safe. The rest of the night passed uneventfully, no bombs dropped and so by eight a tired, nervous Daisy, looking neat and tidy presented herself outside Matron's Office. She knocked on the wooden door, waited for the stern, 'enter', and she turned the knob. She took a deep breath to calm her nerves and entered.

Once inside the warm room the fire lit in the background making the room feel pleasant. She stood upright and rigid and in silence, waiting for Matron to speak first.

"Good morning, Student Nurse Peters, I hear from Night Sister you had an eventful night."

Daisy replied, "Yes, but it wasn't my fault."

Matron sat eyeing the young nurse who stood in front of her. "Oh, I know you weren't, but are you prepared to tell me who was?"

"No, Matron, I didn't see who it was, it was too dark."

Contemplating her next question, Matron waited a moment. "If I was to guess and you just nod your head, you are really not answering me directly?"

"Okay," replied Daisy.

"Was it the medical students?"

Daisy took her time, then nodded, and waited for what Matron had to say next. She said, "I know it is Christmas, and during these extremely difficult times we need to let our hair down and have some fun, and no harm was caused to anyone. In fact, I heard that the patients awake who witnessed the events enjoyed it, it has probably been good for them, they are young as well remember. So with that in mind, you are free to go, and let me deal with the culprits and Night Sister. Remember, I was young once and Happy Christmas," she said smiling.

With that Daisy was dismissed. She said, "Thank you and Merry Christmas, Matron." She turned, leaving quickly before Matron had a change of heart.

Closing the door behind her, she stopped and stood for a moment gathering her thoughts, taking deep breaths and relaxing for the first time since the middle of the night. Lizzie had promised to wait for her in the dining hall. On entering, she felt all eyes on her as she walked to the hatch, she chose her food and glanced around the room, meeting Lizzie's eyes over in the corner. She walked as quickly as she could over to her friend. Placing her tray on the table, she sat down.

Lizzie didn't give her a chance to start eating, before she asked, "Well?"

Daisy took a bite of her fried egg and bacon, chewed slowly and once swallowed she answered and explained what had happened.

"So you were let off?"

"Yes, because it wasn't me and I didn't actually tell her who the culprits were, but she knew already."

"Well, you were lucky?" her friend said.

"And I got out as soon as I could after that," said Daisy.

They finished their food and tidied their trays away and took the normal route to bed walking past all the sandbags that protected the doors.

The next night Daisy was apprehensive about entering the ward, she wanted a quiet Boxing Day night. As she pushed the ward door open, she noticed Jack sitting at the nurse's desk talking with a Staff Nurse from the late shift, he looked at the door and gave Daisy a big smile and wave when he realised who had entered. She smiled back thinking he must have got away with his antics last night.

In the locker room, she rolled her sleeves up and put her clean white apron on over her head, tying it up behind her. Happy with her look in the mirror, she got ready for the night ahead. Saying goodnight to the day staff, she prepared the men for bed and sleep, she did the medicine round and once they were ready, she dimmed the lights. The only light coming from her table, was her lamp glowing.

At nine the siren went off and Night Sister turned up. Daisy took off her cap, putting on her tin hat and with the help of the porters, the patients who could walk, were taken down to the basement, the others either had to take their chance in the bed or get under it. The bombs began to fall, and Daisy got under her table after making sure all her patients were fine. She knew Lizzie was doing the same in her ward and she said a little prayer and waited. The bombs rained down all night, luckily missing the hospital. The all-clear went off at around five in the morning, no major damage was reported and so all the patients were returned to the wards and got back into bed.

The two women finished off the shift and were in bed by nine. This routine carried on, New Year's Eve shift was uneventful, a few injuries caused by too much drinking, and some had to be admitted for observation, both girls had no sympathy as these injuries were self-inflicted.

Chapter 32

They welcomed 1942 with a kiss on the check and a hug, meeting at the door of Daisy's ward. Lizzie thought of Christopher and quietly wished him a Happy New Year wherever he was in the world, unbeknown Daisy was doing the same to Dr Michael Reynolds. By the morning the two friends were ready for their beds, they managed to briefly see Jenny and Claire, who were now also on nights on other wards around the hospital. All four met up in the dining hall and they all wished each other a Happy New Year and they all hoped for a better year ahead.

By summer they would be qualified nurses and where would they be this time next year? No one knew! January was a dark, dreary and what with the grey skies and a chance of snow, it was a miserable month. All the women did was work and revise for their examination, which would take place in June.

Lizzie had a letter from her brother saying he was meeting up with an old school friend who was now in the RAF like himself, he knew Charles very well from school and could cast some light on what happened. He would let her know as soon as he did, he was also taking Glenda home in a few weeks to finally meet their parents. Lizzie wished her brother well with that as it could go either way, she hoped for the best. She also had a letter from Charles, she really didn't want to open it, just touching the envelope made her shake and feel sick, so she asked Daisy to read it.

He was back abroad, relief flooded her as she knew he couldn't get to her at present. He briefly mentioned their time together and he hoped to repeat the experience again soon, Lizzie's face turned ashen, and she breathed quickly. Daisy put the letter down and went over to her friend, who luckily was sitting down before her legs had given way!

Crouching in front of her friend, she took her hands. "He can't touch you while he is away, and Eddie will get the information you need, you'll see."

"I don't know if to write back to Charles. What would I say to him?"

"Well, leave it at present and when you feel ready, reply but stay courteous and polite. I will help you," said Daisy.

The relief on Lizzie's face was present for both to see.

Daisy had been called into Matron's office first thing one morning and she had been told she would be working on the ward which nursed injured prisoners of war, mainly Germans.

When she left Matron's office, she was very nervous and apprehensive but pleased in a way it was her and not Lizzie, as she didn't think her roommate would handle it very well at this moment in time, even she didn't know how she would deal with her feelings towards them! Still, she had a couple of weeks to adjust before she was due on that particular ward, one thing she did know was that she would be the consummate professional as always.

Their revision was going really well, and a few others in the group had asked to join them. They would meet in the common room as it was bigger, and it could hold them all. All four were starting to feel confident about the forthcoming examination.

It was coming to the end of January and the weather was still cold and dreary, the snow was still falling and settling, this was causing havoc in the streets of Whitechapel. There were some injuries caused by the snow, like broken bones and sprains and strains, even getting knocked down by vehicles in the dark, especially when people couldn't be seen due to the blackout. A few people were even being killed while being hit by vehicles in the road, as a result the mortuary was getting rather full.

The four girls were getting expert at putting plaster casts on and bandaging miscellaneous body parts. It was hard to believe that in five months they would sit their final examination and then it would be all over and another chapter in their young lives would begin. It was an exciting but apprehensive time for them all.

Before Daisy started on the new ward, she was given clear instructions to be courteous and professional at all times and not to provoke prisoners, some of them could and would be obnoxious towards the staff looking after them. So, it was mainly male orderlies working on that particular ward, but due to shortages sometimes they had to use female nurses. There were armed guards placed at the entrance and on the ward, as these men were mostly loyal to Hitler and the Nazi party and had been indoctrinated into a certain way of thinking, these were the hardest men you would ever meet, who had been hoodwinked into joining the party. The night before, Daisy was worried, she kept pacing around the room, getting herself more worked up, not knowing how she would react to treating and meeting the enemy.

Lizzie did her best to reassure her friend, but it was difficult when her feelings were all over the place, they had, after all, killed her cousin and her brother had been fighting them in the air. Once she got to sleep, Daisy tossed and turned all night and was up well before she was due to start her shift. Lizzie had listened to Daisy tossing and turning, and it had pulled at her heart to see her colleague so distressed and so she had got up at the same time. Daisy was gratified that her friend had done that kind thing, she knew once she had spent one shift on the ward, she would be fine.

Daisy had been told to leave anything sharp and hair pins back in her room as they could be used as a weapon if got hold of. They sat in the dining hall, eating breakfast. Daisy had hardly touched hers, pushing her greasy eggs around her plate but she knew she had to eat something because it was going to be a long day. Lizzie held her hand and squeezed it reassuringly, they finished eating and headed back to their room to get ready. Daisy made sure she had the bare minimum on her as requested, checking herself in the mirror.

"Well, wish me luck?" she asked Lizzie who gave her friend a hug. "See you later."

Walking down the corridor to the ward, which was situated in the older part of the hospital, it felt like a long way, but she soon reached the entrance. A big sign said, PATIENTS WILL NOT ADVANCE BEYOND THIS POINT, the windows had been additionally barred, to discourage the prisoners from trying to escape.

Two armed guards were positioned out the front and stopped her as she approached. "Where do you think you are going?" They asked firmly.

"I'm to report here today," she replied, looking directly at the two young sentries.

"Can you show us your identification?"

Daisy showed them her identification papers. Once happy, one of

272

the lads pushed the door open and Daisy entered turning around to watch the door closing behind her. The ward was the same layout as she was used to which was a good start, lines of beds on both sides with young men laying on them, all eyes on her as she walked towards Sister's office. There were another two, armed guards at the bottom of the ward. The injured men all had pyjamas on with big yellow triangles on them to show they were prisoners. Knocking on the door of Sister's office, she was called to enter.

Sitting behind the desk was Sister Dors, a harsh-looking woman, Daisy thought. "You will be working with Sidney today, he will show you what to do. Remember this is a difficult ward to work on, it plays with your emotions. If at any time you feel overwhelmed come and see me, do not talk to the prisoners apart from when dealing with them, do you understand?" she said looking straight at the young student nurse.

Daisy stood looking around as she waited for Sidney, the male orderly, who she was to work with. He was a tall, muscular man with a friendly face, he smiled at Daisy as he walked towards her.

"Come on then nurse, let's get to work, just pay no attention to the comments they come out with, understand?"

Some of the men were respectful, others were rude and made unpleasant comments, but the morning went by quicker than she thought it would, once she overcame her nerves. There were two doctors working on the ward, one was Doctor Graham who was in his fifties and was really nice, the other to Daisy's surprise was a German doctor called Hans Schneider, he came across as arrogant and better than everyone else. Daisy tried to keep out of his way, only dealing with him when she really had to.

As she sat eating her dinner, Daisy thought it wasn't as bad as it could have been, Sidney was fun to work with and he kept the prisoners in order, as did the other orderlies that worked on the ward, but Daisy liked Sidney. She had found out that Sidney and Sister Dors could speak fluent German and so did a few other members of staff, so the prisoners knew that their conversations could be listened to. Some of the airmen were actually very pleasant and polite but there was a couple who were die-hard Nazis and were rude and disrespectful.

Their Officer was called Dietrich Schneider, no relation to the doctor and he could speak perfect English as he went to University in England before the war. Daisy thought he was a gentleman and he cared for the well-being of his men. He reminded her of Captain Jameson, and the care he showed towards his men following Dunkirk, which felt like a lifetime ago.

Daisy got friendly with a couple of the men on the ward, two young Oberfeldwebel, or flight sergeants in English, she had learnt that their plane had crashed, and they had bailed out over Kent on their way home. Both had broken bones, Gunther had broken a femur and was in traction. Franz had broken both arms, which were in plaster casts, both these young men would chat with Sidney and Daisy when they were on shift. She had learnt also that they loved flying but didn't want to fight, they had been forced to join up or face prison.

The two airmen who were horrible, Heinrich Meyer and Bernhardt Koch, would sit and sneer at Daisy and Sidney as they worked, and would have words with the others that spoke with them or even got friendly towards them. One shift Daisy had walked onto the ward and Heinrich wore a black eye, but when she enquired about it, no one knew anything, which she thought was odd. Only, 'he had walked into a door'. Sidney thought that it was caused by one of the guards as he had heard Heinrich had tried to escape. That would explain the extra guards who were placed by the doors.

The weather in February was still bleak and grey, dull and snowing. On the BBC News on the fifteenth February Singapore had fallen to the Japanese. The weeks were going very quickly and soon it was the middle of March, the weather had improved. The snow had melted, and it was getting warmer, the sun would come out and cheer people up.

Today was windy and raining and you could hear the birds singing in the morning, spring was on its way. Daisy was on a late shift with Sidney, she had found out when having her breaks with him, he was actually very bright and had done well at school, he would have liked to be a doctor, but his family couldn't afford the training, so he had joined the Royal Army Medical Corps as an orderly.

She felt sorry for him as she thought he would have made a great doctor, and she really hoped that in the future all people would be given the equal opportunity in life and not just the privileged, maybe the war would provide these changes. The previous evening Daisy had spent talking to Lizzie, who had shown interest in the injured airmen Daisy had met on the ward. She still didn't know if she could work on that ward, but when she heard the way Daisy talked about the young men, they seemed normal apart from the two who were offensive and hard-line Nazis.

Lizzie had heard from her brother, he had taken Glenda home to meet their parents, and it had gone better than he could have hoped. Their father had been pleasant and lovely towards his fiancée but their mother had hardly said a word. Her brother was pleased as she hadn't been outright rude. Glenda had been surprised by the size of the Hall and the grounds and he had introduced her to some of the injured servicemen. She had also met cook and her new husband Geoffrey, who both took to Glenda, and they were pleased for Lord Edward.

That had made him really happy, and he knew that Glenda would be a good asset and help him to change things around the place when he was the Lord of the Hall, and they were married. He still knew he had a long way to go and work on his mother but he felt she was changing as the war progressed. Their mother had kept out of their way and only had spent time with them when eating their meals in the kitchen, cook had tried to get Lady Margo to speak with the young woman but to no avail. Their father had also tried to encourage his wife to speak. But he took his son to one side one evening and told him not to worry he would work on his mother, and to bring Glenda back again and just be patient, his father was sure the wedding would go ahead.

Eddie told his father that if their mother didn't come around soon then he would just marry Glenda as soon as he could, his father grabbed his son's arm. "Just don't do anything too hasty, times are changing, she is changing."

Lizzie felt the meeting could have gone better, but she knew it could have been a lot worse, she was sure her mother would come around in the end. Eddie had also written to say he had met up with his friend from school, apparently Charles had fancied a girl from the village near the school and he had got her pregnant, she had told her parents that she had been forced to have intercourse with him. Reading this brought back all the memories from that night and Lizzie felt physically sick, she didn't want to read the rest, but she was curious to what had happened to the girl. Apparently, Charles' family had stepped in and paid the girl and the family to keep them quiet. Lizzie knew that out there was a little child who would never know their father and that the poor girl would have to live with the shame.

Maybe one day she would try and meet the girl and they could talk together but for now she would not let him do that to her again. She knew she had been lucky and was not pregnant because then, she knew, her mother would have made definitely sure that they were married, and she would have had to give up her training for good and be a good wife.

The letter from Charles had been sitting on the desk, she kept looking at it and, in her mind, she really wanted to burn it, but she knew it was best to reply and keep the man sweet. Daisy had sat on her bed keeping an eye on her friend and as promised she helped her write a reply to the awful man.

Lizzie had started by being polite and cheerful, asking how he was and explaining how busy she was. She was glad he was away again and at present not in this country and she quietly prayed that he stayed away as long as possible. Daisy thought it better to not mention that night and so Lizzie had carried on writing about how the weather had been. At the end she wrote, 'yours, Lizzie' and tucked it in the envelope to post.

The hardest letter she had to write was a reply to Chris, she really wanted to tell him about her family and being a lady and what had happened with Charles, but Daisy had told her to do it face to face. Again, she kept the letter light and jovial and told him about her life at The London and wanting to join the army after her training with Daisy. She told him about the German prisoners and how much she loved him and missed him terribly. She hoped he stayed safe and out of harm's way till she could see him again. This letter she signed off, 'yours affectionally, love Lizzie,' and placed it in the envelope, putting a stamp on it. Sitting back on her bed she relaxed the tight muscles that she had been holding, and relief had washed over her.

Chapter 33

Daisy had watched her and now her friend had written the letter she could see the release on her face and her body relaxed. Daisy had received a letter from her brother, George, who had written how he was loving the navy and his training. He would soon be joining a ship and would write to her again to tell her where to send his mail. He had written to their parents and apologised for joining up but he didn't regret his actions.

She knew her parents would soon forgive him and would hope and pray he stayed safe. She too hoped he stayed safe and kept his head down wherever this war took him. Daisy was coming to her last few weeks on the ward and was sad in a way as she had grown quite fond of some of the airmen, even though they were supposed to be the enemy. Heinrich and Bernhardt had been treated and deemed fit and sent to a prison camp, Daisy knew these two would try and escape as soon as they could and the camp's senior officer had been warned.

The two empty beds had been used by two new patients, Faber Becker and a Rudolf Wolf, this had made Daisy laugh as it made her think of Rudolf the red nosed reindeer. Both young men had been injured when they had to jump out of their burning plane, their parachutes had opened but they had landed wrong. One had a broken ankle and the other a broken wrist and concussion. Rudolf had a plaster cast on his wrist but he would like to help around the ward, so Sidney let him help dish the dinners out. he spoke little English, but he was keen to learn so Daisy would help him when she had a quiet moment.

She found out from Sidney, he had just got married and had left his wife in Hamburg working in a factory. They had gone to school together and had fallen in love, they had rushed getting married once they knew Rudolf was going into the air force. He had written to let her know he was safe and now a prisoner of war. Daisy was actually pleased for him as his war was now over and he was at least safe. Now the other two had left the ward, it was actually quite nice, all the men were grateful for the care they received. She enjoyed the last few weeks and was upset on her last day. The young men were all sorry to see her go and wished her all the best for the future, they had grown fond of the nurse from Luton. She would probably get in trouble for telling them where she come from, but she was only being friendly.

On this shift the siren went off just after six in the evening and the airmen had to get under the beds and those who couldn't were left in the bed and moved away from the windows. You could hear the bombers approaching and the look of sheer terror on the young men's faces, Daisy thought, 'Now you know what it's like to be on the receiving end of the bombs'. When they dropped the hospital and the windows shook, the men just kept down low. Daisy kept an eye on all of them and she decided to stay till the end of the raid, which the Night Sister was pleased with.

The all-clear went off at five in the morning, and Daisy said her final goodbyes and headed off to get some breakfast before her day off with Lizzie. The two friends had a lovely day together once Daisy had got a couple of hours sleep during the morning. It was a fresh, late March day, cold and very windy. Wrapping up in warm coats and scarves Daisy and Lizzie went for a walk around the local park, catching up, and getting some fresh air. It was only three months to the exam and they were both anxious, but they believed they were both ready with the amount of revision they had completed the last few months, and they were pleased. The last two months the girls were to be on wards one and two the hospital had just numbered the wards for the duration of the war as it was easier for everyone.

Daisy would have the pleasure of meeting up with Sister Williams and Staff Nurse Johnson again, she knew that she was now not the naive probationer that she was that first year but a competent third year nurse. How she wished Dr Reynolds was there and she could have showed him how she had developed into a consummate professional and extremely good nurse over the last two and half years. One of the reasons she hoped to join the army was that she hoped their paths crossed again, so not long to go now she thought.

The next early morning Daisy arrived on the ward in uniform, looking smart and ready to work. Sister Williams had to do a double-take. "Well, if it's not our very own Student Nurse Peters, a third year now, looking down at her belt with pride. I have planned your off duty to help with your revision, so I have put you on nights until after your exam as this gives you the evenings to revise."

Daisy couldn't believe how nice Sister Williams was being. "Thank you, Sister," was her reply.

"Welcome back Student Nurse Peters it is always nice to see our probationers back and nearly qualified," said Sister Williams as she and Daisy walked along the ward together. "As you can see, it is mainly servicemen on the ward now with a few civilians who have been caught up during the bombing or injured themselves and can't be sent away at present."

Most civilians were still being sent away to be nursed at hospitals away from the cities in the countryside. Daisy stood and took a look around the ward, she found thirty young pairs of eyes staring back at her. There were some whistles and kisses blown towards her, she blushed and smiled cheerfully back at them. She thought it was going to be hard work but fun. Sister Williams glared back at the young men, but you could see she had a twinkle in her eye as she did so, Daisy thought she had mellowed over the years.

"Don't take any notice of them, they are all harmless," she continued. "Mainly they are bored and all they want to do is get fit and get back to their regiments. Right, let's get hand-over and the night shift can go, and we can get on with the morning's work."

Daisy followed the sister to her office and the night nurse handed over the patients. Within half an hour Daisy was back on the ward. A couple of the young servicemen were due in theatre today and had to be prepared for surgery, once ready Daisy gave them their pre-medication which was a sedation to make them sleepy and relaxed and then they waited for the porter to arrive to wheel them down to theatre.

Mr Moses was still around but some of the young doctors had gone off to fight. "Private Kelly you're next on the list, shall we get you into a gown and then prepare your pre-medication?" Daisy asked.

The young soldier gazed back at Daisy, appearing to be full of nerves. Regarding him she said calmly, "You have nothing to fear, you will feel nothing, you will be asleep the whole time, I promise." Then she thought this young person in front of her had been trained to kill and had probably killed many people and now was scared of an operation and was seemingly acting like a little boy. Daisy felt sorry for the young soldier and with some trepidation helped the young man into his white gown and gave him his pre-medication. Within ten minutes, he was asleep and he was wheeled to theatre with the young nurse at his side holding his hand.

Many hours later he returned to the ward with Daisy sitting by his bed till he woke up, behind the screens to give the young airman some privacy. He groggily woke by the end of her shift but she offered to stay till the young man was awake enough for the night staff to nurse him through the night. She offered him sips of water, but he felt sick, she got a kidney dish just in case.

"The anaesthetic could make you feel sick," she said and did his observations again which were fine. The young nurse stayed till ten and wearily headed back to the nurse's home and her bed. Lizzie was already back, and Daisy sat down on her bed and started to explain what had happened.

Lizzie had a similar welcome from Sister Warnock on her ward and she too had been given time to revise for their exam. Lizzie was also put on nights straight after the exam, the results would be out six weeks later. Sister Warnock let her get stuck in straight away, and she had been given more responsibility being a third year. Each week that went by was another week nearer their exam, the closer it got the more tense they both were.

They had both had a go at each other for no apparent reason as the nerves had got the better of them one evening while revising in their room, both felt bad and had apologised to each other very quickly. Both girls had given each other a hug and had promised to work together and to use their time constructively and wisely up to the exam. As even Hilary was being exceptionally nice and had finally succumbed to asking both Daisy and Lizzie for help, the girls couldn't be unkind, but they had laughed about it when they were on their own as they couldn't quite believe the perfect Hilary actually needed their help. So they let Hilary, when she could, join their revision group, which was still growing with more people.

Claire and Jenny had noticed over the weeks that the sparkle had gone from Lizzie's eyes, and she wasn't the fun-loving girl since her trip up to London to see a guy who was a friend of her brothers. Daisy hadn't elaborated and the two girls hadn't wanted to pry, as they would be told when the time was right, but when they had mentioned it to each other when they were alone in their room, they both knew something bad must have taken place.

During April, Sister Tutor had offered extra revision lectures which could be attended if not on shift, Daisy and Lizzie managed a few, so had Claire and Jenny. Jenny had been put on the children's ward which she was loving. Unbeknown to everyone, Sister Tutor was very proud of her girls, they had begun their training at the start of the war and had evolved into very good nurses. She silently hoped that she wouldn't lose too many to the armed forces once they qualified, but she knew a few would make a move.

The month of April also saw the Americans bomb Japan to get back at them for Pearl Harbour, it was called the Doolittle Raid and was on the wireless as the girls sat round listening one evening. The month of May was wet and windy not spring-like at all and in the beginning of June more news came from the Pacific as the Battle of Midway took place. Soon the middle of June arrived, and the weather had improved considerably, and the sun had come out warming up the month.

The exam was scheduled for Monday twenty-second, and the Sunday night before no one had slept well, both the girls had tossed and turned and, in the end, they had both got up and had ended up in the kitchen having a cup of cocoa. They had sat talking quietly but soon more of the group arrived to join in, you could cut the air with a knife with all the nerves that the girls were feeling at that present time, but it felt nice to all be together, there was a sense of closeness.

Night turned into day and the sun soon come up, the young nurses made a slow move to get ready and into their uniforms. No one could stomach breakfast and so they made toast in the kitchen and drank tea. By eight forty-five the whole group gathered in the Preliminary Training School ready to sit their state exam, they had all walked over from the nurse's home together, it had looked a sight, seeing all these nurses. Some other members of staff had wished them luck as they passed, the girls had been thankful for the good wishes.

A room had been allocated in the Preliminary Training School for Nurses taking their exam and they took their allotted seats, Sister Tutor handed out the papers, and dead on nine the exam began. The girls all hoped that the siren didn't go off today as they really wanted to finish the paper by twelve. At precisely twelve, the girls closed their papers, they could do no more and they were collected by Sister Tutor who had sat still all the way through watching the young girls writing hard. They left the room relieved, and they now could relax until the results came out in six weeks.

All four walked back to the nurse's home, they had been given the rest of the day off. Daisy lifted her face towards the heat of the sun's rays and let it warm her face for a few moments. The sun was beating down on them. "What do you fancy doing for the rest of the day?" asked Lizzie.

"I don't know about you, but I am physically and mentally tired so all I want to do is rest and enjoy this lovely weather," answered Daisy. "Maybe have some lunch and then we can come outside and enjoy the delightful weather we are having and the good company because it seems ages since we were all together."

The others now had chance to recover from this morning's mental exertions and all of them could slowly feel the nervous energy ebbing away. After lunch, which had been eaten with gusto mainly because they were all hungry from not having a big breakfast, the girls were tempted to talk about the exam and what answers they had written down but Lizzie, being the sensible one stopped them.

"When I was at boarding school It was tempted to analyse the results before they came out and it's better just to forget otherwise it can play havoc with your mind," she said in a serious tone.

She lit herself a cigarette laid down on the blanket they had brought out with them and let the sun warm her face as she blew smoke out of her mouth. The four chatted away until late afternoon and they were all getting rather hot, and so they headed inside to cool down and to have a glass of cool lemonade that Home Sister had arranged for them as a special treat.

A lot of the other girls had the same idea, and they too were sitting or lying enjoying the afternoon sunshine. Home Sister had been hanging around all afternoon in the background. Once the girls had returned from the examination, she was acting like an anxious parent fussing and making sure they were all fine after their ordeal. Little did the girls know that Home Sister had grown quite fond of them all and would be upset when it was time for them to move into the qualified accommodation, but she knew she would have a new intake to mother and nurture in September.

In the meantime, her thoughts were on this group of girls and keeping her beady eye on them. As they walked past her and climbed the stairs, chatting away to each other, only stopping to acknowledge her as they walked past to their rooms, she glanced at them one by one just to make sure they were all okay. Once she was happy, she moved towards her room for the evening until it was time to walk her dog Henry, who was always at her side. On entering her room, she walked to her shelf and found her sherry bottle and got a glass, poured some into it and raised it glass to the class of 1942. With that she took a swig and let the warmth of the liquid catch the back of her throat.

Daisy and Lizzie were sitting on Daisy's bed, having splashed cold water on their faces to try and take the sting of the heat out, as now they were out of the full sunlight, they could see how burnt their faces were, both were like beetroots. Daisy wanted to cry as her face was extremely red and very sore. Her friend, feeling sorry for her got her flannel and tried to draw the heat out by placing the flannel, which had been soaked in cold water, on her face.

After a short time, Daisy said she felt slightly better, and did the same to Lizzie, whose face was just as bad. Both, girls went down to tea glowing and were the picture of health. They had to laugh as when they saw Jenny and Claire, they looked as bad as they did. The four of them wouldn't forget that day in a hurry, as they sat eating their tea of beef hamburgers and eggless ginger cake. Again, some of the other nurses and students who they knew came over and asked how they had gotten on this morning, so the girls explained the questions they had been given and some of the answers too. Lizzie had tried to stop them, but she was outnumbered. All four stopped outside to enjoy the evening, the sun setting was a beautiful sight, the colours up in the sky were different shades of reds and oranges, it was breath-taking to see and the girls knew tomorrow was going to be another very hot and sticky day.

Lizzie was puffing away with Jenny while Daisy and Claire stood with them a few feet away from the smoke. Daisy had tried smoking but had never got on with it as it made her feel sick. Lizzie and Jenny respected their friends' distance and kept blowing smoke in their direction for fun. Daisy kept shoving her friend in the arm but she couldn't help but laugh as she did it. It was a while since the girls had been this so care-free and they made the most of it.

Once they had finished their cigarettes, they all decided the evening was so nice they would stay out for a while, so they found a spot and sat down on the grass overlooking the hospital's main block. Tonight, they were joined by others who were taking a quick break, grabbing a quick cigarette before bed or also enjoying the evening's warmth. All four listened to the traffic outside the hospital grounds, it was still busy late in the day. Slowly people of the East End were trying to get their lives back on track. By ten it was getting dark and the four girls headed back into the nurse's home that had been home for the last three years, soon they would be leaving and all starting a different adventure. It was a bit sad to think about it, so shaking their heads they didn't dwell on it for too long.

Once back in their room after saying goodnight to the others, Daisy made sure the window was open and letting in the cooling night air to try and cool the room down a bit and make it bearable to sleep in. She pulled back the blackout curtain and looked up at the clear moon above her, how beautiful she thought it was, her thoughts then went to a certain young doctor, and she prayed he was safe wherever he was in the world.

Daisy wondered sometimes if he ever thought of her, as she had caught him staring at her a few times on the ward. He was an attractive looking man, a bit over-confident but he had never been unpleasant to her, and she felt drawn to him for some reason. Lizzie had fallen head over heels in love with Christopher and she hadn't known him long. Was it really love that she felt for the doctor or just a crush? Daisy knew once she saw him again, she would know, she had never felt like this when she was with Bobby, but she had just had a letter from Mary saying how happy she was, and the wedding plans were coming along nicely despite the war. He was still abroad but when he could get home, they would be married, and she hoped that her sister would be bridesmaid.

In her heart Daisy didn't really want to be bridesmaid but she wouldn't be cruel and upset her sister. When she had finished looking out the window, she got ready for bed, she would have a wash in the morning and they were all at a loss for what to do as they had no more revision or study to do, it was a nice feeling.

On the wards the senior staff treated them differently now they were third years and at the end of their training. The sisters gave them more responsibility, and the doctors were even respectful towards them and not treat them as if they were juniors any more. Both girls were due on the ward on Monday to start their stint on nights. Daisy was still worried about her friend. She had recovered from her injuries, her arm and face were better, but she was more worried about her mental state. Daisy would make sure to keep a close eye on her friend.

Sister Warnock was a fair sister and they both knew that now they had taken their finals; they would be given more responsibility which they could both deal with and were relishing.

Lizzie entered the room as Daisy climbed into bed. "Is the window open?" she asked noticing the heat in the room. "It's going to be a warm night."

So she pushed all her covers down to the bottom of the bed and laid on top of the bottom sheet. Lizzie still worried how she would deal with Charles as she would have to announce the engagement by September, if she didn't deal with him soon. She hoped her aunt would speak with her mother. With luck, he would still be out of the country and she could postpone the announcement for a while yet.

Her biggest problem was explaining to Christopher about the rape and her having a title and getting his reaction when she did finally build up the courage to tell him. She had promised herself that when they did meet up, and that was going to be soon hopefully, then she would sit him down and talk to him and tell him everything as she wanted no secrets between them. Lizzie knew once he found out about Charles and what he had done, Christopher would go after him and she could imagine what he would do to him if he caught up with him. Lizzie shivered at the thought because she knew Charles deserved everything that he got but he knew so many, influential people and Christopher could get into serious trouble.

Lizzie put the thought away for another day and settled down on the bed and lay chatting to her mate, it was nice to be able to chat late as they had the rest of the week off. They had decided not to go home, one being the trains were being used to ferry troops around the country and were not running on time, and they had been asked, "Is your journey really necessary."

Lizzie really didn't want a confrontation with her mother at present as she would probably tell her what Charles did to her in no uncertain terms and Daisy was just happy to stay with her friend, as she thought she needed her. Finally, the girls got off to sleep and woke to an exquisite morning. When Daisy pulled back the curtains, blue sky and light cloud greeted them, they stayed in bed until they couldn't lay there any longer and felt guilty for not getting up.

As they were later, they decided to have breakfast in the little kitchen on their floor, they could toast some bread and they had some jam that Daisy had brought back the last time she was at home. Butter was scarce but they found some and sat at the table enjoying their food, sipping their tea and just enjoying the morning.

"I think I will have a bath, or shall we go and enjoy the sun and have one later?" Lizzie asked.

"Later, as we are going to get rather hot out in the sun," Daisy replied.

Clare and Jenny had joined them once they could smell the toast along the corridor and drifting under their door. Feeling full, the girls went back to their rooms, put on their summer clothes and got their blanket ready, they headed out into the sun feeling the heat as they went out the door, even though it was only ten-thirty. Settling down on the blanket, they had brought their pillows to lay their heads on, soon they were laying letting the sun warm their bodies. Lizzie warned them to watch that they didn't burn and so about twelve-thirty they went in as the heat was insufferable.

They decided to stay out of the heat until later in the day and go out after two and see if they could sit in it again. Their patience paid off as they found a shaded area and placed the blanket there. The four spent the rest of the day just enjoying the sunshine, talking and reading and making plans once they qualified as nurses. The birds were singing in the background, it felt just like a British summer's day.

Lizzie was looking forward to tomorrow evening as she was meeting her brother and Glenda up in town for supper at Lyons corner house. It would be the first time they had met since her altercation with Charles and she had found out about the girl from the village and the baby. She was concerned that once she saw her brother in the flesh, he would notice that something had happened to her. It made her think she would have to be a good actress and pretend nothing was wrong, she didn't know if she could pull it off, only time would tell.

The following day was just as warm and the girls found their shaded area and settled down to enjoy the day, Matron had come around earlier and had asked for volunteers to start nights from tomorrow as she was short of nurses. Everyone had readily agreed and so were enjoying their last day off.

Lizzie was looking forward, with some trepidation, to seeing Eddie and Glenda that evening but she hoped that her body language didn't give her secret away as her brother knew her too well. By the time she was ready to leave, she'd had a bath and washed her hair, she felt a bit more relaxed. Daisy had spoken to her and hoped she had a nice evening; the air raids were less now due to the Germans' attention being on attacking Russia.

She had promised to meet her brother at eight, by the time she walked to Leicester Square she was running a few minutes late and was slightly out of breath from the exertion. They were waiting for her as she arrived, Lizzie put a smile on her face and walking up to Eddie and Glenda, giving each one a warm hug and kiss on the cheek.

"Sorry I'm slightly late but the train and the underground got held up," she said.

"Don't worry, you are here now," her brother replied.

"Shall we go and grab some food, I am famished," she said.

Taking hold of both their arms and she in the middle, they talked about how her exam went and what was happening in the war. Looking around they could see more Americans milling around taking in the city sights on this warm evening. Lizzie had noticed the looks she was getting from these young servicemen, some even whistled at her as she passed. Before the episode with Charles, she would have maybe encouraged them, but not now. She noticed her brother looking at her intently, she pretended she hadn't noticed. They entered the restaurant and found an empty table which had just been cleaned, and they slipped into the seats. The waitress gave them each a menu and they sat for a few moments reading it.

While waiting for the waitress to come back Eddie looked at his sister, who looked different, but he didn't exactly know why?

He asked, "What have you been up to?"

"Mainly studying for the exam, I go back on nights tomorrow as we are short-staffed," she replied, not elaborating.

"Have you heard from Christopher?" Enquired her brother, hoping this would get her to open up.

"Yes, he is still away, but I hope we can meet up soon. I'm actually thinking of joining the Queen Alexandra Imperial Military Nursing Service once I have qualified and hope to be sent abroad, maybe even near him."

"That is a bit risky," her brother replied.

"Maybe, but I will be with Daisy to make it easier."

Then he asked the question she had been dreading. "Have you heard from Charles?"

Lizzie tried not to shake at the mention of his name, she hoped her brother hadn't noticed. "Yes," it came out weak, her voice was quiet. "He sent a letter a while ago, he is fine."

She left it at that, and her brother could sense she didn't want to talk about him, so he decided to leave it this time.

"Oh, by the way, I got the address of the woman in the village," he passed Lizzie a piece of paper with an address on it.

His sister took it and looked at the writing. "What are you going to do with it?" he asked interested.

"I don't really know yet," came her reply.

Lizzie placed the paper into her handbag to keep safe. The waitress arrived back, took their order and left them to catch up, it turned into a pleasant evening. Lizzie was sorry when it was time to go their separate ways. Before parting, when he had Lizzie in a hug, he pulled her close, and in her ear, he said, "Remember, you know you can tell me anything."

A tear trickled down her face as she hugged her brother. "One day I will tell you, I promise," she replied wiping the tear away with the back of her hand.

Eddie looked at a loss for how to help his little sister, but he was sure of one thing, Charles had caused this. They said their goodbyes and went in different directions and Lizzie took the underground back to Whitechapel.

Chapter 34

As she sat on the train, relief washed over her. Eddie hadn't pushed, and she knew with time her mind would heal. On the outside she looked fine but, on the inside, she was still deeply upset about what had happened. Blaming herself for getting into the situation and actually letting it happen. Daisy had been brilliant and the best friend she could wish for, they had come a long way together and she hoped they would have many more adventures together.

Opening her handbag, she re-read the address and decided when the time was right, she would go and see this woman and hopefully see the little girl. Walking from the station and heading to the hospital gave her time to contemplate all that had taken place these last three years. How many more would the war go on for? She wondered.

At last, she entered the familiar entrance with the sandbags protecting the front. As she passed Thomas' hut it was empty, and she knew he was home with his family. She climbed the stairs up to her room, turning the handle she slowly entered and there was Daisy fast asleep on her bed with a book in her hand.

Lizzie tiptoed across the room and got ready for bed, it wasn't late, but she still had no wish to wake her friend up. There was still some light in the room as the evenings were lighter now, she got into bed once she had paid a visit to toilet. Sleep didn't come easy for Lizzie that night, she lay in the dark listening to Daisy's laboured breathing, quietly trying to keep the dark thoughts from her mind. She knew Charles would always be there. By about three she managed to drift off, she had a restless sleep but she knew she could sleep all day if she wished as they were not on duty till later that night. Daisy woke refreshed and the first thing she did was look over and see that her friend had returned safely, once she was satisfied, she got up.

Quietly she got herself dressed and decided to leave Lizzie in bed asleep. She headed for the door and breakfast. Lizzie had woken sometime later and she too got herself changed and was just about to head to the kitchen for breakfast when Daisy appeared at the top of the stairs.

"Do you want some toast?" Lizzie asked.

"No thanks, I just had breakfast. But I will join you."

Lizzie was quietly pleased that her friend was joining her as she didn't really want to be on her own today. While waiting for the toast to be grilled in the oven, Daisy made the tea and the two girls sat together in a silent calm.

While placing a small amount of butter on the toast Daisy enquired, "How did last night go?"

"It was really nice, my brother and Glenda were both looking good," Lizzie replied.

Daisy took her friend's hand and asked in an alarmed voice, "How are you doing?"

She looked at Daisy and burst into tears. "Not good today if I am honest."

Daisy looked at Lizzie. "Remember, you are not to blame so don't feel guilty, what he did was unforgiveable. It is going to take a long time for the pain to go but I'm here for you always," she said, as she wiped the tears from her friend's eyes and squeezed her hand.

They could not say any more as just then more girls arrived, they could smell the toast and sat down with Daisy and Lizzie at the kitchen table. Soon there was laughter coming from the kitchen, which had lightened the mood immensely. Most of the girls went back to their rooms once they had finished breakfast and tried to get some more sleep. Daisy, Lizzie, Jenny and Claire all did the same, Daisy found it hard as she had slept all night but Lizzie, now her stomach was full and her mind a lot calmer got back into bed and soon she was fast asleep. Daisy could see that her friend had been distressed earlier so let her sleep as long as she needed to.

By late afternoon both girls headed for the bathroom and both enjoyed their baths and washing their hair. Once they were finished, they dried themselves with a towel, headed back to their room and dried their hair, putting on their clean uniforms and hats and headed for tea. Then to finish getting ready to relieve the day shift. Daisy had been put back on maternity and this time she wasn't so daunted as she had been the first time. Arriving just before eight she put on her clean apron and took hand-over from the staff nurse as Sister was busy with a delivery.

Once satisfied she was left with a junior and they settled the new mothers down for the night. The one woman who Sister was dealing with had just delivered a little boy who was being taken to the nursery. Daisy took over from Sister and made the woman comfortable and settled till feeding time.

Daisy promised her a cup of tea, so headed to the kitchen. Finding a very large cockroach, she found the killer powder that was kept in the cupboard and placed it on the floor. When she first had seen a cockroach Daisy would scream, but now she was used to them but still didn't like them, for when you stood on them, they crunched under the shoe. Daisy made a cup of tea for the patient, which was a mistake because then nearly all the women on the ward decided they wanted a cup as well, but between Daisy and the junior they managed, some of the able mothers even helped, too so long as Night Sister didn't see.

Daisy walked into the nursey at feeding time as she had already made up the bottles, she took one hungry baby and settled down to feeding, soon the bottle was empty, once sorted she settled the baby down again for a sleep. Daisy loved her time in the nursery as it was quiet and gave her time to think. Once all the little ones were fed and winded. Daisy made sure they were all settled and headed back out into the quiet ward.

One of the mothers was crying into her pillow, Daisy heard her as she walked past, it was not a surprise as a lot of women cried following childbirth. Daisy thought that it was because their bodies went through so much trauma. She stopped and pulled up a chair taking her hand and sat with the woman until she had settled again. The women turned over, sat up, and gave Daisy a big hug saying, "Thank you, Nurse."

Daisy rubbed her back and spoke to her in a calm manner.

She just got back to her desk when Night Sister arrived, she checked all was well and left Daisy to carry on. On nights when there were no air raids Daisy would make cheese on toast and scrambled eggs for her and the other nurse on the opposite ward, sometimes a doctor on call would join them. They had a pleasant time sitting around the table enjoying the food and chatting quietly before the next round of bedpans were asked for. They knew as soon as one wanted one, everyone on the ward needed one. That is exactly what happened, as soon as the buzzer went and the bedpan was asked for, then everyone else wanted it too.

This kept Daisy and the junior nurse busy and the least favourite job for Daisy was cleaning the bedpans. She got the disinfectant and got to work, she remembered the beginning of her training spending hours in the sluice room, cleaning. 'Oh, the joys of nursing,' she thought smiling, but she wouldn't trade it for anything else.

Early morning the feeds were due again. Daisy made up the bottles and she was glad of the sit down. She picked up a baby and held it in her arms and fed it the warm milk. Daisy began talking to the baby as she was feeding and the little one looked back at her in awe as if understanding what she was saying. By the time all babies were fed and changed, Daisy left the quiet of the nursery and went back onto the main ward, she sat at the desk and wrote up her report for the night.

Once completed she sat back trying not to fall asleep, she thought of Lizzie and hoped she'd had a good night. Soon they would meet up and walk together to get breakfast then they could climb into a clean bed and then sleep. Before that could happen, she had to wash the patients and get them ready for breakfast, so she handed out the bowls and assisted the mothers that couldn't wash themselves.

Between the two of them it was soon done and by the time the morning staff came on the ward the patients were ready for Sister. Hand-over took time and as soon as Sister was happy then Daisy was free to leave.

Right on time she met Lizzie in the corridor, and they said a cheery good morning to each other, and walked together to the dining hall where a cooked breakfast awaited them. Even though they were dead on their feet and their feet were burning after a hard night, both enjoyed the breakfast and soon they both made a weary walk back to the nurse's home, trying their hardest not to yawn.

As soon as they had changed and got into bed, they said goodnight, and they were both asleep. This was going to be the same routine for the next three months which took them to September. At the beginning of July on the wireless, news had come in that the army was fighting a battle at El Alamein in Africa. Both women hoped that their men were not caught up in the fighting, and they both said silent prayers. Daisy thought of Michael, he wasn't really her man and she should stop thinking of him like that, he probably didn't know she existed.

In exactly six weeks from the exam the letters had arrived and were sitting in the mailboxes. Lizzie picked hers up first and Daisy followed. They rushed up to their room, tired feet forgotten, and they entered it in a hurry, both girls looked down at the envelopes.

"You go first," said Daisy, saying it in a shaky voice, looking over at her friend.

Lizzie gripped the envelope and opened it carefully and read the piece of paper inside, she passed it to Daisy. Lady Elizabeth Margaret Fenton, State Registered Nurse, congratulations. As she read a smile spread across Daisy's face.

"Come on, open yours," Lizzie said impatiently.

Daisy hurriedly opened hers, Daisy Hannah Peters, State Registered Nurse, congratulations.

Both girls dropped the papers and grabbed each other tightly, hugging and crying both saying, "we have passed, we are qualified nurses." It took a while to sink in and both knew they wouldn't get to sleep now if they tried, they were too wound up.

It didn't take long for Jenny and Claire to knock on their door and by the look on their faces they too had passed.

Lizzie pulled up the floorboard and as she was doing it, she said. "This calls for a celebration," and pulled the bottle out.

Four glasses appeared and she poured the golden liquid into them saying, "A toast to us four."

Clinking glasses, the four took a gulp, the warm liquid burning the backs of their throats as it went down, but it tasted good on this special day.

The whole set had passed, even Hilary, by the skin of her teeth, and the girls spent the rest of the day together until utter exhaustion took over and they had to get some sleep, as tonight they would be working as Qualified Nurses.

Once the news had gotten around the hospital, they had received plenty of congratulations and well dones, only Lizzie felt apprehensive because as soon as she told her parents then the engagement announcement would be made in The Times newspaper.

She really didn't want to marry Charles and she knew that she really wanted to carry on nursing for a long as she could. The only answer was to come clean about what Charles had done to her and find the girl with the baby, and then see her mother and tell her the truth. If she met the woman with the baby and heard from her directly, she would have no choice but to believe Lizzie was in fact telling the truth.

It would be good to get her aunt involved and she could come and meet the woman. Even if the woman would not come to the Hall and tell her story to her mother, at least her Aunt Lynn would be her witness and they could confront her mother that way.

Lizzie was relieved and happy now she had a plan, as for Chris, as soon as she saw him in the flesh, she would tell him everything and hope in her heart he still wanted her. The hospital asked them to continue working with them for another six months and in that time, they could apply for the QAIMNS.

Lizzie had written to her aunt asking that they both go to the village near Charles' old school and see if they could meet this woman on Lizzie's next day off. When the reply came, her aunt had agreed to the request and would meet Lizzie at the Hall and Geoffrey would take them in the Rolls Royce. The only concern Lizzie had was her mother seeing Lizzie at the Hall and wanting to know why she was home. Lizzie still didn't want her parents to know she had qualified.

I will deal with your mother it's about time she knew the truth, her Aunt Lynn had put in the letter. The village was up in the Warwickshire countryside, so not far from where Lizzie lived. They could be there in one day but it would mean Lizzie having to stay at the Hall overnight and then back to London the next day.

Daisy in the meantime just listened to her friend and wished her well, her parents on the other hand, had been over the moon when she had written to them. She had written to her brother, George who was now with his ship in the Atlantic somewhere. Mary had written congratulating her and wishing her well for the future. Bobby was still away and so the wedding was on hold until he could get home, that was a relief for Daisy as she didn't want to be bridesmaid just yet. The only sad bit about not getting home was not seeing her parents and her little brother Mark, but the hospital needed her at this moment in time.

Lizzie travelled home on her next day off, she had said goodbye to Daisy, that morning. So far, the journey had been good, no holdups and she was met by Geoffrey at the station. He took her bag and case, and he gave her a warm hug, "Welcome home M' lady."

"Thank you, Geoffrey, how is Edna and married life?"

"Just wonderful," he replied. Looking in the mirror he saw sorrow in the eyes of the young girl in the back of his car and she looked older too, this war was damaging young people's lives he thought.

"How is my mother?" she asked shakily, her voice cracking.

"Oh, she is fine," came the reply. "She is enjoying helping the injured at the Hall, she spends a lot of the day with Edna cooking."

"That is good," was all Lizzie could say.

Sitting back against the cool leather she felt a tightness in her chest when her thoughts returned to either her mother or Charles. She rubbed her neck to try and loosen the knots that were forming from the stress she felt. She couldn't work out between them who was worse, in the end her head was beginning to hurt so she stopped thinking about it and turned her thoughts to pleasant things like seeing her aunt and Edna very shortly.

The car turned into the long driveway and pulled up outside the now familiar kitchen entrance. Before Geoffrey could get around to the door, Lizzie was already out and heading towards the kitchen door. Edna on the other side had heard the car approaching, wiping her hands on a tea towel as she was preparing the mid-day meal she walked towards the door as they both opened it at the same time.

Edna pulled it to her sharply and Lizzie fell through the door into the arms of the cook. Feeling the warmth and tenderness of the elderly woman, Lizzie couldn't help the tears that fell from her eyes freely.

"Whatever is the matter?" asked a concerned cook.

Lizzie was just about to explain everything when she noticed out the corner of her eye her mother entering from the other entrance, tray in hand.

Quickly drying her eye on the back of her hand, she heard, "Oh, Elizabeth, you're home," in her mother's curt voice.

Lizzie answered awkwardly, "Yes, Mother I am here for a couple of days, then I will be returning. I promise I will not get in your way." She couldn't help the frostiness in her voice as she said it.

Passing her mother by, she hurried up to her room, once inside she shut the door with more force than she had wished. Putting her case down, she sat on the bed and cried, the tears kept coming and she just couldn't stop them, all the anguish over the months had finally caught up with her.

Lizzie hadn't realised that her mother had followed her up to talk to her and had heard the crying as she stood listening outside her daughter's room. Margo's heart was breaking for her daughter, and she didn't know what was wrong, or more importantly how to fix it.

As Margo was walking down the stairs her thoughts turned to Edward, she only wanted the best for her children but here they were both going against her decisions and wishes. Glenda was a nice girl but she was not in the social class one expected her to be, but Edward was dead set on marrying her. Margo knew in her heart that her children in the end would do whatever they wanted, like she had, as they were both strong-willed like her. She turned and crept down the stairs, as soon as she could, she would talk to her daughter.

Lizzie got up and washed her face in the sink, took her coat off and hung it on the back of the closed door, she began to unpack the few belongings she had brought with her as she knew she wouldn't be here long. Once satisfied she took a deep breath and made her way down the back stairs.

Edna spotted her as she came in, she could see the red and puffiness around the eyes from the crying and as soon as she could she was going to sit the young girl down and find out exactly what the problem was.

Lady Margo was plating up a dish and looked up as her daughter entered the room, her heart ached. Edna noticed the strain between the two. "Let me put the kettle on," she said, and started gathering the teacups.

Lizzie was relieved and took a seat at the table and was grateful as she felt all the energy drain out of her. Tea was swiftly made, and Lizzie took a sip of the warm liquid, she had got used to tea without or with limited sugar since the rationing, she liked it either way, so she took a spoonful and stirred it into the tea. It relaxed her and she sat back in the chair, waiting for someone to say something.

Edna said, "Why don't you take that dish up into the dining room."

Margo was just going to protest when she could see her daughter really didn't want to talk to her at this moment, so she reluctantly did as she was asked.

Once Edna knew her Ladyship was gone and not listening by the door, she got the chair nearest Lizzie and sat down by her side. "Now we don't have much time, so tell me briefly what on earth has happened?"

Edna listened as Lizzie relived that dreadful evening and all Edna did was hold the poor girl in her arms as she cried all over again. Once Lizzie had finished, she was surprised how well she felt, it felt like a big burden had been lifted from her shoulders. Edna was shocked and extremely angry, good job she was sitting down and as soon as the young girl's Aunt Lynn arrived, she was going to talk to her. No way was this beautiful young woman marrying that horrid man.

Margo in fact did not go back to the kitchen as she knew her daughter didn't want her there at present, it hurt but she respected her wishes. Maybe when her sister arrived in the morning, she could shed some light on what was going on with her daughter. For the rest of the day and evening Lady Margo kept her distance from her daughter, which she was thankful for.

Edna and Geoffrey kept the young girl company and fed her after her long, tiring journey. The only time she saw her mother was to help with feeding the injured servicemen and then she left them alone again. Her father, once he heard his daughter was home, made sure to pop his head in and say hello. He had heard from his wife how his daughter had arrived very upset, he took one look at Elizabeth and felt a stab to the heart, he didn't know what had happened but whatever it was he could see it was making his daughter extremely unhappy. He too would talk with his sister-in-law when she arrived tomorrow, he now was very unhappy with this arrangement with Charles and would do all he could to stop it.

By early evening Lizzie was mentally and emotionally tired and she made her excuses and went up to her room. 'Maybe it was a mistake to come home,' she thought as she ran the bath. Once ready she climbed in, and she felt herself relax. The plan for tomorrow was Aunt Lynn turning up early and then Geoffrey taking them to the village where the girl lived.

Lizzie hoped she was still there as they had no way of knowing until they got there or what would she do if the girl had moved away.

Once she had dried herself and got back in her room, she felt better and found a book to read, she got into bed. It was a warm and humid night as it was the beginning of August, so she pushed the sheets back and opened the window to let the air in before the room got too unbearable. She soon fell into a deep sleep as she was still doing nights this was her time off before she had to return to nights when she got back. She hoped with all her heart tomorrow she would finally get some answers.

Lizzie woke early and was very nervous, to the point of feeling sick, but she pushed herself on and got dressed into comfortable summer clothing. By the time she entered the kitchen breakfast was already laid out and she found a chair and sat down.

Edna placed a cooked breakfast in front of her and said, "Get that down you," which she thought she wouldn't be able to do, but she managed it and she drank her camp coffee. Lizzie grimaced as she drank, she would never get used to the taste of chicory.

Her aunt arrived by nine and headed for the kitchen, seeing Lizzie, she gave her a kiss and hug and she greeted her sister with a kiss on the cheek.

Her "good morning" was breezy and cheerful as she talked to Margo and Lizzie went off to finish getting ready.

As soon as her daughter was out of ear shot, Margo said questioning, "Where are you two off this morning? Lizzie has been very secretive and won't tell me."

"You will know soon enough," came the reply. This was all she got out of her sister as Lizzie came down the stairs and both ladies walked towards the kitchen door.

"Ready? Then let's get going," said Aunt Lynn glancing over at Lizzie, who nodded as they walked out of the warm kitchen. Geoffrey was waiting by the Rolls Royce in all his finery.

Her father appeared and pulled Aunt Lynn to one side. "I hope all goes well today and let me know what happens, won't you?" She nodded. He stood back as the car pulled away down the sweeping driveway and out into the country lane. Aunt Lynn sat back and looked over at her niece, she too thought she was looking tired and hoped today would help her, but she knew it would take longer for her to get over the ordeal she had been through with that ghastly man.

The journey took over an hour before they entered the tiny village of Lower Manton, it was a long winding road and as they drove along it they soon found the cottage they were looking for from the sheet of paper Eddie had given her, it was not far from the village pub.

Both women got out and walked up to the front door, leaving Geoffrey in the car, it was a lovely bright colour thought Lizzie trying to keep calm. Aunt Lynn found the knocker and hit it hard and they both stood back to see who answered it.

They waited a few moments, and they were about to turn and go when a young woman came to the door, she opened it slightly. Lizzie could see she was nervous looking over at the Rolls Royce, maybe they should have come in Aunt Lynn's car instead, her Morris, but it was too late now.

"Hello, are you Gloria Weybridge?" Lizzie asked awkwardly looking down at the paper in her hand.

"Let me introduce myself, I am Lizzie Fenton, and this is my Aunt Lynn we would just like a quick word with you about Charles Holmes."

As soon as the name had left her lips and by the look on the woman's face, she knew she had the right person. Gloria, on hearing that name stumbled back and Lizzie grabbed her before she could fall, she led her into the front room and sat her down on the settee.

"Can I get you a drink?" she asked in a concerned voice.

"No, thank you, it's just I haven't heard that name for a while and had hoped not to for a very long time, or never really."

"If I can explain why I am here?" Lizzie for the second day had to relive the events of that evening, her aunt was holding her hand the whole time. Gloria was watching and listening intently to everything Lizzie said showing no emotion on her face.

Then it was Gloria's turn, it was very similar, but the only difference was that it wasn't in a fancy hotel but in a farmer's barn up the road.

Lizzie heard footsteps and a little girl came toddling in, calling, "Mummy, Mummy," she said, and climbed onto Gloria's lap. She was dressed in a pretty, expensive summer's dress and sandals.

"This is my daughter, Irene who has just turned three. Irene, say hello to these nice ladies."

"Hello," came a timid voice, and both Lizzie and her aunt said "hello" back.

"Go and play with your toy dolly and I will be in soon."

With that the little girl went off happily to the kitchen where her grandparents were waiting. Lizzie saw the likeness; she knew instantly Irene was Charles' little girl.

"His family gave us a large amount of money to go away and never to talk about it, but you can see she is definitely Charles' daughter. Till this day I am not happy taking the money, but we needed it as I wasn't going to give her up for adoption once she was born. His mother was very rude and even suggested the baby wasn't even her sons, but once she saw her, she knew. I think lady muck wasn't very impressed with her precious son's behaviour after that," Gloria said laughing.

This even made Lizzie and her aunt laugh too.

"What do you want from me?" Gloria asked seriously. "Because I can't go against the agreement we made as I am compelled to keep to it."

Lizzie looked at the scared young woman sitting in front of her. "I wanted you to speak with my mother and tell her what happened to you, and I would tell her he did the same to me, he could even have done it to other women we don't know about, but I can see it would put you in a bit of a dilemma. Charles' mother is friends with my mother and if you did this it would get back to him, please think about it but I understand if you won't." With that Lizzie and her aunt stood up and said their goodbyes, heading for the door.

Gloria showed them out and said to Lizzie, "I wouldn't be without Irene, but you were lucky not to be in the family way." With that she wished them good day, and she closed the door.

The two women walked to the car and got in, Geoffrey started the engine, and they made their way back to the Hall.

"I need a cigarette," said Lizzie, pulling one out of the packet and putting it between her lips. She offered her aunt one who declined. Lizzie got her silver lighter out and lit it, taking a deep drag and letting the smoke travel around the car. She felt calmer but Lizzie didn't know what to do, she wasn't going to risk that young woman for her benefit, so they would just have to come up with another plan.

Her aunt looked at her niece, who had a serious look on her face. "Don't worry, we will sort this mess out with your mother one way or another."

Lizzie took hold of her aunt's hand for reassurance. They explained to Geoffrey what had taken place and he said he would tell Edna on the quiet, so her Ladyship didn't hear.

On arrival back at the Hall, Lizzie had the rest of the day to keep out of the way of her mother before tomorrow morning and getting the train back to London. Then she was back on nights for a few more weeks. Her aunt stayed for a few more hours and spent them with her sister, it had been very strained as she wouldn't discuss Lizzie with her.

At one stage her mother was sitting in the kitchen after Lynn had left and she asked Elizabeth straight out, "Have you taken your exam yet?"

This flummoxed Lizzie, so she did the only thing she could do, she lied and said, "No not yet, it is soon."

She didn't think her mother quite believed her but she was relieved when her mother didn't push her to say any more about it. This surprised Lizzie because in the past she would have done so relentlessly.

Much later when Lizzie was in the kitchen on her own drinking cocoa, her father wandered in. Seeing his beautiful daughter gazing into space, he moved slowly to sit by her side. "Elizabeth," he said gently, trying not to frighten her.

She glanced sidewards. "Hello, Papa."

"Are you really that unhappy?" he asked, concerned. "Please, be honest with me."

So Lizzie took a deep breath. "No, I am very happy with Christopher. I still could never marry Charles and Mother needs to realise this as soon as possible," she said, wiping a single tear from her eye.

He held her hand and rubbed the knuckle and then he raised it to his lip and kissed it. "I promise you; you will not marry that man."

"Papa, I need to tell you one more secret, I have passed my State Finals, I am a qualified nurse and soon hopefully will be joining the Queen Alexandra Imperial Military Nursing Service with Daisy and try and get to see Christopher," she smiled.

He smiled back at Elizabeth and hugged her tight, in her ear he whispered, "Your secret is safe, I won't tell your mother until you tell her yourself."

Lizzie hugged him tight and said, "Thank you."

He got up and asked, "I will see you in the morning before you leave?"

"Yes, see you in the morning," came her reply.

Margo felt left out, and she was hurting as she walked around the grounds of the Hall in the warm summer's evening air with Dinky at her side. She wished she could heal the pain her daughter was in so much, but how? She knew she was not an easy person to get on with and she only wanted the best for her children. Seeing Elizabeth so unhappy these last two days she knew something bad had happened and she wouldn't or couldn't open up to her own mother. She also knew her daughter had lied about her exam, she had taken it but again she couldn't tell her own mother, that hurt too. Margo had tried to get it out of her sister, Lynn but she kept her lips tightly shut together, and her husband she didn't think knew.

One way or another she thought, as she made her way back to the Hall, she would find out and hopefully in time make things better. With that she made her way up to her room. As she passed Lizzie's room, she heard crying. She stopped dead and listened, she really wanted to knock, go in and hug her daughter, heal the pain that she knew she had caused, and she wanted to find out the reason why and put that right too. But she knew Elizabeth wouldn't want her at present with the mood she was in, so she walked past with a great ache in her heart.

She promised that she would change but she would find it hard, she only wanted the best for her daughter and that was with Charles. Lizzie had heard footsteps stopping by the door, had waited a few minutes to see if anyone knocked, but they had moved on. She really wanted her mother to see her suffering, she could stop this once and for all if she put a stop to this engagement but Lizzie knew this wouldn't happen anytime soon. With a heavy heart, she turned on her side and had another restless sleep.

Lizzie got up early and packed her clothes. Quickly had breakfast and said her "goodbyes" and met Geoffrey by the car ready to get back to London as soon as she could.

Saying a longer goodbye to Edna she held the young girl tight. "Take care and if you need anything let us know."

"I will, promise," she said, trying desperately not to cry.

"Your mother will change, you'll see, give her time," Edna said reassuringly as Lizzie got into the car. Lizzie still wasn't so sure, but would really like to believe it, but she still had a lot of doubt.

Putting on a brave face she smiled and she waved as the car pulled away. At that moment all she really wanted to do was to see and be held by Christopher and sort this mess out once and for all, but she knew that was still a long way from happening.

Standing on the platform of Warwick station having said goodbye to Geoffrey, Lizzie waited for her train to arrive and again her mind drifted. Could her mother truly change, like Edna had said? Maybe, thought Lizzie, but she knew she was running out of time.

Lizzie lit her cigarette and felt peaceful smoking it, but she knew that wouldn't last long. The train ride was uneventful and she arrived back in London in good time and got back to the hospital in time to get a few hours' sleep before reporting for duty.

Chapter 35

Having promised to stay at the hospital for six months, both girls completed their night duty and were given wards to work on as newly qualified Staff Nurses.

Daisy had gotten home to see her family for a few days break, and her parents had been overjoyed to see her. Daisy couldn't get over how Mark had grown and was turning into a young boy; he was no longer a baby any more. He loved school when he could get there just like Daisy had, and even Mary had been pleased to see her sister home.

On the wireless more news had come through that the Germans were caught up fighting in Russia, and on the twenty-first of August the battle for Stalingrad had begun.

On a morning off both women approached Matron's office and took their seats outside, they would normally have called individually, but Matron had some idea why the two women were there. They both looked professional in their Staff Nurse uniforms, and both checked themselves over before they were called in. Matron stood from behind her desk and walked to the door, opened it to find them sitting patiently for her to address them.

"Staff Nurse Fenton and Peters do come in."

They stood and entered the small room which they had only been in a few times. Two chairs were already in position.

"Please sit," Matron said, pointing to the chairs.

The women did as they were told, sitting ramrod straight, hands clasped on their laps.

"To what do I owe the pleasure of your company this morning?" Matron said from behind her large oak desk.

Lizzie looked at Daisy, and she could see her friend was petrified, so she decided to speak up for them.

"Well, Matron," Lizzie took a deep breath. "We have both decided we would like to join the QAIMNS."

Both women looked across at the stern woman in front of them, keeping their eyes on the fob watches pinned to their uniforms. "Before you say anything, we have taken our time and consideration to reach this decision. We know if you agree we will be leaving you short of nurses, but we both want to do our bit. When the war is over, we would be happy to come back and nurse at The London, but just not yet." Lizzie sat back and had a sideward glance towards her friend, who hadn't moved the whole time Lizzie had spoken, she wriggled in her chair as her bottom was getting numb.

Matron leaned forward and looked back at the pleasant young women in front of her. "Yes, your timing is not the best, but I can see you really want to go, and I will not stand in your way, I will put both your names forward. This doesn't mean you will be able to stay together but I can see it's what you both really want. Remember, this is going to be tough and unpleasant at times, you will be working in harsh conditions, but I wouldn't put you forward if I didn't think you could manage. Leave the paperwork and other requirements with me and I will be in touch."

Both girls knew the meeting was over and stood up to leave the room. "Thank you, Matron," they both said as they left.

Standing outside the closed door, relief washed over them but apprehension was also present as they didn't know quite what they had gotten themselves into. Now all they had to do was wait and tell their friends Jenny and Claire. They also would have to inform their families what they had done.

In Lizzie's case she would have to tell her mother that she was now a qualified nurse, and she could get engaged to Charles.

"If I tell her once we have been taken on, then we can get engaged, but the wedding can be after the war," she said hopefully to Daisy as they walked back to the Nurses' home.

Lizzie, as she walked up the stairs behind Daisy, said a silent prayer that things were going to turn out all right, because at this very moment in time it looked surprisingly bleak. Putting on a happy smile they knocked on their friends' door, only Jenny was in.

Pulling her friends in, she sat them down on one bed. "Well, what's your news?"

"We have been given the go-ahead to join the QAIMNS."

Jenny looked open-mouthed at her friends and sat down on the unoccupied bed.

"Why?" Was the first thing she said.

Lizzie was the spokesperson for them and so she explained why the two women wanted to go to war, the other woman knew it was because Lizzie really wanted to try and meet up with Christopher and Daisy wanted to travel as she hadn't told anyone about her feelings for Doctor Michael Reynolds.

Once Jenny had the time to digest the information she said, "I really thought we would all work together here for a few years at least."

"Sorry," was the only answer Daisy had.

Jenny stood and went over to her two mates, and she got them to stand, and they had a group hug.

"You will write?" In a pretend stern voice.

"Yes," they both replied.

The weeks following the girls kept busy working long hours on the wards, they had both written home and told their parents. Daisy's had been surprised but were pleased for her, they didn't tell her in the letter that they were sick with worry that she had made the wrong decision, but they wouldn't stop her. Lizzie's parents had written back and were pleased she was qualified and her mother would get in contact straight away with Charles' family and put the announcement in The Times.

Reading the letter Lizzie felt sick and wanted to cry, but she stopped herself. Hopefully she wouldn't see Charles until the end of the war and by then Christopher, with a bit of luck would be back.

Daisy once her friend had told her about the engagement, sat Lizzie down on her bed and said, "It's only on paper, and the war will go on for a long time yet, don't give up hope." She hugged her tight as the tears fell.

Lizzie dreaded the next letter she was going to receive from Charles and joining the QAIMNS couldn't come quickly enough. On October twenty-third more news had come that the allies had invaded North Africa. People were thinking that things were happening for the better.

By the end of 1942 the girls would celebrate their last Christmas and New Year at The London, they were both sad but knew a new chapter was just about to begin, even though they didn't know what form it would take.

Lizzie had letters from both Charles and Christopher. She read Charles' first, he had heard from his parents they had announced the engagement in The Times newspaper. Lizzie had seen it as her mother had sent her a cut out. Lizzie in anger had ripped it up and thrown it in the bin. She then had read Christopher's letter. He was still fighting out in the heat and using the code they had decided before he went away, she roughly knew where he was.

She had written back to both and told them she was joining the QAIMNS as soon as she could. The one who would be upset the most would be Charles, but Lizzie didn't give a damn. Christopher, she knew would be more encouraging and so with that, posted the letters at the next available opportunity she had.

The two women didn't in fact have long to wait as within six months of speaking to Matron, letters arrived for them both, getting them to report to Edinburgh on the eighth of January 1943. Daisy sat on her bed in the nurse's home and speaking to Lizzie said that it was going to be very cold up in Scotland. Lizzie agreed, she just wanted to go.

A letter had arrived back from Charles, she had been right he was incensed with her, but he couldn't do anything as he was miles away, and he knew that. On the seventh of January, with tears in their eyes, the two women packed up their belongings and Lizzie pulled the bottle of whiskey from the secret hiding place and gave it to Jenny and Claire.

Jenny and Claire were also moving to another part of the nurse's home for qualified nurses so for the last night together, they all sat on Daisy and Lizzie's beds and drank to their futures. Jenny and Claire didn't stay long as they knew the two girls had a long journey ahead in the morning. Saying their goodbyes, and with a promise to keep in contact, the tears fell.

Matron had come to the door of the nurse's home with Home Sister to see them off as they left to make their way to Kings Cross station, both girls were excited and nervous as they boarded the train to Scotland, but they had each other for support.

The journey was slow as the train had to keep stopping for troop trains to pass, by early evening they arrived in a very dark and unfamiliar part of Britain. At the station they were met by a burly Sergeant Major who was as tall as he was wide. He checked their names off on a list in his hand and showed them to a waiting lorry. Both girls were worn out from the travelling and climbed up into the back, four other women were already sitting on the benches and they said a tired "hello' in greeting and took a seat together.

Another hour passed and two more women arrived. Once they were safely on board and the back of the truck secured, the Sergeant Major sat in the front cab and ordered the driver to pull away. The truck was a bit bouncy, throwing the women around in the back as they drove out of the city, the women didn't say anything as they couldn't see where the truck was heading in the dark and extremely bitterly cold winter's night. They pulled up their warm coats around them to keep the chill out.

Much later they pulled into a gated road and the truck drove up to a large house. From what Lizzie could see of it, it reminded her of her home. The Sergeant Major told them to get out and stand by the entrance, the women couldn't see much but did as they were told with some trepidation. Once assembled they turned, picked up their belongings and entered the building and found themselves in a great hall lit by a bright light, a chandelier, it was nice to get out of the cold.

It was the first chance the women had to take a good look at each other, and Daisy and Lizzie stood close together and took a good look around their new surroundings. The other women were all around the same age as Daisy and Lizzie. An Officer arrived with a clipboard, and the women were allocated rooms up the stairs. Daisy and Lizzie were placed in the same room, and they picked up their luggage and headed up the stairs finding their room on the second floor. It was bigger than their room in the nurse's home but much colder.

There was a fireplace in the corner. "We need to get that lit!" said Lizzie, so she went off to find some wood and newspaper. Daisy, on her own, walked over to one of the beds with linen left on it, she picked up the clean sheets and got to work making the bed to keep her warm.

Lizzie came back a few moments later carrying some wood and got down to making the fire. Using her lighter it was soon ablaze; it was nice to feel the heat entering the room. Daisy helped Lizzie make her bed and Lizzie told Daisy some sandwiches and hot tea were being laid on downstairs in the dining room in fifteen minutes. The women made their way back downstairs looking for the dining room. They found it was a large room with separate tables and chairs so the women entered and helped themselves to food and sat down.

Soon other women joined them, and the room got noisy with the chatter of voices. Both women were grateful for the food as it had been a long day and the hot tea was a blessing, washing the sandwiches down. A couple of new ladies joined Daisy and Lizzie at their table and over the food they made their introductions.

Mary and Gwen had trained at St Thomas' in London and too had wanted more adventure once they had qualified, their friends had said they were mad but both women had been determined to join up. Daisy and Lizzie had pretty much said the same thing, keeping the real reason to themselves.

The same officer who had met them walked into the room and the women stood, they were told to sit. The officer told them to be downstairs in their shorts and tee shirts at seven-thirty for a run and then breakfast and wash. The officer turned and the girls stood and she left them alone again. They said goodnight and the women made their way up to bed. They would have a wash in the morning as they wanted to unpack and get settled in as the two women weren't sure how long they would be here.

Daisy found the toilet, just a few doors down from their room. As she turned the handle and the door opened, she could feel the warmth as she entered, she told Lizzie where it was, and Lizzie went off to use it. They found where the bathroom was situated down the hall from them for the morning. Both unpacked and took out the garments they had been told to acquire before coming on this adventure. It was late when the women had put everything away, and they were in warm pyjamas.

Lizzie by now was desperate for a cigarette and sat on her bed and lit one; it made her feel better and calmer. Once she had finished, she found a makeshift ashtray and stubbed it out; they decided to call it a night and they settled down to sleep, both women knew that when in a new place they slept badly but they had each other and that was worth its weight in gold at that precise moment.

Daisy laid in bed watching the embers as they flicked and the warmth sent her into a sleepy haze, Lizzie was doing the same and soon both were sound asleep. Lizzie woke before Daisy and quietly let herself out of the room, when she came back Daisy was awake. They got into their PT clothes and plimsolls and when ready, made their way downstairs.

The Sergeant Major was waiting for them but luckily Daisy and Lizzie were not the last to arrive. The Sergeant Major checked their names off the list and, once satisfied everyone was present, they headed for the door. What hit them most was the cold as they left the warmth on the January morning, but soon they were running around the vast grounds. Both girls were out of breath and had to stop a couple of times as they had got a stitch. The Sergeant Major had shouted at them to keep going which had the desired effect and the women got around in a respectable time.

On finishing the Sergeant Major said, "Welcome ladies to the army." And they were dismissed for breakfast, quietly he was impressed and had respect for these women.

Walking into the dining room they were given hot porridge and then a full cooked breakfast. Once filled with the delicious food, they could head to the bathrooms to get cleaned up. The women enjoyed the hot bath immensely and once clean they were told to report downstairs, where they were shown into a big room and were supplied with Army uniform. Their measurements had been sent on beforehand, and the uniforms were ready.

Both women were sent to try them on and to come back down if there were any problems. Luckily for them, their uniforms fitted perfectly, and when they looked at themselves in the mirror, they didn't recognise the person staring back. Furthermore, they headed back down to the large room where it was now an empty room and the officer from the night before was back standing at the front.

"Please, come in and take a seat." All the women did. "Let me start by introducing myself, I am Captain Eleanor Cannon QAIMNS, and I will hopefully explain your training and fitness before we ship you out to your destination. You will wear your battledress at all times. From tomorrow you will train in your uniforms and get used to them, tomorrow you will be running out into the hills with full packs on your back and don't forget your tin hats. Over the weeks, we shall teach you to keep and record medical notes in the field, and how a field kitchen works, how to purify water and the layout of a general hospital under canvas. When a serviceman is injured, they will be collected by a stretcher bearer and hurried to his Regimental Aid Post (RAP). Then taken by ambulance to the Field Dressing Station (FDS) or Casualty Clearing Station (CCS) for urgent surgery then down the line to the hospital, where they receive treatment before being evacuated by sea or air to the United Kingdom or back to service with their regiment. Doctors will give lectures describing the injuries the battlefield inflicts and you will be taught about rank to feel and behave like the army officer you are…"

They were to have inoculations for Typhus, Typhoid, and smallpox.

Daisy whispered to Lizzie, "After that lot we will be like a pin cushion," Lizzie had to laugh.

"…It's going to be hard, but you will be prepared," was the last thing the captain said. "Time for your inoculations and then you will be taught to march and salute like an officer this afternoon." With that they stood as the captain left the room.

Both women walked to the room where they were to get their inoculations and as they joined the queue of women, they chatted away, both afraid to admit they were slightly nervous. Daisy went first and dropped her trousers and underwear, the injection when it happened was a sharp scratch and it stung. Once all done Daisy rubbed her bottom, pulling up her clothes, she waited patiently for Lizzie who she could see was pulling a face. Daisy tried not to laugh but she couldn't help it and it took some of the tension from the room.

Once both women were done, they had some free time to recover, get a cup of tea and a biscuit. "I think we have earned it," said Lizzie rubbing her bottom.

Sitting down was a bit uncomfortable for the rest of the day as the two women found out when they attended the afternoon lectures. Lizzie found them some aspirin to take with their tea and by the evening both women were feeling better, and the pain had subsided to a dull ache, which they could tolerate.

Over the next few days, it was full on. Neither of the women had any adverse effects from the inoculations and they were both learning a lot, both had given their relatives their temporary address for their post

312

to be delivered and that evening they sat on their beds reading the post they had received that day.

Lizzie had a letter from her parents, her mother had included a cut-out piece of The Times newspaper with her engagement to Charles printed in it again. She also had letters from Eddie, Charles and Christopher.

Daisy's were from her parents, George and Mary — it took till lights out to read all of them.

Lizzie handed the piece of paper to Daisy who stared at it, looking over at her friend concerned. "So there it is again in black and white," Lizzie said. Lizzie sat back and felt her chest tighten, she couldn't breathe. Daisy told her to take deep breaths, breathe she said slowly. Lizzie did as she was told and felt better. Okay, she thought, it was official even if she kept throwing the notice in the bin, but they weren't married yet and still something could happen, she prayed.

They both decided to reply to them tomorrow as they lay in bed, silently. Lizzie dreaded answering Charles' letter so she would leave that one to last and she hoped silently he was still away. The last few weeks had been good for her as she had been kept busy and she had no time to think about what had happened, but every time he wrote, it brought back the bad memories of that frightful night.

Daisy looked over at her friend and she knew in an instant what letter she was reading. "Come on Lizzie, put it down and get some sleep, you can reply to it tomorrow." Lizzie placed it on her bedside table and rolled on her side and pulled the blanket up around her neck. Finally, she went to sleep. For Daisy it took longer as she still worried about her friend.

The following day the two women attended lectures and in their free time decided to reply to their letters. Daisy's were easy, she first wrote to her parents keeping it cheerful, asking if they were fine and explaining to them what she was up to as much as the censors would allow. George's letter she wrote asking how he was and how he was getting on, the letters being censored made it difficult to write but Daisy knew what joy it was to receive a letter, so she kept plodding along. Mary's letter was more problematic as she found it difficult to communicate with her sister, she was engaged to Bobby, yet again Daisy just politely asked if she was all right and had she heard from Bobby and when was the wedding?

Lizzie on the other hand dreaded writing to her mother and replying to her about the announcement. She first took her letter from Christopher and sat and re-read it. Oh, how she wished he was here with her at this very moment, God she missed him. It had been so long since she had seen him, she was beginning to forget what he looked and sounded like. Sitting at their dressing table with a lit cigarette she took the sheet of paper and began, she found it difficult, normally the words flowed but she had been bothered by the announcement more than she cared to mention.

She wrote how she loved him and missed him terribly and she hoped they could meet soon just so she could be held in his arms. Once the letter was completed, she placed it in the envelope and put it to one side. Then she picked up another sheet and began, "Dear Mother and Father," going on to say thank you for the cut out and asking how Charles' parents are receiving the news of the engagement? They must be over the moon?

It was a match made in heaven according to his mother, Lizzie had pulled a face when she had first read that. Really? If she knew the truth… but she did thought Lizzie, he still could do no wrong in the eyes of his mother. Lizzie wondered how many more incidents had taken place and she quickly put the thought away, but it still niggled in the background.

Lizzie kept the letter short hoping they were well, and she explained how her training was going and finally, she asked if they had seen Eddie? Signing off she began the next one to her brother, she first told him of the announcement making it official between her and Charles and that she really hoped her aunt and father would come through for her. How seeing it again written in black and white sent a cold chill down her spine, making her feel physically sick just thinking about it. She then asked how he and Glenda were and hoping they were both well? While she was writing, her thoughts were on the next letter to Charles and how she was going to say what she felt.

Once she had finished the letter to her brother, she put that to one side with the others, and for the last time that evening, she picked up another sheet of paper. She began with, "Charles," she decided to go for the formal greeting as she didn't feel romantic tonight, "I hear from my parents we are formally engaged but remember there is still a war in progress and things could change again," she silently prayed to herself as she wrote it. Keeping the rest of the letter formal she signed off, "Elizabeth," if they were to be married it was going to be a business arrangement she had decided.

Putting all the letters together and picking up Daisy's they would get posted later that evening, when they went down for their evening meal. Daisy was worried for her friend, the news from Africa where she thought Christopher was stationed was that there had been heavy fighting and last November the allies had invaded North Africa, so Lizzie had put the clues together.

"Stop daydreaming and come for supper," Daisy called cheerfully turning and looked at her friend smiling. They were just about to go on a great adventure together, linking arms they made their way down the sweeping stairs to the dining room for supper, first stopping to drop off the letters for posting in the tray.

After supper, the girls were full, but there wasn't much to do, so they headed back to their room to rest. Both laying on their beds chatting, they were so happy in each other's company now. Lizzie had another cigarette; Daisy was concerned for her friend as she was smoking too much lately since the incident with Charles, Daisy promised herself to keep an eye on her. They reviewed the things they had learned today and over the last few weeks in preparation for when the time came to put their knowledge into practice. Little did the girls realise but the time would come sooner than they expected.

A few days into February more news was heard on the wireless in the mess that the Germans had surrendered at Stalingrad, Russia. That was excellent news all round, maybe the war was going their way at last.

One night, about a week later, both women were in a deep sleep when the lights to their room were switched on, and the Regimental Sergeant Major told them to get up and that they had an hour to pack and be downstairs ready to leave. Both girls, after rubbing the sleep from their eyes, quickly shot out of bed after he had left the room. Just before the hour mark, they were standing with bleary eyes in the hallway with the other nursing sisters all packed, and ready to leave; the room was noisy with nervous chatter.

"I need a cigarette," said a sombre Lizzie glancing at Daisy, who raised her eyebrow. The Sergeant Major shouted to be quiet and he told them to make their way out to the front and climb into the waiting truck, both girls clambered up and sat on one of the benches, it was freezing, and they pulled up their greatcoats to keep warm. Both were nervous but excited but both were wondering where they were going?

Once loaded with everyone aboard, the truck pulled away into the dark spring night and to the docks and their next, unknown destination.

Chapter 36

After travelling for around three hours in the back of a bumpy, cold, dirty truck the girls were pleased when it finally entered the entrance to the docks, the girls could smell the sea in the breeze as they exited the truck.

They were told to stand in a line and then would be given a cabin number and told to walk up the gang plank, find their cabin and get settled in for the voyage ahead. Lizzie looked at the large vessel ahead of them and it looked like an ocean-going liner that would sail across the ocean to beautiful countries far away.

Luckily Daisy and Lizzie were sharing, they boarded, and they soon found their cabin along a dark corridor, it wasn't what the girls expected, it was actually very nice inside, they had a wardrobe, set of drawers, twin beds and a sink with a mirror over it. There was a small porthole which was blacked over to prevent light from escaping. The toilets and showers were down the corridor, they found out. The two women got unpacked and they were so excited they didn't want to sleep so they had a walk around the ship exploring, until they were told to get back to their cabin and stay there by an angry officer in a navel uniform. They had noticed a lot of servicemen milling around so it was a troop carrier. Once they had found their cabin again, they got ready for bed and tried to get to sleep, which didn't come easy to them as they were both still excited.

Lizzie lit her cigarette enjoying the taste and when finished she stubbed it out. Laying down sleep soon claimed her, as her eyes grew heavy, she glanced over and observed Daisy was already asleep.

The next morning, they gathered on the top deck to be told they would be sailing tonight at midnight, so they had the day to get prepared and were introduced to some of the officers they were to spend a lot of time with over the next few weeks till they reached their final destination. Both women were both excited and had some reservation to actually what they had agreed to. They lost some of it when they gradually became friends with the officers onboard. They dined in the officer's mess and all the nurses were treated like royalty.

Their Matron in Chief warned the young women not to start affairs with the young married officers, some of them did look dashing in their uniforms. They were also told not to smoke on deck as the U-boats could see the light. Lizzie moaned as she would have to smoke in her cabin and Daisy would be moaning about the smell.

At precisely midnight the engines came to life and the vessel quietly slipped it moorings and they slipped out of the safety of the harbour beyond the boom and into the dark deep ocean. Both women laid in their beds listening to the hum of the engines as the vessel sailed into the darkness, the vessel was joined by other ships of the Royal Navy, there to protect it from the German submarines that lurked in the depths of the water.

The submarines were the biggest threat and worry to both women as they knew that the vessel could be targeted at any time. By the time the weak sun had come up in the sky, land had long gone. The grey cold sea was not smooth, but it wasn't rough as the vessel cut through the waves, making its way to its journey's end. The women made their way to the officer's mess for breakfast, which was pleasant as there was plenty of food, more than the two women had seen in a long time.

By the end of the first day the weather had changed, and the wind started to increase, the waves were bigger, and it looked like wild horses were riding through the waves, pounding the vessel. The ship was rocking and heaving and so were many of the women, soldiers and crew were feeling ill, seasickness was a major problem and it kept many to their beds. The QAIMNS that had their sea legs assisted the ship's surgeon, but both Daisy and Lizzie were struck down, until they found their sea legs a few days later.

Night time was worse as they lay in their beds feeling ill and hoping that the U-Boats didn't strike. They were told to keep quiet and the only sound they heard was the drone of the engine in the still of the night. The ship took the long route north of Ireland, and down the coast of Africa. Each day that passed was a blessing and it meant they were getting nearer to their destination. Daisy and Lizzie, once they had discovered their sea legs and the weather had improved were allowed up on deck with the other nursing sisters, they all breathed in the fresh warm air and could taste the salt from the sea.

The sea was calmer, and at night the moon shone bright in the sky, which gave the sea a lovely glow, it was also a worry as the submarines were lurking around ready to attack any ship in the convoy. Luckily, they were missed but other ships were not so lucky, it was a frightening time and the two women prayed a lot.

They heard the screams in the quiet of the night as a ship went up like a Christmas tree, they heard people who were bobbing around in the sea and their cries for help which gradually died out. One ship went back to pick up survivors alive and the rest of the convoy carried on. Fresh water was a real problem as the days went on and, in the end, it had to be rationed and you could only have a quick wash in the shower between the hours of seven and eight in the morning.

When not helping in the sick bay, Daisy and Lizzie were up on deck, there were no seats, so the girls used life jackets as rugs as the heat was stifling. Cabin Fever was a real problem, especially with the sticky heat that made people lethargic and irritable. The girls' days started at seven with an hour's PE on the deck before the heat got too much. Then the rest of the morning was lectures and training. The ship was lucky, it had a group from ENSA aboard, they would put on evening shows for the ship's crew, troops and nurses. These shows helped to pass the time and were repeated as the vessel carried on its journey to warmer climes.

All the women were a big attraction for the male crew, especially Daisy and Lizzie, and over the weeks they got to become very friendly with a few of the officers who would try and to seduce both women, but to no avail. Daisy still hoped that she would see her doctor, Michael Reynolds. Lizzie was thinking the same thing, she hoped to see Captain Christopher Jameson and her heart beat a little bit faster at the thought.

It didn't stop the flirting and the fun, but the girls didn't succumb, it passed the time though. One evening the girls were finishing dinner in the Officers Mess when they heard a rumour that they would soon be arriving at their destination; the port of Tobruk, then onto their base in the desert.

The Matron in Chief gathered the women in a room the night before and informed the nurses what was before them. Both Lizzie and Daisy looked at each other, holding each other's hands, while the older woman was speaking, unsure of their future but excited as well. When the briefing was finished, they went back to their cabin to pack.

The girls had an early night, they took a shower which they knew was against orders but they both didn't know when they would have another chance. Some of the other QAIMNS had the same idea and the Matron, on seeing this, turned a blind eye. When they were both safely back in their cabin they climbed into bed and let the sea gently rock them to sleep, both dreaming about the next adventure this trip would be taking them on.

Chapter 37

The next morning was a hive of action and activity. The ship was unloaded and the women were told to line up on the quayside. By eight the sun was already getting very warm, so the women were standing in their battledress and tin hats trying to keep the sun off them.

They were causing quite a storm with the Libyan workmen who were working at the docks. Some nurses with blonde hair, were the fascination as the men were used to their women being dark-haired and covered up. Both women were talking in hushed tones when their truck appeared around the bend, it was a big Army truck with a big cross painted on the sides of the cloth in red paint.

The women were told to climb aboard and sit on the bench to the side. Daisy climbed in first followed closely by Lizzie, Daisy helped her friend up and they found a seat next to each other. It was nice to get away from the rocking of the waves and they both knew it would take a few days to get rid of their sea legs.

All the other women followed and then their kit was loaded and their journey began. The lorry's engine whirled into life, and they turned towards the exit of the port. Canteens of water had been loaded on to the supply truck ready for the journey with all the other equipment they had brought with them from Britain. It took some time to leave Tobruk due to the traffic, it was dusty and very dry sitting in the back of the truck and soon it was getting very hot, it was a good job they were all sitting down. The exotic smells and sights as they left the city were new, exciting and memorable. The women's senses were in over drive with the smell of all the spices it was making the women hungry.

By mid-morning the convoy stopped, and the women were allowed to get off to stretch their legs but told not to wander too far. Armed sentries were put on duty to protect them. Daisy and Lizzie were glad to get off but being scared they chose not to wander far from the safety of the trucks. It was nice to get a drink, even if the water was warm due to the heat but it did the job of refreshing their mouths which were full of sand that had been whipped up from the road. Fires were made and a meal of stew was cooked. The group of nurses stood watching as a procession of camels went by with their owners who took interest in the foreigners especially seeing the female soldiers. The sentries were on high alert just in case there was trouble they all past peacefully.

Once everyone was fed, and it everything was cleaned away the convey carried on into the desert, to their final destination to which they would arrive by late afternoon if all went as well as expected. Finally, as the women were getting tired and irritated with the heat and the dust the trucked pulled into their base, which was to be their new home.

Field Hospital Two would be made over the next few days, everyone worked hard, and it began once the trucks had stopped. The Nurses climbed out and looked at the wooden huts that were already standing, they walked over to the first one and Matron opened the door, behind her she felt the other nurses all pushing to try and get a glimpse inside, so she entered first followed by the rest of the inquisitive women.

Folding bedframes were constructed, mattresses and pillows and blankets were gathered and the forty-bedded wards were created. Old packing cases were used as bedside lockers and an up-turned soapbox was used as a medicine cupboard, for heat and boiling water there was a Beatrice stove.

Each ward was assigned a couple of orderlies who helped the QAs and generally kept the men in check. Many of the service personnel had shortened the nurses to QA's and that was how as they were known now. The nurse's accommodation was tents which didn't keep the sand out and before the girls went to bed, they would check their beds for spiders and other desert creatures. Water again was a real problem, so the water used for washing was also to be re-boiled for the girls' hot water bottles as the nights in the desert were very cold.

Lizzie and Daisy settled into their new surroundings and over the coming weeks settled into a routine, they heard that a new batch of doctors would be arriving at the weekend. Daisy was excited and apprehensive at the same time but then she thought she was being silly; he wouldn't just turn up, so she put that thought to one side and carried on.

Lizzie had noticed her friend's behaviour once the new doctors were mentioned and made a note to herself to speak to her when she next had the chance. The wards were filling up with injured soldiers and they usually only stayed for four days then were moved either back to their regiment or sent home once they had surgery.

That evening Lizzie was sitting at the nurse's desk writing up her notes, when she heard a cough and she felt someone standing behind her, turning around in her chair she looked up into the loveliest blue eyes she had seen, and her face broke into a beautiful smile.

"Oh, Christopher." She jumped up and fell into his open arms.

He pulled her tight and hugged her. "I really want to kiss you, but I know we can't really do it here!" he said smiling.

Lizzie remembered where she was, and he reluctantly let her go.

"I will be due a break in an hour, then meet me in the canteen. I can't believe you are really here!" Lizzie kept looking at him, not taking her eyes from him, her heart was racing.

"I heard that a new set of QAs had arrived and I hoped you would be one of them."

"I will see you soon," she said, and he reluctantly released her and went off to speak to his men.

Lizzie sat back down, watching the man she loved caring for his men. Then she thought to herself, what was she going to do? She really would have to tell him about Charles, the engagement and the rape and her title if they had any chance of them being happy, she wanted no secrets between them. She had thought about this long and hard prior to this meeting in her dreams and soon it would become a reality.

Where was Daisy when she needed her? "No, you can do this, if he thinks the world of you, he will accept it," she mumbled to herself.

At eight she was relieved by another nurse for her break, Lizzie took a deep breath and entered the canteen and saw Christopher looking around as she entered. Her heart raced faster as she walked up to him. He stood and took her in his arms again and this time he didn't care, he pulled her in for a kiss and it was magical. Their lips met and stayed locked together for some time.

The cheers went up from the other service personnel in the tent, so reluctantly they pulled apart, both smiling. "We will carry on later when we are somewhere more secluded," he told her, looking at her lovingly.

Lizzie went and got herself a mug of tea, she refused the food as she knew she wouldn't be able to eat it. Walking back to the table, she couldn't help but still have a big smile on her face.

Taking the seat by Christopher she sat down. "We have a lot to talk about," Lizzie began. She took his hand; she really didn't want to do it here but she had no choice so she just took a deep breath and blurted it all out.

She first explained about Charles and the engagement, and it was all her mother's doing, he seemed to sit and just listen. Lizzie was trying to judge his countenance by his face, but it was a poker face, Chris showed no emotion at all.

Then she mentioned her title and he said, "I'm not bothered, I could care less about the title or the money, I just love you, I have fallen in love with you."

She relaxed a little, she then told him how she had met up with Charles and it had ended by her being raped. Lizzie waited for the reaction on the face of Christopher. At first, he was quiet and then he let her hand go and had a hurt look on his face. As he got up, not saying a word, he just left the tent.

Lizzie got up and followed him. "Christopher," she shouted after him, he didn't turn around and just kept on walking, his shoulders were hunched. She tried to catch up with him, but he walked too quickly for her. Looking at her watch she realised she had to get back, so she turned and hurried back to her ward.

She got back and took over and just got through to the end of her shift, she made it back to her tent and as soon as she saw Daisy she burst into tears. Once she had calmed down, she explained what had taken place.

Daisy took her friend in her arms and hugged her tight. "Let me speak with him," Daisy offered, "when he comes again."

"He may not come back," Lizzie cried looking forlorn.

"He will do, when he has a chance to think things over," Daisy offered.

Lizzie sat on her bed chain smoking, worried with guilt that she had told him everything but, in her heart, she knew she had to honest with

Christopher or it just wouldn't work out between them.

It was a few days until Captain Jameson returned, Daisy found him talking to the Matron, so she waited until they were finished.

As he walked past Daisy he said, "I don't want to talk about it."

Daisy grabbed his arm forcefully. "Please talk to me? Yes, she was a fool to go but she had no choice, he would have made her life hell, she loves you and if circumstances were different, you would be doing things differently. But you are not because of this war."

Christopher stopped and turned, he looked at Daisy. "I still love her but at present I am really angry and cross, and when I see Charles, I will kill him, that is a promise. Tell her I need some time, but we will meet up soon."

Daisy looked the captain in the eyes. "Don't leave it too long as she is really unhappy," she said turning and walked away.

While all this was taking place, Daisy had no idea but one of the new doctors to arrive was Doctor Michael Reynolds and he had stood watching this all unfold.

"Well, I see it's the young Student Nurse Peters, all grown up." He stood in front of Daisy blocking her way.

Daisy's heart was racing, and she looked into Michael's eyes. "It's actually Sister Peters now if you don't mind," she said, pushing past him. 'Why did he wind her up so much,' she thought as she walked on. She could hear him laughing behind her, but it was not in an unpleasant way.

Lizzie had just come off shift and was in their tent, trying to sleep which they'd had little of the past few days.

"I saw him!" said Daisy as she came bustling into the tent and sat down on her bed. "He still loves you but needs time to think things through, and by the way, Doctor Reynolds is here!" She didn't know why she had told Lizzie, but it was too late.

"Take a deep breath and carry on," said a shocked Lizzie. Lizzie had already seen that look in her friend eyes before.

"See I knew he would be okay about things, he just needed time to think," smiling over at Lizzie. "Now do you think you can eat some food as you have had nothing for the last few days and need something inside you? I am getting really worried about you, Daisy said to Lizzie, who nodded her head, she was in fact quite hungry."

Both women stood, hooked arms and headed for the canteen and tea. When they entered the tent, who did Daisy see, but Doctor Reynolds chatting to some other QAs. Daisy got her food, and found a seat near Lizzie, she wasn't going to let the new doctor get under her skin. Out of the corner of her eye she saw the doctor looking longingly and it made Daisy blush the deepest shade of red.

Lizzie looked at her friend with a keen interest but didn't say anything. Both women were hungry and tucked in. Finishing off their food they then sat chatting, Daisy thought it was good to see her best friend starting to be like her old self again, and hopefully the charming captain would soon be back. She knew they had a lot of things to address but this was a start.

As the two women sat at the bench Doctor Reynolds walked briskly by and said, "Good evening, Ladies." His eyes caught Daisy's and she just melted.

Pulling herself together smartly she carried on listening to what Lizzie was originally talking about. Again, Lizzie had noticed the interaction between her friend and the doctor. There was definitely a mutual attraction and Lizzie knew life was precious and so she would do a little match making to help her friend.

The next day both women were busy as they had just had an influx of new casualties, both women worked until they dropped. Once back in their tent they both collapsed on their beds and fell into a deep sleep, only waking when the sky had turned black, but it was lit up with bright stars and a full moon shining high.

It had got very cold, and Daisy pulled up a blanket and wrapped it around herself, she looked over to see Lizzie was still asleep, she pulled her blanket up from the bottom of the bed and placed it over the sleeping form. She felt famished and decided to go and look for something to eat.

As Daisy was walking to the canteen in the dark, who did she run into but Doctor Reynolds, they both stopped before knocking into each other in the blackness.

"Well, hello, Sister Peters," said Doctor Reynolds in a jovial voice.

Daisy, feeling flustered, answered, "Good evening, Doctor."

They stood staring at each other not moving. Doctor Reynolds said, "What is your first name?"

Daisy stuttered, "Daisy."

"Would you like to get a hot drink?" asked the Doctor. "I am just off duty now."

"Yes, that would be very nice," stuttered Daisy, he looked tired.

They both walked towards the canteen at a leisurely pace, Daisy trying to concentrate on what the doctor was saying, his white coat flapping by her side. They entered the tent, which was quiet at that time of night. Once they had their drinks and Daisy got herself something to eat, some sandwiches that were old, they found a seat and sat down. Once the initial shyness and awkwardness was gone the two found they got on really well and had a lot in common, they sat talking well into the early morning.

When Daisy looked at her watch and saw the time, she made her excuses and headed for her tent. Doctor Reynolds walked her back and bid her goodnight. Daisy really wished he had tried to kiss her.

Lizzie had woken up earlier and noticed her friend missing had heard her come back. When Daisy entered the tent, she looked sheepish.

"Had a nice time?" asked her friend.

Daisy blushed and answered, "Yes. It's late, let's get to sleep we have a busy day ahead." With that she prepared for bed.

Lizzie turned on her side and smiled to herself. 'Well! Well!' She thought, maybe I won't have to interfere too much, and soon she was asleep.

Daisy laid in bed unable to sleep as she was extremely happy and excited and she replayed her conversation with the doctor in her head, finally slipping into a deep gratified sleep.

The next morning both girls were up reasonably early and it was getting warm, they both had a quick shower, breakfast and got onto the wards on time. The injuries that the nurses saw, were varying a lot. Mainly they were gun-shot wounds and serious shell injuries which caused limbs to be amputated, there were a lot of tropical diseases like smallpox, diphtheria, typhoid fever and poliomyelitis. Nursing these brought considerable personal risk, and many showed outstanding bravery in this area.

It was while Lizzie was working in the infectious ward that Captain Jameson turned up asking for her. One of her fellow nurses gowned up and entered the tent, Lizzie was busy, and once she had finished, she came over to the nurse and was told a Captain Jameson was waiting for her outside the tent.

Lizzie stopped breathing; she took deep breaths trying to slow her heartbeat down. Taking the gown off and washing her hands she left the tent to find out her fate. As she stood out in the heat, she saw him, he looked so handsome in his uniform, her knees buckled as she got near to him, he walked forward, took her arms and pulled her to him.

Lizzie felt at home in his embrace, and she tipped her head to kiss him, and he didn't stop her. Relief was written all over her face, she really thought she had blown it with Christopher. Once they broke from the kiss, Christopher stood away from Lizzie.

"We need to talk, but not here," he said.

"I'm off duty now," she said looking down at her fob watch.

"I have a jeep coming for me for a short journey to see a small village not far from here, that's if you would like to come? I just want some time alone with you," he said in a deep husky voice.

Lizzie couldn't speak but she nodded her head in a 'yes'.

Chapter 38

Taking her hand, he pulled her close to him and they walked close together, they found his vehicle and climbed aboard, she sat quietly as he put the jeep in gear, and they roared out of the hospital compound and into the desert.

Lizzie didn't have time to tell Daisy where she was going, 'never mind,' she thought, she wondered what lay ahead of them. She let the drone of the engine lull her as her heart was silently racing. They sat together, not speaking as it was very noisy and the sand was blowing up, they had to keep their mouths closed using scarves to cover them and they both had goggles on to keep the sand out of their eyes.

After the last few weeks, it was nice just to be close to Chris and she wanted to re-connect with him whatever lay in store for them. They arrived at their destination, it was late afternoon and Chris pulled up at the small village. It was pretty to view with the palm trees, this was one of the reasons why Lizzie had wanted to join the QAs, to travel, even though it was war time, she was going to appreciate and enjoy every minute of it.

Chris took her hand and as the sand was whipping around them, he made a make-shift tent attached to the jeep, it was cosy, and they made themselves comfortable under the material and enjoyed their surroundings.

"Sorry, we can't walk around not with this wind," he said.

"I don't care came the response." Lizzie was struggling to breathe as she was nervous.

"What was Chris going to say now he was sat very close to her." She could smell his cologne. He looked pensive and she took his hand.

"Whatever you have to say, I will accept it," she said nervously. Really, she wouldn't, because if it was bad, it would break her heart in two.

Christopher dropped her hand. "Let's eat first," he said, he took out a hamper and a flask of tea he had got one of the women he worked with to prepare. Once he opened it; he was really pleased with the look on Lizzie's face. They prepared and enjoyed the food and drinks as both were hungry. Once they had eaten and they had packed away the dirty things, they settled down to talk. They had made small talk while they were eating but both knew they were ready for the main issue.

Chris spoke first, it was his turn to take Lizzie's hand and he rubbed her knuckle. "At first I was shocked and hurt, I will not lie," he said. "I wasn't expecting that news and I really don't care about your title and the money because, like I said, I love you." The next thing he said was, "Do you love Charles?"

"No," she replied straight away. "No! No! It's all my mother's doing, she planned this all along and now I hate him for what he did to me. Yes I was a fool to go but he would have made my life hell and I would never escape him. He doesn't love me, he wants an open marriage, he has already got a little girl who is gorgeous."

"You have met her?"

"Yes, his mother paid to keep it quiet. I was lucky not to get pregnant and I definitely didn't enjoy it." Lizzie couldn't look Christopher in the face as she spoke, "Sorry I hate talking about it. I just want to forget about it and somehow get out of the engagement. I'm hoping my mother, once she gets to see Charles in his true colours, will not want him in our family. My father, aunt and brother are on our side." Chris smiled at that.

He was proud of Lizzie, and he knew how hard it had been for her to talk so openly to him, now he understood more he wanted this brave, beautiful woman back in his life and he pulled her close and their lips met languidly. The kiss was full of hope and burning want, they lay down by each other and the kissing got heated, but this time it was because the two people were in love.

The love making was perfect in every way, Chris was the considerate and romantic lover and they both enjoyed it immensely. Lizzie felt like she was on top of the world, she had wished it had been like this the first time, but it wasn't, and she had to learn to live with it. Christopher hadn't used a sheath so there was a chance of pregnancy, but she was happy to take that risk!

After, they lay in each other's arms, wallowing in the afterglow. "We

330

will deal with Charles together," Chris said, kissing her forehead.

"I really thought I had lost you once you knew the truth," she said, looking into the blue eyes that would always melt her heart.

"Yes, I was upset but I can't stay mad at you for long," he said laughing.

They both sat deep in their own thoughts, smoking a cigarette. "I would really like to stay here but I need to get you back before you are missed and Daisy sets off the alarm." Chris looked at his watch checking the time.

"Next time we will have a weekend in Tobruk," he said grinning, and looking lovingly at Lizzie.

Lizzie looked back and said, "Yes, that would be lovely."

"One more thing before we go." Christopher got on to one knee taking a box out of his pocket. "Elizabeth, will you do me the honour of being my wife?"

Lizzie didn't need to think, she automatically said, "Yes."

They sealed it with another kiss. "We will get married when the war is over," he said.

They cleaned up and prepared to leave. The sand was still whirling around but they made it back in time for a late supper.

Lizzie sat in the front of the jeep and gently leaned over to kiss Chris. "Thank you for today, you really do have my heart," she said pressing his hand to it.

He could feel it beating under her Army battledress and said, "We will sort this mess out, but it may take some time." Kissing her again he pulled his hand away regrettable. "I will see you soon," he said. "And sorry you didn't get to see the village!"

Then she jumped out and watched him drive away back to his command, she turned and headed to her tent.

On entering Daisy was sitting on her bed, she jumped up when Lizzie entered. "Where the hell have you been?" she shouted, unable to hide the worry on her face. "I was worried sick. I was just going to report you missing."

"I have been to look at a village a few miles away with Chris and we talked, everything has been sorted out."

Daisy looked closely at her friend, sensing something more had taken place. "You didn't?" she said.

Lizzie couldn't hide the happiness. "Yes, we did, and we took a risk, but I am happy before you ask. It was lovely." She went on to explain sitting down on her bed, and it was needed after all that had happened. "I don't regret it," she went on to say.

Daisy was truly happy for her friend and didn't comment any more, apart from saying, "Come, let's eat, I am hungry." Grinning at her friend and going over to pull her up off the bed.

She noticed the ring on her finger. "Oh, you're engaged!" she said excitedly, it's a beautiful diamond ring.

Daisy looked at it closely, she was pleased for her friend. They chatted away as they left the tent arm in arm, Daisy was pleased for her friend, but she was slightly jealous as she wanted the good Doctor Reynolds to make love to her.

As they entered the canteen the said doctor was there too, he glanced over at Daisy as they entered, and he smiled to them both.

Lizzie didn't miss the interaction and grabbed her friend's arm. "Come on, let's get food."

Once seated they enjoyed the food and were chatting away when Doctor Reynolds came over.

He again said, "Good evening, ladies" and he looked longingly at Daisy and said, "Would you care to have a walk with me around Tobruk on your next weekend off?"

Daisy looked shocked. "Really?" she answered.

"Yes," he said again in earnest.

She didn't think twice. "I would really like too."

"It's a date," he replied and walked out of the tent not looking back.

Lizzie glimpsed at her mate and said, "Be careful."

Daisy flashed back, "I will be." And they continued to finish their food.

Chapter 39

The next weekend Daisy had off, Doctor Reynolds was true to his word and he picked her up. Saturday morning, she had an overnight bag, Lizzie had helped to pack it before her shift had started. Warning her friend again to be careful she left the tent and Daisy sat on her bed nervously waiting.

He arrived on time, and they settled in the jeep and left the safety of the compound. Then he spoke, luckily the wind was still so the sand was settled and they could talk to their destination. It took a while but Daisy found talking to Michael was rather pleasant and she learned that he had parents who had been given money by an elderly relative and could send him to medical school, he had a sister in the Wrens who was based in Scotland. His parents lived in Suffolk and were proud of their son. They were shocked when he joined up but they respected his wishes. He went on to apologise to Daisy for the way he behaved at The London, but he had really liked her from the beginning, but at the time he was going out with another nurse.

Daisy really didn't have a problem which she told him. She said it was nice to be with him now and that she felt they had a connection. He looked over at her and smiled. Daisy fell in love just a little bit more. They drove in silence, and they arrived in Tobruk by late afternoon.

"I have booked us into a hotel I know." Daisy looked over at Michael, and he quickly said, "Separate rooms of course!"

Daisy was a little disappointed but tried not to show it. He smirked as he had glanced across and noticed the disappointment, maybe things were looking up he thought.

They parked up outside and headed into the hotel and they checked in. The man on reception gave them a wary look but welcomed them, they were given rooms next to each other on the second floor.

Michael stopped Daisy at her door and said, "Freshen up and I will knock in an hour's time."

Daisy nodded, entering the room and closing the door, she leant against it. Her mind was all over the place. What did she want? She really liked Michael, as he told her to call him. She knew she didn't want a quick affair, she wanted it to last. Did he want that too? She would have to find out first, later tonight.

He was on time, and they walked into the city to the sea front which was full of ships of all shapes and sizes. The harbour was bustling! They found a restaurant by the sea front not too badly bombed and ordered some food.

Daisy was slightly worried about what she had ordered, but it turned out to be lamb stew, it tasted really lovely and so they tucked in. The conversation flowed and Daisy talked about her family in Luton, Michael listened intently to what she said. He talked about his family in Felixstowe, his father was a General Practitioner and his mother a housewife, she was a nurse before they married. This bit of news eased Daisy's nerves slightly.

Once the meal was over, they walked amongst the ruins of the city as it was still warm. Michael took her hand and she smiled and let him. They headed back to the hotel and with a quiet understanding, they went to his room. The room, Daisy thought, was exactly the same as hers, it wasn't a plush hotel but comfortable, basic and more importantly clean.

On closing the door, he looked over to Daisy and said, "Are you sure?" he asked, looking adoringly into her eyes.

"Yes, but I am nervous." She rubbed her sweaty palms together.

"Don't be," came the reply. "I will take care of you."

He stepped forward and took Daisy's hand and led her over to the bed, he slowly undressed her, she was in a pretty floral dress with sandals. The dress fell to the floor, and she stepped out of it, all she had on underneath was her white bra and matching knickers.

Michael's eyes wandered over Daisy's suntanned body. "Take them off," he said in a husky voice.

She did as she was asked, standing naked before him. His eyes devoured her and he undressed himself quickly and guided her onto the bed. He laid her down and climbed on top, she could feel his erect penis touching her thigh. He then began to kiss her, their lips touching like fire, god she was in heaven. He moved and touched her, she was excited and ready for him, she could feel the wetness down below.

He climbed back on her, kissing her again. They didn't talk, he just pushed into her gently and she relaxed as he thrust in and out. The pain caught her suddenly but soon it was forgotten. She felt all sorts of nice feelings at that precise moment, and she didn't want it to end. He rubbed her and she felt alive, they both orgasmed together.

Michael slowly recovered and rolled off, he took Daisy in his arms, and she lay with her head on his chest listening to his heartbeat.

"Thank you," she said shyly.

"Are you okay?" he asked, concerned.

"Yes," she replied. "It was amazing."

"Will you stay the night with me?" he asked in a husky voice.

Again, she didn't have to think twice, she said, "Yes." Daisy lay listening to his heart beat in rhythm and she thought how lucky she was that her first time was with a nice man and not what Lizzie had to endure, she felt slightly guilty.

'What if she got pregnant?' Her parents would be shamed, but she didn't care she loved this man with her whole heart.

Later they fell into a deep and contented sleep in each other's arms. In the morning before they got up, they made love again, and once changed they had breakfast.

"We had better make a move back to the hospital or we will be late," Michael said as they climbed into the jeep.

The journey back was perfect. They talked all the way and Daisy knew she had fallen more in love with the doctor for whom she had held a torch for a long time. The only thing she was worried about was she didn't know how he really felt about her? Should she ask him outright or just wait to see if he opened up to her?

On arriving back, he pulled up and he took her hand and pulled her into a tight hug. "I had a lovely time Daisy, and would really like to do that again sometime?"

"Yes, that would be nice," she answered shyly and got out collecting her bag. She headed for her tent, glancing back at Michael who sat watching her.

On entering her tent, she found it was empty and she unpacked her bag and laid down on her bed looking up at the ceiling, reliving the last twenty-four hours. She must have fallen asleep because when she woke Lizzie was asleep on her bed.

Daisy rolled over and looked at her sleeping friend, she really wanted to wake her and talk to her but instead she let her sleep, it could wait till the morning. But now she was having doubts. Had she done the right thing by sleeping with Michael when she hardly knew him? Why had she been so rash and what if she was pregnant! Too late now, she thought and turned over and went into a restless sleep.

In the morning Daisy woke and felt tired as she hadn't slept well at all. Lizzie opened her eyes when she heard Daisy stir.

"Good morning," she said to her friend rubbing the sleep from her eyes.

Lizzie looked at her friend. "Did you have a nice time?" she enquired.

When Daisy didn't answer straight away, she sat up. "What's wrong?" Lizzie asked, looking over at her friend worriedly.

Daisy felt a tear spring to her eye, wiping it away she looked over and said, "I slept with Michael, and I don't really know how he feels about me."

Lizzie looked at the forlorn Daisy. "Trust me, he's mad about you, yes, he really loves you!" she said.

Daisy glanced at her mate and said, "Do you really think so?"

"Yes," came the reply. "Just wait and see."

Daisy glanced worriedly over at Lizzie. "What happens if I am pregnant?"

"Well, we will be pregnant together then." Lizzie said smiling and laughing. "And we will go home in disgrace."

Daisy in fact didn't see the doctor for another few days as he was busy in theatres as they had an influx of casualties. Daisy was pleased as it kept her busy and her mind occupied on other things. When she did bump into Michael, he looked exhausted and her heart went out to him, she felt sorry for him.

"Are you okay?" she asked, concerned.

When he spoke, he sounded worn out. "Let's get a drink."

She led him to the canteen and sat him down. Once she had handed over the mug of hot, sweet tea, she felt only love towards him. They sat talking for a few minutes as she could see he needed rest and then led him to his tent and got him to lay on the bed, she pulled up a blanket and kissed him. He smiled and closed his eyes, he slept.

The next morning, she saw Michael again and he thanked her for her care the previous night, he was very professional, but Daisy didn't mind, she would catch up with him soon. This was torture for Daisy as all she wanted to do was to sit down with Doctor Reynolds and find out how he really felt about her.

On the other hand, Lizzie kept bumping into Chris and they would spend any free time together, planning their future after the war. By the weekend most of the fresh casualties had been treated and patched up and either sent on their way to a hospital ship or were well enough to return to their regiments. This gave the hospital staff some much needed breathing space to recover.

Daisy was sitting in the canteen when Doctor Reynolds walked in, he glanced over at her and smiled, and she smiled back. She thought he would come and sit with her, but he got his food and drink and went and sat by another group of QAs. Daisy was disappointed and upset, she tried not to show it, but she couldn't hide the look on her face, so she got up, cleaned her tray away and left.

She felt his eyes burning on her back as she pushed the flap of the tent and walked out into the heat of the day. It was her day off and she really didn't want to go back to her tent as Lizzie was working and she would only end up thinking bad thoughts. Just as she made up her mind to have a shower and do her hair, she felt a tap on her shoulder, and looking around she saw Michael, standing very close to her. She could feel him breathing on her neck which sent a shiver down her spine.

"Come with me," he said, and pulled her arm. They found a quiet spot away from the main wards. "I'm sorry I haven't seen you since our weekend away, but we have been busy," he started. "I do like you," he said with complete honestly. "I may not show my feelings."

Daisy on hearing these words felt relief. He pulled her to him and kissed her long and hard. Daisy knew then she had found her soul mate and she had done the right thing by sleeping with him.

When they broke apart, she was breathless, and he was smiling at her. "Are you watching the show tonight?" he asked.

"Yes, I was going to see it," was her reply.

"I will catch you later." And with that he strode away.

Daisy watched as he disappeared into a ward, and she headed back to her tent to collect her wash bag and towel for her shower. She wanted to look nice for the show tonight. She headed to the shower with a spring in her step, life was pretty good she thought.

The shower for once had run effortlessly and Daisy came out refreshed, drying herself, then got to work drying her hair. When Daisy looked down, she saw that she and Lizzie had received post from home. Daisy noticed that Lizzie had received a letter from Charles, and she wondered how her friend would deal with it? Will she show the letter to Christopher? Daisy could only watch and hope it turned out well.

Daisy sat herself down on her bed and opened her first letter from her parents. She read the letter through, they were both fine, Mark was growing up and still enjoying school, Mary was still awaiting the return of Robert so they could get married. Daisy wished she had been nicer to Bobby but what she felt for him wasn't real love. What she felt for Michael, now this was pure love.

She read the rest of the letter, how her mother was finding it hard to get material so was just doing alterations for people, if the war carried on then she would have to look at factory work as she wasn't getting enough money. Daisy knew her father wouldn't like it but they knew they had no choice, they needed to keep money coming into the family.

The other letter she had was from her brother, George, his was full of adventure and loving being in the navy, he couldn't say too much but he asked, how she was. She would respond by trying to let him know where she was without getting into trouble with the censor. Putting the letter away, Daisy would reply to them tomorrow as she had to get ready for the ENSA concert that was being put on tonight for their entertainment. Hopefully Michael would be at her side as he had promised a little while ago.

Daisy turned on the wireless that Lizzie and her had acquired and was humming to the music as she got dressed. Putting one of her summer dresses on as she would still be off duty till tomorrow morning. Both had their periods; both were slightly disappointed but she they knew it was for the best as it was not the right time to bring a baby into the world.

More news had come that Mussolini had resigned in July and now it was the end of August, the girls felt maybe the war would be ending soon.

It felt nice to be able to dress and feel like a woman and not be in her Army Uniform, which was made of a coarse material and at times was uncomfortable, especially in the heat of the desert. Lizzie made it just in time to get changed and into one of her summer dresses, she too wanted to get dressed up for Chris as he would be coming to the concert as her guest. She stood at the mirror and applied her make up carefully.

For both girls it was like a date night, in fact it was like their first double date, only Daisy didn't know if Michael would actually be there. The concert was to start at seven and Chris had turned up just before, waiting outside their tent as he didn't want to cause the two women any distress and gossip as he knew what the other QAs were like on any juicy news of romance taking place.

Most of the other nurses knew of the romance between the dashing captain and the Lady Elizabeth, they had just accepted it as normal to see them together all the time. They didn't know the true nature of the relationship forming between Doctor Reynolds and the young nurse. That was about to change tonight because as they took their seats, Lizzie taking the seat next to Chris and Daisy the other side of him. Just as she thought Michael wasn't coming, she felt someone sit down by her side, he squeezed her elbow.

As the lights went down, she looked up into his eyes, falling under his spell. Turning to the front of the makeshift stage the concert began, all four laughed and sang for the next few hours enjoying the break from the reality of war.

When the concert finished all four stood and waited to exit the tent. "Shall we get a drink?" Lizzie asked. They made their way over to their tent; men were not strictly allowed but the two girls wanted to break the rules just for today. Lizzie poured the whiskey into four mugs and she and Chris sat on her bed and Daisy and Michael took the other free bed. The four got on really well and the rest of the evening passed pleasantly. Much later when a lot of whiskey had been drunk, Daisy offered to walk with Michael back to his accommodation as she wanted to give Lizzie and Chris some time on their own.

Pulling Lizzie to her as she left the tent she whispered, "Take as long as you want, I will be back later."

Michael caught her hand and held it tight as they walked in the cool night air through the rows of tents, they arrived at his tent which he shared with another Doctor called Philip. Michael popped his head in and luckily Philip wasn't there, so he grabbed Daisy's hand and took her in. Inside was laid out the same as her tent but only more basic, she and Lizzie had made it like home as much as they could over the few months since they arrived.

Daisy hesitated as she didn't want to get in trouble and the whiskey was playing havoc with her emotions. How she wished she hadn't drunk so much; she would have to be sensible. Michael sat her down on his bed and then he sat by her side, he pulled her towards him, and their lips met. Kissing Michael was like paradise she thought. Suddenly he put his hand on her breast and massaged it, it made Daisy have all sorts of feelings, the only one she knew was that he really wanted her.

He moved his hand down towards the hem of her dress pushing it up, but she suddenly came to her drunken senses and put her hand on top of his. "Not here," she said.

He stopped what he was doing, and he removed his hand and apologised. "I'm sorry but I can't help myself, you are exquisite, and I think I am falling in love with you."

Daisy thought she had mis-heard him as he was slurring his words, "What did you just say?"

"I am falling in love with you," he repeated taking her in his arms again.

This time she hugged him tight and said, "I'm in love with you too, since the day we met on the ward. I really want to spend another night with you but not just this drunken grope," she said looking adoringly into his eyes.

They both seamed to sober up and they sat talking late into the night. Around one, Daisy made her way back to her tent and knocked on the canvas, Lizzie said she was on her own and that Daisy could enter.

Both women got ready for bed, Daisy told her friend what Michael had just admitted. Lizzie was pleased for her friend. Soon they both fell into a deep sleep until it was time to get up and go on duty Sunday morning.

Before they were due to go on shift Daisy noticed that Lizzie held the letter from Charles in her hand, it had been opened.

"I opened it last night and read it to Chris as I don't want to keep secrets from him," she said looking at her friend.

"What did it say? If you don't mind me asking."

"Well, he hoped that I was fine, and he couldn't wait until we met up again, this made Chris very angry, but in the end, I managed to calm him down," she continued. "Then he wanted to know where I was but I'm not going to tell him."

Daisy said, "I give him credit for his persistence."

"Luckily, we are hopefully in different countries." Lizzie crossed her fingers behind her back as she didn't want Chris to meet up with Charles. She wasn't sure what he would actually do to the man if their paths were to cross before the end of this war.

"Did you read your other letters from home?" Daisy asked trying to change the subject.

"Yes, my Parents were the usual stop playing at being a soldier and come home and get married, but that is not going to happen. Over my dead body."

"My brother, Eddie is getting married and my mother is still dead against it, but he says he is going ahead because he loves Glenda."

"Good for him," said Daisy. "Will you get leave to attend?"

"I don't want to go all that way back to England and then Mother stopping me coming back here, so no." Lizzie was adamant about that, so Daisy dropped the subject again.

"Right, are you ready to get to work." They checked each other over and headed to report for duty, both nursing slight headaches.

Once their shift had finished, they were ordered to see the Matron in Chief, they knocked on her tent and were told to enter. They marched in and they stood to attention in front of the tall elderly woman, who then looked up at them with kind eyes.

"Well, Sisters. I have some news for you." Both women waited with bated breath. "You are both being sent to Malta to nurse in the hospital there.

Both women looked across at the Matron but knew arguing would be useless as orders were orders, this is what they had signed up for. At least they were not leaving straight away. They took their paperwork and saluted, turned and marched out.

When they reached their tent, both sat down on their beds. Lizzie had an uneasy feeling about this next deployment, she had a bad vibe which she kept to herself. They would both have to break the news to Chris and Michael, and they knew it would be hard on all of them, but they had to remember there was a war still going on.

So, the girls met up with both men and broke the news to them, they were not going straight away but in a week's time, so they still had a few days for them to be together. It was much harder than they thought, Lizzie kept crying and Daisy had to stay strong for the both of them.

Michael was brilliant, he accepted it quite well, but it made Daisy uneasy as she hoped he wouldn't go back to his old ways of chatting up the nurses, or worse sleeping with them. She had no choice but trust him, he promised that he loved her, and they would meet up again when they could, that night she held him tight, but they didn't make love as they couldn't find anywhere quiet where they could be alone.

Matron was watching them like a hawk, Lizzie was panicking and was making herself ill, and she didn't know why.

Chris was worried about her. He took Daisy to one side, the day before they left. "You will take care of her?" He sounded worried.

"Of course," replied Daisy.

More news had come in that on the third of September, Italy had surrendered. Things were really happening very quickly. The war was still going on, especially in the Pacific.

That night they packed up their belongings, said their farewells to their other colleagues, and in the morning boarded the truck to take them to Tobruk and their ship to Malta.

No one knew where they were going as they hadn't revealed it but her and Chris had made a code of where she was so they both would know, and he could tell Michael once they had arrived safely, both men stood and watched as the truck drove away.

Chapter 40

It took to mid-afternoon for the truck to arrive at Tobruk and they found their ship, they got unloaded and were told to wait on the quayside till they were told to embark and find their cabin. The heat beat down on them making the sweat pour down their backs, soaking their shirts and making them feel uncomfortable.

Lizzie and Daisy were sharing a cabin again. Lizzie, as the journey progressed, began to calm down, but she still had the uneasy feeling. Once they arrived at their destination then she had decided to tell her friend, but not during the voyage, she would keep it to herself. They set sail that night, around midnight and it was dark with a full moon. The sea was like a duck pond silently still, both women hoped that the U-boats were not in their area as they left the safety of the harbour and went out into the open sea.

The journey took a few days, and it was mostly calm, which the girls were relieved about and were happy when the Island of Malta came into view. It was September 1943 and what would happen in their next chapter, Lizzie wondered, looking at the land as it gradually got nearer.

Malta had been bombed by the Germans and Italians the week before Christmas 1941 and it went on till July 1942, the main targets were the naval base and the airfield. The hospital stood on the hill overlooking the dockyard and the staff had endured a year-long bloody battle which had been hard for all of them, that was why they had come to relieve two nurses so they could go home and have a rest from this war.

They docked a few hours later in Valletta and were met by an orderly driving a battered jeep who was to take them up to the hospital and have a meeting with the Matron in Chief. As they drove through the war-torn streets, they saw for themselves the devastation caused by the long bombardment, they saw the ruins and rubble all along the route.

It pulled at both the girls' hearts to see, worse than the Blitz that they had lived through back in London. The orderly dropped them off and told them their suitcases and trunks would be sent up to the room they would be sharing together.

They entered the front of the worn looking off white building and were directed to an area away from the main block. Matron's office was situated along a long corridor. Lizzie knocked on behalf of both of them, they checked each other over one last time and were told to enter by an elderly voice from behind the door.

They stood in front of a thick wooden desk, sitting behind was a plump middle-aged woman. Both women looked and thought at the same time, did all Matrons look the same? They stood to attention and were told to sit, they took the chairs and brought them forward and sat down in front of Matron. She looked at some papers and then, when she noted that the women were ready, she glanced up.

"Welcome to the Island of Malta. I'm sorry you have been transferred but needs must, I have it on good authority you are in fact very good nurses, and you are needed to replace two very good nurses that need some time back home. I have given you their old room in a building across from the hospital, it's basic but warm and clean. You will be wearing your grey dresses, and scarlet-trimmed cape, and white veil caps, until told differently, as I think that they look smart and versatile for the wards."

Both girls glanced over at each other, they had never worn their uniforms yet as they had always worn their battledress out in Libya, it would be a new experience from them both.

Matron explained about the rules and regulations, and both listened intently. Once dismissed they walked back the way they had come to the front of the building, glancing around getting a feel for their new home.

Once they left the hospital, they looked across the road to where their building was, they checked the road was clear and they crossed and entered the front door, clearly the building had taken a battering, but it was still in one piece.

Climbing two flights of stairs that they noticed was moving slightly as they walked up, they found their shared room. Daisy had the key, she unlocked the door and turned the handle. Once inside the women were impressed, it was actually a nice size with two single beds already made with a spare blanket sitting on top, with a small bed side cabinet and a

344

bedside light on it by the side. There was one wardrobe, a bit battered but it was functional, and a sink which stood in the corner.

The window was open and when they looked out, they looked out onto the hospital, well at least they didn't have far to travel to work.

Lizzie sat down on her bed, the mattress was firm but comfortable she thought, looking around the room, it was good and most of all functional. Daisy came and sat on her bed. When there was a knock at the door, Lizzie being the nearest jumped up and walked over to answer it, it was an orderly with their suitcases and trunks. Both girls thanked the orderly and got to work unpacking. In little over an hour everything was tidied away, and their uniforms were hanging up on the wardrobe door ready for the morning.

Lizzie looked around for some stockings and cleaned her regulation black shoes. Daisy had done exactly the same, both were ready for a bath as they felt dirty from all the travelling and they wanted to wash the grime off. The bathroom was along the corridor from their room, Daisy ran the water, the tap took time to fill the bath. When she was happy with the amount, she got undressed and climbed in, laid back and let the warmth cover her. Once washed and her hair washed, she emptied the dirty water down the drain, and made her way back to the room. Lizzie went next and came back refreshed, she dried her hair, and settled on her bed. Her thoughts went to Chris and how she was missing seeing him.

She hoped they would meet up again very soon as she really wanted to sort out Charles and the engagement once for all. Daisy was thinking about Michael and was hoping he was behaving himself with her gone.

Once they were settled, they decided to write to both men and their parents when they had a free moment, but for tonight they would grab something to eat and rest as they both had early starts in the morning.

Since the end of the siege, convoys were getting through with urgently needed supplies, so when the two women walked onto their ward, they were pleasantly surprised how well equipped it was. In fact, the whole hospital was badly damaged where it had been repeatedly bombarded but it was well supplied. The morning had flown by and both women had to have separate breaks. What they saw when they went to the mess was very tired war weary staff, but with a defiance and inner strength to succeed.

The wards were full of injured military personnel brought over by ships from North Africa, men were still waiting to have surgery. The nurses witnessed other injuries like burns, which took ages to dress because sometimes the uniform had melted into the wound, saline was used to soak the cloth off. Forceps were then used to pick out any other foreign matter that was still in the wound. Painkillers were given to the patient, but they usually had to have morphine in the end as the pain was intense.

The biggest fear was that the patient contracted septicaemia and the nurses did all they could to stop the infection. But it was difficult under the circumstances. The nurses tried to keep the men's spirits up as best they could, the men who were ready to go back to their company or go home where full of fun. Underneath, both women knew these men had witnessed unimaginable things that they may never recover from, but time was a great healer.

The wards were similar to any hospital, forty beds were lined up on either side and before Matron's inspection each morning, the nurses went around turning the wheels, so they faced the front. They then had to tidy the patient's lockers, ready for ten when Matron arrived through the doors. It was Daisy's turn to be Sister in Charge so at precisely ten, Daisy stood at the door awaiting Matron,

At ten exactly the said woman arrived and said, "Ready Sister?"

Daisy replied, "Yes, Matron." And they made their way down one side. Matron stopped to pass the time of day with patients and then they made their way down the other side doing the same. Matron sometimes popped into the Sister's office if they had anything to discuss, but today, she got to the ward doors, turned to Daisy who was standing, shuffling her feet nervously. "You keep a tidy ward Sister." With that she pushed the swing door and hurried off.

Daisy felt herself relax as the tightness in her shoulders subsided, she must have been holding them tightly she thought. Lizzie looked over at her friend and gave her a reassuring smile and both women got to work with the dressing round, while the other staff carried on with their duties. On the ward were a couple of orderlies who were friendly enough, the dinner arrived, they got to work dishing out the hot food, the smell making the two women hungry.

After lunch the nurses did the afternoon drug round, making sure the men were given their analgesia and the new wonder drug penicillin which was only available to the military at present as there was not enough for everyone, but it was saving men's lives.

The wards were warmed by stoves positioned at each end, now that they had coal to keep stoking them in the winter months, that was the job of the orderlies.

It was still very hot even in September and the wards were warm from the late summer heat. At the end of their shift both women left the ward, tired but satisfied as they headed across the road to their room.

"I really need to write my letters," said Daisy. She was looking forward to writing to Michael. "Let's get changed and get something to eat." They both wanted to get out of their dresses and back into their battledress as the dresses were only practical for the wards.

Once changed the two women headed back to the hospital and entered the dining hall, the food was all right, they were both hungry and they soon finished it and they sat talking, still getting used to their new surroundings.

"We had better get back and write those letters," said Lizzie. "Our families will be wondering what has happened to us."

The women left the hospital, crossed the road and headed up to their room. Once they had their writing paper, they settled down to write.

Lizzie kept her parents' letter short and only informed them she had moved and that she was fine and in good health, she wished them well, she left out about Charles. She then wrote to her brother, hoping that the wedding plans were going well and that she hoped that they would both be home to come to the wedding. She wanted Daisy there and Chris, if he was back in the country and everything was sorted, and that the engagement was off. But she knew in her heart that was a long way from happening.

Lizzie then wrote to Chris, she wrote she was missing him and very much loved him, she told him she was fine, and the journey had been uneventful. She had decided that she wouldn't write to Charles this time as she hadn't received a letter recently. She hoped that something bad had happened but her mother hadn't informed her.

Daisy sat and wrote to her parents, saying the same, she was well and in good health. Mary had written and she replied to that letter, wishing Bobby and her all the best for the future. Then she had written to her brother, George and told him to keep safe. Finally, she wrote to Michael, telling him she missed and loved him deeply and she wasn't sorry for spending the night with him. She hoped they got a chance to do that again very soon.

On completion, they inserted the letters into the envelopes ready for posting. It was getting late, and they both had been up since early. Lizzie was on a late and Daisy had another early tomorrow.

Lizzie, once laying on her bed listened to Daisy snoring quietly, she was a little worried she had not heard from Charles, and it was beginning to make her anxious. He normally wrote regularly and this was very out of character. If he been killed his family would have let her parents know and they would have written to her. Maybe it was a good thing as he didn't know where she was, and she had kept that quiet for as long as she could.

Rolling on her side she closed her eyes and drifted off to sleep but she slept badly that night, suffering from bad dreams, she finally got to sleep in the early hours of the morning.

Daisy was quiet when she got up, not wanting to disturb her sleeping colleague, she got dressed and made her way across the road to the dining hall for breakfast. On the way she dropped off the mail for posting, she noticed that Lizzie had not included one to Charles.

She decided that when she saw Lizzie later, she would ask her about it, but for now she had to get to the ward, or she would be late.

It was late evening when Lizzie arrived back to the room, Daisy was laying on her bed reading, she had thought about going for a walk but Valetta was so badly damaged that she had decided against it and had done some washing instead.

Lizzie looked around the room, observing the washing hanging on a make-shift line. "You have been busy?" she said to Daisy, pointing to the washing.

"Thought I would get a head start, it will dry very quickly in this heat." Looking at the underwear hanging and drying. The heavy laundry got washed in the hospital but things like underwear the girls liked to wash themselves.

Lizzie got changed and put her pyjamas on, hanging up a clean uniform for the morning.

"How was work today?" asked Daisy.

"Very busy," came the reply. "Some of the dressings were pretty bad but they are slowly improving which is good."

Daisy glanced over to her friend, she could see dark lines under her eyes, she was concerned and wanted to know what was troubling her. She sat back against the pillow, resting her book on her knees.

"What's bothering you?" she asked, looking over at Lizzie concerned.

Lizzie took a minute to answer. "I'm worried I haven't heard from Charles for ages, and he would normally have written by now."

Daisy watched as her friend rung her hands together nervously. "It could just be that he is really busy," she replied, but she quietly doubted it.

She anxiously believed he was up to something; she would keep an eye on her friend. They spent the rest of the evening talking, till they both felt their eyes getting heavy, Lizzie got off the bed and turned the light off. "Goodnight," she called into the darkness.

Over the next few days, the girls settled into their routines; they didn't go out much as the streets were still badly damaged, but the girls were surprised how the Maltese people were so resilient, just like the British had been during the blitz. A few weeks later Lizzie got called to see Matron, she left her ward and walked down the corridor. What could she want? She pondered as she walked to her office. She gave herself the once over, and when happy knocked on the door.

"Enter." She opened the door and walked in. "Good morning, Sister Fenton." Matron seemed to be in a good mood she thought.

Standing to attention Lizzie waited to be told to sit. "Please come and sit down," she said, pointing to the chair by the fire.

Lizzie sat down, letting the warmth of the fire calm her nerves a little.

Matron joined her, seeing the worry etched on Lizzie's face, she said, "Don't worry, you are not in trouble." Relief seeped through Lizzie.

"I have some news for you, your fiancé is here in this hospital." Lizzie grabbed the chair arms tightly.

Matron noticed and so proceeded with caution. He has sustained some injuries that required surgery, but he is on the mend now. "He has only just woken up and was asking for you, would you like to see him?"

"How did he know I was here," she thought to herself. Lizzie was filled with dread, she hesitated, which Matron noticed again.

Seeing the distress the young woman was in, she said, "My dear girl, what is the matter?"

Lizzie, pleased she was still sitting down, knew her legs would have given way if she had been standing. She looked at Matron and said, "Yes, we are engaged, but it's not through choice, my mother has arranged this marriage but I love someone else."

Matron sat listening and kept quiet.

"He also did something bad to me a little while back." Lizzie felt the tears prick her eyes and a tear rolled down her check.

Matron was quick to hand her a handkerchief which she took with gratitude. Matron didn't pry but she had a pretty good idea what had occurred and let Lizzie compose herself. When Lizzie was ready; she went on to explain what had taken place and then the tears came. Matron sat still and listened intently not interrupting the young nurse.

When Lizzie had composed herself once more, Matron took her hand and asked, "Do you want me to accompany you?"

"Yes, please," she replied.

Lizzie went to stand, and her legs buckled, she gripped the seat, getting her balance, and she stood straight.

Matron made sure Lizzie could walk before both women left her office and headed down the long white-washed corridor, both were lost in their own thoughts. Matron promised she would not leave this young woman with that man.

They stopped at the ward door and Lizzie took deep breaths, the hairs on her arms stood up. He can't hurt me here she kept telling herself.

Matron said quietly, "Are you ready?"

Lizzie nodded and they entered together, Matron had called the ward ahead, so the nurses knew to expect them. Both women stood at the end of the ward, Lizzie was scanning down the beds to try and spot Charles, her eyes stopped at one bed, and she begun to walk towards it, followed by Matron. Lizzie stood by the bed and Charles had felt her presence, he turned his head.

"Well, if it isn't my beloved, what took you so long to come and see me?" he said in a menacing way.

Lizzie felt physically sick, Matron kept back a safe distance but still could hear what was spoken, but Charles had spotted her and quietly said "Brought a chaperone?"

Before Lizzie could answer Charles grabbed his chest as if in pain, Lizzie just stood and watched not offering to do anything. She wanted to smile but she stopped herself.

Matron called the Sister over, and requested pain relief for him, which she hurried off to get.

"Sister Fenton, I think we had better go, you can visit again once the captain is feeling better."

She said her "goodbyes" and turned, walking as quickly as she could to get out of the ward. As she was leaving, she could feel Charles' eyes burning a hole in her back.

Chapter 41

Once outside the door, she took a deep breath, it was as if she had stopped breathing in there, she couldn't stop shaking. All she wanted to do was see Daisy.

Matron started to speak, "As you have had a shock, you are relieved of your duties today, go back to your room and rest. I will get a massage to Sister Peters to check on you during her break."

"Thank you, Matron," said Lizzie, and now feeling utterly physically and mentally drained, headed off towards her room. She wanted to run down the corridor, but she knew Matron was standing and watching her.

Walking back her emotions were all over the place, she knew one thing, she despised Charles with all her heart, and she would never marry him. She made a promise to herself, once she got home, she would tell her mother everything that had taken place and she hoped the truth would be enough to call this sham marriage off. Lizzie would get the help of her Aunt Lynn and would write to her with her plan.

Feeling a little better, once back in her room Lizzie lit a cigarette to calm her nerves. She was still shaking; the nicotine made her feel better. Lizzie undressed and in only her underwear crawled under the sheets to sleep. She must have dozed off because when she woke, Daisy was sitting by her bed, holding her hand.

"How long have you been here?" she enquired.

"Not long, I popped in earlier, but you were asleep, and you looked peaceful, so I left you, now I am off shift. Let me get out of my uniform and then we can get something to eat, and you tell me what has happened. Matron filled me in that Charles is here and that she took you to see him."

"It was awful, he was horrible to me, luckily Matron was there, otherwise I don't know what he would have attempted to do to me."

"Listen you are not to visit on your own, hopefully, once he is well, we can get him shipped off back to England, where he can continue his convalescence."

Daisy, seeing the distress in her friend's eyes promised to keep an eye on her. "Right, get some clothes on and we can go and grab some food."

Lizzie wasn't particularly hungry, but she got out of bed and got dressed while Daisy sat and waited.

"Are you going to write and tell Chris that Charles is here?" asked Daisy.

"I really want to, as I promised no secrets from each other before I left." Lizzie pulled up her trousers and put her boots on, doing up the buttons of her shirt.

Daisy could see how torn her friend was, just considering what was the best option. She knew that she would have to tell Chris, but she was going to keep away from Charles as much as she could.

That evening Lizzie sat and wrote to Chris, it was not an easy letter to construct, and the words didn't flow like they normally did but once finished she put it in the envelope. She had read it through to Daisy and her friend had agreed it was the right thing to do, she still didn't know how Chris would react to the news. Daisy later sat on her bed, while Lizzie slept, dropped a quick line to Michael explaining what was going on and asking him to keep an eye on Chris.

The next morning both women were up early, ready for their day on the ward. Daisy looked at her friend, her complexion was shallow with a tinge of grey. "I think you should have today off!" said a concerned Daisy.

"No, really, I'm fine," replied Lizzie in a harsher voice than she had intended. "He is not going to go away any time soon, so I had better just get on with it."

Daisy left it at that, but she was still troubled as they checked themselves over in their full-length mirror and proceeded to the dining hall for breakfast.

Lizzie collected her cooked breakfast like she normally did, but she picked at her food, pushing it around her plate as Daisy spoke to her, "Are you actually listening to me?" Queried Daisy, glancing over at her friend.

Lizzie truthfully was only half listening as her thoughts were on

Charles. "Should I go and visit him today?" she asked.

Daisy didn't want her friend to go but she didn't really know what to say. Thinking swiftly, she finally said, "Let me know when you go and I will go with you so you are not on your own with him."

"He won't like that," answered Lizzie.

"Well, at this moment in time he can't do anything whatsoever about it. Have you finished, as it's time to go?" Looking down at the fob watch pinned to her uniform.

Picking up their trays, they stopped off to clear them away and made for the exit.

The day went surprising fast for both women. When they were finally relieved of their duty, they had agreed to meet by the door and then go to visit Charles. His ward was the other end of the hospital and the two colleagues walked in silence. When they arrived at the entrance, Lizzie stopped. Daisy looked at her friend with concern and squeezed her hand reassuringly. "Remember, I will be by your side all the time and when you are ready, we can leave."

Looking at her friend one more time, Lizzie nodded, pushing the ward door open. As they entered Charles was slightly sitting up, supported by pillows, really all Lizzie wanted to do was suffocate him but she kept a poker face. She felt Daisy by her side as she walked over to his bed. "About time you got here?" he hissed.

"I have been working," she replied trying to keep the anger from her voice.

"Well, you are here now, another chaperone I see!" he said raising an eyebrow. "Do I get a kiss?"

Lizzie leaned forward to kiss him on the cheek, but he turned his head and she caught him on his lips, she felt sick, and he grinned. He grabbed her arm and pulled her in for a longer kiss, she tried to pull away.

Daisy spotted what was going on and told him to release her immediately, luckily, he did, but he whispered in her ear, "Wait till we are alone again." He laughed, but this caused the pain to shoot through the wound on his stomach.

Lizzie stood frozen by his bed, Daisy took her arm and led her out, getting the attention of the ward Sister that they were leaving.

The Sister, seeing Charles in pain went over to his bed, neither of the women looked back, they didn't talk till they were back in their room.

Daisy sat her friend down on the bed and went to find the whiskey and poured two glasses. Lizzie drank it down in one, letting the feel of the strong liquid run down the back of her throat.

Daisy soon emptied hers. "Are you feeling better?" she asked her friend.

Lizzie liked the feel of the warmth in her stomach, settling her nerves. "I detest him!" she said decisively.

Daisy couldn't wait till the captain was shipped back to Britain, she would have a word with the doctor looking after him and then a quiet word with Matron to see if he couldn't be shipped out sooner, once he was medically able to cope with the long journey. Daisy thought maybe a little discomfort during the journey wouldn't be a bad thing, laughing, she pulled Lizzie off the bed, and they got changed.

Lizzie noticed the smile on Daisy's face. "What has made you laugh?"

"I had an unpleasant thought towards your fiancé," she replied.

It was nice to see the whiskey had put some colour back on Lizzie's face, come on tea time.

That night Lizzie dreamt that Charles was attacking her, she was fighting him off, shouting, "No! No!" The sheets, and blankets were pushed off the bed, and it woke Daisy. She rubbed the sleep from her eyes got up and went over to her friend and shook her awake.

"Lizzie, wake up you're dreaming." Daisy kept shaking her friend to wake. Lizzie woke with a start.

"You had a nightmare," she said, glancing at Lizzie concerned. "Are you okay?" Daisy was holding her tightly.

"Yes," came the reply, but she could see that her friend was shaken up.

Daisy sorted the bed out and got Lizzie settled. "I can't sleep yet." So Daisy climbed into her bed beside her and laid down by her side and they talked till Lizzie had fallen asleep.

Daisy hoped that a letter from Chris would arrive soon, as Lizzie needed reassurance that they were still all right together. The next day Daisy had a different lunch time to Lizzie, and instead of going to the dining hall, she made her way to Charles' ward.

On entering she found the doctor and asked him, "When will it be likely be that Captain Holmes will be fit to travel back to Britain?"

The doctor replied, "Give him a few days and he will be fit."

Daisy couldn't have been more pleased, thanking the doctor as she left the ward. Her next person to see was Matron, she wanted to make sure he would definitely be sent on his way when the time was right. Daisy knocked firmly on Matron's door, and waited. When she was told to enter, she opened the door and walked into Matron's office.

Matron was sitting at her desk, looking up she welcomed Sister Peters, Daisy stood to attention awaiting orders to sit down. "Please sit." Daisy sat down as gracefully as she could.

"How can I help?" she asked Sister Peters looking directly at the young woman in front of her.

Daisy went on to explain, that for the good health of Sister Fenton, then the captain needed to go as soon as possible. Matron sat back taking it all in, and once Daisy had finished, Matron agreed to get Captain Holmes away from the hospital and Sister Fenton as soon as she could.

Daisy said, thank you, to Matron, checking the time on her fob watch, standing up, she waited for Matron to dismiss her.

Before opening the door Matron said, "Sister Fenton has a good friend looking out for her."

Daisy turned. "We look after each other Matron."

Striding back to the ward, she reflected on the good news, Daisy didn't even mind foregoing her lunch, but she wouldn't rest until Charles was aboard a ship bound for England.

Daisy felt much happier and couldn't wait to tell her friend the good news. On arriving back on the ward, she heard her stomach rumble, but she quickly got herself ready for the afternoon's work. Leaving the staff room where her locker was, she put her cuffs in place and tied her apron around her back. The afternoon flew by, and she didn't have time to speak with Lizzie as they were working different sides of the ward. When at last their shift had finished and they were told to leave by the Late shift, Daisy found Lizzie in the staff room taking off her cuffs and apron.

"At last, I can talk to you," said Daisy as she slipped her apron off. "I saw Matron at lunch, and she has agreed to get Charles out of here and back to England probably in a few days."

"What about his doctor?" enquired Lizzie. "Oh, he has agreed as well," came Daisy's reply smiling at her companion.

"Really!" said Lizzie surprised. The two young nurses walked back across the road to their room, stopping to collect any mail.

"Did you not want to see Charles today?"

"No, not really," came back the reply. "Let him stew!"

"He will be really cross if you don't pay him a visit," her friend warned.

Lizzie looked back over at her friend. "I don't love him and can't stand the sight of him, so let him stew today."

While she changed out of her uniform she turned to Daisy, relenting. "Will you come with me tomorrow?" she asked Daisy, who agreed straight away. They settled into a comfortable silence, while they finished getting changed.

What broke the silence was Daisy's stomach rumbling. "Sorry," she said. "But seeing Matron, and Charles' doctor, I missed lunch."

"No worries, we can get supper early if you want?"

Daisy smiled at her friend. "Oh, yes please."

Lizzie looked down at the mail she had picked up, it was from Christopher, he must have written a reply straight away.

"Can I open it or are you really hungry?" Lizzie asked.

Seeing the happy face of her friend Daisy relented and said she could wait for supper, so she sat on her bed while Lizzie sat on hers and tore the envelope open.

Lizzie was concerned what Chris had to say but she wanted to read it, so she scanned through it and then re-read it in full.

Daisy sat waiting patiently and kept looking at her friend's facial expressions to see if she gave away any clues to what the letter was saying. Finally, Lizzie looked up.

"Well?" asked a concerned Daisy.

"Well, he isn't too pleased as you can imagine, and he's not happy that he wasn't here to support me and I have to deal with the situation by myself, but I have you and Matron, so I don't feel I am alone." she finished by saying. He said again, "that when he does see Charles, he is going to kill him or do serious harm, so I really hope they never meet." Lizzie said in an anxious voice. He wanted to get on a ship and come over, but to her relief he couldn't leave his men at the moment which Lizzie was delighted about.

Finally, "He says he loves me very much and can't wait till we are married." Lizzie looked up with a slight blush to her cheeks. "Now Matron has agreed to send Charles home, I can write and tell Chris the good news."

Daisy's stomach rumbled again loudly, which broke the tense situation, and make both women laugh.

"Come on, let's get supper before you fade away," she said, pulling Daisy up from her bed.

The dining hall was quiet as it was still early, both women chose their supper and found a place to sit together.

Daisy turned to her friend as she put her fork in her mouth, waited while she chewed her food. "Do you think Chris would really hurt Charles?"

Lizzie contemplated for a few minutes. "I really think he would after what he did to me." She went on. "I wouldn't blame him if he did!"

Daisy nodded and carried on eating her supper, happy now that her stomach was full. Once finished both women cleaned away their trays and headed back to their room, so Lizzie could reply to the letter and they could get it posted in the morning. Daisy was on a late shift but had promised to meet Lizzie when she had her supper break and pay Charles a visit, as he would be in a terrible mood. Lizzie finished the letter and decided to have a bath, the hot water and bubbles revived her and she came back to the room feeling cheerier, which hadn't gone unnoticed by Daisy, who grinned to herself.

That night Lizzie slept well; Daisy slept listening just in case her friend needed her but she did think that perhaps Lizzie was coping better now Charles would soon be gone. In the morning Lizzie got herself up and ready without waking her colleague, her morning went quickly.

Daisy woke much later. She had her breakfast, came back to her room and settled on a bath which she thoroughly enjoyed. On arrival back to her room she dried her hair and got herself ready for work, at the back of her mind there was a worry, of how Charles would react to his fiancée not going to see him yesterday. She thought they would deal with it when they saw him later that day. Once dressed in her uniform, Daisy checked the time on her fob watch, noticing it was time to get to the ward. She picked up her key, locked their room and hurried to the hospital and her ward. Pushing the door to the ward open Daisy entered and heard a blood curdling scream, she saw Lizzie and an orderly trying to hold down a patient so Lizzie could give him a sedative to try and calm him. Daisy was just about to rush over and help when Lizzie managed to get the injection in him, and he soon settled.

Daisy caught up with Lizzie as she headed to dispose of the syringe. "What happened?" she asked.

"He was fine, then all of a sudden he heard a plane landing at the airport, and he thought they were coming to fire at him, and he started getting distressed. At least he is sleeping now," she said glancing over at the sleeping man who looked at peace.

"Right, I had better get ready or Matron will be on my back." Daisy walked to the locker room and got herself ready. Taking a look in the mirror, pleased how she looked and taking one more look at her fob watch she hurried to the office. Once hand-over was complete Daisy got settled into the afternoon routine and soon it was time for Lizzie to leave. Daisy found the other sister on duty with her and checked to see if she could go to her break.

She found Lizzie waiting by the door, looking very pale and drawn. Daisy took hold of her hand and said, "Come on, let's get this over with."

They walked down the corridor to Charles' ward, Daisy didn't say anything, but she could see her friend was distressed by the look on her face. When they reached the door, Daisy glanced over. "Are you ready?"

Lizzie nodded, her heart was racing, and they pushed the ward doors open. Lizzie looked over at Charles' bed and saw him sitting up against the white pillows. He watched as the two women walked towards him, Lizzie felt like he was undressing her as she walked towards him, she felt physically sick. When she reached his bed, Lizzie kissed his cheek.

Charles hissed, "Give your fiancé a proper kiss." And he pulled her to him roughly. Lizzie let her lips meet his and he kissed her hard, there was no feeling to it and Lizzie wanted to cry but it took all her strength not to let a tear fall.

"I see you brought your chaperone again?" he said looking daggers over at Daisy who looked straight back at him, she wanted to smile but she didn't want to cause any more difficulties for her friend.

Daisy pulled up a chair for her and Lizzie and she sat down by his side. He wanted her to hold his offered hand, but Lizzie just patted it.

Charles glared. "What is wrong with you?" he whispered. "Don't you get it? I hate you!"

She scowled. "How are you feeling," she asked sarcastically.

"Better, they will be shipping me home very soon and then I can rest and recuperate at my leisure. Will you be coming back to England soon?" he enquired, sneering.

"Honestly, I don't know."

"Why, my family wish to meet you," he said with a venomous voice. "So we can make this engagement official."

Lizzie was getting unsettled by his behaviour and Daisy could see she needed to get her away from this hostile situation as soon as possible.

Charles seized her arm again and said, "We will be married, Lizzie, as soon as you are back in England. That is a promise." He must have jerked himself because he clutched his stomach where the bandage was and his face twisted in pain.

Lizzie took that as her moment to leave. "We will pop in tomorrow," she glowered at him and called the nurse.

They left the ward in a hurry. Once through the door, Daisy pulled Lizzie into a hug and the tears fell.

Chapter 42

They stood for a good ten minutes, Daisy never let her go, only to pull a handkerchief out for her friend to blow her noise and wipe her eyes.

"Oh Daisy, what am I going to do? What if we are sent back home and he finds out, then he will force me to meet his family."

Daisy could hear the anguish in her friend's voice.

"What do I do?" Implored Lizzie.

"Come on," said Daisy, trying to cheer her friend up. "Let's get you back to our room and then I need to get back to the ward."

"No," said Lizzie. "I can manage by myself I know you are really busy you have helped me enough."

"Will you be all right getting yourself back to our room? I will try and get off as soon as I can," said Daisy.

"You promise?" Lizzie looked at her friend through tear-stained eyes. "Yes, I will be all right until you get back."

"See you later and then we will sort it out, if we are sent back to England."

Lizzie left and Daisy felt happier as they parted at the main entrance.

Back on the ward, Daisy had trouble concentrating as she was really concerned for her friend, and as soon as she was relieved by the night shift, she couldn't get back to their room quickly enough.

Earlier, once Lizzie had returned from seeing Charles she had got back up to their room and gone straight to her bed and curled up and cried again. She really wanted Chris to be there but she knew she was lucky as she had the next best thing, Daisy.

Once all the tears had dried again, she got changed. She wasn't hungry, so decided to skip supper and sat on her bed trying to work out what to do. Her mind was in disarray and thoughts kept playing on her mind, she really needed Daisy to make sense of it all.

'Just when I think it's all sorted, I get myself upset again. I must not let Charles get to me,' she thought.

Daisy arrived just after eight and didn't know what state Lizzie would be in, so she opened the door slowly and peered inside.

When she saw her friend sitting on the bed, the first thing she said was, "I have been really worried about you and thinking that you would be still upset. How are you feeling?"

Lizzie, raising her eyebrow. "One minute I know exactly what I want and then I don't," she answered honestly.

Daisy took her friend's hands in hers. "You know what you want? You want to marry Christopher. Remember he loves you and you love him. Charles is a nasty person, and you are best without him. Let's get the letter from your parents and we can decide what's next."

Lizzie agreed. In the next few days, a letter did arrive for Lizzie from her parents and Daisy got one from her parents and one had turned up at last from Michael.

Both girls sat on their beds reading. Lizzie's Mother was still determined for her daughter to marry Charles as soon as she was back in England. Lizzie decided when she did get back to England, she would have to explain everything face to face. Her mother would not be happy with her decision but it's what she really wanted and so it was going to happen.

Daisy's parents were doing fine just both very tired. Mary was still getting married as soon as Bobby was home, Daisy was pleased, she didn't feel jealous at all, she had Michael, who she loved with all her heart. Mark was growing and George was still somewhere in the Atlantic Ocean. Daisy grabbed Michael's letter and opened it, it read he was really sorry not to write earlier but he had been extremely busy and when he did have time off, he slept, he went on to say he missed her and that he loved her very much. He said they would be together again soon; she really did hope so as at the moment it didn't look like happening.

Folding up the letter she placed it back in the envelope and put it away. Her first letter from Michael, she would treasure it! Daisy thought she should reply to her parents, write to George and Michael, so she got writing but she didn't get far as she was tired, and emotional, especially for her friend and what she had been through today.

Putting her writing things away, she spotted that Lizzie was already asleep which was good, as she thought she wouldn't sleep well, Daisy climbed into bed and still promised herself to keep an eye out for Lizzie, soon she too was fast asleep.

The next day when Lizzie and Daisy went to visit Charles, it was raining slightly, it was still warmish as it was mid-October and when they arrived on the ward, the doctor and Matron were by Charles' bed. "Good afternoon, Matron," the two nurses said as they walked up to her.

She turned. "Good afternoon, Sisters, we were just telling Captain Holmes that he is being shipped home tomorrow, and he is happy to go."

Lizzie was extremely happy and couldn't hide the smile that spread across her face, large as anything. She wanted to cry but held it together in front of Matron. Daisy was smiling too as she was pleased for Lizzie and Charles was finally going.

"Right, I will leave you to talk." She winked at Daisy as she walked past. Daisy couldn't believe it, but she smiled and nodded.

Lizzie walked to where Matron had stood and looked at Charles. "So you are off tomorrow?'

"Yes," he sneered back. "I will see you back in England for our marriage."

Lizzie shivered and just nodded but she knew she couldn't do it; she would write to her aunt and then when she was back in England, she would speak to her mother, there would be no wedding, she was resolute in that decision.

Charles sat up and he winced as he pulled his wound. Lizzie didn't want to speak to him, so she made some excuse and her and Daisy hurriedly left the ward.

Charles called after Lizzie, "I will see you back in England and we will be married."

Lizzie didn't turn around, she felt sick. "Let's get back to our room and I can write to my aunt."

That evening they wrote their letters and got them ready for posting in the morning. Reading through the letter one last time, before she placed it in the envelope, Lizzie had written that she really hoped her aunt would now speak to her Sister, and explain that Lizzie was very unhappy and couldn't marry Charles because of the harm he had caused her, and that more importantly she didn't love him. She wanted her mother to know about his daughter and how he wanted nothing to do with her. Lizzie was quiet but she was ecstatic that Charles was going, but she had some doubt still. She knew her life would be hell if she did marry him, he was cruel, sadistic and heartless, she could never marry someone like that, Chris was the opposite, kind, caring and loving. If she was to meet Chris, she surely would like him, she needed her aunt and hoped she would send her reply quickly. She should have written sooner but she had been busy.

Lizzie promised herself she wouldn't see Charles off tomorrow, but she would make sure he had gone. Both women slept well, and in the morning they both had the day off, so they got up late, had a late breakfast and had a long bath. Once ready, they decided to post their letters and go for a walk, dressed in their battledress with tin hats just in case of an air raid, they headed for the docks.

It was a nice morning, blue skies and a light breeze but it was starting to get chilly. They walked past all the bomb damage and piles of rubble and ruins of what were once buildings, it was a struggle to not fall over. Luckily the two women had their sturdy Army boots on which protected their feet. At the docks they watched the ships being loaded and unloaded, and Lizzie just wanted to see for herself that Charles' ship was actually in, the docks were heaving with vessels and activity.

Once satisfied that the hospital ship had arrived the women walked for a few minutes and found a small café near the docks that was still standing between the ruins. On entering they found an empty table and decided to have a coffee and piece of cake, sitting and taking in their surroundings, it was a small quaint building with a few tables, and chairs, the tables had tablecloths. There was only Lizzie and Daisy sitting drinking, feeling lucky that they were seeing the world.

When the war was over their lives would change for sure. Walking back to the nurse's home, Lizzie felt relief like she had been holding her breath for days, now Charles was gone she could live a little. When they arrived back at the nurses' home, they were both told to report to Matron at three o'clock today, no need to change. "What could Matron want with us?" They both thought as they headed up to their room. "We will soon know."

At two forty-five the two nurses walked over to the hospital and walked along the corridor, they ended up outside Matron's office, and they sat down on the chairs positioned outside. Both women wiped their sweaty palms on their trousers, why did they always get nervous, when they had to see Matron?

Dead on three they knocked on her door. "Enter," she called from inside.

Once inside the room, which was becoming known to them, they were told to sit down. Matron took her seat and looked directly at the two nurses, she began by saying, "Thank you for your hard work the last few months, but you have orders to return to England after Christmas and then to work in a hospital back in London for a while. It has been a pleasure to work with you both and you will be greatly missed. I hope you enjoy your last few months with us before you leave. I know it is a lot to take in." Matron must have seen by the look on their faces that they were indeed shocked at the news. "Sister Peters, I need you on night duty for a few weeks, starting tomorrow night."

"Yes Matron," came the reply.

"Well, that is all, enjoy the rest of the day." With that the two sisters were dismissed and they left the warm room.

Walking back the two women talked about going home and wondered which hospital they would be working at? Would they be together? They hoped so! All these questions would soon be answered. Right now, Lizzie prayed that her letter got to her aunt quickly and she replied fast, so she could make a plan to go and see her parents as soon as she could and end this farcical engagement.

Daisy too wanted to go home to see her parents, it was over a year since she had seen them, she hoped they were well. Would young Mark actually remember who she was? She hoped so. Walking up the stairs, talk turned to Christmas which was a few months away.

"We will have to decorate the wards the best we can, could some of the orderlies actually get Christmas trees?" They would ask when back at work.

The rest of the day flew by and once they'd had supper, the women sat on their beds reading. Daisy would be going on to nights knowing that her friend was fine as Charles was no longer here, and she could sleep well tonight, in fact they both did.

Lizzie was on a Late shift and Daisy was starting nights, so they would not see each other for at least two weeks, only in passing. At lunchtime Lizzie went off for her shift, and Daisy tried to sleep, but found it difficult, the first night was always difficult. In the end she got up and laid on her bed reading till it was time to get herself ready.

Just before eight, Sister Peters walked onto the ward to start her first nightshift. Stifling a yawn she took hand -over from the departing day shift. With the help of an orderly they settled the men down. There was only one incident during the night which Daisy dealt with quickly with the help of the orderly. Nightmares were a common occurrence amongst the men. Next morning Lizzie arrived to a very tired looking Sister Peters who handed over to the day shift and hurried to her bed she was exhausted.

A few weeks later Lizzie had a letter waiting for her when she got off her shift; she knew the handwriting was her aunt's, Lizzie couldn't wait to get to her room and read it and raced up the stairs as quick as she could and her uniform would allow. Fumbling to find her keys she opened the door and strode in, closing the door behind her. Ripping the envelope, she pulled the paper out and opened it. Scanning the page, she then skimmed it, holding her breath as she did so, her aunt had written back saying that as soon as Lizzie could get a visit home, she would be there with her and then they would talk to her mother together.

Lizzie released a breath, she knew her aunt was right, and it was better to do it together. As soon as she got back to England, she would head home and face her mother head-on once and for all. Lizzie felt relief, she usually did when she felt strong but facing her mother was a different matter face to face. Lizzie knew her mother normally came out on top, not this time she said defiantly.

Daisy arrived back later and listened attentively as Lizzie explained the plan to her, inwardly she hoped it would all go smoothly for her friend, but she had her doubts which she would keep to herself. Both women got ready for bed, and they both dreamed that night of getting back home to England. Daisy wished she could see Michael before she left, but she knew that would be impossible, so they would have to keep writing to each other. Daisy hoped he wouldn't tire of her while she was gone, only time would tell.

The middle of November and the weather had turned colder, it was still warmer than England, but you still needed your greatcoat if you ventured outside. The talk on the ward was of Christmas coming up, and Daisy and Lizzie had found some decorations for the ward. They had seen better days, but they would have to do. More injured arrived and many more were sent back to England on the ships, soon it would be the two nurses' turn.

They worked tirelessly to patch up the wounded and get them home to their families or back to their regiment. Both girls had decided to work on Christmas Day as it was better than just sitting around in the nurse's home, so on Christmas Day morning, they were both up early and ready for work. On arrival to the ward, hand-over was brief as nothing major had happened during the night. There was a tree in the corner by the door, but it was barely decorated, the young soldiers didn't mind; it reminded them of home.

The orderlies had made some decorations from old newspapers, and they hung around the walls. However, in the morning, the mood on the ward changed because a young soldier succumbed to his wounds. The others on the ward were troubled, and it tainted the day. Once the porters had removed the body to the mortuary, Lizzie had managed to arrange a supply of whiskey so the soldiers who were allowed to drink it could have a drink.

This cheered the men up no end and the rest of the day went really satisfactorily, the tomfoolery on the ward brought much laughter. Both women had separate breaks and had been served Christmas dinner in the dining hall. The nurses were relieved by the late shift, and they were tired and happy when they got to their room. Daisy sat on her bed and rubbed her feet; she wanted to soak them in warm water, Lizzie got up, found the whiskey she kept in their room and poured them a glass each, toasting each other a Happy Christmas.

Daisy let the amber liquid burn the back of her throat as it slipped down; it felt good.

"Let's have another," she said when her glass was empty, Lizzie poured out some more. By supper, the women were slightly drunk but were able to get to the dining hall unnoticed, they could still walk steadily. After food, the two women walked back to their room and spent the evening talking and opened the presents that they had been sent from home and bought by each other. The week between Christmas and New Year dragged as the weather had turned wet and windy, the sky was very grey and dark, it still felt warmer than England this time of the year. The two women were stuck inside once their shifts were finished, so they were starting to go crazy for some fresh air.

By the start of 1944, the weather had changed, the rain had stopped, and the sun had come out, the women had gotten out for a walk after weeks being cooped up, it felt nice to see the blue sky and have the winter sun warming their faces. Their surroundings looked bleak in the winter, it was just nice to get out and walk amongst the ruins and rubble down to the docks, soon they would be on a ship sailing to England.

The rumours were, the Germans were up against it, and the tide was turning in Britain's favour. The war was still raging on in the far east; the Japanese were still battling against the Americans in the Philippines. Over the next few days, the women began to pack up their belongings and, on Saturday, they said their "goodbyes" and looked around at their room for the last time. A driver loaded their belongings on a jeep and drove them down to the docks.

Chapter 43

They had to wait all day at the docks until they were told to embark onto their ship, the weather was cold but dry, the sky was blue with a few clouds swirling around, 'at least it wasn't raining,' thought Lizzie. Lizzie lit a cigarette while they waited inhaling the smoke, it made her relax a little. Both women were glad to be wearing their battledress and big warm greatcoats, both pulling them up around their necks to keep the wind from the sea blowing against their skin, keeping the warmth in.

The emotions the two were feeling were split, on one hand, both were excited to be going home, Lizzie was also apprehensive as what would be the reaction of her mother when she saw her, Lizzie was determined to do it. She was scared to see Charles because if he knew she was back in England he would make sure they were either married or he would harm her in some way because of the way she had treated him while he was in hospital.

Daisy was pleased to be going home, she could see her family, but on the downside, she was missing Michael terribly. She hoped one day soon her family would be able to meet him and she could be introduced to his family. She also knew she would do anything to protect her friend from Charles but most importantly he must not find out she was back in England at any cost.

Lizzie had written to her brother; he had replied that Glenda and himself, once Lizzie was home, would get married. They had waited for her to be present at the wedding. Lizzie would make sure she was there; she just hoped her parents would have the decency to come. Lizzie knew her father and aunt would attend but she was not so sure about her mother, but she prayed she had changed.

As the time got near to embark both were silent with nervousness, lost in their own thoughts, they both hoped the journey would be acceptable but this time of the year it could be unpredictable. Both women would miss Malta. They would like to come back after the war when they could see it without the war-torn buildings and air raids, which had been luckily few now. Malta was a lovely country, war had torn the heart out of it, but it would recover.

A Sergeant Major stood shouting for them to walk towards the gang plank and up into the waiting vessel, it was like the others they had travelled on, dark grey and battle weary. They found their cabin again with ease, they were lucky to be sharing together, their luggage was already waiting for them in the room. They didn't bother to unpack, just sat down on their beds and waited for the time to be under way. The port hole had been taped up so they couldn't see out, so they just sat talking, they couldn't even be bothered to go up to see the ship sail out of the harbour into open sea. It was calm at present while the ship was sitting in the port but the women could feel the slight swell of the water hitting the ship.

By midnight they could hear the engines starting and the anchor raising up, they would be under way very soon. Slowly they felt the ship move and soon they were making their way through the harbour and out into the open sea, where the vessel would be at the mercy of the elements, and more importantly the German U-boats. At last, the vessel picked up speed and the women knew they were out into the open sea; they could now feel the waves hitting the ship and the ship was rocking more.

Both women hoped this was the worst it was going to be as they both couldn't face being seasick, they just wanted the journey to end and get home safely. Every night the women prayed before going to sleep, they were not religious, but it made them feel safer.

Lizzie had a cigarette prior to getting ready for bed, it made her feel less nervous. The women got undressed into their warm pyjamas and climbed into bed, pulling the sheets and the blankets up to their chins they were sent to sleep by the movement of the ship. Both slept well considering they kept one ear open just in case the ship was hit during the night. By next morning land had disappeared and there was only water all around them, when they felt brave, they ventured up the stairwells, they pushed the thick door open that lead them out onto the deck of the ship. The wind was blowing so they pulled up their greatcoats tightly around their necks and looked out to the horizon, there were other ships in the convoy. It was nice to feel the wind blowing through their hair but soon they were getting cold as it was still early January and so they headed back down to get something to eat. There was not much to do so they sat in their cabin, they asked if they could help in the hospital but at present, they were not needed. If any nurse was to get seasick or ill, they would be asked to help only if they were not affected. By mid-week they were making good time and they were to stop at Gibraltar, to drop off troops and to pick up some more to take home for long overdue leave.

On entering Gibraltar harbour, it was nice to see land and the Rock standing majestic above the port, but the women were told not to go ashore, they stayed on deck watching all the movement around the busy harbour. By the evening the ship was ready to leave so again, late that night the ship slipped out into the sea. On the second night, around midnight, the ship's alarm sounded, Lizzie and Daisy were fast asleep but they soon woke on hearing the shrilling. They found their life jackets and put them on over their pyjamas and a jumper, a sailor knocked and opened their door and told them an enemy submarine was in the area and to keep in their cabin and keep quiet.

They heard explosions in the distance and the two women sat holding each other. They were not happy sitting in their cabin, so they pulled on their greatcoats and headed up onto the deck, in the distance they saw the vessel on fire and then it disappeared into the waves and vanished into the dark sea. On the deck it was bitter, with the cold wind biting into them, and it was very dark with no moon in the sky. Sailors were running around manning their post and guns ready to aim and fire when told. Much later they were told the threat had been disposed of, the submarine had been blown up by the destroyers in the convoy. The women made their way back to their cabin, but they didn't sleep what was left of the night and kept their life jackets on for the rest of the journey. At last, they were told they were heading into British waters and the escort had done its job, the women felt nothing but relief, this journey had been tiring and their nerves were frayed.

Chapter 44

The next morning, they sailed into Portsmouth's harbour and docked. Lizzie and Daisy had to wait to be disembarked from the vessel. Once on dry land it took some time to get their land legs. They had been told to report to an office situated at the harbour, they knocked and waited. On entering it was a small office with five Wrens sitting at desks working at typewriters, they all looked up and they stopped talking, there was silence when the two women entered. The officer got up, adjusting her tunic as she did so, picking up an envelope which had been sitting on her desk, she walked over to the two nurses.

"Are you Sister Fenton and Sister Peters?" she spoke with a clipped accent.

"Yes," replied both women pulling out their identity papers.

The officer took them and looked at the names, happy she had the right people, she handed over the envelope. Lizzie ripped the envelope open and pulled out the paper and quickly read it, putting the paper back in the envelope they said, thank you, and turned and left the warm office.

The Wrens and their Superior watched as the two Lieutenants left, envious of the suntans the two women were carrying.

"Well, what does it say?" Once outside in the cold.

"We are to report to Goodwood House in West Sussex for training," said Lizzie. "But before that we have a five-day leave."

"You had better contact your brother to organise that wedding and your Aunt Lynn so she can meet you to speak with your mother," said Daisy.

Lizzie felt excited for Eddie but also apprehensive at facing her mother but she knew it had to be done.

Daisy was looking forward to going home for a few days, she was looking forward to seeing her parents and brother, she was still unsure how Mary would take to her, but she had Michael now and she hoped once her sister learnt that she had a boyfriend her attitude would change!

Neither of the women had time to telephone their families to let them know they were coming, but Lizzie found a telephone box and called her brother at his base.

Once connected she hoped he wasn't flying. It took a few seconds to register and when he came to the phone, he said, 'Hello!"

On hearing his voice, she started to cry. Once she regained herself, she said, "Hello, Eddie, I'm home."

"Lizzie, is that you?"

"Yes, I will be home for a few days, can you get home with Glenda and get married? I know it is short notice for both of you?"

"We will try, something big is about to happen but it's all hush hush."

"I know, I have to report down south in a few days and that's all I can say."

They talked a bit longer till the operator cut the call. Lizzie then called her aunt who agreed to attend the wedding and then tackle her sister at the same time. It was decided not to telephone her mother, because if she knew Lizzie was coming then she would get in contact with Charles' family. Putting the receiver back, Lizzie turned and pushed the door, she walked out and explained all to Daisy who had been standing outside with their luggage.

Daisy had decided to just turn up at home and surprise her family. Their trunks were to be sent on to Goodwood House, so they had packed lightly in their suitcases. Both women were to travel to London together and then go their separate ways.

Portsmouth harbour was busy and both women were glad to be standing at the station awaiting the train to London but couldn't help but notice the attention they were getting from the young soldiers. They looked beautiful with their sun-drenched skins. The train arrived, it was busy and the women couldn't get a seat so they found a spot and stood together talking. The journey took forever as the train kept having to stop. Much later they arrived in Waterloo Station, which was heaving with uniformed personnel. This is where both women said their goodbyes and promised to meet back there in four days to travel back down south and the next part of their adventure.

They hugged each other tightly and Daisy said, "I hope all goes well with your mother, if you need me send a telegram and I will come."

Lizzie promised she would, but she knew she had to deal with this situation herself.

Once Daisy had made her way on the underground to St Pancras, she was happy to be back in England, she had missed her parents very much. She went to the ticket office and bought her ticket. She found the station buffet and ordered a slice of cake and cup of tea; and found a seat. The waitress behind the counter enquired, "If the young lady had been away?"

The other waitress carried on preparing the teas. Daisy couldn't answer but she just smiled at both of them, taking a sip of her hot tea. Daisy sat looking around her surroundings, the cake tasted all right, it was a bit stale but still edible, the hot tea washed it down. She sat back and watched with fascination the people all around her as she quickly finished eating.

Her train was called, and she picked up her luggage and gas mask, leaving the warmth of the buffet and headed along the concourse to her platform. Again, the train was packed but she found a spot and watched as the scenery turned from grey buildings to countryside through the window. As the train pulled into Luton, Daisy had been chatting to two sailors who were heading somewhere up north. She wished them well, picking up her luggage she climbed off the train.

Luton Station was much busier than when she was last at home, it had been damaged during the bombing but was still in working order. Daisy walked towards the exit and out into the late afternoon. It was still very cold but at least it was getting lighter in the evening. Walking through the familiar streets, minding the rubble and ruins as she went, Daisy felt a pang of uneasiness, she was excited to see her parents but worried too as it had been a while since she had been home.

What would they think of their daughter going out with a doctor? She hoped they would be fine with it. As she entered their street, she noticed some spaces where houses once stood. She noticed the rubble and ruins and looked for her house, she held her breath and scanned the street… there it was, still in one piece. The only damage she could see was on the roof where there was plastic tarpaulin covering part of it. Checking her uniform, she walked down the entry by the side of the house, she clicked the latch and entered.

The back door was closed, she turned the handle and entered.

"Hello," she called out in a loud voice as she walked into the kitchen, she heard footsteps.

Daisy looked at the door to the kitchen, it opened and her mother stood in the doorway. Once she registered who was there, she raced forward to hug her daughter, who hugged her straight back. Tears sprang to Daisy's eyes and she could feel her mother's face wet with her own.

Her mother took a step back and looked at her daughter all over, once satisfied she was in one piece. "Well, you look well, maybe could put some weight on?" she said looking lovingly at her daughter,

Daisy just looked at her mum and smiled.

"Come and sit down, why did you not tell us you were coming?" She scolded her daughter, but not in an unpleasant way. Hannah noticed how more confident and mature she had become, being away had done her daughter some good, or was there another reason? She would soon find out thought Hannah.

Putting her case down Daisy took her big greatcoat off, sat down, and noticed her mother looking at her uniform, she felt proud to be wearing it.

"I can't tell you too much, but I am home for a few days and then I need to be down south."

Hannah sat herself down at the kitchen table, while Daisy was talking and made the tea. "Where is Mark?" enquired his sister. The house is quiet, Daisy waited for the water to boil.

"He is at friends; I will collect him soon; you can come with me if you want," said her mum looking over at her daughter. Daisy now placed the full teapot on the table.

"Yes, I would like that," replied Daisy.

Hannah placed a cup in front of her daughter and one in front of herself. "Do you want some cake?" asked Hannah.

"No, thank you, I had a slice at the station."

Once all the tea was drunk, Hannah stood up. "Let's go and collect your brother and you can fill me in with all your news." Hannah reached for the kitchen door and Daisy went and put her greatcoat back on and her mother got her coat.

"Right, let's go." And they headed out the back door.

When out of the entry, they turned to the right, Daisy filled her mother in with all her news, the travel, the places she had seen and the people she had met.

Daisy's tone changed; Hannah noticed, and said, "What's the matter?" She glanced over at her daughter concerned.

She waited for Daisy to speak. "Mum, I have met someone, he is a doctor, he worked at The London, but now he is overseas with the RAMC. We met up when I was abroad, we love each other very much and I hope someday that you both will get to meet him."

Hannah wasn't surprised her daughter had met someone, but a doctor, now that was a turn up for the books. Daisy stood blushing.

She knew her daughter was stunning to look at and she had a lovely personality to go with it. "What's he like?" she asked with interest.

Daisy went on to explain how they met but she did say they hadn't spent a lot of time together due to the war. Hannah smiled and was generally pleased for her daughter, at least now. When Mary married Bobby, it wouldn't cause too much tension between them.

They arrived at the front door of Mark's friend Harry. Hannah knocked on the yellow door, Agnes come to the door with Mark and Harry was closely behind her. As soon as Mark spotted Daisy he ran and jumped into her arms, he was getting heavy. "You have grown!" she said laughing.

"Daisy, Daisy," he said looking at her in her uniform, he was proud of his eldest sister, he still grabbed a hold round her neck, and she hugged him tight.

"Come on, shall we go home for tea?" she asked.

Her mum finished talking to Agnes and the three of them walked back to their house. Mark settled in the middle, making sure he held Daisy's hand and telling her what he had done at school today. Once home, Daisy got the range on and her mother prepared the stew for tea so there was enough to include Daisy.

Daisy handed over her ration book and sat down with Mark in her lap. Dead on six-thirty Jack walked through the kitchen door, he was just about to say hello when he noticed his eldest daughter sitting at the table, holding her brother in her lap.

"Well, hello stranger!" he said, and Daisy jumped up, knocking

Mark off her lap and walked into her dad's arms. He held his daughter tight, not quite believing she was actually here.

"How long have you got love?" he asked first.

"A few days Dad then I have to report down south, that's all I can say."

"I know, I won't keep on, but that uniform suits you," he said smiling proudly.

Hannah glared at her husband. "I don't want her in the army, risking her life. I want her safe," she said angrily.

"Mum, I am safe as can be and I am saving lives," Daisy tried to explain.

"I know you are," her mother said in a tired voice. She carried on, "I'm sorry love, I know you are doing a good job."

"Right, we just have to wait for Mary, then we can sit down for tea," said Jack breaking the tension in the room. "Set the table Daisy." Which she did with pleasure.

It's just like old times, she thought, but one person was missing, her brother George.

Mary walked through the door a few minutes later, spotted her sister and her whole demeaner changed. "Oh! You are home. You could have informed us!" she said bitterly.

"I only got back to England this morning," Daisy said trying to justify herself. "Anyway, I will be on my way in four days," she said angrier than she wanted too.

Mary shrugged her shoulders as if she didn't care and sat down at the kitchen table with a glum look on her face. Hannah served the food and they all sat round eating the hot stew, it was amazing what her mother could do with food being rationed thought Daisy. Once they were all full, Hannah had made an apple pie for pudding, which was delicious, served with custard.

Daisy took a deep breath. "I have some news for you, I have met someone, he is a doctor and was at The London but now is overseas in the RAMC. We met up just recently while I was overseas myself, he is called Michael and I really hope you get to meet him one day very soon."

Once finished she took a breath, she waited for the reaction from her father and especially her sister. Her father sat back with a glass of beer and looked at his daughter. "Well, I hope you are happy?" Was all he said.

Daisy answered, "We are Dad, extremely happy, but I would like you to meet him as soon as possible."

Jack took his daughter's hand and rubbed her knuckle. "As long as he treats you well then I am happy." He looked over to his wife, who smiled back in agreement.

Mary sat back and was taken back on hearing her sister's news. She hated to admit it, but she had always been jealous of her older sister, but today she felt happy for her, she no longer felt threatened. Mary knew Bobby was now hers wholeheartedly and her sister was in love with this doctor, life was looking up.

The two women cleared the table and helped with the washing up, as their parents sat at the table talking, the tide was turning, and people were hoping that the war would be over very soon.

Daisy asked her sister genuinely, "How is Bobby?"

She hoped he would soon be home and then they could be married replied her sister.

Her parents sat at the table, observing the two women getting on better than they had for a long time. Hannah was relieved, she really thought that Bobby would cause a rift between the two and it nearly did happen, she was looking forward to meeting the doctor. Silently she felt honoured to have a doctor as a future son-in-law, if it got that serious. Hannah had also observed her older daughter the last few hours, she had changed in so many different ways, her girl was now a young woman.

"Have you heard from George?" Enquired Daisy.

"Yes, we had a letter, here, read it." Her mother passed it to her and she put down the damp tea towel. Daisy made a pot of tea for them all and read the letter, he was doing all right, very cold but well and most of all he was really happy.

Daisy then took her brother up to bed as he was yawning, he brushed his teeth and she read him a story, soon his eyes were heavy. "Will you be here tomorrow?" he asked tiredly.

"Yes, I will take you to school in the morning, promise," she replied.

Heading down the stairs she heard them talking. "She looks well, but what about this Doctor, what's he like I wonder," asked Jack.

"I'm sure he is really nice," she heard her mother reply.

Yes, he is, she thought to herself. "You will like him when you meet him."

She opened the door to the kitchen. "Marks's gone to sleep. Can I have a bath?" she asked. "I have been travelling a week and need a bath, the showers were not very good on the ship."

"Yes, of course you can."

Daisy had only brought her uniform with her and clean underwear, as most of her clothes were in her trunk and on its way to West Sussex. It didn't take long to prepare the bath, it was heaven she thought, while she laid back in the hot water and let it warm her. This was luxury Daisy thought, she would never take it for granted ever again, soon the water cooled and Hannah had given her daughter a towel to take upstairs with her.

She found the pyjamas she had brought with her, and she got dressed into them, her mother had warmed them. She had also put a stone hot water bottle in the bed to warm the bottom for the girls. Daisy, once clean was tired from all the travelling, she came back downstairs and said her "goodnights" and made her way up to bed. Climbing into her old bed she smiled and smelt the sheets, it was nice to be home, she pulled the sheets up and laid on her side, she was just going off to sleep when she heard her sister enter the room.

Mary quietly got undressed and sorted herself out, she climbed over her sister and got into bed on her side, and turned and gave her sister a hug, Daisy smiled and soon fell asleep. She knew tomorrow her sister would be asking more questions about Michael so she would brace herself.

Daisy was up early in the morning, dressed and downstairs with her sister, Mark raced down the stairs to the kitchen to make sure that Daisy was still here as promised. When he opened the door, she braced herself for a hug and he ran at her, she picked him up and hugged him tight.

"You are still in uniform?" he asked, inquisitively.

"Yes, I have no other clothes here," she replied.

He went off to play with his toy car and seemed happy with that explanation, soon Hannah got breakfast and they all sat around.

Jack had already left for work, Mary soon had to leave as well, which left Hannah, Mark and Daisy. Daisy got herself ready, put her greatcoat on as it was still very cold, and Mark got his coat and shoes; Daisy put on her Army boots.

They were allowed out the front door and they said goodbye to their mother. "Remember to write to George."

"I will," came the reply.

Daisy pulled the collar up, to stop the biting wind getting to her neck and walked down the road towards the school. Mark was beaming, holding his sister's hand tight, he had his scarf on which had been knitted by their mother, he kept glancing up at her, taking in her uniform and quite not believing she was here.

Soon the school building came into sight. "I hope you are working really hard?" she asked him seriously.

He answered nervously, "Yes, but I do struggle sometimes. Mum helps me when she can and I have you for a few days."

"Yes, you do," she replied smiling.

Leaving Mark at the gate, she had watched as he ran into the building, stopping when he saw his teacher. She stopped and spoke to a few people she knew, who wanted to know what she was doing. It seemed like forever till she managed to get away. Walking back to their home she felt contented, her mind went to Lizzie, and she hoped she was managing her mother.

Her mother had given her a list of shopping to get on her way back, Daisy first went to the butcher and joined the long queue, she managed to get some sausages and then made her way to the bakery where she joined another queue, once she had her loaf of bread, she hurried home.

Daisy was surprised that she had to wait so long for everything, she felt exhausted as she entered the kitchen door. "Mum, I'm back," she called as she put the bag onto the kitchen table.

"Did you manage to get some sausages?" her mother called.

"Yes, I did," she replied.

Daisy heard her mother coming down the stairs, and entered the warm kitchen. "I was just upstairs making the beds. I will make toad in the hole for tea tonight, the milkman has just been."

Daisy found that her mother still had work as people had donated old clothes that they didn't wear any more, and Hannah would fix and mend them to look as good as new, then sell them again. She was working on wedding dresses as more girls were getting married.

When Daisy entered the front room, she noticed sitting on the manikin was the most exquisite wedding dress Daisy had ever seen. "Mum, did you make this?" she asked.

"Yes," her mother replied. "Out of silk from a parachute."

"Where did you get it from?" she asked.

"A young woman came with it given to her by her American fiancé."

Daisy touched it. "It's lovely." Her mind wandered to Michael and wondered if they would get married once the war ended, she really did hope so.

Looking at her mother, she asked, "Will you make my dress for me?"

"Of course, love, but you have plenty of time yet." Hannah got to work, and Daisy headed for the kitchen to prepare tea.

Hannah stopped for lunch, which she ate with Daisy. Daisy cleaned up and Hannah sat at the table finishing her cup of tea.

She glanced at her daughter. "You look different," she observed. "More grown up."

"Mum, so would you be if you had observed the things I have."

"Tell me more about Michael? About his family?"

She told her mum again how they had met and that his parents live in Suffolk, and they were given money, so they sent Michael to Medical School. "He's got a sister in the Wrens." Daisy went on, but she really didn't know him well because they hadn't spent a lot of time together, and Daisy remembered it was mostly them making love, and she couldn't tell her mother that. She thought her mother had guessed her secret, she was trying not to blush the darkest shade of red.

On finishing her tea, her mother headed back to the front room to work, while Daisy sat reading. Then when the time was right, she would go and pick up Mark, he was old enough to walk back on his own, but he wanted his sister to collect him. She only had two days left then she would be meeting up with Lizzie at Waterloo to continue their journey, or adventure, as she liked to call it.

Mark had been waiting at the school gate for his sister to arrive, as soon as he saw her, he ran out. The rest of the day passed uneventfully; Daisy couldn't get over Mary being so nice now she wasn't a threat any more.

The rest of her time at home flew by and soon it was time to say goodbye. Daisy had said her farewells to her dad and sister that morning,

Mark had gone off to school upset, she could see he was trying not to cry but a stray tear rolled down his cheek, she stopped it with her finger.

"I will see you soon, I promise," she said, hugging him tightly.

Then it was only her mother left in the kitchen. Her mother grabbed her eldest child and held her tight. "You take care," she said. "And more importantly, come back safe." It was as if she knew where her daughter was going.

"I promise, Mum." She felt tears prickling her eyes and then they rolled down her cheeks, she wiped them with a hanky her mother given her from her apron.

Daisy composed herself, picked up her packed case, handbag and gas mask and walked out of the warm kitchen, down the entry and out into the street. Daisy stopped, pulling up the collar of her greatcoat and waved goodbye to her neighbour across the road. Looked up and down the street as if it was the last time, she would see it. Turned and walked into town towards the railway Station.

On arrival it was busy, and she found a space to wait for her train. A station master walked down saying the London train was delayed and would be here as soon as it could. Daisy patiently waited. Another hour went by, and when the train arrived, she climbed aboard and found a space in the packed carriages. They made good time and arrived in London only an hour late. Daisy handed her ticket in at the barrier and made for the underground and Waterloo station, she was so looking forward to seeing her friend, even after this short time apart she had missed her.

Chapter 45

Lizzie had said her goodbyes at Waterloo and hugged her friend tight. "Wish me well," she said.

Finding the sign for the underground, she disappeared down the stairs. On arrival to Marylebone station, she too had to wait and found the station buffet. Ordering a cup of coffee, she sat down and waited, she was joined by a young woman in an Army uniform ATS who struck up a conversation with Lizzie. The young woman was interested in Lizzie being a nurse, and in the army, as well, the time flew by. Soon Lizzie heard the announcement for her train, and she said her goodbyes and picked up her luggage, handbag and gas mask.

Finding the platform, she too couldn't find anywhere to sit so she stood in the corridor for the journey. She was nervous, her mother now knew she was a Qualified Nurse, knowing she had lied to her, and she didn't know what response she would get once she arrived home. Oh, She felt sick. Lizzie looked out of the window, watching the countryside pass as the train got nearer to Warwick, she would hope that a taxi was around to take her home as she'd had no time to let Geoffrey know she was coming.

Well, no one knew apart from Eddie and her aunt that she was home, and they wouldn't say anything to her, only to her father so he was prepared for the showdown. Lizzie felt dirty, the showers on the ship had worked, but you didn't feel clean, all she wanted was a bath before she faced her mother. On exiting the station, she noticed that Warwick station too was busy, she looked around for any vehicle that resembled a taxi. One pulled up and she climbed in. "Where to young lady?" asked the driver cheerfully.

"Newton Hall, please, do you know it?" she asked as an afterthought.

"Yes," came the reply. "Are you going to work there?" asked the driver.

"Yes, something like that," replied Lizzie. She didn't want people to know who she really was.

Lizzie sat back and let the few short miles go by, she didn't really want to talk but the driver asked, "Have you been abroad?" But she only nodded her head as a reply.

As soon as the taxi was sweeping down the long driveway, she felt sick again, soon it was time to face the music.

"Do you want the front entrance miss?"

"No, the back entrance will be fine, thank you." The driver looked at Lizzie in his mirror, surprised but didn't comment.

Lizzie handed the money over and climbed out and the driver got her luggage from the boot and placed it at her side. He tipped his cap and climbed back into the driver's seat and drove off with Lizzie standing watching him go. She looked around and picked up her things and headed for the kitchen door. She prayed her mother wasn't inside.

Pushing the door, it opened and to her relief Edna and Geoffrey were the only two in the room. Edna looked up and as soon as she saw Lizzie, the young nurse fell into the open arms of the cook. "My dear girl, why did you not tell us you were coming, and Geoffrey would have collected you?"

"I only knew this morning," she replied through the tears that were flowing freely.

Edna produced a handkerchief and Lizzie wiped her eyes.

"You look well if a little underweight?" Edna said, standing back observing Lizzie.

"Well, you both look really well, married life must suit you well."

Edna smiled and agreed with her. "Yes, we are very happy. Come, take off your greatcoat and sit a moment."

"I really want a hot bath, but I will come down when I am finished."

Leaving her greatcoat on the chair, she headed up the back stairs to her room. Finding some fresh towels, she ran a bath and waited for it to fill. Once ready, she headed back into her room where her case had been brought up and laid on her bed. Lizzie opened it and pulled out fresh knickers and bra as she was putting her uniform back on again. Within ten minutes she is laying in a hot bath full of bubble bath, Lizzie was enjoying the feel, she heard a noise outside the door.

Her heart stopped, then she heard a familiar voice, her father. "Darling, is that you?"

"Yes, papa," came the reply with relief. "I will see you downstairs once I have got changed," she called.

With that, she heard footsteps walking away towards the back stairs and the kitchen. Lizzie washed herself, her hair and headed back into her room, where she got re-dressed. Not bothering to dry her hair, she put it in a ponytail. Instead of putting her Army boots back on she went down in her socks.

As she entered the kitchen, she felt the warmth and she then spotted her father. "Papa," she called, and he stood up. She nearly ran into his arms, and he held her tight. Lizzie felt the tears coming again and she cried making the shoulder of his shirt wet.

When he spoke, he whispered her name, she pulled away to look at him, and walked him to the nearest chairs.

First, he looked at her again and then he said, "You look well, if a little underweight." He then asked how she was and where had she been?

She explained as best she could, and they sat in silence drinking the tea Edna supplied.

"How long are you home for?" he asked.

"Only a few days and then I need to report south, I think something big is about to happen, especially with all the troops moving about."

"I spoke with Edward, and he is coming up tomorrow with Glenda to get married the day after, which doesn't give us much time."

She looked shocked. "But what about Mother?"

"Well, she is not happy, but Edward has said that he will never set foot in this house again, if he is not allowed to marry Glenda, and they will go off and elope. Your mother has given in and has agreed."

Lizzie couldn't believe it, was there hope for her and Christopher after all?

"Your aunt and uncle are arriving tomorrow, as are Glenda's parents. There is no time to plan a big wedding because Eddie says they have waited long enough."

Lizzie sat listening as her father carried on filling her in with all the news. She didn't notice or hear her mother enter until it was too late.

"Well, if it isn't my runaway daughter who has finally reappeared!"

Looking directly at Lizzie.

"Mother, you know where I have been. And yes, I have come home for Edward's wedding, then I am off again till the end of the war."

Her mother didn't answer, she just looked at Lizzie and mumbled something nasty like. "We will see." And she turned and walked out.

Her father said, "That went well! It could have been a lot worse."

Lizzie wasn't so sure, she was really worried now and wanted to speak with her aunt when she arrived tomorrow.

Lizzie didn't see her mother again until the morning when she arrived down in the kitchen for breakfast, her mother was already sitting in the room drinking tea and eating her food.

Lizzie sat down by her side. "Mother, let's not fight," she said. "Yes, I didn't tell you I had qualified and that I have a fiancé and it's not Charles." Lizzie sat looking directly at her mother as she spoke. "His name is Christopher and is a captain in the army and I love him very much." Lizzie waited with bated breath for her mother to speak.

"What about Charles? You are engaged to him remember," her mother hissed.

"You agreed to it, not me, Mother," Lizzie threw her hands in the air.

Just as the voices were getting louder, Lizzie's aunt walked in through the door. "What in the dickens is going on here?" She glanced at her sister.

"Aunt Lynn," she cried, the relief on Lizzie's face when she saw her aunt! "Now Aunt Lynn is here, I will tell you what Charles Holmes is really like, he is a womaniser, he has a love child, he is a psychopath, and he is a rapist." Her mother sat in stunned silence all the while Lizzie talked. "If you make me marry him, it will be a life of misery. Can you really make me do it?" Lizzie asked looking directly at her mother. "Aunt Lynn has seen the little girl, who is lovely by the way. He raped me, Mother, a while ago, and I nearly lost Christopher because of it."

Margo looked at her sister. "Is this all true?"

"Yes," she replied."

"Let your daughter marry for love and be happy. I'm sure when you meet Christopher, you will like him, and the next thing you need to do is end this phoney engagement with Charles, so you can carry on with your lives."

By now her father had entered with Eddie and Glenda, who had heard some of the commotion, and were filled in by Edna who had been sitting at the table the whole time. Lady Margo stood abruptly, looked around at everyone, didn't say a word and left the kitchen hurriedly.

Lizzie's father was reassured that his wife was doing the right thing at present by leaving, and so the rest of the day was taken up with frantic wedding preparations. No one saw Lizzie's mother again for the rest of the day, until tea.

Everyone was quietly relieved. Glenda was shown up to the guest room, next to Aunt Lynn and Edward's rooms. Edward was in his usual room near Lizzie's. Glenda's parents were arriving from Devon and Geoffrey was picking them up from the station.

Much later they were all sitting around eating tea in the warm comfy kitchen, when Clifford stood up and raised a toast to the happy couple.

"Tomorrow is a big day," he said, looking around at all the happy faces, apart from his wife's, Margot was still smarting as her best laid plans were laying in ruins.

This war was changing people's views and actions, a few years ago both her children would have done as requested by her without any arguments. Lizzie was observing her mother, she knew that her mother wouldn't accept Christopher but she was determined to spend the rest of her life with him.

She looked away and looked over at the happy couple, they only had eyes for each other. Tomorrow would be interesting, maybe her mother would thaw? Lizzie doubted it, she hoped maybe with the help of her aunt. Most people turned in at ten o'clock as the wedding would be held early, both Eddie and Glenda only had forty-eight hour passes which they would be spending here. Then the following day they would be travelling back down south to their base.

Glenda's parents were very nice, but Lizzie wondered if they could work out her mother? They didn't let on what their feelings were, they sat talking to her father and aunt. Eddie and his fiancée said their goodnights and made their way, accompanying Lizzie upstairs, once they got to Lizzie's room she stopped and turned, welcoming them both inside. The room was warm from the fire slow burning and Eddie and Glenda walked over to her bed, sitting on it, while Lizzie made herself comfortable on a chair.

It was nice to spend some time together, Eddie sat examining his sister closely, she looked healthy that was contributed to by spending months out in a hot country.

Her eyes told another story he thought. "Come on, Sis, tell us what's bothering you?"

Lizzie took a deep breath, she didn't want to upset her brother prior to his big day, but she wanted to be honest with them. Lizzie sat with her hands in her lap, mainly to stop them shaking while she talked.

"Please don't get too angry," she began. "But some time ago I met up with Charles in London, we went to a hotel where we had drinks." Lizzie could see her brother working it all out in his head. Lizzie carried on. "He had booked a room. I know I was naive to go up there with him, once in the room he wanted sex, and when I refused, he raped me." Lizzie felt the tears streaming down her face.

Eddie rushed off the bed and went over to her on the chair, he knelt down and gave her a hug while the tears kept coming.

Once Lizzie felt better to continue, she carried on. "I have told Christopher, he wasn't happy, and at one stage I thought I had lost him, but things are good between us. He wants to kill him if their paths ever cross each other."

Eddie nodded in agreement. "I feel the same."

"I have told Mother I want to marry Chris. Her reaction was the same, she wasn't happy. I am determined to do it as soon as the war is over, and Christopher is back home."

Eddie took hold of Glenda's hand, he fiddled with her engagement ring as he absorbed what his sister had said. "Thank you for sharing this personal information, I know it was hard for you."

Glenda got up and went over to her future sister-in-law and held her tight.

"Welcome to the family," Lizzie said with a rueful smile.

Lizzie tried to stifle a yawn, and Eddie pulled Glenda up. "Get to bed," he said, looking over at his sister.

They kissed her on the cheek and said, "Goodnight, and see you in the morning."

Once the door was closed, Lizzie sat back down on her bed, she felt mentally drained. She still didn't fully know how her mother would behave tomorrow, she got undressed for bed. Once between the crisp white sheets she pulled the blanket up to her chin and said a silent prayer, praying their mother behaved.

Lizzie woke early listening to the birds in the garden, she looked over to her uniform hanging on the wardrobe door, as it was short notice, they had all decided to wear their uniforms, including the bride.

Her brother didn't want to take any more chances and wanted to get married as soon as possible, and it here it was. Lizzie pushed the sheets and blanket off her and wrapped her dressing gown around her, she headed for the bathroom with her wash bag. The bath was refreshing, she didn't spend too long as she knew others would need it soon. Back in her room, she got dressed in her uniform, taking a look in the full-length mirror, she was content with what she saw, her hair was fine as she had rollers in all night. Lizzie didn't like them as they were really uncomfortable to sleep in, but needs must she thought.

Picking up her cap she headed for the door, and downstairs for breakfast. On entering the room, she heard voices, Edna had laid a cooked breakfast out on the table and it looked enticing. Lizzie said her "good mornings" and took her place at the table.

Edna placed a full plate of food in front of her, Glenda's parents were already tucking into their food, Lizzie was grateful her mother was yet to make an appearance.

Her father entered followed closely by the bride and groom, both looking resplendent in their pressed uniforms. Customarily it was bad luck for the bride to see the groom until the church, but these were not normal times, so they would all be walking to the church together. Last to arrive was Aunt Lynn and Uncle Edward, Lizzie looked around the room for her mother but she still hadn't made an appearance.

Lizzie was worried, what was her mother up to? Soon they couldn't wait any longer, her father and aunt had already searched the rooms along with Lizzie.

"Come on, we need to get going." They all proceeded towards the door and out into the fresh air.

It was cold with a few drops of rain. They were all covered by their greatcoats, to keep the cold out. Lizzie's father had handed out umbrellas for the journey to church. It didn't take long, but there was still no sign of their mother.

Sir Clifford came up to Lizzie and whispered, "Where the hell is she?"

"I don't know!" Whispered Lizzie. I will never forgive her if she doesn't turn up for her own son's wedding.

Aunt Lynn had overheard them and agreed. "She still might arrive at the church." Lizzie and her father weren't convinced.

The vicar was waiting for them at the entrance, they all entered apart from Glenda and her father, they held back waiting for the music to start.

Soon Glenda was being supported down the aisle to join her future husband. All too soon the wedding was over and the happy couple exited the church.

Edna had laid on a wedding breakfast for the happy couple as it was nearing lunchtime. Eddie was joined by some of his friends from the base who had stayed at a guesthouse nearby and the atmosphere was joyous. Back at the House, the festivities were in full flow, Margo was still missing. Lizzie was beyond being upset; she was livid. How her mother could be so insensitive was beyond her. Luckily Glenda and her brother didn't seem bothered with it and had a lovely day.

Much later into the evening they made their apologies and escaped to Eddie's room.

Lizzie sat talking to her aunt, in a concerned voice, "Is this is how she is going to behave when I finally bring Christopher home? I promise I will not be marrying Charles."

Her aunt looked over to her niece and could see the anguish in her face, she promised she would do all she could to help when the time was right.

Lady Margo finally turned up the following morning, she was sitting at the kitchen table when Lizzie entered the room. Lizzie didn't even acknowledge her, and sat down for breakfast, Edna put a plate of food in front of her.

"I'm leaving today," she said, not even looking at her mother. "I need to get back."

Edna said that it was a shame, but she understood.

Her mother didn't even acknowledge her, so as soon as Lizzie had finished, she went back to her room to pack. She bumped into her brother and new wife, she explained why she was leaving and they too decided to share the journey with her as far as London.

All convened in the kitchen with bags, their father, aunt and uncle had arrived. Geoffrey brought the car around; he collected all the luggage, placing it in the boot.

Glenda's parents had already been dropped at the station so now it was the turn of Lizzie, Eddie and Glenda to be dropped off. All three said their farewells. Lord Clifford had already apologised for the behaviour of Lady Margo to Glenda's parents, now he had to do it again to his daughter, son and his new wife.

Eddie's heart ached for his father; Lizzie was still incensed. Once they had put on their greatcoats to keep the cold out, they hugged their father, aunt and uncle and climbed into the waiting car. It didn't take too long to arrive at Warwick station, they all clambered out.

Geoffrey was already getting the luggage out and placing it on the ground for them. He turned to the newlyweds. "Sorry you couldn't stay longer and I hope to see you back soon."

Eddie and Glenda replied they would be back, they had a lovely time seeing everyone, and Glenda had a great fondness for the Hall, in fact she was already falling in love with Fenton Hall, which she knew would become her home one day.

Eddie had told her that they would live somewhere else, until the death of his father, then they would have to come and live at the Hall. Eddie hadn't told her, but he really wanted to turn it into a hotel in the future.

Geoffrey walked over to and gave Glenda a hug and kiss on her cheek, which made her blush. Geoffrey then went over to Lizzie. "Take care of yourself?" he said fondly. "See you soon hopefully, with your young man."

"I promise to bring him as soon as I can."

He grabbed hold of her and hugged her close to his chest, she could smell his cologne, which made her feel protected. Lizzie felt her eyes water and a stray tear rolled down her cheek. When he released her, she wiped the tear away, collected her suitcase and joined the others waiting to walk together, to join Glenda's parents already on the platform.

The train luckily was running only slightly late, they didn't mind as they stood getting to know each other better, Lizzie apologised again for the way her mother acted and she lit a cigarette to calm her nerves. Glenda's parents took it well, but Lizzie could see they were embarrassed by the way her Ladyship had acted. Glenda's parents invited Lizzie to Devon and she promised once the war was over, she would love to visit with Christopher.

The train arrived, and slowly pulled into the station. It was nice to get out of the cold, they found, by luck an empty carriage for all of them. They all took off their big greatcoats, placing them in the overhead storage with their cases. Eddie helped his new in-laws to settle and waited for the train to depart. Soon they were picking up steam and they were travelling through the countryside back to the city. It turned out to be a delightful journey, the company was very pleasing, it made Lizzie feel slightly better, but she was still very cross with her mother.

Soon the countryside turned to grey, dreary looking buildings, as Marylebone station approached. They all stood and collected their belongings and gathered up their greatcoats putting them on, ready to enter out into the cold. At the station entrance they all said their goodbyes, and Lizzie hugged her brother and then Glenda.

Again, she apologised but Glenda just brushed it aside. "I married the most wonderful man, and I am extremely happy," she said, looking towards her new husband with love and pride, she was happy for the war, as it had brought them together. Lizzie felt slightly jealous, but she soon shook those thoughts away, she headed for the underground with all the other military personnel to make her way to Waterloo and where Daisy would be waiting. Lizzie's heart felt happier than it had done recently, the last few days had been very arduous.

Lizzie came up the steps from the underground and proceeded towards the main station clock. Glancing around, she didn't see any familiar faces, so she put her suitcase down on the cold station floor and waited. Lizzie must have drifted off and daydreamed as she heard her name being called, looking around she spotted Daisy advancing towards her, carrying her suitcase and she had her handbag and gasmask on her shoulder weighing her down.

Daisy put her case down and turned to her friend and gave her a big hug, Lizzie hugged her back, and both women felt each other's warmth. Daisy felt her friend tighten the hug and then the tears came. Daisy held her while she sobbed, and she guessed that the visit home had gone very badly.

"Come on." Once Lizzie had settled and the tears had stopped.

Daisy gave Lizzie a handkerchief and she dried her eyes. "We have time to get a pot of tea and slice of cake in the station buffet which is over there," she said pointing in the direction of where it was situated.

Lizzie followed her finger. "Come on, let's go." Walking towards it swiftly arms linked.

Lizzie held the door for her friend, and they entered, once inside the air was full of smoke and it was very warm, the buffet windows were steaming up with condensation. Glancing around they found an empty table in the corner, with a couple of chairs. Placing their suitcases by the chairs they headed to the counter to place their order.

The older woman behind the counter asked for their order and she wrote it on a pad and took the table number. Both women went back to the table and took their seats.

Once settled Daisy glanced worryingly at Lizzie. "Now tell me exactly what took place at home?"

Oh, Daisy, where do I begin. When I arrived home, I waited for when my aunt was going to arrive, so I had some moral support. It ended up that my mother and I got into an altercation, and it all came out how I wouldn't marry Charles and that I was going to marry Christopher, my father tried to back me up and so did my aunt when she arrived. I also told her about the rape and Charles' little girl, but she didn't like it. She never showed for the wedding of Eddie and Glenda, her own son! Can you believe it Daisy? She is so cold!"

Daisy just sat and listened not sure what to say as a response. She felt very sorry for her friend, she only wanted one thing, to be loved by her mother. Daisy was very sure Lizzie would end up marrying Chris, but the biggest question was, would Lady Margo agree to it in the end? Daisy hoped that her aunt came through. Lizzie having re-capped the story, felt despondent again and she felt tears prickling her eyes.

Lizzie took the hanky that Daisy had given her and she wiped them. "I just want this war to end so we can get on with our lives. I want

Christopher here," she said despondently.

Daisy sat looking at her friend and her heart went out to her. Lizzie was glad that she had gotten all of it off her chest. They both sat in silence and finished the tea and cake which was slightly stale.

They heard the train being called on the tannoy, and what platform, picking up their belongings they headed for the door and out onto the station concourse.

Chapter 46

The two nurses found their train and headed along the platform to the correct carriage but were unable to find any available seats, as the train was full of military personnel heading south, so they stood in the corridor. Daisy was trying hard to lighten the mood a little, for which Lizzie was grateful to her friend. The last few days had been tough emotionally for the young woman.

Lizzie dreamt that she was being held by Chris, suddenly she heard Daisy's voice in the background she must have drifted off, looking at her friend, her mind drifted again, she knew that would be impossible due to him being thousands of miles away, but she could dream.

The two women spent the rest of the journey chatting and watching the countryside pass by out of the window, now the blackout blinds had been removed. The rest of the trip passed uneventfully, and the train pulled into the nearest station to Greenwood Manor.

It was a late January afternoon when the train stopped, and it was starting to get dark. The women did up their greatcoats, gathered up their belongings and waited in turn to exit the hectic carriage. At the end of the platform, standing with a clipboard was the Regimental Sergeant Major, both of them picked up their suitcases and walked forward towards the foreboding looking man, he asked their names and he scrolled down the list. Once he found them, he pointed to the awaiting truck, they walked over and climbed into the back using the steps. They found a space and sat down, having to wait for the others to arrive.

Both pulled up the collars of their greatcoats to keep the cold weather out as the wind was still getting through the canvas roof and it was bitterly cold seated in the back of the truck. Once everyone was on board, and the Regimental Sergeant Major had climbed into the front next to the driver, the truck set off through the town and out into the wintery countryside. A couple of miles outside the truck slowed and turned right up into a long sweeping road, the two women thought this is going to be home for the foreseeable future, until they got their next set of orders. After listening to the wireless and seeing the large movement of vehicles around the country, both thought it was going to be France but no one had admitted definitely. Both women were trying eagerly, to see what their new accommodation was like, through the small slit in the canvas. The large house came into view, and soon the truck had parked up outside,

Lizzie thought it reminded her of her own home but kept that thought to herself. The Regimental Sergeant Major shouted for them to disembark and form a line which the women obediently did, once satisfied they were given a room number and told to settle in and be back downstairs in the ballroom at eighteen-thirty hours for supper.

It turned out that Daisy and Lizzie were both sharing again, they had a room up in the attic where once the servants used to sleep. Heading up the stairs the women could hear their heavy boots pounding on the beautiful flooring, they took their suitcases up as their trunk was already placed in their chosen room. Lizzie stopped by the door and unlocked it with the key they had been given and entered. Both women glanced around, getting their bearings, there was some furniture, but it was a sparse room, a wardrobe to share, bedside cabinets with a light on top and two single beds which had been made, on top were fluffy eiderdowns for warmth.

Lizzie sat on the bed she had chosen, and she thought they would be happy here and then she felt the relief hit her that she was now away from her mother and she couldn't hurt her at present. Maybe she would have a change of heart Lizzie thought, but that wish was for another day. In the corner there was a small two bar electric heater which had warmed the room, the two young women took off their greatcoats as they were now feeling very warm, dropping them on their beds.

Daisy walked over to her bed and sat, the mattress was comfortable, she jumped up and down on it to test it, at least she would get a good night's sleep she thought smiling. Both women got to work unpacking, once they were satisfied with the room, they were ready to head back downstairs for some food, they were both hungry as it had been a long time since they had eaten. Daisy's stomach rumbled which made both girls laugh.

"Come on," said Lizzie. "We will feel better once we have eaten something hot."

Getting up they left the cosy room and found the stairs, all they heard was their boots clanking as they descended downwards. At the bottom, they heard the noise coming from the room to their left, so they followed it, the ballroom was large and majestic looking. In its heyday it would have been magnificent and held some wonderful dances, but now had rows of tables and chairs, it was full of other Army personnel, they walked up to the front and joined the queue, the catering staff had made a beef stew and dumplings with bread and butter.

Picking up a plate they walked to the chef who placed some stew on their empty plate with bread and then they made for two empty spaces. Greeting the others nearby, once seated they tucked into it as they were ravenous. The food was all right that was the main thing, it was hot and edible and more importantly filled a gap, they washed it down with a mug of tea, Lizzie had coffee. Pudding was apple pie and custard with no sugar, that too was all right, the apples made it slightly sharp tasting, but it was edible.

When satisfied they were full, the two women made their way back to their room and were told to be downstairs at seven a.m. in their full battledress for a run around the grounds.

The girls found a bathroom along the corridor and toilet next to it. Lizzie ran the bath first and then Daisy would follow after. She collected her toiletries and towel that had been left on the bed. After the long journey it was nice to have a long soak in the bath, it gave her time to think. She wondered what her mother had planned for her, following her news about Christopher? In a few days she would write to her aunt for some advice and to gauge how her mother had reacted, at least she couldn't hurt her here. Once she was finished, she got herself dressed in her warm pyjamas and headed back to the room, Daisy was ready and she then had her turn.

When they were back together in the warm room and refreshed, they found a small clothes-horse to put their damp towels on.

Lying on the bed Lizzie glanced over at her friend and said, "Thank you for today, and for listening to me go on about my mother," she said, and in a sombre mood. "You are my best friend and I know I can rely on you."

Daisy listened bringing a tear to her eye. Wiping it she thought seriously and then replied, "You are my best friend too!"

Daisy would do anything for Lizzie, and she knew Lizzie would do anything in return. As both women drifted off to sleep, they had left the heater on with one bar to keep the room warm, it left a lulling feel to the room.

The next morning both were up early and were downstairs at precisely seven, all their other colleagues were there. The Sergeant Major was standing by the front door waiting for a few stragglers, when everyone was ready, they followed him out into the cold morning, his booming voice scaring the local wildlife, it made a few of the nurses jump as well. Lizzie and Daisy kept pace and soon they were running around the acres of land in record time.

By half eight they were back sitting in the warm ball room enjoying bacon and eggs, and a mug of steaming tea washed it down. The women went back up to their room for a quick wash and got ready for the rest of the day. The next job for today was to collect the equipment they would need, so they were on the move again. They were back down just after nine and were told to go into another room which had the Quarter Master, they were each given a canvas valise, bath, washstand, bed, bucket, these were all packed in a trunk with their name and number on it. These were then stored away until they were needed, after that the women were free for the rest of the day.

Lizzie thought this was a good time to write to her aunt so she made her way back up the stairs to their room. Daisy followed as she wanted to keep an eye on her mate as she was worried about her mentally, she had been through a very difficult time dealing with her mother and Daisy really hoped that it would all get sorted out very soon.

In the room Lizzie found her paper and pen and got to work, she asked firstly how her aunt and uncle were and enquired about her cousins. Then she asked about her father and finally she brought up the subject of her mother, the main question she was dying to ask though was would her mother ever change her mind about her marriage to Charles? Because Lizzie was getting to the end of her tether and thought death was better than a lifetime spending it with Charles. Lizzie hadn't said anything to Daisy or her family but she sensed that her friend knew how she was really feeling. Finishing the letter, she placed it in the envelope and sealed it down.

Daisy wrote her letters making sure that they had given everyone their new address. Lizzie ran back down the stairs and found the post tray and placed the letters in it, then ran all the way back to the top. Daisy made a suggestion to go for a walk but upon looking out it had started to rain slightly so that idea was rejected.

The girls went down to the library and found some books to borrow on the promise to bring them back in one piece. They were told that Matron was arriving in the morning, and she was giving a talk first thing at ten. The rest of the day went quite slowly, and they were in bed early as they wanted to be at their best for when they had the talk by Matron. Again, they were downstairs by seven, ready for their run, Sergeant Major Patrick was barking his orders to the late arrivals, both girls winced.

Once again, they did really well and were back in record time. Following breakfast and their wash they smartened up their uniforms in the long mirror and made their way back down to the room designated for the talk. On arrival it was filling up and the two women found two spare chairs and quietly sat down.

Whispering, Daisy said, "What do you think she is going to say?"

Lizzie shrugged her shoulders and replied, "We will know soon enough, because she is here." As she looked over to the entrance.

The room silenced and everyone stood as the woman in her well-groomed uniform entered the room and made her way to the front so everyone could see and hear her.

Matron Smart first said they were entering a very important time and the war was now turning in the Allies favour. Everyone cheered, she held up her hand to silence the room.

"For the next few months, we have been asked to help at a hospital nearby as they have a flu outbreak and are short of nurses and we have been asked to help cover until we are told to move."

Daisy glanced at her friend next to her and knew it would mean them. Matron Smart finished off by saying that they would be back in their dresses and then when they were due to travel, they had to be back in battledress.

Once the talk was finished both women waited to be told where they would be positioned and then they headed back to their room to prepare for the next day. They went into their trunks found their dresses and got to work with the iron, pressing them for the morning. After supper both women had baths and did their hair ready for the next day and their early shift, the truck would be leaving at six-thirty, sharp to take them to the local hospital.

They both had slept well and were up and ready on time wrapped in their capes, to keep the biting wind off them. Both looked impeccably well turned out. It was the first day of February and the two women set foot inside the local cottage hospital to begin their shift. It had been fun trying to climb into the back of the truck in their dresses, both had fallen about laughing but they had managed it with some help and steps.

The hospital wasn't particularly large, but its function was to get the injured better and then shipped out. The corridors all smelt of carbolic and it was quite soothing for both nurses who were slightly nervous of starting on a new ward, even after all this time. Daisy was on ward one and Lizzie was sent to report to ward three.

Daisy entered through the swing doors onto the ward, tightly gripping her apron. The beds were lined up on both sides, the layout like any other ward, she looked around to get her bearings and found the staff room in the corner. First, she glanced to her right and found Sister's office, Daisy walked briskly over to the door. Knocking she waited for the command to enter, she waited and hearing it, turned the handle.

She entered trying very hard to hide the nerves that had resurfaced. Sister Norman sat at her desk, Daisy thought she had been brought out of retirement, she looked that old, she was taking hand-over from the night staff, once complete she let the young nurse get off to her bed. Daisy stood ramrod straight in front of Sister Norman, waiting for her to speak.

Looking up and down as if inspecting Daisy, she said, "So, you are Sister Peters? It is highly irregular to ask for help but needs must," she continued. "As some of my staff have been struck down ill. Take yourself to the staff room and get your apron on and then meet Mr Lockhart back on the ward."

Daisy knew she was dismissed and turned and exited the door, one of the orderlies came over as she was making her way to the staff room. "Don't mind her she is all right really," he said, his eyes wandering over to Sister's Office.

Daisy smiled and then introduced herself to Graham Lockhart. "Let me show you the locker you can use and then meet me back here to start the bed baths," said Graham.

He left her in the locker room and she got to work rolling up her sleeves, putting on her cuffs. She then placed her apron on, taking a quick look in the mirror, happy with her appearance she headed back out onto the ward. Graham was talking to another orderly called Gerald who was working with another Staff Nurse called Maria Wilson, and there were a couple of VAD Nurses who were at that precise moment down the other end of the ward.

Graham called Daisy over and he made the introductions, they both said a cautious, "Hello."

Graham showed Daisy where the linen cupboard was situated and prepared their trolley. The ward was full with wounded soldiers who had already had some surgery at the field hospital, now some needed more surgery or just needed care to get them home or back to their regiment. Daisy and Graham got to work with the two bed baths, once they were done, sheets changed and bed pan round completed, she left Graham doing the temperature, pulse and respiration round followed by blood pressures, while Daisy started on the medicine round and then wound round.

She let Graham go for first break, then headed for the canteen next, following Graham's instructions on where to go. Getting near she could smell the toast and licked her lips, Daisy was looking forward to a slice of toast and cup of tea, glancing around she tried to spot Lizzie as she entered the canteen but to no avail, she wasn't there, maybe she would be there at lunch.

Daisy finished her break and rushed back to the ward. She was asked to put up a drip which she did straight away. She noticed out the corner of her eye that Sister Norman had been studying her all morning, so it wasn't a surprise a bit later when she said, "Well done, Sister Peters."

Daisy had to hide the smile,

"You have worked hard this morning, now please, off you go to lunch."

Daisy remembered where to go, again she could smell the lunch cooking, joining the queue she walked up to the hatch and chose her food taking it back with her she found an empty seat and sat down. She got talking to some other nurses who were interested in why some Army nurses were seconded to their hospital.

Daisy explained it was only for a few months while they had this outbreak of flu but she thought it might be for longer. Daisy finished up and made her way back to the ward, with a full stomach and with the help of Graham they got the back-round completed in record time.

Once Sister Norman was satisfied, she then looked at her fob watch and let Daisy, Graham and the other staff off, apart from the VAD nurses whose shift finished at eight.

While the late staff were left to hand over to the night staff. Sister Norman stopped Daisy. "See you tomorrow on the late shift."

Daisy nodded and made her way to the locker room, where she rolled down her sleeves, taking her cuffs off and took her apron off, leaving it in the locker for tomorrow. Checking the time on her watch she quickly placed her cape around herself and rushed down the ward saying "good night" as she went, she made it to the front entrance and the waiting truck.

Lizzie was already sitting up in the truck as Daisy was helped aboard, Daisy was pleased to see her friend and they spent the journey catching up. Both were on late shifts the next day. They were both extremely tired and their feet ached terribly, but both girls were happy to be back nursing. Lizzie had had a similar day to Daisy and both agreed that they could do this until they were given new orders to move on.

It was dark when they arrived back to Greenwood Manor, it was in darkness and the women climbed off the truck and opened the front door. Once inside the two women had to shield their eyes as it was bright from a lovely crystal chandelier up in the ceiling in the hall. Both weary from a long day they headed up to their room and to get change ready for tea. Lizzie had hoped for some mail but realistically she knew it was too soon.

Both women were pleased to sit on their comfy beds, taking their regulation shoes off and rubbing their tired feet to get the circulation back into them. Once satisfied they got changed and proceeded to the ball room for tea. Back upstairs, both sat on the bed reading their books borrowed from the library until they couldn't keep their eyes open. At least tomorrow they could both have a lie-in.

Over the next few weeks, it was the same routine for both women and they settled into their new surroundings very well. The staff were beginning to get used to them and more importantly accept them.

One day following an early shift, Lizzie had a letter waiting for her from her aunt, she recognised the handwriting. She was alone in their room as Daisy was on a late shift and wouldn't be back till much later. Lizzie placed the letter on her bedside cabinet while she undressed and changed into her battledress for tea. She kept glancing over at the letter, she was in a dilemma, she really wanted to know what her aunt had written but her head was telling her to wait till Daisy was with her, so she had support.

It had been difficult but in the end her head won, and she decided to wait till Daisy returned. Putting the letter back on the bedside cabinet she made herself busy until much later she heard Daisy coming up the stairs. Lizzie watched as the door opened, and an exhausted looking Daisy entered, Lizzie gave her friend time to get into her pyjamas and while she was doing that, she had run downstairs and got her a mug of Horlicks.

On her return she sat on her bed and Daisy, seeing how Lizzie had a worried expression on her face came and sat down by her.

"What's wrong," she asked an anxious Lizzie. "Have you had bad news?"

"No. No," replied Lizzie seeing how apprehensive her friend had become. "I've had a reply from my aunt," she said, glancing over to her cabinet by the bed.

Lizzie leaned over and picked up the envelope, she slowly opened it and pulled the sheets out, careful not to rip them. Daisy let her friend read the letter through and waited patiently giving her time to digest the contents. After what seemed like a lifetime, Lizzie looked up. Daisy watched as the tears came to her eyes and slowly rolled down her cheeks, she passed the letter to Daisy to read.

Apparently, her aunt had written, she had spoken with the help of her father to her mother once Lizzie had left. Her mother was adamant that Lizzie was going through a phase with Christopher, and she would soon come to her senses. Her mother was still determined that she would

403

marry Charles even knowing about his little girl and what he did to her daughter. Her words were that Lizzie had encouraged him! Finally, her aunt apologised and said, "She would still carry on and would still try to get her to change her mind." She told her niece, not to lose hope.

Lizzie, now she knew the contents of the letter was pleased she hadn't opened it on her own.

Daisy dropped the letter on the bed, turned to face her distraught friend and pulled her into her arms and held her till the tears had dried up. Once Daisy could speak to Lizzie, she pulled her back so she could face her fully.

"Now listen to me, you do have a future with Christopher, and you will marry him. You do not need your mother's permission."

Lizzie looked at Daisy and said, "She would never trust or love her mother again." Lizzie was angry and said in a determined voice, "I will have to sort out Charles myself the next time I see him." She carried on. "I have no plan." Looking at Daisy. "So, I will have to think about how to deal with him carefully. He will pay for raping me," she said in an unwavering voice. "Or Christopher will do something if he ever gets his hands on him."

Lizzie sat their shaking and lit a cigarette to help calm her nerves as she was talking and was feeling physically sick with worry.

Daisy prayed that Chris would never come across Charles for she feared he would kill Charles or get hurt himself trying, because she knew Charles would not play fair.

All Lizzie knew was Charles was still in England, recovering from his injuries and would be able to return to his regiment soon so the letter said.

At present she was safe and soon they would be on the move. Lizzie dried her eyes with the handkerchief that Daisy had handed to her, she had stopped shaking but you could hear in her voice and see in her actions she was still visibly upset.

"Let's sleep on it and you will feel better in the morning, maybe you can write to Chris and your brother."

"I will not write to my mother," said an adamant Lizzie.

Daisy couldn't blame her so didn't say any more. It was late so they climbed into bed and turned the light off, in the dark Lizzie laid there with all sorts of emotions going through her mind. She hated her mother with a vengeance and that would never change. She lay listening to Daisy's breathing which soothed her to sleep. Over the next few weeks, the two women were kept busy, which Daisy was pleased about as she was concerned for her friend, she had written to her family, George and Michael to tell them what had happened. Lizzie had written to Eddie and Chris to inform them of her news from her mother. They both waited eagerly for replies.

It was now coming to the beginning of March and the weather was still unpredictable, but it was getting lighter, so all the women did was stay indoors and read when not working.

The next day, when they returned from the hospital, they found they had letters. Both, even with tired legs rushed up the stairs. Lizzie had letters from Eddie and Chris, she opened Eddie's first. It said that Glenda and himself were well, he wasn't surprised at their mother's behaviour and that she should still go ahead and marry Chris and be happy.

Chris had written that he was disappointed with how her mother was acting but it didn't stop him, he still wanted to marry her as soon as they could. His family really couldn't wait to meet her and when Lizzie finished the letters her heart felt lighter and she had a smile on her face, which she hadn't had for a long time. Daisy, looking over saw her friend smile and it made her feel reassured as she had been very anxious for Lizzie.

Daisy's letter from her parents was good, everyone was well, and they hoped she was too. George's letter was short, he was still on the convoys and he was doing all right, he had made some good friends, and he hoped to be home soon for some leave.

Daisy was relieved they were all fine, hoping to be home when George was next there. By the middle of May the weather had improved and their time at the hospital was supposed to be coming to an end, both would miss the other colleagues they had met and had got to know.

Matron had come to see everyone last night and had informed them that all the sick staff were well again and their services would no longer be needed.

As of Monday, they were back preparing to leave at a moment's notice. As the weather was better Daisy and Lizzie would take a walk around the grounds, it was just nice to get out in the fresh air and to keep fit, and blow some cobwebs off them when the wind was blustery.

Chapter 47

On June 6th, known as D-Day, American and Allied troops had landed in Normandy to fight the Germans, everyone hoped this was the beginning to end the war once and for all. News was getting through that on the thirteenth of June, Germany sent over the first flying bomb, it landed in London killing and injuring many people, the government tried to keep it quiet as they didn't want to frighten everyone. These attacks went on for many weeks and were frightening the people of Britain as they didn't know quite where they would land, they were called V1s.

All the women were on tenterhooks, something big was about to happen, none of the officers were saying a word and three weeks after the invasion the women were told to dress in battledress and pack up their belongings as quickly as they could as they were travelling to Portsmouth. The transport stopped in the new forest later that day, they were told they couldn't write letters or receive phone calls. That night they had to sleep in tents, but the food was exceptional, both women were apprehensive.

Before they embarked all of the women were given money which would be their spending money in France, now they knew the destination. Lizzie wondered if her French would come in handy, she hadn't spoken it since her school days. The next day they made their way to the harbour to wait their turn to embark on to a troop ship. That night they were on the ship sleeping on a bunk that was metal, very hard and extremely uncomfortable not like the one they had when they travelled home from Malta, the women weren't too bothered but were nervous and settled down for the voyage over the channel, it was rough and many of their colleagues were seasick.

Both women were lucky with all their travelling they had found their sea legs very quickly. It was funny to see the others wishing the journey to be over with and to be on dry land as they all looked very green indeed. The next morning, they entered French waters and were told to come up on deck, what Lizzie and Daisy saw was the Mulberry harbours had been constructed, these were artificial harbours, they went back to gather their belongings and waited to go ashore. Once ashore they were loaded onto the back of a waiting truck and observed that some of their colleagues were still looking a bit unwell, and were still feeling queasy from the voyage, the weather was very unsettled for June.

The truck drove to a field beyond Bayeux and Caen, which was covered in mud. Daisy and Lizzie got off the truck and had a walk around their new accommodation to get their bearings, they noticed the tents were already up and the pioneer Corps had already set up the operating theatre, as the field was not level, they laid a concrete float in the middle of the theatre and placed two operating tables on it, side by side.

The surgeons worked back-to-back. The engineers set up the generator which gave light to the operating theatres and wards. It was raining heavily and the tarpaulin on the ward floors turned it into a sticky layer of mud. The women were taken to their tents and told to leave their luggage and get to work getting the hospital set up as soon as possible. All the nurses worked together and in record time the hospital was up and running and accepting casualties. Each wounded man, when he arrived had a label attached to him which was tied to his buttonhole, describing the time and treatment he had already received at the field dressing station. If a soldier had been given morphine to treat pain, then M had been written on their foreheads in indelible pencil. Many of the injuries were terrible and most of the young men went to theatre still in their clothes to keep them warm, the only area that was cut off was the area that was being operated on like a sleeve for the arm or trouser leg for the leg area. Many injuries were caused by standing on land mines and these needed surgeries very quickly.

Lizzie and Daisy were working flat out and were using the new drug called penicillin to help fight infection. At night while they were sitting at their desk on the ward, the light from the lamp gave a pretty glow, Daisy jumped when she heard the gunfire start up in the distance, that caused the battle fatigue cases to start desperately digging the tarpaulin that covered the ground, trying to escape the noise. During the day they were very drowsy and lay quietly, Daisy tried desperately to calm the young soldier down, but in the end, she used sedatives and a soothing voice, a young orderly had to help her to keep the soldiers still.

These men were always evacuated within twenty-four hours back home. The nurses didn't have time to think, they were often dead on their feet at the end of the day, Lizzie had an uneasy feeling that she was being watched since she had arrived, but being so busy and more often tired, she put it out of her mind and carried on, she didn't think to bother Daisy as she was probably just shattered.

Daisy and Lizzie couldn't get used to the guns firing in the distance it was like a constant bombardment. Daisy's thoughts, when she had a quiet period, went to Michael and she wondered where he was? And was he safe and well? She wished with all her heart that he would walk through these tents doors and she could see him. She knew she was being selfish, but she couldn't help it, she loved him. Lizzie in her free time, which wasn't often, would think of Christopher and wonder where he was? Oh, how she wished he was here. Both Nurses were kept busy over the next few weeks, many casualties kept coming and going and the beds got full, there was no let up. The wounded made very little noise and were very brave and uncomplaining, the ones who were dying wanted only a cigarette, which Lizzie was happy to assist with, Daisy had to borrow from Lizzie or she bought a pack.

Each morning Matron would tell her staff where they were working that day, there was no regular routine. One day Daisy was working on the head injuries ward and another day she could be working on the amputation ward. The toilets and washing facilities were very primitive, it was a board with holes in for the toilet, fixed across a trench a tarpaulin shielded them from the men. Sometimes if the wind blew it would raise up and the men could see, but the women just carried on. Both Women could see the funny side, which was good, they hadn't lost their sense of humour. The contents of the bedpans were just thrown into the bush which would shock people, but this was the reality of the situation.

A few weeks later the women received letters, their post had finally caught up with them. Daisy received a letter from Michael, she popped it into the pocket of her battledress until she found a quiet time to read it, so when she had the chance she went back to her tent, Lizzie wasn't about, she had the tent to herself. Daisy sat on her canvas bed and read through her letter. It turned out Michael was here in France and once he found out where Daisy was stationed, he had made arrangements for him to borrow a jeep and drive over to see her, he also had a surprise for Lizzie as Chris' regiment was very near his clearing station and they had become good friends when the two women had left them in Libya, he too was coming to see them this Saturday. What day was it? Thought Daisy as she been so busy, she had lost track of time.

It was Thursday so in two days they would be here. Daisy couldn't wait to tell Lizzie or should she keep it a secret? No, she would tell her friend. Daisy hurried off to find her, first, went to the ward where she thought she was working, Lizzie wasn't there, the other sister told her Lizzie was on her break in the canteen, Daisy rushed there as quick as she could. On entering she found a tired Lizzie, who was surprised to see Daisy. Waving the letter Daisy stopped at her table and handed the letter as she was out of breath. Lizzie read the letter and couldn't believe it, Chris was coming here to see her this Saturday with Michael, she jumped up and hugged her friend tightly. It was not surprising that both women didn't sleep well that night or the next with the excitement.

Both women were given some time off on Saturday after they had spoken to Matron. So, at midday the jeep came into view, both women were waiting apprehensively as they hadn't seen the men for a long time. Michael pulled up, turning off the engine and jumped out, grabbing a crying Daisy and hugging and kissing her as if his life depended on it. Chris did the same with Lizzie. Once they were reconnected, they headed for the canteen where they could talk and catch up.

Lizzie was slightly concerned about Charles because if Chris was here, then there was a big chance Charles' regiment would be too, and she knew Chris would kill Charles if he got his hands on him. Lizzie explained all that took place while she was at home and her mother's reaction to the news that Lizzie was marrying someone else and not Charles. Chris sat and listened intently; he still couldn't believe this woman even after hearing all the facts she still wanted her daughter to marry that man. He was incensed and he knew in his heart that if he ever met Charles or even worse if he hurt Lizzie, he would harm him.

Michael sat listening and all the time he kept glancing over at Daisy, he thought she was most beautiful woman he had ever seen and knew he wanted to spend the rest of his life with her. First, he wanted to meet

Daisy's parents and her family and she had to meet his family. He would arrange that once this war was over and then they could plan the wedding, the only problem being he hadn't asked Daisy yet. Michael felt in his trouser pocket where the box was sitting nicely, he was waiting for the right moment. There was an awkwardness between them to start with but they talked some more and it felt so natural and then before they knew it their time was up, both men had to get back, Michael didn't think this was the right moment to propose, he wanted to do it when he was on his own with Daisy.

As all four walked to the jeep, they made a promise to meet up in a few days. They kissed and they all knew they would meet up again, both women stood and watched the jeep drive away. As she watched the jeep drive into the distance, Lizzie had that feeling something bad was going to happen, and she knew it would involve Charles for sure, and she couldn't shake the bad feeling off. Over the next few days, the women were kept busy and they only had time to sleep and work it was very tiring. Lizzie still kept having a feeling she was being watched but every time she glanced around, there was no one there. She didn't tell Daisy or Chris as she thought she was going mad, or even worse imagining it, she just thought she was tired.

Matron had informed the women they were going onto nights starting Monday. Chris and Michael turned up over the weekend and they had a few enjoyable hours before going back on duty.

Chris grabbed Lizzie's arm gently. "Can you give me a few minutes alone?" he asked.

"Come with me." She took Chris's hand and they walked to a secluded area away from everyone.

Chris took her into his arms, their lips met in a languid kiss. Kissing Chris was a delight, it started to get heated and then his hands began to wander, he opened her trousers, pulling the zipper down, and pulled them down, followed by her knickers. Chris knew this was a risk but he wanted her, badly, he unzipped his trousers hurriedly and he took her against the wooded building. It wasn't pretty or romantic it was a desperate need.

Afterwards they had no regrets, as they had both wanted it, they both knew they could be dead anytime soon. They tidied themselves up and headed back to join the others. Michael was still carrying the ring and he

410

was still waiting for the right time to propose but he kept putting it off for some reason. He would do it soon, he promised himself.

Monday the sisters went on night duty, they were on separate wards. They settled into a routine and over the weeks, Lizzie still felt as if she was being watched. She started to worry as she had missed her last period, she hadn't said anything to Daisy as she would wait and see as it was still early. The next week, Lizzie walked onto her ward, the night started off fine for both women, Daisy had her break like normal and Lizzie went later. On her way to the canteen, she popped her head in to see Daisy, coming out she had that feeling someone was following her, but she continued walking.

Lizzie was just about to turn around when she felt someone's breath against her neck, then she felt the revolver pressed against her back. Then she heard his voice, no surprises, it was Charles, but he sounded different, like his was drunk! He put his hand in front of her mouth to stop her from screaming, she tried to fight him off, but he was just too strong, she hoped someone would hear the commotion but there was no one around, it was eerily quiet.

"Keep moving," he growled, stabbing the revolver in her back. Lizzie did as she was told, automatically her hand went for her stomach. Nearby was a jeep. "Climb in," he ordered sneering, she did as she was told, and he put a gag around her mouth so she couldn't scream, and he tied her wrists together so she couldn't escape.

She was hoping Daisy would realise she was missing and raise the alarm. Lizzie was shaking and the tears had started to fall, they were streaming down her face, why was he doing this? Charles, climbed into the jeep by her side still pointing the revolver at her, she thought about running but she knew he would shoot her. He started the engine and they headed away from the hospital into the French countryside, it was pitch black, only the moon for light. About a mile or so he drove off the main road and headed for a deserted farmhouse. He pulled up and helped Lizzie out, she refused to walk so he grabbed her arm and pulled her to the front door, she nearly fell, her tied hands went automatically to her stomach.

Once inside he pulled her to a seat and made her sit down, tying her up he kept pointing the revolver at her, he said, "If only you wanted to marry me, things would be so different."

Lizzie was petrified, she really hoped Daisy had raised the alarm by this time.

Charles keep ranting, "Why didn't she want to marry him?"

She thought he had gone mad and was very dangerous and possessive, he kept stroking her hair. Back at the hospital, by the morning Daisy finished her shift and went straight to find Lizzie, when she wasn't at her desk on her ward, she asked the other orderlies if had they seen Sister Fenton? They replied they hadn't seen her for a while, this news raised alarms in Daisy's head and she rushed off to check the latrines and showers, including the canteen to see if she was eating breakfast. She asked everyone had they seen her, but no one had, she wasn't anywhere around the hospital.

Daisy by now was very worried, she started to shake, she wanted to cry but held it together, she rushed to Matron's office. Daisy rushed in without knocking,

Matron looked up. "What's the meaning for this intrusion Sister Peters?" she asked. Seeing her nurse distressed she didn't say any more.

"Lizzie is missing," she said in a hurry.

"Sister Felton is missing?"

"Yes, Matron," she said again.

"When did you last see her?" Matron enquired in a soothing voice, she could see the terror in the young woman's face.

"Last night, we parted to go to our relevant wards, apparently she went for her break and never came back."

"Why did no one raise the alarm then?" Thought matron but kept that to herself.

"I asked the patients and her cover, but she never came back from her break, her cover thought she was just ill and gone to bed. "I need to inform her fiancé and Dr Reynolds as soon as possible; I think I know who has taken her."

Daisy by now was crying. Matron's eyes bore into Daisy. "Nurse," she shouted looking directly at the young woman. "Well, who is this person?" Waiting for a reply.

"It's a man she is supposed to be engaged to, but she doesn't love him, we think he's slightly unhinged."

"Well, carry on and get a message to these two men quickly."

Daisy hurried off to get the message to Chris and Michael, Daisy knew time was against them, she kept trying not to cry but it was no use the tears came streaming down her face, she couldn't stop them. Daisy wanted Lizzie back in one piece and unharmed.

Once she got the message sent to Chris and Michael she waited. Daisy sat in Matron's office so Matron could keep an eye on her and get every spare member of staff looking around the camp just in case she was there. Daisy was still shaking and crying, Matron passed her a handkerchief which Daisy was grateful for.

Chapter 48

Back where Christopher was, Sergeant Hibbert couldn't help but overhear the conversation between the doctor and his captain. He cautiously approached the captain and stood to attention. When the captain waved his hand to approach the Sergeant marched forward and saluted. Sergeant Hibbert had been a patient at The London just after Dunkirk and had met Lizzie, he thought she was a lovely girl and the captain was a very lucky man.

"Sorry, Sir." He was told to stand at ease. "I've over-heard everything, and I would like to come along as your driver."

Sergeant Hibbert waited patiently, Christopher sat back looking at his Sergeant and thought it would be a good idea to take him with them.

Finally, he answered, "Yes."

Sergeant Hibbert stood to attention and saluted, turned and marched out. Once out of the tent he headed back to his tent and collected his kit and his service revolver which was an Enfield number two revolver. He then went to find a working jeep for them to use, in under thirty minutes he was back outside the tent ready to head off.

Within the hour Chris and Michael had turned up, so had the military police. Daisy went to greet Chris and Michael and filled them in with all the patchy details. Once done she fell into Michael's open arms and cried her heart out, he hugged her tight rubbing her back soothingly. Chris on the other hand was absolutely livid, he was more worried about where Charles had taken Lizzie and particularly what he had planned to do to her, he was also scared he would lose her, he promised he would do everything to find her.

The military police checked around the hospital but to no avail, she wasn't there. We need to widen the search area they decided, but where? The French countryside was vast. Michael and Chris decided to take the jeep and drive around just to see if any nearby troops had seen anything, it was a long shot, but they had to try.

Daisy asked permission to go with them and Matron, seeing the anguish on the young woman's face, reluctantly agreed.

Glancing at Michael and Chris she said in a stern voice, "Take care of her!"

So the four of them set out.

Charles had thought the plan through very thoroughly and he had built up a supply of food over the past few weeks and warm clothing as he dare not light a fire because that would locate them. He kept Lizzie quiet with the gag as he couldn't trust her, he kept mumbling to himself. Lizzie could hear him, she thought he had really lost his mind.

"I need to keep him calm because if he loses his cool it might make him more dangerous." She thought.

He kept looking over at her, she was very pretty but why did she not love him? It kept playing over in his mind, if only things were different, why was he hearing these voices telling him things? He held his head to try to silence them but to no avail. Lizzie was watching this with keen interest.

He came over to her and pointed the revolver. "I am going to remove the gag, if you make a noise, I will shoot you."

Lizzie nodded, so he came close and removed it, it felt nice to let her jaw muscles relax. She was too frightened to say anything so she just looked at him, pleading with her eyes to let her go.

"Let's get some food." He pulled some Army rations out of a rucksack and warmed the food up on a thermos heater, Charles handed her some, she was very hungry, but she could only manage a small amount as she felt physically sick.

Once finished she asked Charles for a drink, he handed over a water canteen and she took a sip. Once she'd had enough, she passed it back. He placed the gag back into position and went to look out of the window to check if anyone was about, but it was silent and all clear. He had hidden the jeep in a barn next to the farm, he dared not keep it out in full view, for fear of being exposed. All the while Lizzie sat back in the chair and watched him with interest, she wished he would show some remorse, she wondered what had tipped him over the edge? Lizzie would find out somehow.

Sergeant Hibbert, Michael, Chris and Daisy pulled out of the

415

hospital, turning onto the road. Where to begin? Chris was angry and frustrated, if anything was to happen to Lizzie he would kill Charles, he prayed she was unharmed, he instructed the Sergeant to continue to drive, Lizzie could be anywhere, but they knew they had to find her, as they didn't know the extent Charles would go to in harming her.

Michael sat in the back with Daisy and didn't let go of her hand, she gripped his tight. They drove to the outskirts of Caen and pulled up, the town was completely devastated by the bombing and the town lay in ruins, it was unsafe for them to enter. Chris didn't think she would be here, so where would Charles hide her? And more importantly how are they going to find her?

They decided to leave Caen and concentrate on and around the hospital as there were plenty of old farm buildings that could be ideal for a hiding place. On the journey back they stopped by a company of soldiers walking along the roadside and they enquired if they had seen anything abnormal but no luck. By the time they returned to the hospital, it was late afternoon, it was still very warm and muggy, there were dark clouds in the sky, and it looked like rain.

Daisy was getting worked up, desperate in fact to find her friend, she was also very tired as having had no sleep. Michael advised her to go back to the hospital and get some sleep, but Daisy gave him such a look that he backed down. Sergeant Hibbert saw they were running low on fuel and needed to refill the jeep by the docks, and they decided to carry on looking for a while longer.

The rest of the day they kept driving around the countryside checking out all the nearby derelict buildings but no luck, as it was late July it stayed lighter into the evening and Michael and Chris met up with the Military Police to liaise. More soldiers joined in the hunt and it went way into the night. It had started to rain lightly, but they knew they had to keep on searching as time was running out.

Charles was getting more agitated, Lizzie must had fallen asleep because when she woke up it was very dark. Charles kept the farm in darkness, but Lizzie wanted a cigarette, she tried to get Charles' attention, he came over and took the gag off her. He fed her some food and gave her a drink, which she was grateful for.

"I need to use the toilet," she said.

Charles looked at her unbelieving.

"I really do," she said again trying to convince him, she had needed to go more lately, this was a sign of being pregnant. He untied her and followed her into the darkness.

"Don't try anything heroic, because I will fire," he said in a menacing voice, once outside, pointing the revolver sharply into her back. She used the toilet, looking down inside her knickers she spotted blood. Her first thought… Was she losing the baby? Lizzie started to cry, they returned to the farmhouse.

Now was her chance to talk to him calmly and try and coax him to release her. "What happened?" she asked in a gentle voice.

"Your mother, when I was home on sick leave, spoke with my mother and myself and told me she had decided to let you marry someone else."

Lizzie was astounded by her mother's actions; she didn't quite believe it. This news must have pushed Charles over the edge, now she needed to keep him relaxed and rational.

Nearby, Chris, Michael and Daisy were still trying every empty building they could find. Christopher was becoming more anxious as the hours ticked away.

Lizzie knew she needed to shine some light with the hope of attracting attention as there must be men around in the forest, she had to come up with a plan and fast. "May I have a cigarette?"

Charles glanced at her but lit one and handed it to her, she took it with thanks, and she puffed on it. Slowly in small movements she moved nearer the window, hopefully the glow would be seen.

The four were nearing an old farmhouse not far from the hospital, it was their last chance of looking that night and were on the verge of abandoning the search. Chris had an uneasy feeling about this place.

Daisy could have sworn she saw a small light coming from the window, Sergeant Hibbert turned off the engine and climbed out of the jeep, taking his service revolver and headed for the undergrowth.

Charles heard the footsteps and pulled Lizzie roughly away from the window, Chris and Michael pulled their service revolvers from their holsters and walked to the front of the building, trying to get a better view.

Charles grabbed Lizzie's arm and she cried out in pain, causing her to be heard by the three of them. Chris shouted to Lizzie who cried out that she was unharmed. Charles was getting more agitated and was pacing around the room, talking to himself. Lizzie kept talking to him and begged him to open the door and let her go as he was outnumbered.

Charles grabbed her and pulled her to the door and shouted, "We're coming out!" He would take his chances outside.

Lizzie went first, closely followed by Charles, she could feel his breath on her neck and the revolver in her back, she shivered.

As they stood outside Charles shouted, "Stand back, or I will shoot her."

Both men stood still, they could hear Charles mumbling to himself and saying Lizzie was his and nobody could ever have her.

Lizzie was frightened and shaking with fear, she closed her eyes wishing this was not happening, she really needed a pee, but she fought the urge, and it took all her will-power to be strong.

Charles pointed the revolver at Michael and Charles. The two men took aim ready to open fire if need be. No one saw Sergeant Hibbert raise his revolver and aim it at Charles, he knew he only had one chance at this, a bead of sweat ran down the side of his face... all of a sudden, a shot rang out!

At first, Lizzie thought she had been shot by Charles, she felt all over her body but couldn't feel anything, she felt no pain. She felt some sticky warm fluid on the side of her face, she put her hand up and when she pulled it away, she saw blood. Lizzie looked down and she saw Charles' limp body and blood oozing from a head wound. Lizzie on impulse ran towards Daisy, both were overcome with emotion.

Daisy held her friend tight. "I really thought I would never see you again." Both began to cry with relief and realisation that her ordeal was finally over and that Charles, she hoped, was dead.

Chris and Michael rushed over to Charles' motionless body, Michael examined him, but it was too late, he was already dead.

After a while the military police arrived and took over the investigation, they would need to speak with all five of them, and especially with Lizzie when she was up to it.

Michael glanced at Lizzie and said in a steady voice, "We need to get you back to the hospital and checked over."

No one disagreed and all five headed back to the hospital with Sergeant Hibbert driving. Michael sat in the front while Chris sat in the back of the jeep holding Lizzie tight, her mind went straight to the safety of her baby.

Daisy sat beside them, just happy she had her friend back. Matron was waiting for them when they arrived back at the hospital, news had got around and many of the nurses were also concerned for their comrade and pleased that she was unhurt.

Matron stood watching and she felt a tear come to her eye, she was overcome with emotion that her nurse had returned in one piece. "I must be getting soft in my old age," she thought.

Chris helped Lizzie out of the jeep as her legs were like jelly and he supported her to her tent. Once they were alone, Chris guided her to her bed and sat her down, he sat by her side and took her face in his hands and kissed her tenderly.

"I really thought I was going to lose you today." He had to fight to stop the tears from falling as he loved this woman with all of his heart.

"While I was held captive, Charles mentioned my mother had given her blessing for me to marry you. It was this news that pushed him over the edge as he knew he could never have me and knew I never loved him."

Chris hardly believed the good news that they were finally allowed to marry.

"I have missed my period," she said, slightly embarrassed. "But before you get excited, I'm bleeding, I could be losing the baby." They both sat heads together, trying to digest the news.

The first priority was to make sure that Lizzie had no side effects from her ordeal and that the investigation into Charles' death cleared all three of them. Chris had no regrets that Charles had died, now they were free to start afresh, and with the war coming to an end, things were looking up for all of them.

Matron arrived carrying some medicine which she ordered the young nurse to take. "These will make you sleep and once you are rested Dr Reynolds will check you over, and then you can talk to the military police."

"No, I need to see Dr Reynolds now," Lizzie said urgently.

Matron called Dr Reynolds over and he entered the tent. Lizzie told him she was bleeding, he checked her over and told her she was in fact losing the baby.

Lizzie sat on the bed crying; she would talk to Daisy in the morning. At the moment she was distressed and inconsolable, she got a terrible pain in her stomach and needed the toilet badly.

Lizzie rushed out. "I will be back," she called.

Once on the toilet she had an urge to push, and Lizzie cried. Once back in the tent she sorted herself out and took the medicine and laid down on her bed, she was exhausted, and she soon fell into a deep sleep.

Chris didn't want to leave her side, but Matron persuaded him to come to the canteen and get a drink and something to eat. Daisy had watched as Chris had led Lizzie to their tent, she found Michael talking to Matron and she went over to see them. Matron saw her coming and made her apologises saying that she had things to attend to.

Michael caught sight of Daisy and pulled her into his arms, kissing her tenderly and languidly on the lips.

"Today has made me realise that life is very precious and that I love you very much." With that he knelt down on one knee and asked, "Daisy, will you marry me?" Pulling out the ring and offering it to Daisy.

When she was over the shock she immediately said, "Yes." He placed the ring tenderly on the ring finger on her left hand. Daisy looked down at it and Michael kissed her again and never wanted to let her go again.

"I'm sorry it wasn't the fancy proposal I wanted to make, but it just felt right," he said. "Once we are home I would very much like to meet your family and then you can meet mine."

Daisy yawned; the past events had finally caught up with them and he knew they needed to get some rest. He walked Daisy to her tent and kissed her goodnight with the promise he would see her tomorrow.

Before they parted, she asked, "What happens with the investigation. Charles had died, and all three of you are suspects?"

"As we thought he was aiming his gun at us it was classed as self-defence."

When Daisy was alone with a sleeping Lizzie to her side, she recalled all that had taken place. a little of their actions made her think: Did one of them really want Charles dead? The guilt washed over her but she knew she was being stupid as he thoroughly deserved it, she put that thought out of her mind. She tried to sleep but she was so excited about the engagement that she knew it would be impossible tonight, so she chose to watch over her friend and keep her safe.

Lizzie woke refreshed, whatever Matron had given her had definitely done the trick. Daisy on the other hand looked tired but happy, Lizzie couldn't place why her friend was extremely happy until Daisy flashed her hand at her, and she caught the glare of the diamond ring.

"When did this happen?" she asked, holding Daisy's left hand, quizzing her friend. Daisy happily replied on our return to the hospital.

"I am so happy; we can be each other's bridesmaids."

Lizzie liked that idea.

"Firstly, when I get home, I must see my mother to make sure she has really agreed for me to marry Chris, and then I need to explain what took place last night."

Daisy noticed her friend looked sad. "What's the matter?" she asked concerned.

Coming over all emotional she cried, "I lost the baby last night!" Laying her hand on her stomach she let the tears fall.

Daisy just held Lizzie tight and let her tears fall too. Daisy, after a short time laid her friend down. "Just lay here and rest." Daisy asked. "Do you want me to get Chris?"

"No. I will see him later, thank you."

Daisy wanted to ask her friend one question before she left. "Do you feel guilty about what took place?"

"No," Lizzie replied. She was sure. "No, he deserved it, but I don't want anyone to get into trouble. It was self-defence, he would have pulled the trigger and tried to shoot someone, he was mad, he kept talking to himself. I will speak with the military police as soon as I can and clear everything up."

"You must rest first," said Daisy, and she left her to rest.

Later, they both got washed and changed their clothes and got some food. "I'm sure Chris and Michael will be back very soon, and I really want to celebrate your engagement." Both women picked up their wash things and headed to the showers.

Once refreshed, and in clean clothes, the two women made their way to the canteen. When they entered all eyes were on them, Lizzie felt anxious, and she kept by the side of Daisy, who put a protective arm around her.

Neither thought they would eat but surprisingly they were extremely hungry. Matron entered and walked over to them, she checked to make sure Lizzie was all right after her ordeal and losing the baby, but she still wanted Michael to check her over again one more time for reassurance.

By ten Sergeant Hibbert, Michael and Chris arrived in their jeep, they had already spoken with the military police. Michael took Lizzie into her tent and examined her. When he was satisfied, Daisy was allowed in. Now it was time for Lizzie to speak with the military police, Chris drove her over to the farmhouse, and he mentioned the baby.

"We will have other opportunities said her fiancé tenderly." He held her hand and kissed it, he spoke softly "Darling try not to beat yourself up too much, with what has taken place, this all-Charles's fault". "It still very raw and my heart is breaking" said Lizzie trying not to cry. Knowing that with Chris by her side, the future looked brighter. "We need to walk you through the events is that okay with you?" She nodded her head.

A young police Sergeant was waiting for them to arrive. Chris helped Lizzie out of the jeep while Sergeant Hibbert waited by it, and they all introduced themselves. Lizzie then had to retrace her steps; Chris stayed by her side the whole time not letting her out of his sight. Once complete, Lizzie couldn't help the tears and Chris held her as she recalled the previous night's events. The young Police Sergeant taking notes as she spoke.

It was an exhausting morning and a very emotional one, Lizzie was relieved when they were free to go back to the hospital, the young Sergeant said he would be in contact in a few days as he had to inform Charles' parents. The mention of Charles' family made Lizzie feel uncomfortable, guilty and sick, all these emotions playing havoc because they really needed to know the truth about their precious son, but Lizzie feared it would be swept under the carpet and Charles would come out the hero. The young Sergeant had passed the case to an older officer because, in relation of who Charles was, the only thing that concerned

422

Lizzie was that all three came out of the situation exonerated of Charles' killing, it was self-defence.

Late morning, they were released from helping the military police, so Chris took her back to the hospital. Once back Lizzie was trying to get used to all the other members of staff staring at her and talking about her behind her back. Chris knew he would have to leave her as he needed to get back to his regiment, his commanding officer wanted to speak with him about the recent events and he thought he had better get it over with as soon as possible.

Lizzie didn't want him to go but Daisy talked some sense into her and after joining them for lunch he left shortly after.

Michael was back on duty at his casualty clearing post in the next town and he had promised to come back as soon as he could. When the two women were left on their own that was when Lizzie had time to think and they were sitting in their tent, she just started to shake uncontrollably and everything become so overwhelming she found it hard to breathe.

Daisy was worried and told her to take deep breaths which she did, and it got her breathing back under control in no time. Daisy reassured her friend by saying what took place wasn't her fault, it was all Charles' doing and the outcome was his fault as well. Daisy knew that it would take a long time for Lizzie to physically and mentally recover from this ordeal and the rape, now losing the baby on top, but with the help of her friends, and time was a great healer, she would be okay.

The military police hoped to wrap up the investigation very quickly and without too much fuss as it was wartime, both women were nervous until all three were cleared. Over the next few days Michael was spoken to and so was Daisy. Sergeant Hibbert was also spoken to but Christopher made sure he stayed with him the whole time.

The police spoke with Charles' colleagues in his regiment and it turned out he had been behaving oddly the last few days prior to the incident. In the end the military police concluded that it was self-defence, and that the official version would be he died in battle. Lizzie thought that perhaps Charles' family had something to say about the final conclusion, but she had no proof, so she just let it go reluctantly.

Lizzie was extremely reassured that Sergeant Hibbert had been exonerated, as she was very thankful to him for saving her life. But she was angry that Charles' family would be able to say he had died like a hero. When she mentioned it, Daisy and Chris told Lizzie to forget about it and look towards happier times.

The Allies were making good progress across Europe and before long they would be entering Holland. Night times were hard for Lizzie she suffered from nightmares, which caused her to wake in the night covered in sweat and always crying. Daisy would get up and get in beside her, holding her friend tight, until she settled. This troubled Daisy immensely so she mentioned it to Matron and Michael, who prescribed some sleeping tablets for a few days to help.

Life slowly returned to normal, Lizzie asked to go back to work but Matron thought she should work closely with Daisy as she was still fragile and planned for the two women to return to England as soon as they could be released. She felt it was better for Lizzie to get home. Chris would be moving on with his regiment and Michael would also be following with the field hospital, so their war was far from over. Lizzie handled being back at work very well under the supervision of Daisy, but she was happy when Matron called them into her Office at the beginning of August.

It was a hot, sultry day and all Lizzie wanted to do was get into a cold shower. They stood outside the office with beads of sweat slowly trickling down the sides of their faces and knocked on the door.

"Enter," Matron shouted.

They made their way in. Standing to attention they waited to be given the order to sit.

Sitting side by side, Matron's look softened and she said, "I have news for you both, you are to be on tomorrow's hospital ship back to England, and then you are to have a week's leave. Following that you are to return here and continue your duties."

The women couldn't quite believe what they had heard. Once it had sunk in, they were ecstatic and couldn't wait to be going home. It was just a shame Chris and Michael were not coming as well.

Matron dismissed them to go and get ready to leave, Lizzie really wanted that shower. By the evening it was still very warm, though the heat had slightly gone out of the sun. Lizzie had her shower and had put clean clothes on and felt refreshed, they had done their washing the day before and it had dried on their makeshift clothesline hanging between two tents.

Daisy had gone off to have her shower and Lizzie sat on her bed, they had the flap open to let some air in, and she thought about her mother for the first time. Did she really say those things? Soon Lizzie would know, and she hoped that her mother had really changed, she also wondered what she felt once she had heard Charles had died, and on top of that had kidnapped her daughter and nearly killed her.

Lizzie had written to her brother and Glenda to tell them what had happened, she was waiting for a reply, perhaps when she was home, she would try and telephone him, but she knew he would be busy with the squadron. Lizzie while on her own sat on her bed glancing down at her stomach, she ran her hand gently over it, her heart ached for her lost child, and she hoped she could have children in the future. Michael had reassured her everything was all right.

Late that night the two women had tried to sleep but it was so warm in the tent they gave up and lay talking to each other, their sleeping bags pushed under them as they were too warm. They wished they could say goodbye to Michael and Chris but they had hardly seen them since they went back to work. Reality was it was very doubtful they would see them before heading home, so Daisy got one of the ambulance drivers to give Michael a letter. There was one for Chris that she asked Michael to pass on.

Chapter 49

The next morning it was slightly cooler, which made it pleasant and made it easier to travel. The two women were ready and waiting for their lift to the docks. They were touched, as some of their colleagues had made the effort to come and wish them a safe journey and a safe return.

So here they were sitting in an Army lorry being driven down to the docks with their suitcases, as the rest of their equipment would be staying for when they returned. The docks were a hive of activity and the two women had to show their identity papers and travel passes giving them permission to travel, security was very tight. Both women were allowed through and were told to wait to be boarded, once onboard they were taken down to a cabin where they were left to settle in.

The cabin was very basic, but it was fine, they wouldn't be in it during the day as they wanted to help the injured, the vessel was a hospital ship. Late afternoon they set sail, the sea was like a mill pond, very smooth and calm. The following morning, they arrived back in Portsmouth, and once they were off the ship, they were off to catch a train to London. Neither of the women had time to let their families know they were coming so it was going to be a complete surprise for everyone.

Lizzie was getting nervous as she had left under unhappy circumstances, but other events had happened since then and she just prayed it would work out, it made her shiver with anticipation.

By luck the train journey wasn't too bad and at Waterloo the two women said a tearful goodbye. They promised to meet back here on Saturday and then travel down to Portsmouth and then on to Normandy. Lizzie got off the underground making for the station, she stopped at the station buffet and bought a cup of tea, her thoughts turned to her mother, how would she react to her daughter coming home? Only time would tell, Lizzie picked up her suitcase and headed out on to the concourse.

The train journey was uneventful, and she actually got a seat, all the young men would be fighting over in France or in Asia. She said a silent prayer for their safe return. On arrival at Warwick station, she manged to get a taxi, when she told the driver the address, he raised an eyebrow but kept quiet. Soon she recognised the scenery and the driveway came into view, Lizzie's mouth was very dry, and she had goosebumps on her arms, it will be fine she told herself.

The taxi driver pulled up by the back door as instructed, Lizzie paid, and the driver retrieved her suitcase. Opening the back door, she stood quietly as she spotted Edna, she waited for her to turn around and notice her. Edna had heard the door go and when she turned, putting the rolling pin down on the bench, she broke into a lovely smile when she saw Lizzie standing there.

Edna rushed forward. "Oh, welcome home, lass," she said, and took the young woman into her arms. Lizzie's head resting against her warm breast.

"Well, this is a nice surprise, we didn't know you were coming!"

Lizzie looked lovingly at the older woman. "I didn't have time to let you all know; it was all very sudden," she replied guiltily.

Looking over, Edna noticed the dark rings around Lizzie eyes. "Are you not getting enough rest and sleep?" she enquired worriedly.

"We have been kept very busy with a constant stream of casualties," she replied.

Lizzie wanted to tell Edna and Geoffrey about her ordeal, but she felt it was only right that she did it when her parents were present. Edna sat Lizzie down at the kitchen table and placed some home-made cake in front of her and a mug of coffee. Lizzie realised she was very hungry and picked up the cake and popped a piece in her mouth relishing the taste. She took a sip of her hot coffee and sat back feeling her shoulders relax and the stress disappear for the first time in weeks. Perhaps being home was a good thing, she really hoped so.

Once she was satisfied, she sat talking to Edna and Geoffrey, recalling what she had witnessed over the last few months. They all agreed that they hoped the end of the war was actually now in sight. A little bit later, Lizzie heard her parents' voices, they walked into the kitchen.

Her mother, on seeing her daughter, stopped suddenly. Lizzie went to stand but she was stopped by her father who told her sit back down.

Her parents made their way over and took their seats at the table. Lady Margo turned to her daughter and took a few moments to compose herself before she spoke, the silence was unbearable.

Margo gazed at her daughter lovingly for the first time in Lizzie's adult life, her expression changed, and she began by saying she was sorry with the way she had behaved.

Lizzie hearing these words couldn't stop the tears from stinging her eyes, she forced herself not to cry.

"You have to know I only did it for you, and I wanted the best for you," Lady Margo continued. "I had a call recently from Charles' mother who filled me in on what happened over there."

Lizzie tried to compose herself before she spoke, she was shaking, and she badly needed a cigarette. She shuddered and took a deep breath. "Charles kidnapped me at night and held me prisoner using his service revolver, he wanted to kill me to stop me being with Chris at all costs. I also lost a baby," she cried. "And if it wasn't for Chris, and Michael, Daisy's fiancé and Daisy herself I would be dead."

Lizzie couldn't stop the tears from falling. That was when her mother came around the table and wrapped her arms around her daughter and said, "You are safe now and I'm sorry you had to go through that on your own."

This action caused the floodgates to open, the tears came, and she didn't stop them, she just leaned into her mother for comfort, it was comforting and for the first time it felt right. Lizzie hugged her mother back and she for once was blissfully happy.

The rest of the week was about discovery, she cried many tears for her unborn baby and her mother just comforted her. It was nice, her parents really couldn't wait to meet Chris, she promised as soon as she could, she would bring him home. Lizzie had even learned that her mother had welcomed Glenda into the family and at last accepted her. She was delighted for her brother.

Lizzie rested as much as she could, her mind underwent different emotions. The atmosphere around her home had changed, it was a happy place. Her mum was smiling, this is the mother she wished she had known as she was growing up.

The rest of her break flew by, and she found that she was

disappointed to be returning. she didn't want to leave this happy place but she knew she had to, and she really hoped that Chris would still be around, but she doubted it. His regiment would have moved on by now.

On the Saturday morning all packed up, Geoffrey had gone to get the car, she stood in the warm kitchen waiting to go.

Her parents walked into the room and, walking over to them she said, with a beaming smile. "Next time I come home it will be with Chris." she promised. "I can't wait for you to meet him."

She hugged her father and he whispered in her ear, "All is well?"

"Yes," she replied happily. Lizzie knew what he was saying.

Lizzie stood in front of her mother, she couldn't hide the happiness on her face and her mother hugged her tightly. "Just come home safe," she whispered in her daughter's ear.

"I will do," she replied sincerely. She hugged Edna who had lovingly taken care of Lizzie all week. Wiping the tears from her eyes she picked up her suitcase and headed for the door, Geoffrey stood waiting by the open door, and she climbed in. Sitting in the back of the cool car it was nice to get out of the August heat, a lot had happened over the week and she was still digesting all that had taken place, her emotions were still reeling. Lizzie was glad her mother had seen that Charles was not right for her even under the present circumstances.

Geoffrey looked at her through the rear-view mirror. "I'm really pleased for you, Lady Elizabeth; your mother is a great lady once she lets you see her real side."

"Yes, she is Geoffrey. I just hoped she keeps this up!" The doubts had started to creep in again, it would still take a long time to trust her again.

"She will, you'll see." Geoffrey dropped her off at the station. As he helped get her suitcase out of the boot, he placed it down and turning hugged her tight. "Take care and come home safe, and make sure you bring that young man with you!"

Lizzie picked up her suitcase. "I will, I promise." She smiled.

Standing on the platform waiting for the train, she lit a cigarette, it soothed her, it gave her the time to reflect on the past few days quietly, it couldn't have gone any better and she felt elated that things were finally looking up at home. It had actually been a nice week, Lizzie looked up at the sky, it was very blue with hardly a cloud about, she let the morning heat warm her face. Lizzie couldn't wait to see Daisy and update her on her news, she would be surprised how her mother had reacted.

The train was empty with just a few people travelling, Lizzie managed to get a seat, it was very warm in the carriage, so she took her jacket off, placed her suitcase in the overhead rack, and she sat back to enjoy the journey. Lizzie noticed that there were hardly any service personnel travelling, her mind drifted to how the war was developing in France and beyond.

On arrival into London, Lizzie made her way to the underground and her meeting spot with Daisy at Waterloo station. Arriving a little early she put her suitcase down and waited patiently. Glancing around she spotted Daisy walking towards her, she smiled in greeting.

"Well, you look happy. I take it all went well at home?" asked an excited Daisy, questioning her friend.

"Yes," came the happy response. "It went extremely well and my mother has changed, very much for the better."

Daisy was delighted for her and it made a nice change from her crying and being upset every time she came back from being at home.

"I will tell you all about it over a sandwich and mug of tea in the buffet if we have time," said Lizzie looking down at her wristwatch. "But first, how was your visit home?"

"It went really well, firstly the train was empty and I actually got a seat. Once home my parents were pleased to see me but when I explained what had happened, they were very concerned. It took a while to calm them, and they told me to be careful in the future, I did tell them I actually wasn't in any danger. They loved my ring and can't wait to meet Michael. It was nice to see Mark and to catch up with Mary, she is waiting for Bobby to come home then they will have the wedding, I can see a baby arriving not long after." Daisy glanced over at her friend, concern etched on her face, "Sorry," she said.

Lizzie put her hand up as acknowledgement that it was fine.

"George, as far as we know, is still fine, and finally they can't wait for me to bring Michael home and introduce him to everyone."

Glancing at her watch again. "Let's get that sandwich and sit down for a minute, I'm hungry."

Lizzie and Daisy headed for the buffet, pushing the door open they entered, it was very warm inside. Looking around they spotted empty seats and advanced to the table. Dropping their luggage by the chairs they proceeded to the counter. They ordered and waited while the lady served them, and once sitting back down, they both took a sip of tea.

Lizzie couldn't contain her excitement, she wanted to explode, but she took a deep breath to calm herself before beginning.

Daisy sat and listened intently, her friend was so animated that she just let her continue until she stopped and took a bite of her sandwich.

"My mother was very supportive about me losing the baby." Looking over at Daisy, she said, "You can mention it, though it still hurts but it's getting easier with each day."

Daisy nodded that she understood, and she spoke, "Well, I am pretty shocked your mother has really surpassed herself and done well!" Smiling over to Lizzie. "You must be overwhelmed with it all!"

Lizzie took her time to respond. "Yes, I was, but I am really happy, and I have my mother being nice and I know now that I love her very much." she said honestly.

Daisy was truly pleased for her friend and the future was finally looking good for both of them. They had just finished when they heard their train being called.

"Come on, we had better not be late as we will miss our ship."

Quickly picking up their belongings and rushing to the platform, they boarded the train. Again, they were surprised to get a seat, the journey sailed by and soon they were back in Portsmouth harbour, waiting to board their ship back to France.

They both hoped that Chris and Michael would still be around but realistically they knew it was very unlikely. It didn't stop them from feeling ecstatic and looking forward to getting back in the thick of the action, the rest had truly done them both good.

The channel was calm for the journey to France, they both spent a lot of the trip out on deck enjoying the warmth and the sun beating down on them made them feel well.

Chapter 50

They arrived back in Normandy refreshed and ready to go, an ambulance had been sent to collect them from the port and it took them to where they were based. The young driver was a friendly lad who couldn't stop talking all the way, the women were pleased to fill him in on their trip home.

They found out he had a young daughter who he had only met once since her birth. That was three years ago and he hoped soon to be allowed to go on leave and meet her again. This made the two women realise that they were very fortunate, they both looked out the window onto the French countryside, lost in their own thoughts.

On arrival back at the hospital they were met by Matron, who was pleased to have her nurses back. Having inspected them both over, she was happy that they both looked refreshed and well, because she had a surprise announcement to make, they would be moving out and making a fresh camp in Holland as the soldiers had done a good job in pushing the German Army back. They would be moving out in two days' time.

Lizzie enquired if Chris and Michael were still around and the answer was, no, they had both moved forward with the rest of the battalion.

Both women retrieved their belongings and found their tent and settled back in. They would be back on duty first thing in the morning, with that Matron left them to it. It didn't take them long to unpack and get settled, Lizzie checked the time and told Daisy it was time for supper, so they headed to the canteen and all their colleagues wanted to chat and catch up on their news from home.

They spent a pleasant evening talking to everyone. Soon they were yawning and saying their goodnights and made their way to their tent. Before turning in Lizzie stood outside the tent holding a lit cigarette. Looking up at the full moon and the shining stars, she said a silent prayer for Chris to keep him safe and for their unborn child that she would never meet. On entering she got changed and climbed into the sleeping bag, she knew it would soon be kicked back as it was a warm night. Both women lay talking until sleep took over, tomorrow was another day.

Both were awake early ready for their shift; parts of the hospital were being dismantled today ready to be loaded up and moved. The pioneer corps were coming to collect the items that were ready. All the nurses were the last to be moved so they had another day, most of the patients were already either being sent home or re-joining their regiments.

At the end of the day both women were exhausted, they had worked extremely hard, they had showers and got changed ready for some supper and then sleep as tomorrow they had a journey to the Belgium/Holland border. They had been told they were just going over the border and then to set up the new hospital, they were both excited and neither slept well, they wanted the next chapter to start.

The journey was in fact not too bad, there was an awful lot of troop movement but they made good time, soon they reached their destination at Baarle, and the pioneer corps were nearly set up, it helped that the weather was pretty good and that the ground was very dry.

The layout was the same as their last hospital, so getting around it wasn't too bad. The fighting was further ahead, and once the casualties arrived, they had been patched up at the casualty clearing station. Within a few days more men were arriving and being treated, they were then sent on their way to either home or their regiment, life settled into a routine.

The weeks passed and just before Christmas the Germans tried one more defensive, known as the battle of the bulge, but it didn't succeed.

Well after the New Year of 1945, all the nurses and doctors were getting to hear disturbing news that was coming out and revealing more information about concentration camps that kept being discovered all across Germany and other countries in Europe. Many nurses and everyday people from all around the world got to read about it in the papers, people couldn't believe that human beings could be so cruel to each other. The British Army soldiers and nurses that went into these camps to liberate them were horrified by what they saw, and they knew it would stay embedded in their minds for the rest of their lives.

By the end of March there was a blustery wind blowing but no rain, it was still very cold. Daisy and Lizzie were shocked and when they started to see these prisoners for real, it shook them to their core.

One evening while they were resting in their tent, they had both received post, this had cheered them up as they were both missing their men. Lizzie scanned her letter, apparently Chris was just entering Germany and he hoped very soon that the war would be at an end, he really wanted to get home and back to her in one piece, most of the German army were surrendering on sight. Hitler was still in Berlin — little did they know that very soon, he would be dead.

Daisy read her letter and found out Michael was attending to the prisoners from the concentration camps. Daisy's heart went out to him, and she wished she could be with him and actually work with him. On the first of May news was coming through that Hitler had in fact committed suicide, nobody could quite believe it, after six years the war would soon be over.

On the seventh of May the news came through everyone had been waiting and hoping for, the Germans had unconditionally surrendered and the war in Europe was finally over.

Daisy and Lizzie ran to find each other, and they hugged and cried with joy. Daisy and Lizzie knew they would soon be going home to await the return of their fiancés. That night there was very little sleep as everyone was celebrating the news and the good fortune that they were alive.

Over the weeks the injured got less and less, and by September the women got the news they had been waiting for, they would soon be on their way home.

One night while sitting in their tent, Daisy looked over to her friend and with a serious look she asked, "What are your plans once you get home?"

Lizzie took her time to respond. "Well, if all goes well, I want to get married as soon as we can. I then want a honeymoon and when I get back, I hope Christopher goes back into teaching."

Daisy asked, "What is going to happen with your home now the war is technically over."

"That is down to Mother and Father with a consultation with Eddie and Glenda."

"What about you?" she asked looking over to Daisy.

"Like you, get married and then Michael spoke about being a general practitioner back in Felixstowe, working within his father's practice, maybe I could be the practice nurse or even train as a midwife and work on the district!"

"I promise you one thing, we will keep in contact and see each other regularly," said Lizzie, smiling warmly at her friend.

Daisy looked back and smiled. "I would like that very much." She was overcome with emotion, and tears came to her eyes, which she wiped with a hanky.

The next few months went by very quickly, and then one morning Matron called the nurses together. Standing in front of them, she began by saying how very proud she was of all of them. She carried on by saying that it was time to pack up and finally go home. "As of next Saturday, we will be on a ship heading back to Dover."

There were sighs everywhere, they were going home, their duty was complete! Lizzie and Daisy were overwhelmed with emotion and so were most of the other women, they had been through a lot together and now the journey was coming to an end. Back at their tent they realised they had five days to pack up and be ready to move out, they had no time to write home so again they would be surprising their families.

The next four days the nurses didn't stop, they were run off their feet, but they were proud they had completed the task and Friday night they were ready to leave. Both women stood and looked around, they would never forget this place and they were slightly sorry they were leaving. The truck was waiting, and all the women climbed aboard, they were to travel through the night to Calais and get the ship to England tomorrow.

Lizzie took out a cigarette and smoking it she sat looking out through the slit at the passing countryside, and excitement was building. She was going home and was actually quite happy about it for the first time. She wondered what would happen to her home now the war was nearly over, there was still fighting in the far east.

Her parents were getting older, and she knew Eddie and Glenda wouldn't want the responsibility of keeping the house running as it was, unless they turned it into a hotel, she would speak to her brother once he was demobbed, he may even want to keep on flying? She thought.

Daisy sat opposite deep in her own thoughts, she was really looking forward to spending her life with Michael, she couldn't wait to get married and start their next chapter. The truck travelled on into the night and by the time the sun was coming up they had arrived at the port of Calais.

Again, they had to wait to get their ship, the port was a hive of activity, they all climbed off the truck and stood around waiting on the dock. Lizzie, being her usual self, lit another cigarette and Daisy stood very close to her, chatting to her as she smoked. About lunch time they were ordered to get aboard their awaiting vessel, it was a short crossing to Dover and both women stood on the deck watching as England came into view.

It had been a rough trip as the sea had been rough. As they approached Dover they looked up at the white cliffs, they were finally home. The ship had to wait its turn to dock. Gathering up their belongings, their trunks would be delivered later to their homes, the nurses stood together and said their goodbyes to each other.

Matron stood watching, she was proud of what these women had accomplished. She shook hands with each one of them, and the tears came, she watched as they disembarked from the ship. Lizzie and Daisy went to the station to wait for the next train to London. They were lucky they didn't have to wait long. The train journey was quite sombre, they sat in their seats quietly, lost in their own thoughts, they had both been doing a lot of that lately. The two women were sad to be finally saying goodbye to each other for the present.

Chapter 51

On arrival at Charing Cross, they stood on the concourse, and they hugged each other tightly. Both had tears streaming down their faces, they didn't even bother to wipe them.

"Now you promise to come as arranged on the twenty-fifth as arranged?" said a forlorn Lizzie.

"Yes," replied a distressed Daisy. "I will be there, promise."

"Now you know where I live, and I will have Geoffrey at the station to meet you."

"You really don't have to but thank you. I really appreciate it."

It was time to say goodbye, they held each other again. Finally, releasing each other, they walked to the underground and went their separate ways.

Once sitting on her train, Daisy looked back at her life, from growing up, until she trained as a nurse, which led her to meet Lizzie and the journey they had been on and finally meeting Michael. What she wished most for was that Michael would be home to come with her when she went to visit Lizzie at her parents' house. Daisy was really anxious about the upcoming visit as she had never met a real-life Lord and Lady, and more importantly how should she behave, especially in front of Lady Margaret. That's why she really wanted Michael by her side, for support.

Daisy had noticed that the train was arriving into the underground station, she gathered her thoughts, picked up her handbag and her suitcase and made her way up to the concourse. Once she had bought her ticket, she walked to her platform. The train was already in, looking around she found a quiet carriage and climbed aboard, choosing a seat, placed her case on the rack above and then sat down. A young lad in a sailor uniform came into the carriage, he looked over to Daisy, and smiled as he sat down, Daisy returned the smile.

A few more people entered the carriage, and the whistle blew. Daisy was excited and apprehensive, she was going home. Matron had given them all their demob papers and now she was to be a civilian again. On entering Luton station, she stood, gathered her items and waited for the train to stop, making her way to the door. It was early October, and it was still warm as she made her way out of the station, she began her walk home.

Daisy pulled her greatcoat up against the slight wind. Everywhere she thought, looking around, looked tired and old, the war had definitely left its mark, ruins and rubble were all over the place. There would need to be a lot of rebuilding.

The Americans had dropped bombs on the Japanese in August.

Turning into her street she noticed it hadn't really altered since the last time she was home, which meant it hadn't got any worse. Stopping by her front door, Daisy chose to use the entry to the back. She walked through and clicked the back gate. On entering she stopped by the back door, taking a deep breath she knocked out of courtesy, and entered.

Her mother was busy standing at the range, she turned when she heard the door open, and was surprised when she saw her daughter standing in front of her.

After getting over the initial shock, she asked, "Why didn't you tell us you were coming?" She rushed over to take her daughter in her arms.

"Mum, I didn't have time, I only knew myself a few days ago."

Looking at Daisy. "Well, it's lovely to have you back home."

Daisy then broke the news. "I'm home for good, Mum."

Hannah, on hearing this was overjoyed, her family would soon be complete, as George too would be home soon, she hoped. Hannah went on to say that Bobby too was being demobbed anytime soon and Mary couldn't wait, Daisy was really thrilled for her sister.

"Where's Mark?" she said, glancing around. "It's very quiet!"

"He will be home soon," replied Hannah.

"Your father will be home soon with your sister as she now works in the same factory with him." That was news to Daisy. "It was more money." As if to read Daisy's mind.

"Mary wanted to save more money for the wedding, and it was war work," continued her mother.

Daisy dropped her suitcase and helped her mum make a pot of tea. Once sitting at the table her mother had a good look at her eldest

438

daughter.

"You look better than the last time you were here."

Daisy smiled. "Yes, Mum. I feel all right, I just want you to finally meet Michael and to get married as soon as we can. I'm hoping he will be joining us in a few days, he will send a telegram to let us know," she went on.

By late afternoon and after many cups of tea, she had caught up with all the local gossip, and had enjoyed spending this time with her mum. Daisy felt relaxed and was waiting for her father and sister to come home.

Mark had arrived earlier and when he had spotted Daisy, he had run into her open arms.

"You're home," he shouted excitedly. "For good?" he queried.

She nodded placing a kiss on his head. He sat by her side and she looked him over, he had grown up and was nine now, but in her eyes, he was still her little brother.

At six her father entered with her sister walking behind, he couldn't believe his eyes, his eldest daughter was home! He took his coat off and then he pulled her too him and hugged her very tightly. He stepped back while keeping hold of her and took a good look at her, she looked worn-out he thought, and the sparkle from her eyes had gone.

Mary sat watching while this was taking place, when her father finally let her go, Daisy turned and went over to Mary and hugged her sister. The whole family had tears in their eyes, Hannah had prayed for this moment for a very long time, looking around the room.

After tea, Daisy helped Mary to clear up, they both talked about their fiancés. Daisy hoped Michael would be here soon, she wanted her sister to meet him desperately and for her to see she was really over Bobby. Daisy had enjoyed spending time with Mary, they had gotten along better, and she didn't feel any unease with her.

Later, up in their bedroom, Daisy was getting ready for bed, it felt strange that she wouldn't have to rush to get out of bed in the morning. Mary was already in it when Daisy climbed in beside her, she used to love the warmth shared between them.

"It's nice to have you home, what do you plan to do next?" Enquired her sister sincerely. This surprised Daisy but she was silently pleased.

"Well, once Michael is demobbed, we will probably marry and then live down in Felixstowe."

Her sister peeped over at her Daisy, she indeed looked very happy. Daisy talked some more with her sister, it was nice catching up and reconnecting, they fell asleep soon after.

Daisy rose early the next day. Once everyone had left, it was only her left with her mother, for the first time in a long time she actually felt at a loss. Michael couldn't get here soon enough, then they would travel to see Lizzie. After a few days Daisy did in fact receive the telegram, Michael's demob had come through, he was arriving in two days. First, he had to go home to see his parents and then he was free to come up. Daisy took the telegram and read it to her mother, who was excited for her daughter. He was finally coming to meet her parents but where would he sleep?

Her father had told her Michael could sleep in the front room on the settee. Daisy really wanted to spend the night with him but that was definitely not happening under her parent's roof.

Another telegram arrived the next day for Mary, it was good news, Bobby too was being demobbed and coming home. Mary couldn't contain her excitement, both sisters were ecstatic. The whole house was excited with the upcoming news both men were turning up on the same day.

Hannah hoped George would be home too, she hadn't had any news when he would be demobbed. Hannah had a deep feeling that he would continue in the navy as a career.

The morning of the day of the men's arrival came, it had turned colder, Daisy was dressed warmly and she left the house to walk to the station to meet Michael's train, he had wanted to drive up, but his father needed the car. During the walk, Daisy started to have the old doubts creeping in. Was she good enough for a doctor? Would he like her family? Would she like his family when she met them? Which would be in a few weeks. Would they like her? All these questions were reeling around her mind.

Daisy stopped and looked around, she had arrived in good time, waiting on the platform she was getting nervous and her hands were sweaty, she felt sick. He would be here soon, she looked down at her watch another ten minutes. The time went very slowly until she heard the train pulling into the station, it was on time.

Daisy was looking as the people disembarked from the train and came through the barrier, then she spotted him, he was wearing a blue suite and black overcoat, his dark hair hidden under a trilby hat, he saw her, she waved, and he gave the guard his ticket. He raced towards her, dropped his case, taking her in his arms he kissed her like his life depended on it. After a while they pulled apart, and they looked at each other, taking each other in.

"I can't believe you are really here!" said Daisy rubbing his cheek.

Michael smiled in return. "Where else would I be?" he replied laughing. "I love you."

"I love you too," she replied tenderly. "Come on, you need to meet my family." And she took his hand with a big smile plastered on her face.

He scooped to pick his case up. As they walked to her house, she showed him all the damage caused by the war, he said it was very similar to Felixstowe, they had it bad due to the docks. The war had affected an awful lot of people she thought, in many different ways.

Arriving at her home she still couldn't believe he was really here and she kept looking at him. They entered the back door where he was met by the whole family, apart from George. Bobby would be popping over later.

Her parents stood and the introductions were made, Hannah and Jack were impressed by the young man standing in front of them. Their daughter had made the right choice and they were very happy for her. Mary took a keen interest in Michael and found he was nothing like Bobby, which made her slightly relieved. She actually liked him as she got to know him more during the day. Mark was introduced and he instantly liked the man who was going to marry his big sister. Michael went to the pub with Jack so they could get to know each other better, while the ladies, prepared dinner.

When they left Daisy quizzed her mum, holding her breath. "Well, do you like him?"

"Yes, very much," came back the reply.

Daisy was extremely happy, she smiled over at her mother, they would sit and plan the wedding this afternoon. After dinner they sat around the kitchen table, Daisy only wished two things, to have a small private wedding and wanted to get married as soon as possible. Mary and Lizzie were to be bridesmaids. Within a few hours it was all decided, tomorrow they would talk to the vicar to get the banns read. They wanted the wedding a month from today.

Hannah offered to make the dress for Daisy and the bridesmaids; she had some material kept from a previous job. Daisy wished George would be home by then, Bobby arrived after tea and he was introduced to Michael, they got on really well and by the end of the evening were good friends. Daisy and Mary were pleased, later they left to go to Bobby's house and Michael was alone with Daisy in the front room.

They were sitting on the settee and the fire was sending out a very low glow, the room was comfortable and homely. They were sitting holding hands, and kissing. They both wanted more but not with her parents next door.

It was very hard to keep their hands off each other. Michael was glad the wedding was only a month away. They sat and talked about the war, their experiences and what they wanted for the future. Surprisingly they actually wanted the same things, Daisy enjoyed getting to know Michael without being in a dangerous situation. She helped him make his bed with the bedding her mother had popped in with. Once made they sat down again and said their goodnights, the kissing and heavy petting they were doing was getting them carried away, and Michael reluctantly finally pulled away.

Daisy moaned but didn't protest. She made her way up to bed; she knew she wouldn't stay their long, not with Michael sleeping downstairs. As Daisy got into bed Mary came up, they were talking as Mary got undressed.

"Michael is really nice," she said sincerely.

Daisy took a gamble. "If I go downstairs for a while, you won't tell Mum or Dad?" she asked carefully, glancing at her sister.

"No, I would do the same, just be careful," she replied.

"I promise," she said back with a big grin on her face.

As soon as she thought everyone was asleep Daisy crept downstairs. Watching out for any creaking stairs, she knocked on the closed door and entered. Michael couldn't believe what he was seeing, he wanted to send her back to bed but when he saw her in her nighty he was gone.

Daisy climbed in beside him, it was a tight squeeze. Michael ended up on top and they slowly kissed and made love by the glow of the fire. Afterwards, Daisy and Michael lay there for a while, before she crept back to her bed. Mary woke as her sister got back into bed, they didn't say anything, she just smiled, and Mary turned over and went back to sleep.

The next day they saw the vicar and they had a date by the time they left the church and for the banns to be read. The date was booked for Saturday, Twenty-fourth November. On arrival home, more plans were made, and Mary also had gone to the church and got her date a week later and for her banns to be read. Daisy was only going away for a few days honeymoon so Michael and herself would be back for her sister's wedding, they thought about a joint wedding but decided against it.

Mary and Bobby went out which left her parents and them to have lunch, the more they got to know their future son-in-law the more they liked him. Later they packed to get ready to go to Lizzie's, they were leaving in the morning, Hannah took her daughter's measurements and Daisy promised to get Lizzie's measurements and send them to her.

That night Daisy did the same again and spent part of the night with Michael, she knew she was taking a big risk, but she knew they would be married soon, and she didn't know when they would get a chance again before the wedding.

Again, Daisy climbed into bed, her sister turned over and said in a sleepy voice, "Good job you are leaving tomorrow as you will soon be caught out, Dad's not that naïve," Mary said laughing. Smiling, Daisy fell into a deep relaxed sleep.

Monday morning Jack and Mary said their goodbyes as they had to leave for work. Mark left for school, and Hannah made breakfast for them.

Chapter 52

At nine-thirty they said goodbye to Hannah, and they walked to the station. The journey took till mid-afternoon with all the changes they had to make. Daisy was happy and relaxed being with Michael, they talked and talked the whole journey as if still making up for time. As promised, as the train pulled into Warwick, Geoffrey was waiting, he greeted the friends of Lady Elizabeth, Michael and Daisy couldn't believe the luxury they were being driven in. Both sat back and let the cream leather seat encase them.

Geoffrey spoke to the couple, and he felt he and Edna would like these two very much.

"We are here," he said as they drove down the sweeping entrance that led to the Hall.

Daisy and Michael looked out of the window; they couldn't believe what they were seeing.

"Most of the hospital has been emptied and they are retuning the house into a home again. Lady Margaret isn't too keen to live there any more as it is too big for just the two of them," Geoffrey enlightened them. "Once Lord Clifford dies; we think Edward will turn the house into a hotel." He carried on. "I think they will do this before, as what else to do with this big house? Edward wants to live here with Glenda his wife."

Daisy hadn't realised how big the house was, when it came into view, she was speechless. Michael was astonished, and Geoffrey drove them to the back door. Lizzie hearing the car, hurriedly ran to greet her friends. The car just stopped, and she had the door open, she pulled Daisy to her. They hugged and kissed each other on the cheek, Michael too got a hug and kiss. Lizzie took them into the kitchen while Geoffrey brought in their luggage. Lizzie introduced them to Edna, she hugged them both tightly. They sat talking and getting to know each other while they waited for Lizzie's parents to arrive. Lizzie told them Chris was arriving tomorrow and then they too were planning the wedding.

Daisy told Lizzie her date for the wedding and that she wanted her as a bridesmaid with her sister Mary.

Lizzie was over the moon to be asked. She said, yes, straight away.

They were sitting drinking tea and coffee when they heard Lady Margo approaching; Daisy was getting nervous, Michael held her hand and when she entered, they all stood, they were greeted with a smile and "Welcome."

Lady Margo was the perfect hostess, and she made them feel at home, she was grateful for the care the doctor had shown her daughter following the incident and sad loss of their grandchild.

Michael replied, "It was his pleasure and duty." Daisy was very proud and couldn't stop smiling.

A few minutes later, Lord Clifford entered. Daisy thought he was a lovely man, very similar to her father. Both Lizzie's parents made them feel welcome. Later, Lizzie showed them to their rooms and Daisy knew she would have to behave herself tonight, this made Michael smile as he went down the landing to his room. Daisy sat on her bed; it was a beautiful bedroom, not at all like the room she shared with Mary. It was tastefully decorated, and all the furniture fitted perfectly.

Daisy got to work unpacking, when she heard a knock on the door. "Enter," she called, and Lizzie popped her head in.

"Can I come in?"

"Of course you can," she said, going over to pull her in, Lizzie was laughing.

Lizzie sat on the bed by Daisy's side. "How have you been?" she asked seriously.

"I'm fine, thank you, it's nice to have Michael here. To be honest I was worried, but when we met up, it was all fine. I worried for nothing."

This information put Lizzie at ease. Looking at her friend she carried on. "Seeing Chris tomorrow will be fine, just you see."

Daisy pulled Lizzie to her and hugged her tight. "I have missed you," she said. "Now come on, or Michael will be worried where we are." Daisy grabbed her arm playfully and pulled her up off the bed.

They met Michael on the landing, coming from his room. "Eddie is here, come on, he is in the kitchen with Glenda, he wants to meet Michael," said Lizzie.

Lizzie led the way down the back stairs; she thought her family would probably always use these now. When they entered the warm kitchen, Eddie and Glenda were sitting at the table talking with Lizzie's parents; it was a nice picture she thought, it was only a few months ago her mother would have nothing to do with them.

Once introductions were made all round, they all sat around talking. Edna got up and made sandwiches for lunch, they were eating a big meal later.

Eddie said Glenda had been demobbed a few weeks ago and she was dressed in civilian clothing. They were staying at the house until a decision was made for its future and theirs. Once Lizzie was married then the decision would be made, her brother had said. Eddie liked Michael, and he was excited to be finally meeting Chris tomorrow, he owed the two men a huge debt of gratitude as they had both saved his sister from Charles' clutches.

It was a dry afternoon, so Daisy took Michael for a walk around the grounds and a tour of the house, they even took Dinky with them. Daisy wanted Lizzie to have time with her brother and Glenda, so it was late when they got back, it was getting darker earlier now as they were heading towards the beginning of November.

Edna had tea ready, and they all assembled around the large table. Lady Margo glanced around at everyone, this is what family means, she had been so wrong pushing Lizzie onto Charles, and she was eager to meet Chris. Later, Lizzie joined Daisy and Michael in Daisy's room, Eddie and Glenda had headed off to their room earlier.

"What time are you collecting Chris tomorrow from the station?" Enquired Daisy.

"Eleven-thirty, Geoffrey and I will be waiting for his train to arrive. I'll be honest with you; I don't think I will get much sleep tonight."

They sat talking until quite late into the evening, Daisy sat by Michael holding his hand, she kept looking down at her sparkling engagement ring, she felt fortunate to be here, safe with the two people who meant the most to her.

Daisy stifled a yawn and Lizzie then chose to say goodnight. "I will see you both in the morning," she said, and left the room.

Michael stayed sitting on the bed; he pulled Daisy into his arms. "It's a beautiful house, and the grounds are magnificent." He gently touched Daisy's chin and tipped it up so her lips could meet his, they gently kissed, and when they pulled apart, they were breathless.

"Come on, she pulled Michael up; you need to behave and sleep in your own bed." Michael pulled a face and he kissed her again and let himself out.

"See you in the morning. I love you." Then he was gone.

Daisy got ready for bed; she fell asleep smiling. It took Michael longer as he really wanted to go to Daisy's room, but it took all his determination not too.

Lizzie slept badly as she was so excited. Chris would be here soon, then he would meet her parents.

The following morning everyone was up fairly early, they intended to liaise in the kitchen. Eddie and Glenda, Michael and Daisy were already seated, eating breakfast made by Edna. Her parents had arrived and joined them, and Lizzie was the last to attend, she had gotten to sleep late and had slept in.

Geoffrey was waiting out the front with the car; when Lizzie turned up, he climbed into the front and Lizzie let herself into the back.

Geoffrey went on to say, "It's a big day for you Lady Elizabeth, we finally get to meet your young man," he said eyeing Lady Elizabeth with a keen eye.

"I am very nervous, Geoffrey to be honest, what if my mother doesn't like him?" She looked back at him.

"Now don't you fret, young lady, she will."

Lizzie looked back at Geoffrey and prayed he was right; she had many a bad dream recently that it all went wrong, and her mother was rude to Chris, and he left.

Lizzie sat back and was deep in her thoughts when Geoffrey pulled into the station car park. Without waiting she jumped out and ran to find out what platform the train was arriving on. Lizzie stood smoking a cigarette to calm her nerves and waited, it was on time. She heard it in the distance, and she started to get sweaty palms.

Geoffrey stood by the car, watching, keeping a watchful eye on her from a distance. The train pulled in, Lizzie waited patiently as everyone got off, she spotted him before he saw her, and she ran towards him, He dropped his bag, and on impulse he pulled her to him and kissed her lovingly. Geoffrey watched and smiled as she let him go reluctantly and grabbed his hand and led him to be introduced to Geoffrey.

Chris, once he saw the Rolls Royce was impressed, but nervous to meet everyone, and he sat in the back with Lizzie, holding her hand securely the whole journey. It was nice to have the time to acquaint with each other after so long apart.

As they drove down the sweeping driveway, Chris was speechless, he sat in awe taking it all in. "Is this all yours?" he enquired, trying to keep the surprise out of his voice.

"Yes," replied Lizzie.

Lizzie was embarrassed by all her family's wealth; she hoped Chris wasn't frightened or put off by it.

"Wow!" Was all he said.

Geoffrey stopped the car and they climbed out. Lady Margo and Lord Clifford had been waiting in the kitchen for them to arrive, they had been talking to Daisy and Michael. Lizzie took hold of Chris' hand, and as they walked towards the kitchen entrance. Suddenly, it opened, it was her mother, closely followed by her father.

Once introductions had been made and handshakes all around completed, Lizzie led Chris into the kitchen where it was warm. They spent the rest of the morning getting to know each other over a cup of tea.

When Lizzie went to take Chris up to his room, Lady Margo spoke, "I really like him," she said from the heart.

Everyone was relieved, and Daisy couldn't wait to tell Lizzie when they were on their own. After a lovely lunch, the family sat around the table, making wedding plans. The date was set for the third week in December. Daisy had her wedding and then her sister's coming up in November.

Lizzie wanted it earlier but, in the end, she gladly settled for that date. The vicar put his head in and agreed on the date; they would have to have the banns read as soon as possible.

Daisy and Michael were leaving tomorrow to travel to Felixstowe to meet his parents. Lizzie would have Chris all to herself, until they were also to travel to meet his parents up in Edinburgh, Scotland, in three days' time. Lizzie was excited, she had never been to Scotland, and she couldn't wait.

After supper, Lizzie took Chris on a tour of the house; it was imposing he thought, a lot of history within these walls.

Back in the kitchen, Eddie and Glenda were talking to Daisy and Michael. "What are you going to do with the house?" Michael enquired.

After a few moments' silence, Eddie answered. "Well, we have decided to turn the house into a hotel with the help of Mother and Father. Edna and Geoffrey are also going to stay on and help run it, for a few shares in the place and a wage. We are hoping Lizzie and Chris would also want to help but only time will tell."

"Have you spoken to them yet?" asked Daisy.

"No, I was going to do that tomorrow."

Daisy mulled over the information. "I think it is a good idea."

Much later, Lizzie's father had gotten out his spirits, and they sat around the table toasting the forthcoming weddings. Lizzie was tired, and she and Chris said goodnight to everyone and headed up to their rooms.

They had agreed to meet downstairs for breakfast, and Geoffrey was taking Daisy and Michael to the station.

Lizzie lay in her bed later and was pleased with how the day had gone. Her mother had been charming towards Chris, and it had made her feel very happy. Lizzie had said goodnight by her door.

Chris had hoped to come in, but Lizzie had stopped him. "I want to wait till we are married because of what Charles did to me."

Chris wasn't happy but respected her wishes. Yawning, she turned on her side and soon fell into a deep sleep.

In the morning, once breakfast was finished, it was hard to say goodbye to Daisy and Lizzie couldn't stop the tears falling. Daisy was crying too, the next time they would see each other would be at the wedding. Lizzie was coming down to see Daisy for a dress fitting, as her mother was making Lizzie's wedding dress.

Hugging each other tight, they kissed each other on the cheeks. it had turned colder, and it was trying to rain. Geoffrey took their suitcases and placed them in the boot of the Rolls Royce. Everyone had come to the door to see them off, with a promise to see them very soon. They all watched as the car drove down the driveway and out onto the main road.

Daisy was crying but with happiness, as she had seen her friend and she had appeared so happy. Geoffrey left them at the station with a promise to take care of Lizzie for her.

The journey took forever as they had to keep changing, but by early evening they were in Felixstowe. Michael's father picked them up at the station following doing his rounds, he was a handsome man, and Michael looked very much like him, so Daisy thought.

He dropped them off at the house saying he would see them later. Michael's mother was beautiful and was very kind and made Daisy feel very welcome; Daisy could see why Michael's father had fallen in love with her. Over tea, they all got to know each other better, Catherine and Eric were engaging, and made Daisy feel at home. They were excited about the wedding and would travel up the night before and stay in a hotel; Daisy apologised that her family couldn't put them up.

The next few days the couple spent looking around ideal houses for them to buy for, as soon as the honeymoon was over, Michael would be starting work with his father, once Mary's wedding had taken place.

Daisy was happy just to be a housewife for a while until she was ready to decide what she wanted to do. They would be travelling up for Lizzie's wedding as well, a few weeks later, and she couldn't wait. The trip to meet Michael's parents had gone very well, and the next time they would meet up would be at their wedding. His parents and the rest of Michael's family were all looking forward to meeting Daisy's family and being at the forthcoming wedding.

Michael was to stay with his family and travel up with them the night before, as Daisy had to be at home to get her wedding dress finished in time.

She sat in the front room, observing her completed dress sitting on the tailor's dummy, her mother had done her proud, she had already made Mary's too. Lizzie's was nearly finished. The bridesmaid's dresses were made as well, Hannah had worked long into the nights to get them ready, and she had turned down lots of work to get them finished on time.

On the twenty-third of November, Michael and his family arrived for the wedding. Both families had met at the hotel and enjoyed a meal together, and they all gotten on well together. They didn't stay late as Daisy wanted to get home and rest; they still had things to do; she was just happy that Michael had turned up.

Lizzie and her family were also staying there; it had been nice to catch up, Lizzie would be arriving first thing in the morning to help get the bride ready. The reception was to be held at the hotel as well.

The next morning it was a dry, crisp day but very cold with frost on the pavement, and the sun had started to come out. When Daisy woke, she was ecstatic, she was getting married today! Her mother brought her breakfast in bed, which Daisy never had. By nine, Daisy was up; she was excited and with the help of her sister and Lizzie, who had arrived about ten minutes before, prepared for the day's events.

Most of the family had a bath last night, apart from Daisy who had a bath when she was ready, she lay in the hot water thinking of how far her life had come. She was brought back from her dreams by Lizzie calling her through the door to hurry up. By eleven, Daisy was in her dress and so were the bridesmaids, they looked beautiful. Daisy's mother had made herself an outfit; she looked lovely.

Daisy cried when she saw her. "Thank you, Mum," she said from her heart.

Hannah looked lovingly at her daughter, and she too cried, even Mary and Lizzie had a tear in their eyes. Her father wore his best suit, so did Mark but the one thing missing was her brother, George.

Just as they were leaving for the church Daisy got a big surprise, a taxi pulled up outside, she opened the front door, and George stood there in his Navy uniform looking extremely smart and very handsome.

After all the hello's the cars arrived to take the family to church. Leaving just Daisy and her father behind. Daisy stood to wait for the car to come back to take them. Her father stood and looked at his daughter, and he beamed with pride. She had achieved so much he thought, Michael was a fortunate man.

Daisy peered out the window for the car had returned and she called her dad. The journey was short, and they walked up to the entrance, and they stood waiting to hear the organ begin.

"Ready?" asked her dad with pride.

"Yes," she replied with happiness.

Daisy took his arm and they entered. The service was beautiful, Michael had stood at the front looking so smart, her heart had jumped when he turned around to see her for the first time in her dress, she knew she loved him deeply. The reception went long into the night, and Michael and Daisy were staying at the hotel until the morning.

They went on honeymoon for a few days and made it back in time for her sister's wedding. She spoke to Bobby after and wished him all the best and no hard feelings, and he wished her a happy life with Michael, it was nice as they had been good friends for many years. Daisy also got a chance to speak with George who had decided to stay in the navy, which hadn't surprised her.

Daisy and Michael found a house and they settled down to married life; Daisy found out very shortly after the wedding she was, in fact, pregnant, the morning sickness giving the fact away. Daisy and Michael travelled up to Warwick in their new car, a wedding present from Michael's parents, and they were to meet her family at Lizzie's home.

Her mother had brought Lizzie's dress with them in their new car. Lizzie had tried it on; it fitted well. Looking in the mirror she had fallen in love with it. Lady Margo, seeing her daughter in the dress had become teary, and she was very impressed with Daisy's mother's handiwork. Lady Margo and Hannah over the course of the day had become firm friends, much to the pleasure of their daughters.

The next morning was Lizzie's wedding, the sun was shining but it was very cold, and it too went very well. Lady Margo had spent the morning organising Lizzie to the point where she asked her mother to stop, which she did reluctantly, with guidance from Edna and Hannah.

Everyone left for the church leaving Lizzie and her father. Lord Clifford was in awe when he saw his daughter in her dress and was proud to walk her down the aisle. When Chris saw his bride at the altar, he knew she was the one for him.

Lady Margo had actually behaved herself at the reception which Lizzie was relieved about, she couldn't have coped if her mother had been unpleasant to any of her friends. Claire and Jenny had made it to the wedding, and it had been nice for the four of them to catch up with each other. Both were working in different hospitals around London and were seeing doctors.

Later, Daisy told her friends and her parents her good news as to why she wasn't drinking, she knew her mother would have guessed something was up. Hannah did spend the rest of the day fussing around her daughter, and Lizzie was over the moon for her friend, she hugged her tightly. She felt a little stab in the heart at the memory of the baby she had lost.

Lizzie and Chris had decided in the end to help run the Hall as a hotel. Chris could go back into teaching later if he wished. So, once they came back from their honeymoon, the couple would settle down to running the hotel.

Both women stood together in the reception room with a glass of champagne and lemonade listening to the band. Lizzie looked over to Daisy and raised her glass saying, "Forever friends and to forbidden love that wins in the end." And they clinked the glasses together.